The Journey Home

A Heart's Journey Book Two

Andie Young

SUNFLOWER LANE PRESS

To the men and women who've had to leave their uniforms hanging in the closet

Chapter 1

Paul

Agonizing moans woke Paul Thompson. It took a moment to realize the sound was coming from his own mouth. Pain he'd never known had taken over his body. Another moan slipped past his lips. Light peeked through the darkness that surrounded him. He vaguely recognized that he was in a room. Something squeezed his upper arm and a beep sounded next to him. *Blood pressure cuff*. He was in a hospital room.

A nurse appeared at Paul's bedside, holding a syringe. "Sergeant Thompson, I've got something to take the pain away. It's morphine and fentanyl. You'll have relief soon."

Paul watched as she injected a syringe into the port of the IV. Why was she giving him two powerful drugs? Holding his breath, Paul grabbed hold of the bedrail and squeezed until his knuckles burned. Tears gathered in his eyes. "Where…am I? What happened to me?" his voice cracked.

After she dropped the syringe into the sharps container on the wall, she walked over to him and rested her hand on his arm. "You're in the hospital at Walter Reed in Maryland, and scheduled for surgery early tomorrow morning. There are several broken bones in your left leg and a large laceration down the side. You were stabilized at Landstuhl Regional Medical Center in Germany, and you'll have surgery to repair the broken bones and laceration. You don't remember talking to the doctor?"

Paul shook his head. How did he get from Afghanistan to Maryland? Within a few seconds, warmth flowed through Paul's veins and the pain eased. His eyelids fluttered and closed.

Paul shivered awake. The hospital gown he was wearing and his bedding were soaked with sweat. His heart felt like it was going to explode. The room was full of medical staff, darting around and shouting orders. The nurse from earlier walked up to the side of the bed and leaned close to his ear.

"You've developed sepsis from a severe infection in your left leg. Dr. Morganson and Dr. Godfrey are your surgeons. They'll take good care of you." She patted Paul's shoulder. It made little sense. A moment ago, he was in Afghanistan on the ramp of a cargo plane. What was happening? Some kind of nightmare? It felt too real to be a nightmare.

Paul closed his eyes when the nurse unlocked the wheels on the bed and began pushing him towards the door. The movements as she maneuvered the bed through the halls brought on a wave of nausea. He opened his eyes when he felt a rush of cold air. An operating table was in the middle of the room, waiting for him. For what, he didn't know. He swallowed down the nausea and braced himself as people surrounded him.

The team transferred Paul from the bed to a table, bringing out a moan when a searing pain shot through his leg. A man came to the side of the table and introduced himself as the anesthesiologist. He explained what his job was and how he would keep Paul sedated.

Two of the staff in the room approached Paul and introduced themselves as his surgeons. They informed him of their treatment plan and the outcomes. Before Paul could digest the doctor's words, the anesthesiologist placed the mask over his mouth and nose. Who would he be when he woke up? The same person or someone else? Or would he wake up at all? When Paul breathed in, darkness enveloped him.

Genny.

Opening his eyes, Paul closed them again, hoping to clear his blurry vision. A nurse checking his vitals noticed he was awake.

"How do you feel?"

He turned his head in her direction.

"Dr. Godfrey will be in shortly to talk to you."

"Okay," Paul said, his voice gruff. The nurse brought over a small cup with a straw and raised his head so he could take a few sips of water. The only surgery he'd had was a tonsillectomy when he was twelve and he didn't remember what had happened. Paul tried to move his legs, but he felt nothing from the waist down. A wave of panic pushed through his veins.

"You've had a spinal block. It helps minimize pain during recovery."

Paul glanced around as he sipped water. The room was large and the patients were separated by curtains. The curtain at the foot of his bed was partially open, and he saw a large clock hanging on the wall behind the nurse's station. He strained to see the time. *Ten minutes after ten?* Was it in the morning or afternoon? He didn't know what day it was, much less the time.

The nurse came into his recovery area again. "The doctor is talking to the patient next door, and she will be here soon."

He was about to learn his fate. "Is it ten in the morning?"

"No, it's in the evening."

"What's the date?"

"September eighteenth." She went to the standing desk next to the bed and began typing on a laptop.

"Twenty-sixteen?"

Removing her hands from the keyboard, she stepped over to him. "That's correct. Do you know where you are?"

"Walter Reed?"

"Yes. Who is the president?"

Paul drew a blank. He couldn't remember who was at the top of his chain of command? He squeezed his eyes shut, and it came to him a moment later. "Barack Obama?"

"Who is your emergency contact?"

"My wife, Genny Thompson. Genevieve."

"Okay. You have a concussion. It's not uncommon to be confused." She smiled and started typing again.

Paul closed his eyes and thought about Genny and his children. Did Genny know that something had happened to him? He prayed she wouldn't fall apart. She'd come a long way since she'd lost her family, and he was afraid that his injuries would open an old wound in her heart. A woman's voice grew louder, and he opened his eyes. The woman from the OR walked up to his bedside.

"Hello, Sergeant Thompson. I'm Dr. Godfrey. I'm your orthopedic surgeon."

"Hello, ma'am. I remember you."

Dr. Godfrey talked about the surgery. Paul now had a rod and screws in his left arm, and for the first time, he felt the weight of the cast. He didn't remember the nurse from before surgery saying anything about his arm. The doctor mentioned life-saving measures. Were his injuries that serious? As she talked, Paul remembered the nurse had told him he'd developed sepsis. He wasn't knowledgeable about sepsis, but he knew it could be serious.

"Sergeant Thompson?" Dr. Godfrey's voice held a tone that scared Paul.

"Yes, ma'am?"

"Do you remember Dr. Morganson and myself talking to you about the worst-case-scenario prior to surgery?"

Moisture filled Paul's eyes when he understood what she meant. "Yes, ma'am," he choked out the words. A continual stream of tears fell down the sides of Paul's face as the doctor talked. The nurse grabbed a tissue and began blotting the tears, but there were too many for her to keep up.

Paul was not the same man he was before the surgery, and he never would be. He prayed Genny would still love him, and that his children wouldn't be afraid of him.

CHAPTER 2

Genny

To help close the distance between them, Paul and Genny had picked nine o'clock Sunday evenings for their weekly Skype date. Twelve-hour night shifts and the time difference could make it difficult for their schedules to work. When it was nine in the evening in Charleston, South Carolina, it was six-thirty the next morning in Afghanistan. Three months and this deployment would be over.

Staring at the laptop screen, Genny waited for Paul to come online. Lately, she'd been missing him more than usual. Looking into his blue eyes on a screen wasn't ideal, but it was the best they could do.

"Mama? Is Daddy there?" Three-year-old Katie leaned over to get a look at the laptop screen.

"Not yet, baby girl."

Katie sighed and picked at the frayed yarn covering her doll's head.

While she waited, Genny pulled up Facebook to check her notifications. A few updates from high school friends didn't grab her interest. Closing the browser, she opened Skype again and stared at Paul's name. It was now nine forty-five. Their video dates had been like clockwork during the deployment.

Caleb stirred, and Genny picked him up from the portable crib next to the bed.

"Hi, Bubby." Katie kissed her brother's head. Yawning, she slid down under the covers.

"Tell Paul hello for me," Tricia, Genny's mother-in-law, said as she walked up to the side of the bed.

Katie flung the covers back. "Daddy's not here, Mimi."

"He's not?"

"I'm sure he's running behind at work." It made sense. Paul had no control over the planes' schedules.

"You're probably right."

"It's time for bed, Katie."

"No, Mama. I wanna talk to Daddy."

"He's probably still at work, baby girl."

"Kiss Mama goodnight, and I'll tuck you in."

After a goodnight kiss and hug, Tricia and Katie headed down the hall and Genny laid Caleb back in his crib. Sliding the laptop under the bed, she pulled the covers up and rolled over. It was almost seven-fifteen in the morning in Afghanistan. Paul's shift ended at six-thirty; he should have been in his room by now. Her mind wandered to dark places.

Over the years, Genny had lost all of her family, with the most recent being her brother Brandon, who was killed in Iraq six years earlier. It was the main reason she dreaded Paul's deployments.

Thinking about the unknown would send her anxiety through the roof. She closed her eyes and pushed out a breath. Why didn't Paul send a quick email to let her know he wouldn't make their Skype date?

Startled awake by her ringing phone, Genny reached for it, hoping Paul's call wouldn't go to voicemail before she could answer. A number from the military base showed on the caller ID. Through the fog of sleep, a few moments passed before Genny realized that Paul wasn't the one calling.

"Hello?" Genny ran her fingers through her hair and glanced over the edge of the bed at Caleb.

"Mrs. Thompson?"

"Yes?"

"This is Lieutenant Colonel Torres. I'm Sergeant Thompson's squadron commander," the woman on the other end said. "I'm sorry for calling so early."

Genny pulled the phone away from her ear to check the time. *Five forty-seven.* "It's okay." Why would the base be calling? Genny sat up in bed and softly cleared her throat.

"We've received word that Sergeant Thompson has been injured on deployment."

"Injured?" Genny's arms went weak and she fumbled with her phone.

"Yes, ma'am. His injuries are critical, but he's stable. He's been transferred to Walter Reed National Military Medical Center in Maryland. Senior Master Sergeant Johnson, the superintendent of the squadron, is contacting the Air Force Wounded Warrior Program to assist with travel arrangements. Someone will be in contact with you within the hour."

After the call, Genny sat quietly for a moment. Grabbing her head, she squeezed her eyes shut and rocked back and forth. What was she supposed to do? She'd never had a loved one in critical condition. Drawing in a deep breath, she climbed out of bed, and headed down the hall to Tricia's room.

Genny knocked and rested her hand on the knob.

"Yes," Tricia said after a moment.

Genny froze.

Opening the door, Tricia looked down as if she expected Katie. Her gaze lifted to Genny's face. "Sweetheart, is something wrong?"

Genny gasped and covered her mouth with her hands when she began sobbing. Dropping her hands, she said, "It's Paul."

"What about Paul?"

"He's been hurt."

Tricia's lips parted and she gasped. The women sat on the bed holding hands while Tricia prayed. Genny closed her eyes and tried to force all the scenarios out of her head. All she could think about was losing Paul.

Paul and Genny's neighbor, Mrs. Baker, offered to care for the children, and their friends Trevor and Tamika planned to help in the evenings and on the weekends as needed. The Air Force Wounded Warrior Program had arranged a flight out of Charleston in a few hours, and Tricia reserved a seat on the same flight. Paul's father Brian, who was at home in Murfreesboro, Tennessee, would fly out of Nashville in late afternoon.

"Genny." Tricia slipped her hands in Genny's, pulling her away from packing her suitcase. "God's got this."

Does He? Genny forced a smile. "I know, but—"

"Paul is my only child. I don't know what I would do if I lost him, but I have to put my trust in the Lord."

"It's still hard." Genny stepped forward and gave Tricia a hug. "I need to finish packing."

Tricia reached up and rested her hand on Genny's cheek. "I love you, sweetheart."

"I love you, too."

Katie walked into Genny's bedroom holding her baby doll. "I wanna go." A smile broke out across Katie's face and her eyes pleaded with Genny.

How could she possibly understand what was happening? Genny picked Katie up, brushed strands of dark hair away from her forehead and gave her a kiss.

"No, honey. Daddy's sick and in the hospital," Tricia said.

Katie's smile fell.

"It's okay, baby girl. You'll see Daddy soon, I promise. Mrs. Baker is coming over to stay with you and Bubby. Uncle Trevor and Aunt Tamika will help."

"Okay, Mama," Katie mumbled, wiggling out of Genny's arms onto the bed. She crawled to the head of the bed, sat on the pillows, and brushed her fingers over her doll's face. Genny's chest tightened when Katie began singing to her doll.

Placing her suitcase and carry-on bag by the front door next to Tricia's luggage, Genny went to the living room. She picked Caleb up and sat on the couch next to Katie. Wrapping her arms around her children, she fought back tears as she held them tight. What did the future hold for their family?

A large blue SUV pulled into the driveway. After kissing her children and hugging Mrs. Baker, Genny and Tricia followed the driver out the door to the vehicle. Once their luggage was loaded, Genny settled in the front seat and Tricia sat in the backseat. Genny stared out the window, trying to rein in her thoughts. Critical was one step above fatal. What did that mean for Paul?

The driver took the exit for Charleston International Airport and a mixture of fear, dread, and helplessness hit Genny at once. She drew in a ragged breath and blinked back tears. Pulling up to the curb, the driver found a cart and loaded the luggage. After Genny and Tricia received their tickets, they headed to the entrance of the concourse.

Tears burning her eyes, Genny stared out the windows, watching the traffic on the runway. She couldn't fall apart now. Not here. Closing her eyes, she drew in a deep breath. The temperature around Genny soared and a wave of nausea hit her. Slipping the elastic hair band from her wrist, she pulled back her long auburn hair into a low ponytail.

An agent called for boarding and Genny and Tricia made their way down the jetway to the plane. She found her row and slipped into her window seat. Tricia reached over and patted Genny's arm before heading toward the rear of the plane to her seat. Settling in, Genny closed her eyes and leaned her head back against the headrest.

Opening her eyes, Genny sighed and looked out the window, focusing on the blinking lights on the plane's wing.

A sound got Genny's attention and she saw a young man put his bag in the overhead bin in her row. When he sat in the seat next to her, he powered off his phone, pocketed it, and smiled.

"Hi, I'm John."

"I'm Genny."

After a few more pleasantries, the two quieted and settled into their seats to prepare for takeoff.

The plane taxied down the runway and lifted off, causing Genny's stomach to drop. She closed her eyes and prayed for strength for what they were facing. This flight would start her journey down a road of uncertainty. Was she ready? No.

The hum of the engines relaxed Genny, releasing a rush of emotions she'd been pushing down. What exactly did critical condition mean? Images of Paul lying motionless in a hospital bed flashed in her mind, pushing a soft moan from her throat. She drew in a deep breath and slowly released it.

"Motion sickness?"

Genny pinched her lips together for a moment to hold in a sob. She turned to John and wiped her cheeks. "No," her voice wavered, and she cleared her throat.

"I've been told that I'm a good listener. If you need or want to talk, say the word."

Without a second thought, Genny opened her heart to this stranger. "I received a call a little before six this morning that my husband was critically injured in Afghanistan. He was transferred to the military hospital in Maryland late yesterday and I'm going to see him. To be honest, I'm scared to death."

"I'm so sorry. I'm a physical therapy tech in the rehab unit at the same hospital."

"Really?" Genny said as she tucked her hair behind her ear.

"Yes, ma'am." He smiled. "There's a chance I'll see him."

What were the odds that she'd be sitting with someone that worked at the same military hospital? God had placed John in the seat next to her to comfort her.

"I'll tell you this. More make it through rehab than don't. We've worked with some pretty serious cases." John straightened in his seat. "I'm not saying it will be easy. It takes both the physical therapist and the patient. We can't do it for them."

A flight attendant announced the pilot would begin the descent into Dulles International Airport shortly. Genny realized that she and John had talked for most of the flight.

"Maybe we'll see each other again."

"Probably so." He smiled and stepped aside so Genny could exit the row. She looked down the aisle behind her, but didn't see Tricia.

As they were walking up the jetway, nausea tightened Genny's throat. There were no more distractions, and her mind was back to filling her head with devastating thoughts. Soon, she wouldn't have to guess Paul's injuries. Genny and John parted ways at the restrooms, and Genny made it to a stall in time to vomit. She hated it was the way her body reacted to anxiety.

The bathroom door squeaked open, and Genny heard someone pull paper towels from the dispenser and the water turned on. She unlocked the door and stepped out.

Tricia was standing near the sinks holding a wet paper towel. "Here, sweetheart."

Genny took the paper towel from her mother-in-law and wiped her face. "Thanks."

Heading to baggage claim, Genny saw a young woman in an Air Force uniform holding a sign. She was told that someone was picking her up at the airport. When Genny got closer, she saw her name on the sign and approached the woman. She pushed out her breath. One step closer to seeing her husband and the truth of what she faced.

CHAPTER 3

Genny

"I'm Genevieve Thompson, and this is my mother-in-law, Tricia."

"Hello, ma'am." The woman inclined her head to Genny, then Tricia. "I'm Sergeant Mayfield from the Air Force Wounded Warrior Program. I'll be your liaison while you are here. Let's get your bags and we'll go to Fisher House so you can get settled in. If you don't know, it's the military equivalent of a Ronald McDonald house."

"Oh. Okay." A rush of tears filled Genny's eyes as she led the sergeant to the carousel for their flight. Each step led her closer to the truth. She fought back her emotions and maintained her composure. Sergeant Mayfield loaded Genny's and Tricia's bags into the trunk of a sedan.

"To help set you at ease, Mrs. Thompson, I'll let you know what to expect tomorrow." Sergeant Mayfield drove out of the parking lot.

"Thank you. You can call me Genny."

"And I'm Tricia."

"You can call me Angela when it's just us." She glanced at Genny and smiled. "In the morning, I'll take you to meet the social worker you'll be working with. Her name is Anna." Angela slammed on the brakes and laid down on the horn when a car cut them off. Genny tightened her grip on the armrest.

"Oh, goodness," Tricia mumbled under her breath.

"You'll meet with your husband's doctor, and you should be able to see your husband tomorrow."

"Okay." Genny saw a tall building in the distance and figured it was the hospital.

"That's Walter Reed National Military Medical Center. Everyone calls it Walter Reed for short."

The building in the distance stretched into the sky, and Genny scanned the full height as they approached. Angela slowed and turned into a parking lot of a building that was close to the hospital. The sign out front read: *Fisher House*.

"You are a five-minute walk from the hospital."

"Oh, that's nice." Genny opened the car door when Angela pulled up in front of the building.

Angela unloaded their bags and led them to the reception desk. "I'll see you in the morning."

"See you then." Genny turned her attention to the clerk and checked in.

Within an hour, Genny and Tricia had settled into the suite. Tricia had gone to the dining area earlier and brought back dinner. Eating a few things, Genny threw the rest into the trash when her stomach rolled. After a long, hot shower, she walked into the living room where Tricia was talking to Brian on the phone.

"Hi, sweetheart. All settled?" Tricia asked after she ended the call.

"Yeah."

"Dad said he should be here in about an hour."

"Ok, good." She excused herself and went back into her bedroom and sat on the foot of the bed.

Directly across from the bed hung a mirror over the desk. Genny studied herself, turning her head from side to side. Her pale skin emphasized the bags under her eyes.

Genny walked over to the window, drew back the curtains, and opened the blinds. In the distance, Walter Reed hospital stared at her. Her husband was in there somewhere. What was happening to him? Genny closed the window coverings and made her way to the living room. She couldn't shake the feeling that their lives would never be the same.

Grabbing a bottle of water from the fridge in the kitchenette, Genny opened it and drank the water in three gulps, but her mouth was still dry.

"I don't know why I'm watching that." Tricia clicked off the TV.

"To get your mind off the unknown." Genny sat on the couch next to Tricia. They talked about the children. Genny had called Mrs. Baker earlier to see how they were doing. "Katie is so confused."

"It may take a little while, but she'll get there."

Get where? Where is this going?

The lock released on the door and Brian walked inside. He dropped his luggage when Tricia rushed to him. Several minutes passed before Brian released Tricia. He wiped the tears from her cheeks and kissed her.

"You look beautiful, my love. I have missed you." Brian kissed Tricia again.

"I've missed you, too."

Genny took a deep, pained breath. She'd gone to Tennessee for a month after Paul deployed. Caleb was three months old and Katie was almost three and a half and becoming a handful. They felt it was best if Katie was in her own environment and Tricia wanted to go to help Genny. Brian hadn't seen his wife in nearly two months.

"Any news?" Brian asked.

"No. We'll meet with his doctor tomorrow." Genny slipped her arms around Brian's neck and hugged him. Genny pointed to a bowl of fruit on the small table. "I had a few bites of a banana and a slice of garlic bread from the meal Mom brought from the dining room. I can go grab something for you."

Brian shook his head. "I'm afraid I'll get sick if I eat anything heavy. Maybe I'll have an apple." He walked to the table and picked up a red one.

They settled in for the night and Genny tried to prepare herself for the long, hard day ahead. Looking at the small framed photo of her and Paul on their wedding day she'd brought along, she picked it up from the nightstand. "My love, I pray it's not as bad as I think." Tracing his face in the picture, she kissed him and set the frame back on the nightstand. Turning off the lamp, Genny stared at the ceiling. The last time she looked at the alarm clock on the nightstand, it was almost three in the morning. It was going to be a long day.

Dragging herself out of bed after three hours of sleep, Genny held a cool washcloth over her eyes, but the dark circles remained. In the rush to pack, she'd forgotten to grab her makeup bag from the bathroom counter. Dressed in a pair of jeans and a short-sleeved pullover top, Genny walked out of her room, and saw

Brian and Tricia sitting at the small breakfast table. Brian had his hands wrapped around a coffee cup, and Tricia was staring at the bowl of fruit.

"Are you hungry, honey?" Tricia asked. She picked up a banana but put it back in the bowl.

"No. Thanks."

"Us either." Brian sipped his coffee.

Genny heard Angela and the receptionist talking when they stepped into the hall. Angela looked their way when they walked into the lobby.

"Good morning. Are you ready?"

"I'm not sure." Genny gave a little laugh and glanced at Tricia, who already had tears in her eyes. Genny reached for Tricia's hand, and they headed for the door.

"After you, ma'am, sir." Angela held the door open and gestured outside.

On the walk, Angela talked about everything from what to expect at the hospital to options for meals and worship services. Genny took in her surroundings as much as possible. When the automatic doors to the hospital opened, Genny stopped, and Brian rested his hand on her upper back. Angela turned around and stopped.

"Sorry." Genny inhaled deeply, then blew out her breath. "I'm ready." It was one of the worst lies of her life. She'd never be ready to see Paul in a critical state.

Angela led them through the hospital lobby, down corridors to the social worker's office, and knocked on the open door. "Good morning, Anna. This is Sergeant Thompson's wife, Genny, and his parents, Brian and Tricia."

"Come in."

"Text me if you need me," Angela said.

"Okay." Genny swallowed the knot swelling in her throat. The trio took their seats in front of Anna's desk. "Do you know what happened?" Genny asked.

"The report is still open, but what I see here is that there were several personnel on a cargo plane getting the cargo ready for the flight. The hydraulics malfunctioned and the ramp of the plane fell, sending several full pallets down the ramp." Anna was quiet for a moment. Genny watched as her eyes scanned the words on the screen. She must be searching for information specific to Paul. "Sergeant Thompson was hit by a full pallet and knocked to the ground." Anna looked up at Genny and bit her bottom lip, then returned to reading. "The pallet fell on top of him."

Genny's mouth hung open. "It fell on him?"

"Those things weigh thousands of pounds." Brian gulped.

"It says here that there was a fatality and several critical and minor injuries."

Why did Paul's injuries have to be critical?

"What about his injuries?" Brian asked.

"I don't have that information. I'm sorry. The treatment team will fill you in on everything related to his medical condition."

"Okay, thank you," Brian said.

It took a team to treat Paul? Genny crossed her legs to keep from shaking. "Will we see him today?"

"You'll have to ask his doctors, but I believe you will see him today."

"Okay, good." The thought of seeing Paul tightened Genny's stomach. The last time she saw him was at the end of June. What would her strong, healthy husband look like now?

Anna talked about the hospital, information that Angela had already given them. Genny listened anyway. Something had to fill the thirty minutes until they saw Paul's doctors. She looked at Brian, noticing him blinking every few seconds. He turned to her, tears welling in his eyes. She reached over and rested her hand on his knee. This was as painful for Brian and Tricia as it was for her. Genny imagined Katie or Caleb in Paul's place. She'd be devastated.

"The hospital has a state-of-the-art rehabilitation center," Anna said and described the facilities in detail.

Did that mean Paul needed rehab? She remembered John from the flight. Maybe she'd see him again.

Anna glanced at her wall clock, and Genny's eyes followed. It was ten minutes until ten o'clock. Nausea rose in Genny's throat, and she blew out her breath when Anna raised to her feet.

Genny felt as if she was floating down the hall next to Anna. She'd fall to the floor if Brian wasn't walking next to her. They stepped onto an elevator and passed several floors. When the doors opened, Genny tensed at the sign that greeted them: *Intensive Care Unit.* Which room was Paul in? She kept her eyes forward to keep her gaze from drifting into patient rooms as they walked by. Anna slowed her steps when they entered another hall that looked like where the administrative offices were located.

Genny glimpsed a small conference room through an open door. A woman and two men in white coats sat across the table. Anna stopped at the door and gestured for Genny and her in-laws to walk in ahead of her. The man wearing an Air Force uniform sitting close to the door smiled and stood when they approached the table.

"Doctors. Chaplain. This is Genny, Sergeant Thompson's wife, and his parents, Brian and Tricia."

"I'm Chaplain Zhang." The man wearing the Air Force uniform held out his hand. He smiled when Genny accepted, and reached toward Brian and Tricia, shaking their hands.

Pulling out a chair, Genny sat down. Brian and Tricia sat to her right, close to Anna, and Chaplain Zhang sat to her left. She laid her shaking hands on her lap.

"Mrs. Thompson, I'm Dr. Morganson. I'm a general surgeon. This is Dr. Abraham. He's a neurologist and on the end there," Dr. Morganson smiled at the woman, "is Dr. Godfrey. She's an orthopedic surgeon. We are your husband's treatment team."

"Hello." Genny tilted her head to each physician. Resting her hands to the arms of the chair, she tightened her grip. Feeling as if her heart was tearing out of her chest, Genny glanced down the front of her shirt; it was moving to the beat of her heart. Was she about to have a panic attack?

"Sergeant Thompson was scheduled for surgery this morning, but we had to take him into emergency surgery early in the evening yesterday. He's stable now." Dr. Morganson straightened his glasses.

Yesterday?

"Why wasn't I contacted earlier?" Genny twisted her wedding set. She glanced at Tricia and saw the lines in her forehead deepen.

"I'm sorry Mrs. Thompson. The time difference between the countries and flight times can make it hard to notify loved ones." The doctor pushed up his glasses. "Notification must take place within twenty-four hours."

Twenty-four hours? Genny swallowed hard and rested her arms on top of the table.

"As far as a head injury goes," Dr. Abraham began, "he has a mild TBI. A traumatic brain injury, that is. It should resolve in time. However, he could experience symptoms for up to two years. Some things to look for are headaches, forgetfulness, problems concentrating. Comprehension. His moods might change, too. Remember that it's the TBI, not him."

Genny nodded. The doctor made it sound like Paul would come home as a different person. She shifted her gaze to Dr. Godfrey. The doctor's lips pressed together, forming a thin line, causing Genny's heart to race. There was only one person who knew how to calm her, and he was the person they were talking about. Genny drew in a deep breath and calmly blew it out.

"Sergeant Thompson's radius is broken in two places in his left arm. I placed a steel rod in his arm and I expect him to regain full use." Dr. Godfrey rested her hands on top of the table. "His pelvis is fractured, but it will heal with bedrest."

What did a fractured pelvis mean? Would it prevent him from walking? Brian's hand rested on top of Genny's, the warmth calming her for a moment. Genny glanced at Brian and saw that he was holding Tricia's hand.

"His left leg received the brunt of the trauma."

Genny's breath caught in her throat as she looked at each doctor.

"All the bones from the knee down in his left leg were broken. Some were crushed. There was nothing to put back together. And the laceration on his left leg became severely infected and—"

A ringing started in Genny's ears and increased in volume and pitch as Dr. Godfrey spoke. Genny caught a word here and there. Fever and infection. Blood clots and sepsis. No choice but to amputate. *Amputate?*

Brian pulled Tricia into his arms when she gasped and cried out.

The ringing drowned out Dr. Godfrey's voice and Genny slammed her hands down on the table, causing everyone to jump. She thrust herself to her feet.

"*You're wrong!* You have the wrong Paul Thompson." Genny shivered and broke out in a cold sweat.

"Mrs. Thompson," Dr. Godfrey said.

"No! You're wrong." Genny's ears began ringing again. She closed her eyes for a moment.

"Mrs. Thompson."

Genny felt a gentle hand on her back. She turned and saw the chaplain standing at her side. "No," she whispered, and sat down. "He's a runner and…and we have two small children. How is he going to play with them?" How was he going to walk? Or drive? Could he stay in the Air Force with one leg? What was going to happen to them? She looked in the chaplain's direction again and saw his bowed head. Although she was terrified, a sense of peace came over her.

The doctors discussed Paul's treatment plan. Physical therapy would start working with him once he was out of ICU to help prevent scar tissue and to stretch the skin on his residual leg. Three to four weeks post-surgery, he'd start practicing with a prosthetic in short increments. His residual leg should be completely healed by week twelve. He'd get his permanent prosthetic once he could walk unassisted for most of the day.

Paul would remain in the ICU for several days. They were drawing blood several times a day and the infection was improving. The doctor didn't want Paul to move to a regular room until the infection was gone. Genny drew in a ragged breath and blew it out. Brian slipped his arm around her shoulders and Genny reached over and grabbed Tricia's hand.

Chaplain Zhang leaned toward Genny. "Would you and your family like to go to the chapel for a while? We can pray for your husband."

Genny glanced at Brian and Tricia, and they nodded. The family made their way to the chapel with Chaplain Zhang, spending time in prayer. Brian and Tricia went back to Fisher House so Paul and Genny could have time to themselves.

Chaplain Zhang looked at his watch. "It's getting close to lunchtime. I'm sure Sergeant Thompson has had lunch or is about to. Are you ready?"

"Umm…yes…I think so."

"You're nervous and it's perfectly normal."

Genny smiled and followed the chaplain out of the chapel. As they walked to the elevator, images of tubes, beeping machines, and a flurry of activity around Paul kept popping into Genny's head. Did he look like an ICU patient on an episode of *Grey's Anatomy*?

Genny's heart pounded each time the elevator beeped as the floors passed by. The doors opened to the ICU, but it was a different area than when they were with Anna. They made their way down the hall; Genny's pace slowing with each step. Chaplain Zhang stopped by the nurse's station and asked about Paul. A nurse stepped out from behind the desk and walked with them to a room.

"You must be his wife." The nurse looked at Genny.

"Yes." Genny's mouth went dry.

"I'm Kayla. I bet he'll be ready to eat his lunch now. He was too nervous earlier. He knows you're coming today, but not exactly when."

For the first time since stepping off the elevator, Genny noticed the aroma of food drifting through the halls. Kayla stopped at a room, pushed open the door, and stepped aside

"He's been napping some so he could be asleep. He's doing well considering what he's been through, but the doctor wants him to stay in the ICU until the sepsis has cleared up. I'll be at the desk, so push the call button if you need me." She smiled and turned to walk back to the nurse's station.

"I'll stay here." Chaplain Zhang's smile reached his eyes.

Genny's lips parted.

"It's okay. You've got this."

Genny's steps were heavy and labored—like she was trudging through thick mud. Why did she feel like she was approaching a stranger? This man was her husband. The love of her life, and the father of her children. Why was she scared? Trembling took over her body, and her stomach dropped as if she was on a rollercoaster. *Calm down Genny.*

Forcing herself to focus on Paul's face, her heart rose to her throat at what she saw. His eyes were closed, and she could see bruising on his ashen skin. As she passed by the couch against the wall, she saw his lunch on the tray table. The cover was still on, and an unopened bottle of water was placed next to the dish. Turning back to Paul, she finally made it to the side of his bed and drew in a deep breath.

A blue blanket over a white sheet covered his body. He was wearing a hospital gown loosely tucked under his upper body. Cuts and scrapes dotted his face, neck, and right arm, and bruises covered all of his exposed skin. The cast on his left arm stretched from above his elbow to his fingers.

A tuft of hair was standing up on top of his head. Genny reached to push it back down, and her fingers found a line of stitches in the center of a bald spot. She drew in a shaky breath and wiped her cheeks. Slowly turning her head, her gaze fell on his hips and ran down his right leg. The blanket lay flat where his left leg should be. Dr. Godfrey had said that Paul's leg was amputated between the hip and knee, but she wasn't prepared for what she saw.

Genny clenched her teeth to keep from sobbing. Turning toward the door, she stepped over until she saw Chaplain Zhang. He pointed down the hall and she nodded, giving him permission to leave her alone and head back to the chapel. She could do this. They were going to deal with Paul's amputation for the rest of their lives. Today was day one.

Genny turned back to Paul and leaned down, kissing his forehead, then his cheek. Brushing her nose against his, she eased back, and Paul opened his eyes.

"Genevieve," he whispered. Immediately, his eyes filled with tears.

"I love you." Genny said. Life was going to be different. Not only because of Paul's injuries, but because she was looking into the eyes of a broken man.

CHAPTER 4

Paul

Paul was staring into the beautiful face of the woman who had stolen his heart. Anticipating this moment, he knew he would be emotional, but he didn't expect tears to start the moment he saw her. Would she still love him as an amputee? Peace and fear warred within his soul.

"Hi, my love." The warmth of her breath soothed him. She kissed him, letting her kiss linger.

Tears rolled down the sides of Paul's face. Genny pulled a few tissues from the box next to the bed and wiped the tears away. He began sobbing, and she eased down on the bed next to him. "I'm not the… man you married," he rasped and cleared his throat.

"Yes, you are." Genny laid her hand over his heart. "You are the same man here, and that's what matters."

"But…"

"Let's concentrate on getting you better so we can get you home. Your babies miss you."

Paul wiped his eyes and lifted the corners of his mouth, attempting a smile. He pointed at the controls for the bed. "Can you… raise the head…of the bed?"

Genny pressed the button until Paul told her to stop. He wiped his face with a fresh tissue and drew in a deep breath.

"Do…" Paul cleared his throat. "Do you know what happened?" He swallowed.

"Yes. The social worker told me. Did you know the person who died?"

"Died?" Paul's chest tightened, squeezing the air from his lungs.

"You didn't know? One person died. There were several with severe injuries like you. A few with minor injuries. Here, I bet you're hungry." Genny sat up and reached for his lunch tray.

"I haven't had much of an… appetite."

"You need to eat." She pulled the top off of the plate and grabbed the banana. Peeling it, she broke off a piece and held it to Paul's mouth.

He smiled and took the piece of banana from her hand. "I can feed myself, love." Easing it into his mouth, he took his time chewing and swallowed it. Sucking in a quick breath between clenched teeth, he felt as if the banana was made of glass, a side-effect of the breathing tube used during the surgery.

Genny's shoulders fell. "I'm sorry."

"It's okay." He let it go. Genny was doing what she did best—taking care of those she loved.

"I'm a little hungry. Can I have this?" Genny pointed to the chocolate pudding cup.

Paul nodded.

Genny handed the banana to Paul and reached for the pudding cup. Her hand shook as she pulled the top off. "Mom and Dad are at Fisher House. They didn't want you to get overwhelmed and wanted to give us time. They'll be here after lunch."

"Okay."

"I love you." Genny smiled.

"I love you too, sweetheart." Paul ate another piece of banana. Looking at Genny, he saw tears rolling down her cheeks. He laid the banana aside and took the pudding cup from her hand. Patting the mattress, Genny laid down next to Paul again and began sobbing.

A few minutes went by before Genny quieted. Resting her head on his chest, she softly hummed as she traced the neckline of his hospital gown. "We Won't Be Shaken" by Building 429, was one of his favorite praise and worship songs.

A knock sounded on the door and Genny sat up. "Anna." She smiled at the woman as she walked into the room. "She's our social worker."

"Nice to meet you, Sergeant Thompson. I'm here to help you and your family during your stay here. I'll also help get you set up with a social worker in Charleston for when you return home." She walked to the edge of the bed.

"Thank you."

"We're here to help." She smiled and handed Genny a folder, and explained the information inside.

Anna left, and Paul was alone with Genny again. She turned to him and wiped her eyes. "I'm sorry."

"Cry all you want. I do." He reached a shaky hand out and ran his fingers down the side of her face. The love he felt for this woman was indescribable.

"I was so close to losing you." She laid next to him again. "I don't know what I would have done."

"But you didn't." Paul cleared his throat and reached for the bottle of water. Genny opened it and he took a swig. "We have to remember that." Paul winced when a sharp pain ran down his residual leg.

"Are you okay? Want me to call the nurse?"

"I think it's time for my medication," he whispered.

"I'll call Kayla." Genny pushed the call button.

After receiving pain medication, Genny returned to Paul's side, and he felt himself drifting off to sleep. Peace won the war this time, but fear wasn't far behind.

⸺ℯℓℯ⸺

Paul was settling into his new room. He'd spent four days in the ICU receiving antibiotics. A long, hard road stretched out in front of him for rehabilitation. He had no choice but to hit it head on—giving up wasn't an option.

Tricia was determined to pat down the tuft of hair on the top of his head. He'd told her twice that it was standing up because of the cut and stitches, but she insisted on taking care of him. She'd taken care of him until he enlisted in the Air Force when he was eighteen, and she'd reminded him several times since visiting him that he was still her baby.

"You're looking like a hippy." Genny grinned. "I've never seen your hair this long since you've been in the military."

"I can't wait to shave it off." Paul ran his hand over the top of his head, wincing when his fingers found the stitches in the cut.

Genny's phone rang, and her eyes brightened. "Hi, baby girl. How—. Yes, he's—Okay, just a—" Genny handed the phone to Paul and pressed her lips together. "That girl."

"Just like her mama." Paul laughed and took the phone from Genny's hand. For a moment, he hesitated, not knowing what to say. He didn't know what Genny had told Katie about his injury.

Taking in a deep breath, Paul steadied his voice. "Hello, baby girl."

"Daddy! Are you okay?"

"Yeah, I'm okay." He felt as if he was sinking into the mattress from the weight of the lie. How could he put what he was feeling into words for his own benefit, much less his little girl?

"When will you be home?"

"I'm not sure." Paul heard Caleb squeal in the background.

Katie was quiet for a moment. "Mama said you have a owie on your leg."

"Yes, I do."

"Are you coming for my birthday?"

"I don't know, sweetheart. I hope so. Mimi and Papa will be back tomorrow."

"Yay! I'm having a super sleepover with Mrs. Baker tonight. Bubby's staying with Uncle Twevor and Aunt Tamika. I wish you can come home tomorrow, Daddy."

"Me too, baby girl."

"'Kay, bye bye!"

"Bye." Paul heard Mrs. Baker's voice in the background.

"Well, I guess she's done talking." Mrs. Baker laughed.

"Thank you so much for taking care of the kids. It means a lot."

"Of course. I love those kids as if they were my flesh and blood. You and Genny, too."

After the call, Paul placed Genny's phone on the nightstand. Genny rose from the couch and walked over to the side of the bed. Leaning down, she kissed him. "We're going to head out so you can rest. I'll be back later on."

"Okay, sweetheart."

"Son, work hard. You'll be home before you know it." Brian hugged Paul.

"I will, Dad."

Tricia kissed his cheek and he watched his family walk out of the room.

Paul had received transfer orders shortly before Caleb was born, and they were scheduled to move after the new year. They were supposed to be getting ready for his transfer to New Jersey. Now they'd be adjusting to a life they never imagined. The thought scared him. He liked his old life. God's plans were perfect, but what purpose did it serve for Paul to lose his leg?

CHAPTER 5

Genny

Two weeks had passed since Paul's amputation. Spending as much time as she could at the hospital, Genny left Fisher House early in the morning and returned late at night. The times Paul was being tended to by the aids, she'd visit the chapel or walk around the grounds of the hospital.

Genny laid on the couch in Paul's room with a book she'd borrowed from the chapel. When a knock sounded on the door, Genny placed a tissue between the pages to hold her place. She was surprised to see who walked in. The man knitted his eyebrows together when he saw her.

"I'm John. I'm going to be working with you, Sergeant Thompson."

"You can call me Paul. This is my wife, Genny." Paul gestured toward Genny.

John walked over to her and offered his hand. "You look familiar."

Genny grinned and shook his hand. "I'm Genny from the plane."

"What's going on?" Paul let out an awkward laugh as he shifted in bed.

"That's where I know you from. I had a feeling we'd see each other, remember?" John grinned.

"Yes, I do. John and I were on the same flight when I flew up."

"Small world." Paul lifted his brows.

"I was flying back from visiting my family and I noticed a woman who appeared lost sitting in a seat by the window. When I got closer, I realized I was assigned to the seat next to her."

As John talked about their encounter, Genny's feelings from that day came back. She was broken and scared. She'd had a strong feeling that God had used John to bring her comfort. Now she was sure God had sent him. Genny refocused when John began explaining what he would do and why. She grimaced at the thought of Paul's healing wound being manipulated to keep the skin pliable. Being in the room while John worked on Paul made Genny queasy. She excused herself and went to the chapel.

A chaplain was sitting with a family at the front of the chapel. Genny glanced around and didn't see Chaplain Zhang. Sobbing reverberated throughout the chapel. As devastated as Genny had been when she found out about Paul's injuries, she was surprised she hadn't cried as much as she thought she would. It didn't mean she wasn't scared.

"Genny?"

She looked up and saw Chaplain Zhang's smiling eyes. She slid over and he eased down next to her. He was an older man in his late forties or early fifties, Genny guessed. She'd never asked, but assumed that he was Korean or Japanese. He wore a wedding band, but they'd never discussed his family.

"How are you?" Genny noted he was more upbeat than usual.

"Our grandbaby was born this morning."

"Congratulations. That's awesome. Grandson or granddaughter?"

"Granddaughter. Emma Lynn James."

"That's a beautiful name. You and your wife must be excited."

"Yes, Jeanette is on cloud nine."

Genny glanced at the time on her phone and wondered if Paul's physical therapy was over. How long did it take to manipulate Paul's skin? She shuddered. "Paul's having his first physical therapy appointment and I made the mistake of being there when the therapist said what he'd be doing to Paul." She laughed.

"Ah. I understand. Would you like to grab a cup of coffee to get your mind off of it?"

"I'd love to."

Genny found a table while Chaplain Zhang bought their coffee. She looked around as she waited, there were people everywhere. The medical staff were obvious, but she wondered how many were patients or loved ones. Not every patient was like Paul. In her time at Walter Reed, she had learned that the hospital treated all kinds of patients, not just combat injuries. She smiled as Chaplain Zhang approached, and handed her a cup as he sat across the table.

"First grandbaby?" Genny brought the cup up to her mouth and sat it down when she felt the hot steam brushing across her lips.

"Yes, she is. Savannah, Emma's mom, is our oldest. She was two when Jeanette and I met, and I adopted her not long after we married. Two years after that, we had Scott." He took a small sip of coffee and grimaced.

"Is yours as hot as mine?" Genny grinned.

"Yes, it is." Chaplain Zhang pulled the top off the cup and blew into the liquid. "You and Paul have two children, right?"

"Yes. Katie and Caleb." Genny pulled out her phone and brought up the photo album. Scrolling through the photos, she found one of Katie and Caleb together and handed the phone to the chaplain.

"My goodness. Katie looks like you, and Caleb looks like Paul."

"Everyone says that." Chaplain Zhang handed the phone to Genny. "But Caleb is adopted."

"Is that so? He favors Paul with his black hair and blue eyes?"

"After Katie was born, I had a hysterectomy, but we knew our family wasn't complete. Close to a year ago, we had become foster parents. But before we had the opportunity for a placement, we removed ourselves from the list when our friends approached us about adopting their niece's baby. We brought Caleb home when he was two days old." Paul and Genny would forever be grateful that Trevor and Tamika had thought of them when they found out their niece was giving her baby up for adoption.

"Katie will be four on December first and Caleb is five months."

"Beautiful children."

"Thank you." Genny smiled. Wrapping her hands around the cup, she looked into Chaplain Zhang's kind brown eyes. "Paul and I appreciate your support. It means the world to us."

"My pleasure. I have enjoyed getting to know you and Paul these past few weeks. Paul is a strong man and I have no doubt he will come out stronger. It's going to be hard, but with the Lord and a strong support system, he'll do well."

"I know He's with us through all this. He uses other people, like you. Believe it or not, Paul's physical therapist was sitting next to me on the flight up here."

"He works in mysterious ways." Chaplain Zhang winked.

"Sure does. I'm heading home tomorrow, but I'm conflicted. I want to be here for Paul, but I miss the kids."

"I can imagine how hard that is."

"I want to get back here before the holidays, if I can. I'm thinking about bringing the kids since it could be a while before Paul's able to walk well enough to come home." Genny wrapped her hands around the bottom of the cup and lifted it to take a sip. Changing her mind, she set it down and thought about how she would juggle the kids and spending time with Paul. She tugged on the hem of her long sleeves and eased out a breath.

"I have a feeling he will be home before you know it." He patted her arm.

Genny checked the time and figured Paul's physical therapy should be over. "Well, I think I'll head back to Paul's room. Thank you so much for the coffee."

"You are welcome."

Paul's room door was closed except for a crack. Leaning close, she couldn't hear anything and slowly pushed the door open. Paul was sitting on the side of the bed, gritting his teeth. He had a hold of his residual leg close to the wound.

"Baby," she whispered.

He looked at her and wiped his cheeks.

"Oh, sweetheart." She walked up to Paul and eased down on the bed next to him.

Blowing out his breath, he said, "It's okay. A little more intense than I thought it would be. According to John, I did well." He let out a sad laugh. "I broke a sweat, so I need to take a shower."

"Want me to call for an aid?"

"No…"

"Want me to help?"

"You know, I think I'm going to try it by myself."

"Honey—"

"I can wheel into the shower and use the hand sprayer. I just need a little help to get into the wheelchair."

"Okay." Genny helped Paul into the chair and watched him wheel to the bathroom. It was hard for her to respect that Paul didn't want her help. She corrected her thoughts. Not that he didn't want her help, he needed to do this on his own. Paul was strong, and she was sure he would recover physically. It was his mental recovery that scared her. He hadn't said a word about what had happened since she first arrived at the hospital.

The dark circles were a little lighter than when she first arrived in Maryland. Genny dotted the concealer under her eyes and rubbed it into her skin. Angela had taken her shopping and she'd picked up some much-needed makeup. A yawn watered her eyes and she noticed crow's feet. Grimacing, she wasn't thirty and already had wrinkles. She felt as if she'd already lived a lifetime with all the loss she'd experienced.

Genny did another once over in her room and picked up her suitcase and carry-on bag and made her way to the front desk. After she checked out, the receptionist brought her luggage behind the counter, and she made her way to the hospital to spend some time with Paul before heading to the airport.

On the walk, Genny breathed in the cool morning air. It was still dark and reminded her of the life-changing call she'd received over two weeks earlier. She made her way through the doors of the hospital to the elevator. Pushing the button, she waited for the elevator to descend to the ground floor.

"Good morning, Genny."

She turned her head and watched Chaplain Zhang walking up to her. "Hello. You're here early."

"I start at six, but I like to come in half an hour early to get a cup of coffee and settle in."

"I'm visiting Paul before I leave for the airport." When the elevator doors opened, Genny stepped inside, and Chaplain Zhang followed behind her. They chatted as the elevator traveled to the floor where the chapel was located.

"Be blessed. You, Paul, and your children are in my prayers. I'll see you when you return."

"Thank you."

The chaplain stepped off the elevator and smiled as the doors closed. The elevator stopped at the floor of Paul's room, and Genny made her way down the hall.

"Hello, Mrs. Thompson." A nurse at the nurse's station smiled as Genny walked by.

"Hello."

Paul was still asleep. Genny walked over to the bed and brushed her fingers through his hair. She hadn't seen his hair this length since he was a teenager. He had told her he'd gotten used to it, but she was sure that he'd get a high and tight as soon as he was home.

"Hey, you," Paul said in a groggy voice.

Genny leaned close. "Good morning."

Paul raised his head and kissed her. "I wish I was going with you."

"So do I."

"I promise you I'll work my tail off to get home to you and the kids. I'm ready to get my life back."

"I know, babe." Genny sat on the side of the bed, and stretched out, resting her head on his shoulder.

"I've missed this."

Genny felt his voice vibrating against her cheek. "Me, too. I don't know what I would have done if…"

"Let's not go there. I'm here and that's what matters."

"I know." Genny sighed.

Paul held Genny for a long while. She sat up and picked up her phone from the nightstand. In less than fifteen minutes, Angela would be at Fisher House to take her to the airport. She sighed and kissed Paul's cheek. "It's that time."

Paul insisted on going with her to the elevator and wheeled alongside Genny. As they waited, Genny leaned down and kissed Paul. "I'll be back soon."

"Not soon enough." He smiled.

The elevator doors opened, and Genny stepped inside. "I love you, Paul Tyler Thompson."

"I love you, Genevieve Marie Thompson." He winked.

"I'll call when I get home."

"Okay, love."

Tears filled Genny's eyes as the elevator descended to the ground floor. Paul was going to be okay, but she was scared about his mental health. He could have died, and that would scare anyone. His behavior seemed normal when she'd been around him, but that didn't mean he'd not experienced symptoms. And then there was the fact that he wasn't a whole man, as he'd put it. How would that affect him in the future?

⸺ℓℓℓ⸺

Genny made her way down the concourse to baggage claim. The trip to Charleston was different from the trip to Maryland, but she still faced uncertainty. What would happen if Paul was discharged from the Air Force? They were a single income family. Maybe she should look into getting a job. She shook the thoughts from her head for the time being.

The crowd was thick with passengers from different flights. Genny spotted Brian and Katie. He smiled and pointed in Genny's direction. Katie's eyes lit up and she grinned, trying to pull away from Brian. Genny couldn't hear her voice, but she knew Katie was calling for her. By the time Genny was within a few yards of Brian, Katie was grinning and giggling as she jumped up and down.

"Mama!" Katie slipped her arms around Genny's neck as soon as she picked her up.

"I missed you, girl!" Genny laughed. "Where's Bubby and Mimi?"

"At home." Katie moved from side-to-side looking around Genny. "Where's Daddy?"

"Remember what I told you? He has to stay in the hospital until he is well enough to come home?"

"Oh." Katie hadn't been told that Paul had lost his leg. Only that his leg had been hurt. As time neared for Paul to come home, Genny had to prepare Katie to see her daddy with a prosthetic leg.

On the ride home, Katie chattered about everything from her Sunday school class to what she wanted to be for the church's fall festival.

"Mama, I wanna be a princess."

"A princess?"

"Uh-huh."

"I'm sure we can find a costume. Or maybe Mimi can help us make one."

Katie giggled and clapped her hands. Settling into her booster seat, she started singing "Jesus Loves Me," and Genny and Brian joined in. When Brian turned onto the road leading into their subdivision, everything seemed different. Genny had been gone less than three weeks, yet it looked as if she'd been gone for months. It was her imagination, of course. The houses looked the same; it was their lives that had changed.

As they headed down the hill, Genny caught sight of Paul's truck in the driveway. Tears stung her eyes when the image of him climbing in and out of the truck with a prosthetic leg filled her mind. The new truck was lower to the ground than his old truck, which should make it easier for him.

Brian shifted the car into park. Leaning forward, Genny looked through the windshield at the front door. A moment later, Tricia appeared with Caleb in her arms. Stepping out of the car, Genny hurried to the front steps. Caleb focused on her face and his little mouth stretched into a smile.

"Hi, little man." Genny took Caleb from Tricia's arms. Cradling her baby boy, she kissed his cheek. He was two months old when Paul deployed. She hoped it wouldn't take long for him to bond with Paul again.

Genny walked down the hall to her bedroom with Caleb on her hip and Katie trailing behind. Brian had placed her suitcase next to a large box on her bed. Genny sat Caleb on the bed and Katie climbed up and crawled over to the box.

"Papa said this is Daddy's."

Genny leaned over and read the address and realized that it was Paul's address from the deployed location in Afghanistan.

"It's Paul's items he had with him, I imagine," Brian said from the doorway.

"Oh." A tremble started at the base of Genny's neck and ran down her spine. She'd received a similar box from Iraq when her brother Brandon died.

"Open it, Mama." Katie ran her hands across the top.

Genny pulled open the drawer of her nightstand and picked up a small pair of scissors. Slicing the tape across the top, she pulled back the flaps and stared at the contents.

"Daddy's phone!" Katie grabbed the phone and tapped on the screen several times.

"It's off. And I'm sure the battery is dead by now."

"Oh." She tossed the phone aside and pulled out a stack of cards, pictures, and drawings. "Look, Mama." Katie showed Genny the drawing she'd put in the last care package they'd sent.

"I see." Moisture blurred Genny's vision when she noticed the remnants of tape on each corner. Genny pulled out several uniform items and Paul's civilian clothes and laid them aside.

"There's Daddy's laptop!" Katie reached deep inside for the laptop, nearly falling headfirst into the box.

"Katie, slow down," Genny pulled Katie out of the box. She picked up the laptop, reclined against the pillows, and opened the top. The stickers Katie had used to decorate the areas next to the trackpad were still there.

"What's this?" Genny looked up and saw the toiletry bag in Katie's hands.

"That's Daddy's bathroom stuff like shampoo, soap, shaving cream."

"I 'member when Daddy put the cream on my nose."

"You do?" Genny smiled at her daughter.

"Uh-huh."

Caleb giggled. He was on his hands and knees rocking back and forth. Genny prayed Paul would be home in time to see their son crawl for the first time.

"Ready for lunch?" Tricia asked from the doorway.

"Yes!" Katie slid down from the bed and scampered down the hall ahead of Tricia. "I want chicken nuggets."

"Want me to put that against the wall?"

"Sure." Genny put the uniforms back into the box and Brian picked it and set it against the wall. "I guess his uniform and boots he was wearing were thrown away."

"I imagine so. Probably had to cut his uniform off of him," Brian said.

The image in her head turned her stomach. "I'm sure you're right. They couldn't have undressed him with his injuries."

"Let's go get some nuggets." Brian held out his arm and slipped it around Genny's shoulders when she joined him.

Where would she be without her in-laws? More importantly, where would she be without God?

CHAPTER 6

Paul

Paul gritted his teeth, his face filling with heat. One more trip between the bars that might as well be the length of a football field. Gripping the bars, his knuckles whitened. He had to hang on. One stumble was a setback he didn't need. He had to get home to his family.

"You got it. No need to grip the bars so tightly, and you can slow down." John laughed. "You're ahead of the game. You've already made five trips."

Paul felt John's hand on his back and fought the urge to shrug him off. He didn't need help; he had to do this on his own. "I just want to get back home."

"I hear ya."

Dr. Godfrey had told Paul that he'd be in rehab for at least six months. It took everything in Paul not to scream at the top of his lungs when she told him. He had been at Walter Reed for two months. He didn't have it in him to stay another four. The longing to hold Genny and their children overwhelmed him.

"Okay, that's good for today. Are you going to stay to work your upper body?"

"I think I'll wait until tomorrow." Paul wiped the sweat from his forehead with a towel.

"Tomorrow's Saturday."

"I know." Paul balled the towel and pitched it into the soiled laundry bin.

John shook his head. "Good shot. Just don't overdo it."

"I won't." At the end of the bars, Paul waited for John to push his wheelchair over. He turned around and dropped to the seat, exhaling hard.

"You okay?"

"Yeah."

"Do you need help?" John pointed to the prosthetic.

"No, I'll take it off when I get back to my room."

"All right. Have a good weekend. And don't work too hard."

"You should know me by now." Paul chuckled and wheeled the chair around to face the doors.

John laughed and began gathering up the equipment.

Paul wheeled into his room and saw that housekeeping had been in to change the sheets. He wheeled around with his back to his bed.

"Hi, Sergeant Thompson."

Paul looked up as Kayla walked in. "How was PT?"

"Tiring."

"I bet. How are the kids? Is Genny coming back for a visit?"

"Kids are great. We've talked about her coming up, but I'm not sure. My mom went back to Tennessee for a week, then she'll be going back to Charleston. I wish I was there."

"You'll get there soon." Kayla smiled. "How's that arm?"

Paul straightened his left arm and turned it over, revealing a nasty scar. "A little sore. I've lost some muscle, but I'll get it back. Getting that cast off was the best birthday present."

"Did I miss your birthday? Wait." She tilted her head. "You got it off on Halloween."

"Yep. I'm a Halloween baby."

"No way." Kayla laughed. "Well, I'm glad you are doing well. You have really been working hard. Who knows? Maybe you'll be home by Christmas." She smiled and headed out the door.

"That would be a Christmas miracle," Paul mumbled. He grabbed the socket of the prosthetic and gently pulled. He sucked in air through clenched teeth. Holding his breath, he tugged a little more and the prosthetic slipped off of his residual limb. He sat still for a few moments, then removed the compression sock. The wound was red and inflamed, but according to Dr. Godfrey and John, it was normal.

Grabbing the remote for the bed, Paul lowered it enough where he could move onto the mattress from the wheelchair. A sharp pain shot through his residual leg and he tensed. He still dealt with pain, but it was nothing like the first few days after surgery.

The notification light was flashing on his phone, and he grabbed it from the table. A smile filled his face when he opened the text from Genny. He was happy she'd mailed him his phone. It made keeping in contact with his family easier.

Genny: Here's a kiss from your daughter.

Paul laughed when he saw the picture of Katie's puckered lips. Holding out his phone, he puckered his lips and took a picture.

Paul: Right back at you, baby girl.

He held the phone out again and puckered in a way that only Genny would appreciate. A few moments later, she replied.

Genny: Can't wait to feel your lips on mine!

Paul: Me too baby, I love you so much

Genny: I love you too

After a shower, Paul laid down to cool off. He groaned when he lifted his arm to grab his Bible from the side table. Setbacks happened, but in the shower? While shifting from the shower bench to the chair to dry off, he slipped. Grabbing the safety handle to keep from falling, he must have strained a muscle.

The thought of pulling the call chain crossed his mind but he made it onto the chair, dried off, and dressed himself. It didn't matter if he had to call for help. He'd lost his dignity two months ago. Sighing, he flipped through the pages until he found the first of the highlighted verses that had become his life verses since the accident.

"Second Chronicles chapter fifteen, verse seven: 'But as for you, be strong and do not give up, for your work will be rewarded.'" Reading aloud seemed to help with focus. He flipped to the sticky note and read the next verse. "First Peter chapter five, verse ten: 'And the God of all grace, who called you to his eternal glory in Christ, after you have suffered a little while, will himself restore you and make you strong, firm and steadfast.'"

Glancing out the window at the sun-filled sky, Paul's eyes fell to the couch below the window. Memories flooded his mind of the times he'd found Genny napping on the couch in his ICU room. In his confused state, he had thought he was dreaming. As he'd approached the end of his time in ICU, he knew she had been by his side from the beginning. God had truly blessed him with Genny and continued to bless him with her every day.

Tears stung his eyes as he thought about the possibility of missing Christmas with his kids. And it was Caleb's first Christmas. Looking at his Bible, Paul read over the verses again. An overwhelming peace filled his heart. Everything was going to work out.

When Paul woke up Saturday morning, he decided to skip going to the PT gym. John was right. He'd pushed himself hard and it was catching up with him. Slipping in the shower the day before didn't help.

Squeezing his eyes shut, Paul rubbed his temples and let out a slow breath. At least once a day he had a severe headache, thanks to the TBI. According to the doctor, the headaches should go away. Paul groaned. Not soon enough. He slipped on his prosthetic and walked around his room for fifteen minutes, bracing himself on his wheelchair. His residual limb was still painful, but he had to wear the prosthetic every day, gradually working up to wearing it most of the day. That was the main reason that an amputee was in rehab for at least six months.

Paul spread shaving cream across his face. He smiled when he remembered the time that Katie was curious about him shaving. He'd put a blob of shaving cream on her nose, and she ran out of the bathroom squealing.

After shaving, Paul wiped his face and wheeled out of the bathroom and up to the side of the bed. Locking the chair, he maneuvered onto the bed. This was the part that was the most challenging. Struggling, a few moments, he slipped on his best pair of athletic pants and his nicest t-shirt. He grabbed his Bible and made his way to the chapel.

Paul wheeled around the outside of the pews and took his place next to the front row. There were a handful of people in attendance. As Paul listened to Chaplain Zhang's sermon, the same peace he'd felt before filled his heart.

"Looking good, Paul," Chaplain Zhang said as Paul wheeled up to him after the service.

"Thanks, Chaplain." Paul stopped and shook the chaplain's hand.

"How have you been? How's the family?"

"Genny and the kids are great. I'm working hard to get back home. I miss them so much and don't want my son to forget who I am."

"I can understand that. Are you busy this afternoon?"

"No plans. Just lay in my bed and watch TV." Paul lifted his brows and smiled.

"Why don't we grab a cup of coffee?"

"I'd love to, Chaplain."

"Give me a minute and we'll head to the coffee shop."

After Chaplain Zhang bought their coffee, they found a place to sit and talked about the sermon and Paul's spiritual walk after the accident. Paul shared that despite everything that had happened, he clung to God to get him through.

"It's obvious that you and Genny love each other deeply. Tell me your love story. How did you two meet?" Chaplain Zhang's brows rose when Paul grinned and shook his head.

"It's different, chaplain. We've told our best friends, but that's it."

"I'm curious now." He took a sip of coffee.

"We grew up together. Genny and her brother Brandon moved to the house next door when we were kids. Brandon and I became best friends. Over the years, they'd lost their family and Brandon was all Genny had left. Brandon was killed in Iraq in twenty-ten."

"Oh, my goodness. I'm so sorry."

"Thank you. She had no one, so I brought her to Charleston to help her like I had promised Brandon I'd do if anything happened to him. Well…it was becoming a financial burden and she needed surgery and we got married so she could use the clinic on base, and we had extra money."

"You don't say?" Chaplain Zhang's lips parted.

"I know. A big risk. But we fell in love and the rest is history." Paul smiled and sipped his coffee.

"The Lord knew what He was doing."

"Yes, He did. And here we are. Two kids and almost six years later."

"I experienced a tough situation myself." The chaplain tilted his nearly empty cup towards Paul.

"Oh, yeah?"

"I was a rebel, according to my parents." The chaplain laughed.

The corners of Paul's mouth lifted into a smile and he sipped his coffee as the chaplain spoke.

"I was born in the U.S. two years after my parents immigrated from China. My father was a physician and my mother stayed home with us children. They are traditional and wanted me to marry a nice Chinese woman and go to medical school. I started down that path to make my parents happy and was entering my sophomore year. One night, my roommate invited me to a Bible study group at the chapel and a month later, I gave my life to Christ. I met my wife, Jeanette, at that group."

"Oh, wow." Paul took a sip of his coffee. "How did you become a chaplain?"

"Toward the end of my sophomore year, I felt His calling and withdrew from university and entered seminary. I heard about the shortage of military chaplains and became a chaplain in the Air Force. It was hard with my parents for a while. They finally came around. I'm working on bringing them into the fold." Chaplain Zhang smiled.

Paul's thoughts went to the person who had died in the accident. Why that person and not him? They were in the same area, so why was that person killed?

"Something on your mind?"

Paul shook himself from his thoughts. "I know God's plans are perfect, but sometimes I wonder. Why did I lose my leg and not my life?"

"Because God's not finished with you. He could have special plans for you."

Paul shook his head. "Like what?"

Chaplain Zhang was quiet for a minute. "Maybe God will use you to reach someone."

"Why me?"

"Why *not* you?"

Paul sighed. Chaplain Zhang was right, and Paul wanted to find the answer.

The men chatted as they finished their coffee and went their separate ways. Their discussion brought Paul back to how broken Genny was when she first moved in with him. She overcame a lot, especially her anger toward God for losing her family. She was a stronger woman because of what she'd been through. He prayed her strength would sustain her as they faced the unknown.

Jiggling his leg, Paul sat in his wheelchair, focusing on his watch. Dr. Godfrey was fifteen minutes late. A moment later, a knock sounded on the door and Dr. Godfrey walked in.

"I'm so sorry, Sergeant Thompson. I had to do a quick consult with my colleague on an emergency surgery."

"No problem, ma'am."

Paul watched her gaze fall to his prosthetic. "Let's see what you've got."

He walked the length of the small room several times. The wound was slightly painful, an improvement from the day before. Dr. Godfrey instructed him to sit on the table, and she pulled off the prosthetic and compression sock. After thoroughly inspecting his residual leg, she sat up and stared at him. He held his breath as he watched the contemplative look form on her face.

"Sergeant Thompson? I have never seen someone work as hard as you. You have made great progress. Rarely do I do this, but I believe you are at a point where I can change your treatment plan."

A wide grin stretched across Paul's face.

"Don't get excited yet." She laughed. "You still have a little way to go, but I'm considering transferring you to the VA at Charleston to finish your treatment. It would be outpatient. That way, you can be with your family."

Tears stung his eyes. "Dr. Godfrey, you have no idea how happy this makes me. I have missed my family so much. My little girl will be four on the first and my son was only two months old when I left. I'm so scared that he won't know me." Paul rubbed his eyes.

"Your determination is what led to me sending you home. Don't slack off when you're around those babies of yours."

"Oh, don't you worry, ma'am. I won't let you down."

Paul wheeled towards his room and decided halfway there that he was going to walk the rest of the way. When he was settled in, he grabbed his phone and tapped on Genny's name. It rang five times and Paul held his breath. After the sixth ring, it would go to voicemail. Genny was out of breath when she answered.

"Hi, baby."

"Have you been running a race?"

Genny laughed. "Katie decided to take Lucy outside for a potty break when I was in the bedroom changing Caleb's clothes. Of course, it started raining. Katie came inside, but I had to go out and chase Lucy back into the house. Mom was napping, so she had no idea what was going on." Genny blew out her breath and laughed. "How was your appointment?"

Paul had practiced this conversation many times since he'd left Dr. Godfrey's office. His attempt to remain calm backfired. "I'm coming home!" his voice boomed.

"What?" Genny let out an awkward laugh.

"Dr. Godfrey said that I've progressed so well that she's transferring me to the Charleston VA to finish treatment. I should be in my permanent prosthetic shortly after the new year.

"What?" Genny's voice turned serious.

"I'm coming home to you and our babies."

She screamed, and Paul pulled the phone away from his ear for a moment. He heard his mom's voice in the background.

"Oops," Genny said. "I woke Mom."

"Mama?" Katie said in the background. He heard Genny say something, then Katie came on the phone. "Daddy?"

"Hey, baby girl. Daddy's coming home."

"Yay!"

After Paul talked to Katie, he shared a few words with his mother and Genny came back on the phone. "Babe?"

"Hmm."

"Have you told Katie about my leg?"

"Not yet."

"Gen."

"It's just…I don't know what exactly to say. I'll talk to Mom."

"She's our daughter. It's our job to prepare her."

Genny sighed. "I know."

"I wish you would have agreed to Skype."

"I don't know how that'll help. Are you going to show her your missing leg? I think it would scare her."

Paul sighed. "I should be home by her birthday or shortly after. I know you're doing your best."

"I'd be lost without Mom."

"Yeah. She's a pretty great lady. I love you, baby."

"I love you, too."

After Paul ended the call, he looked around the room and mentally packed his belongings. When would he be released?

CHAPTER 7

Genny

Genny's favorite thing about living in Charleston was the climate. Mid-November brought temperatures in the high sixties. She walked past the SUV and truck to the side of the house where the Jeep was parked. The Jeep hadn't been driven since before they'd brought Caleb home late April, just an occasional crank and idle to circulate the fluids. And the last Jeep club outing they'd attended was late summer the year prior. Genny was still a member of the club, but motherhood had put Jeep life on the back burner.

Genny walked around the Jeep, unfastening the Velcro straps that held down the cover. It took three tries before the cover released its grip on the Jeep. The lights flashed and alarm chirped after she hit the remote. At least the battery wasn't dead. The garage door rolled up and Brian walked around the corner of the house.

"Ready?"

"Yep."

They heaved the hardtop off the Jeep and carried it inside the garage. Genny walked back out to the Jeep and rested her hands on her hips.

"Want the soft top on?"

"Hmm. Yes, but let's fold it back some."

"What about the doors?" Brian smiled.

"Will it be too open for the temps? What do you think?"

"I say go for it." The lines around Brian's eyes crinkled when he smiled.

"You're right." She was out of practice. In the past, she had no problem deciding what to remove for a day of leisurely driving. Brian ran his hand across the treads of the left front tire. "Paul checked the tires before he left in case I wanted to go to the beach. With a newborn and three-year-old, it wasn't happening." Genny laughed.

"I'm sure they're fine. Have fun."

"I will."

Genny stepped onto the running board and pulled herself up. Settling in the driver's seat, she looked around. The memory of the first time she'd driven the Jeep after her brother died filled her mind. Reflective belts and packs of ear plugs had been replaced by a booster seat and car seat.

Bequeath. What a strange word. That was what Brandon had done with the Jeep. He'd bequeathed it to Genny in his will. All these years later, a part of her still felt that it was his Jeep. Genny turned the key, and the engine sputtered a second until it fully turned over. A smile tugged at her lips when the sound of the mufflers echoed off their house and the neighbor's house.

Genny pulled up to the stop sign, leaving the subdivision. In the short distance from their house to the stop sign, her hair had slapped her in the face a few times. It'd be worse when she was on the highway driving fifty-five. Or sixty. She smiled and pulled her hair back into a low ponytail. Glancing at the clock on the console, Genny decided it was time for an afternoon pick-me-up and pulled into the coffee shop where she used to work.

At least ten cars filled the drive thru at The Roasted Bean, but only a few cars were taking up the spaces in the parking lot. One car brought a smile to Genny's face. She spotted a car backing out close to the front door. Genny waited impatiently and maneuvered the Jeep into the parking space once the car had pulled away. Before she turned off the engine, the door to the coffee shop flung open, and her friend Julie ran out and up to the driver's side of the Jeep.

"Come here!" Julie opened her arms.

Genny climbed down and threw her arms around Julie's neck when her feet were planted on the ground. Although they didn't see each other often, they texted a few times a week.

"How's Paul?"

Genny let out a long breath. "It's hard. But you know Paul."

"Yes, I do." Julie draped her arm around Genny's shoulders and led her inside. "You're in luck. It's time for my break." Julie grinned.

Julie was a barista when Genny had worked at The Roasted Bean after she moved in with Paul. It was the owner's only coffee shop back then. Over the years, they'd built three more shops. Renee, the previous store manager, had moved up to manage all four shops, and Julie was now the manager of the original. Genny chose a table in the back by the fireplace while Julie ordered their drinks.

"Here." Julie set a fresh brewed cup of Americano in front of Genny and placed the small pitcher of cream next to the cup. She dropped a few packets of stevia on the table and took her seat. A few moments later, a young man with green hair and piercings in each eyebrow placed Julie's cup of vanilla cappuccino in front of her.

Genny fought to keep her mouth from falling open and grabbed a packet of stevia.

"Braxton is a sweetheart."

"I'm sure he is. I guess the Fletchers relaxed the employee dress code."

"Yeah. They aren't as strict as they used to be. And they don't come by as often." Julie smiled behind the cup as she held it to her lips.

Genny glanced past Julie to the parking lot at the side of the building. Julie rested her hand on Genny's hand. "He's not here."

Genny sighed. "I know. He has seventeen more years without parole, but I can't help myself."

"I'm sure being here doesn't help."

Genny had been assaulted by an acquaintance while leaving work one night. She couldn't keep herself from looking for him everywhere. It was hypervigilance—a symptom of PTSD—her therapist had said.

After Genny visited with Julie, she made her way to the beach. Not much had changed in the way of landmarks, giving Genny a sense of nostalgia. The Jeep club had a few spots where they gathered, but there was one place in particular she wanted to visit today. Pulling into the parking lot, Genny chose a specific parking space and turned off the engine. Five years ago, Paul was parked in the space.

Genny closed her eyes. She could see herself running up to the parking lot where Paul had parked and kissing him as soon as he got out of the truck. Their feelings had grown for each other, but neither would make the first move—until then. And Genny was the one bold enough to do it. Well, not really. It was as if her lips had a mind of their own. She smiled and brushed her fingers across her lips.

Genny's phone rang and she pulled it out of her purse. Paul's ears must have been burning.

"Hi, baby. Guess where I am?"

"Hiding out in the bathroom." He laughed.

Genny laughed along. "I'm at our spot."

"Really?"

"Yep. I took the Jeep out."

"That's awesome, babe. You know? I can still feel your lips on mine from that day."

"Mmm. Me, too."

"I love you, Genevieve."

"I love you, too." Genny focused on the sailboat in the distance, rocking in the choppy waves. What would life be like when Paul was discharged from the hospital? It wasn't like they would pick up where they'd left off.

"You're quiet."

"Just thinking."

"What about?"

Words were flying around in Genny's mind. Should she share her heart? Paul didn't need any pressure as he faced the unknown with the Air Force and adjusting to their new life.

"Babe?"

Genny sighed and pushed the hair off her forehead. "Just wondering about life."

"We'll be fine."

She didn't have to explain herself. They understood how each other thought and often knew what one was going to say before the words left their lips. "I know. I can't wait until you are home."

"Me, either."

Genny set off for home. At the traffic light, a familiar song played on the radio and she couldn't help but smile. "Cold" by Crossfade was one of the many songs she'd listened to as she burned up the roads of Charleston in the Jeep. The song took her back to her and Paul's first summer together.

When Genny topped the hill by the house, she saw Brian and Katie at the mailbox. Katie's face brightened and she jumped up and down when she saw

Genny. There were times she looked at her daughter and thought about her road to motherhood. Genny went from not wanting children, to desperate to have children with Paul.

She doubted her ability to be a mother when she found out she was pregnant with Katie. Through therapy, she had realized it came from the loss of her mother when she was five. Genny's grandmother had raised her with love, but she had desperately wanted her mother in her life.

Brian and Tricia took care of dinner and the kids for the evening. Genny tucked the kids in and got ready for bed herself. She lay staring at the ceiling and counted the blades on the fan. Paul was coming home a few days before his original return date. It was strange to think about. She had thought he'd return in the same condition as he'd left. That sounded bad. She rolled over and stared at the shadow of the lampshade against the bathroom wall.

The past three months seemed like a dream. More like a nightmare. Not long ago, she'd thought about the timeline of events that sent her to Maryland. When she was checking in at Fisher House, Paul's leg was being amputated. How crazy was that? Why wasn't she contacted? She could have been with him. She breathed out. Anxiety was getting ready to put her through the ringer as she prepared for Paul's release from the hospital.

She forced out a long, hard breath. Lucy lifted her head and looked at Genny. "Sorry, girl. Mama's mad at the Air Force and the doctors. Basically, anyone who has to do with the military." Genny reached over and scratched Lucy behind the ear. "The last time Daddy was home; we were a happily married couple with two kids and a dog. I'm excited and scared at the same time about him coming home. That's silly, right?" Genny sighed and rolled onto her back.

Would they be the same family when Paul came home? When she and the kids saw him off on June twenty-third, they didn't know how drastically their lives would change in three months.

⁓ℓℓ⁓

The following day, Dr. Godfrey had signed discharge orders for Paul, and he had a flight scheduled to arrive in Charleston late the next afternoon. Genny could no longer put it off. She had to tell Katie about Paul's amputation.

Sweet singing floated down the hall into Genny's bedroom. Katie was singing "Jesus Loves Me" again. She'd been singing the song off and on since she'd learned it in Sunday school a while back. Genny's heart thudded as she walked down the hall to her daughter's bedroom.

"'They are weak, but He is strong.'" Genny walked in as Katie flexed her arms. She looked up and smiled. "Hi, Mama."

"Hi, baby girl. How would you like to go to Dairy Queen?"

Katie's eyes brightened. "Yes! Is Bubby coming?"

"No, he's staying with Mimi. It's mama and daughter time."

"Let's go!" Katie bolted from the room. Genny laughed and went into the living room to grab her purse.

Genny picked a booth in the back corner and they sat down. Katie chattered on about Paul returning home. "I can't wait to see Daddy. I miss him."

"Me, too. You know that something's wrong with Daddy's leg." Genny's heart pounded and she tucked her hair behind her ears.

"Uh-huh. He has a owie."

"Yes, he does." *Lord, please give me strength.* "Daddy's leg was hurt too badly to save it. Do you know what that means?"

Katie shook her head.

"His leg…his leg would not get better, and they had to remove it." Genny leaned down to read Katie's face, but she was staring at her ice cream cone. Genny's hands fell to her lap, and she raised them, resting her elbows on the table. The long, silent moment that followed rolled Genny's stomach. She should have told Katie sooner than the night before Paul was flying home. Why did she wait? Katie looked up at her.

"Like when Lucy chew Barbie's leg off?"

"Yes. Like Barbie." A knot formed in Genny's throat.

"Oh." Katie licked a drip of ice cream rolling down the side of the cone. "How does Daddy walk?"

"He has a pretend leg." Couldn't she have come up with something better than a pretend leg?

Katie wrinkled her nose. "Oh." She paused for a moment. "Can I go with you to get Daddy?"

"I think that's a good idea."

They finished their ice cream and made their way home. Katie asked a million questions on the drive. Could Paul wear his pretend leg in the shower? What about swimming? Will he wear it while sleeping? Genny had asked herself the same questions. Their family would adjust. They had to. There was no other option.

Later in the evening, Genny was putting away the laundry and stepped into the closet to hang up a pair of jeans. She spotted one of Paul's favorite shirts and grabbed the collar, taking a sniff. A hint of Paul's cologne filled her nose. Butterflies fluttered around in her stomach, and she glanced at the bed. Tomorrow she'd have her husband sleeping by her side again.

Genny got the kids ready for bed and laid Caleb in his crib. Reaching to turn off the lamp, she noticed her journal under a stack of books. It had been a while since she'd last written anything. She pulled it out and found the last entry. Touching her neck, Genny stared at the date.

Sep 9, 2016

Happy birthday to me! Paul sent me sunflowers today. He wants to take me out to eat when he gets home. My present is supposed to be delivered tomorrow. I tried to get him to tell me what it is, but he said I had to wait. I miss him so much. I'm ready for our life to get back to normal.

Genny shook her head. A part of her felt that her words were naïve. Anything could happen at any time. She continued reading as tears gathered in her eyes.

Katie drew a picture for me. It's our family. All of us are round with stick people legs. It's so cute. Caleb gave me an extra big smile today and it melted my heart. I love my little family.

Genny found a pen and closed her eyes. The two entries would be as different as night and day. One full of hope and the other full of fear.

Dec 11, 2016

So much has happened in the past three months. September 18 at 5:47 in the morning, I got a call that has changed me forever. I was so scared and, to be honest, I still am. I don't know what to expect.

I told Katie this evening. She's comparing Paul to her Barbie with one leg. I want to laugh and cry at the same time, but it's how she understands. I hope she is happy to see him. He should be wearing his prosthetic, so he'll look the same to her. Maybe it will confuse her.

I know Paul is struggling ten times worse than me. Maybe a hundred times worse. He's missing a part of his body. He has to deal with that on top of everything else, so I don't feel that I have a right to be scared. I know that sounds silly. Deep down, I know I have a right to my feelings, but I feel guilty when I let fear into my heart. Sometimes I feel like I have no arms. There's so much I want to do, but no way to do it.

I can't wait to see him and hold him.

—ℓℓ—

Standing at the foot of the bed, Genny walked over to her side and tugged on the comforter. She stood back again and went to Paul's side of the bed to straighten the lampshade. Genny yawned and held her hand over her mouth. Last night, it seemed she woke up every hour. Her stomach churned and she took a couple of deep breaths. Her anxiety wasn't so much for herself. She was unsure how their children, Katie especially, would react to seeing Paul.

"Mama." Genny turned around and saw Katie standing in the doorway wearing her favorite purple sundress.

"It's a little cool to wear a sundress. Why don't you wear the white sweater Mimi bought you over the dress?"

"Okay." Katie hurried down the hall to her bedroom. Genny helped her slip on the sweater, and they went to the living room where Tricia was playing with Caleb on his mat.

"Bye bye, Mimi! We gonna get Daddy." Katie yelled as she ran past the couch to the front door and down the steps before Genny could catch her. After Genny said goodbye to Tricia and Caleb, she found Katie standing by the back passenger door, pulling on the handle.

"Girl." Genny shook her head and hit the remote to unlock the doors. Katie grinned and climbed in and buckled herself into her booster seat.

"Let's go, Mama!" Katie rocked back and forth as if she could make the SUV move.

On the way to the airport, they sang songs and talked about what all they could do as a family now that Paul was returning home. At the airport, Genny pulled up to the swing arm for short-term parking. She plucked a ticket from the machine and found a parking space.

"Hurry Mama!"

Genny laughed. "You're excited." Genny helped Katie out of the car and held her hand as they made their way to the entrance. The closer they got, the harder Genny's heart beat. She'd wanted to wrap her arms around Paul's neck and kiss him.

They made their way to baggage claim and stayed close to the concourse, where passengers entered the area. According to the monitors, Paul's plane landed not long ago. A rush of passengers came down the concourse, but she didn't see Paul.

Sweat beaded on her forehead. The temperature in the airport was fine, but Genny felt like she was on fire. She fanned herself when she felt dizzy. It reminded her of how she felt as a teen, waiting for Paul to come home on leave for a visit. Of course, he only saw her as the little sister he never had, but she was head over heels for him.

Katie pulled on Genny's hand. "Is that him, Mama?"

Genny saw a tall man with black hair wearing a uniform. "No, baby. Daddy won't be wearing his uniform." Would he be walking with his prosthetic or in his wheelchair? Genny glanced behind her in case they'd somehow missed him.

"Mama?"

Genny turned back around and saw Katie pointing at someone in a wheelchair. The person was too far away to make out the face, but she could tell that they had short, dark hair. Genny tried not to stare, but curiosity wouldn't let her look away. A smile brightened the person's face and Genny knew it was Paul. "That's Daddy!"

Katie stuck her finger in her mouth and stepped behind Genny. As Genny watched Paul wheeling up to them, his smile slowly disappeared. Genny gently pulled Katie from behind her, and Katie stared at her daddy wide-eyed.

Paul locked the wheels and braced himself to stand. When he pushed himself up, he held out his arms and Genny rushed to him. He kissed her and pulled her against his chest. A few moments later, she pulled away and squeezed his biceps. "You've been working out?"

"Yeah. And using the wheelchair helped." They looked at Katie. She was still standing where Genny had left her with her finger in her mouth. "Gosh, she's gotten big."

Paul took a few steps toward Katie, slightly limping. She dropped her hand to her side and Genny saw her chin trembling. Paul walked the rest of the way and scooped Katie up in his arms. "My baby girl. I missed you." Paul held onto Katie and lowered himself into his wheelchair. "Want to go for a ride?" Katie nodded and sat on his lap as he wheeled to the carousel for his flight. Genny loaded Paul's luggage onto a cart, and they exited the building

"Stay here and I'll drive up."

"It's okay."

"Are you sure?"

"Yep." He led the way across the crosswalk and Genny pointed toward where she'd parked the car.

Genny glanced at Katie. She had her finger in her mouth and was sitting straight up, away from Paul's chest. She didn't want to push Katie, but she had to find some way to ease her fears. Paul wheeled up to the back of the SUV. He lifted Katie off his lap and Genny hit the button to open the back.

"Do you need help?" Genny asked.

"Nah." He lifted himself from the chair. Folding the chair, he heaved it into the back. Genny stepped around him and loaded his bags on top of the chair.

Paul sat in the seat sideways and swung his legs into the car. He looked at Katie and smiled. Genny watched her daughter's eyes. It was as if her daddy was a figment of her imagination. After they left the airport, Genny glanced in the rearview mirror. She could tell that Katie was staring at the back of the passenger seat. *Please Lord, calm her nerves.*

Paul turned toward Katie. "Mama said you love your preschool class."

Katie pulled her finger out of her mouth. "Uh-huh."

"I'm glad you like it. I talked to Uncle Peter and Aunt Melissa. They are coming for a visit after the new year."

"Asher and Izzy too?" Katie asked.

"Yes."

Genny glanced in the rearview mirror again and saw Katie grinning. She prayed Katie would warm up to Paul. He began asking questions, trying to engage her. Her mood perked up, and she leaned forward each time she said something to Paul.

Genny pulled into the driveway, and Paul stepped out of the car, opening the back door for Katie. Genny reached for Paul's hand and slipped her fingers between his. Making their way to the steps, Genny unlocked the door and Katie ran inside announcing Paul's arrival. Finally, their family was together again.

CHAPTER 8

Paul had seen Caleb while Skyping with Genny, but seeing him in person was like looking at a whole different child. Paul's heart swelled when Caleb grinned. Did he recognize him? Walking up to Tricia, Paul held out his hands and Caleb leaned over to him.

Taking Caleb in his arms, Paul rubbed his back when he laid his head on his shoulder. He walked into the living room and saw Katie on the couch. She looked up at Paul and seemed to withdraw into herself. Sliding off the couch, she hurried down the hall to her bedroom. It made no sense. She was happy and talkative on the way home from the airport. Paul looked at his mom.

"It's okay, sweetheart. She needs a little time to adjust."

Genny took Caleb from Paul's arms, and Paul hugged his mom and dad. Tricia brought out a plate of chocolate chip cookies, and Paul talked about his flight home. He glanced down the hall but didn't see Katie.

Lucy whined from the patio. She started barking, yipping, whining, and yelping—pretty much every sound that'd come out of her mouth since they'd brought her home. Paul walked over and opened the door. She jumped up on him, causing him to stumble backward. Brian braced him before he fell.

"Come here, girl." Paul bent down and accepted Lucy's many kisses. "I missed you too."

Easing down on the couch, Paul petted Lucy when she jumped up on the couch next to him. "I thought about walking in the airport, but it was faster with the wheelchair. And walking with the wheelchair would have been a chore." He glanced down the hall again. He looked at Genny and she handed Caleb to him and headed to Katie's bedroom. A moment later, Genny and Katie walked into the living room holding hands.

Genny urged Katie to sit between Paul and his mother. Katie took tentative steps and sat down next to her grandmother and wrapped her arms around Lucy's neck. Paul's heart squeezed tight. There were times in his past that he'd felt rejected, but this was different. His daughter was acting like she was afraid of him.

"Can I get you anything, sweetheart?" Tricia asked.

"A tall glass of milk to go with these cookies would be nice."

Tricia went to the kitchen and returned with a glass of milk. Paul took the glass and studied the various sizes of painted sunflowers on the outside, then took a long drink.

"I bought them not long before you were hurt. Maybe I forgot to tell you with everything that's happened," Genny said.

"They look nice, babe."

Lucy hopped down, and Paul noticed that Katie had moved a little closer to him. It was probably an inch but progress. Pain shot through his residual leg, and he winced.

"What is it?" Genny asked.

"Some pain. I think I'm going to take my meds and lay down for a bit." Paul took his medication and yawned as he headed to the bedroom. When he walked to his side of the bed, he reached to turn on the lamp and realized the lamps were different. He liked the pull chain on the old lamps. Why change a good thing?

"What do you think of the lamps?"

"They're nice." He raised his brows.

"Why don't I believe you?" Genny frowned.

"I'm sorry. I liked the pull chain, but it's okay." He smiled. Genny pulled back the covers. "Are you napping with me?"

"Caleb will. He missed his nap." Caleb started crying. "See." She smiled and went down the hall and brought him into the bedroom.

Paul slipped under the covers after removing the prosthetic and Genny laid Caleb next to him. Quieting, Caleb's eyes slowly closed. Kissing them both, Genny left the room, closing the door behind her.

A few moments later, Caleb opened his eyes and stared at Paul. He brushed his finger along Caleb's cheek, and he grinned and flailed his arms. Soft wisps of black hair, long fine eyelashes, and chubby cheeks brought a smile to Paul's face. "Gosh, little man. You are so big."

Since Caleb came along, it had been harder to leave his family. Especially since Caleb was so young when he left. Paul didn't have to worry about that any longer. He'd be home with his family from now on.

Paul woke up gasping for air. Resting his hand on his upper chest, he forced himself to take deep breaths until his heart rate slowed. He sat up and wiped the sweat from his brow. He had been dreaming, but he couldn't remember the details—only that he was scared. Scared of what, exactly?

Looking beside him, he smiled at Genny's half-open mouth and wild hair. He barely remembered her slipping under the covers last night. He noticed Caleb wasn't laying between them and put on the prosthetic. Walking around the end of the bed, Paul saw Caleb sitting up in the crib. He looked at Paul and grinned, showing his two bottom teeth that had recently pushed through his gums. Paul picked him up and headed down the hall.

Brushing his hand across Paul's face, Caleb cooed and leaned over, pressing his open mouth against Paul's cheek. His baby boy had kissed him. Genny had said that Caleb had begun giving kisses a few days earlier. As he passed Katie's room, he looked through the crack and saw her black hair peeking out from under the covers. His baby girl. At least Caleb wasn't afraid of him.

Paul laid Caleb on his play mat and went into the kitchen to make a cup of coffee. He shook his head when he noticed it wasn't yet six in the morning. Opening the cabinet next to the fridge, instead of coffee mugs, he found the glasses. He glanced over the counter and saw that the Keurig had been moved to under the cabinet to the left of the sink. Common sense told him to look in the cabinet over the Keurig, and sure enough, the coffee mugs were in the cabinet where the glasses used to be.

Why had Genny changed everything around? The glasses, mugs and Keurig had been in the same place since they'd moved into the house five years earlier. Paul picked up a Community Coffee K-cup and dropped it into the Keurig and closed the top. As he waited for the cup to fill, he glanced out the dining room window into the backyard. He glimpsed Felix zooming around Mrs. Baker's backyard next door. He went to the window and laughed to himself when he saw Mrs. Baker standing on her patio in her housecoat and slippers with her hands on her hips. Her son had given her the beagle last spring. She was frustrated, but ended up falling in love with the dog.

Paul looked at Caleb and back at Mrs. Baker. He picked Caleb up and wrapped him in his blanket. Paul slipped on his shoes and made his way outside. Mrs. Baker's face brightened when she saw Paul and she walked over to the gate that separated their yards.

"Paul!" She drew him into her arms when he stepped through the gate.

"Hello, Mrs. Baker. You look lovely as usual."

Pink graced her cheeks. "It's so good to see you. How are you?"

"Improving every day."

"Good to hear. It looks like this little one has bonded quite well." She grabbed Caleb's hand and gave it a light shake. He grinned and babbled.

"Yeah. Katie's a different story."

"She's old enough to know something has changed. Give her time."

They chatted for a few minutes and Paul went back inside. He sat Caleb on the mat in the living room and made his way to the kitchen to prepare his coffee. Taking a sip, he grimaced and put the cup in the microwave. Caleb squealed and Paul looked in his direction, noticing Katie as she walked into the living room, and plopped down on the play mat next to him. Caleb giggled when she held up a stuffed dog and pretended it was barking at him.

Sipping his coffee, Paul watched Katie's interaction with Caleb. Jealousy had crept in not long after they had brought Caleb home. Genny had told him that Katie's behavior had gotten worse shortly after he'd deployed. She'd caught Katie with Caleb's pacifier in her mouth. When she was told to give it back, she had jerked it out and threw it at Caleb. He was glad to see the change in Katie.

Caleb waved his arms and when Paul leaned forward to grab his foot, he saw Katie staring at his legs. He was wearing athletic pants, so his socks and the prosthetic weren't showing. "Do you want to see?" Katie shook her head as if he'd asked her if she wanted to throw her toys in the trash. "You can look at it whenever you want to, okay?" Her green eyes widened, and she turned toward Caleb. Paul sighed. *Baby steps*, he told himself.

Paul turned on the TV and picked up his coffee cup. The thigh muscles on his residual leg cramped, and he placed the cup on the side table and began rubbing the muscles.

"Having some pain?"

Paul looked over and saw his dad walking into the living room. "Yeah. Just some cramping."

"Papa!" Katie shot to her feet and ran to her grandfather.

"How are you this morning, baby girl?" Brian leaned down and picked her up.

"Good. Me and Bubby are playing." She pointed toward Caleb.

"I see that." Brian put Katie down, and she went back to the play mat. After he got his coffee, Brian joined Paul on the couch. "When's your appointment again?"

"Christmas Eve eve." Paul laughed and drank the last of his coffee, placing the empty cup on the side table. "I'm a little nervous about getting into the VA system. It's like I'm sealing my fate."

"What do you mean?" Brian took a sip of coffee.

"Going to the VA is ending my Air Force career."

"It's not over yet." Brian tilted his head toward Katie.

Paul looked down and saw her staring at his prosthetic. It took a moment for him to realize that she had raised his pant leg.

Katie looked up at Paul. She climbed onto the couch and sat next to him. "Mama said your leg is gone." She pointed to his residual leg.

"My leg was hurt from here down." Paul gestured down his leg. "Here. Feel." When he reached for her hand, she pulled it away. "It's okay. Tap here." The socket thudded when he tapped it. With a hesitant finger, Katie gave the socket a light tap. Above the socket, she poked Paul's residual limb several times.

A shy smile spread across her face. "You have a little leg now."

"Well, I guess you could call it that."

Katie looked past Paul. "Mama! Mimi! Daddy has a little leg."

Paul looked toward the hall and saw Genny and his mother.

"That's right sweetie," Genny said as she walked into the living room.

"But you said Daddy's leg is gone."

"I meant most of it."

Katie seemed satisfied with Genny's answer. She slid down from the couch and crawled over to the mat, and sat next to Caleb.

Genny walked over and kissed Paul. "Good morning."

"Good morning, love." Genny reached for his empty coffee cup. "I'll get it. I want another cup," he said and followed her into the kitchen.

"You'll have to stand in line." Tricia laughed. She grabbed her cup of coffee and walked into the living room.

"I see you changed things around." Paul slipped his arms around Genny's waist.

"Well, I thought it would work better if the glasses were next to the fridge, since that's where the drinks are. And I moved the Keurig over here. You don't like it? I can move it back."

Paul heard a hint of frustration in her voice. "No, it's fine. I'll get used to it." He smiled and kissed her.

Brian and Tricia took the kids Christmas shopping to give Paul and Genny some alone time. Paul stretched out on the bed and rolled onto his left side. He winced and rolled onto his back. It was too soon.

When Genny came out of the bathroom, Paul patted the mattress. She climbed onto the bed and laid on her side next to him. Pulling her close, she rested her head on his chest and ran her fingers down his arm.

"I love you."

"I love you too, Genevieve."

It felt good to be home and to have his wife in his arms. Thinking about the future overwhelmed Paul. The VA had scheduled an appointment with the orthopedist, and he would be starting physical therapy soon. Part of him wished he could skip the next year. Recovery was going to be hard. But the hardest thing would be recovering from losing his Air Force career.

CHAPTER 9

Genny

Resting her head on Paul's chest, Genny slipped her arm around his waist, and her leg over his legs. It was her favorite way to snuggle, but it would take some getting used to. The prosthetic was hard and cold and a reminder of how close she had come to losing him. They lay quiet for a moment.

"What are you thinking about?" Paul asked.

Closing her eyes, Genny smiled at the vibration of his deep voice against her cheek. "I would have missed this if—"

"Hey." He raised her chin until their eyes met. "We said we would not talk about it anymore. I'm here and that's all that matters."

"I know, it's just…"

"God said it wasn't my time. I don't know what His plans are, but I trust Him."

Did she trust God in this? Truly trust Him? She had to. Doing it on her own would end in disaster. "Do you have a date yet for your medical board thing?"

"Medical evaluation board? Not yet. I have to meet with the doctor first."

"Oh, okay."

A flash of pain crossed Paul's face when he eased Genny onto her side. But before she could say anything, he pulled her close and kissed her in a way that she'd desperately needed. A way she'd been afraid she'd never experience again. Thankful to God for this moment, she was once again in the arms of the man He'd chosen for her.

"Daddy!" Katie's voice echoed from down the hall.

"They're back already?" Paul laughed.

Katie ran into the room and climbed onto the bed, sitting between her parents. "Guess what I got you for Christmas, Daddy."

"Don't tell him." Genny laid her finger across Katie's lips.

"Just kidding!" Katie started giggling.

Paul slipped his arm around Katie's waist and pulled her over to him. "You're something else, girl."

She looked at him and a slow smile spread across her face. "I love you, Daddy." She kissed his cheek.

"I love you too, baby girl."

A moment later, Genny heard Caleb crying.

Katie held her hands over her ears. "He cried all the time, Mama."

Tricia brought Caleb into the room and Paul met her, taking him from her arms. "He feels a little warm."

"He's teething," Tricia said.

Paul sat on the edge of the bed and patted Caleb's back as he rocked back and forth. Katie narrowed her eyes at her brother and slid down from the bed, hurrying out of the room.

"I'll get the Tylenol," Genny said.

After Genny gave Caleb Tylenol, she carried him into Katie's room to rock him. He gnawed on a teething ring while she hummed.

Paul walked in and smiled. "I can take him if you need a break."

"We're okay." Genny eased the teething ring from Caleb's grasp. "He's almost asleep, anyway."

"I've missed out on this. I'd like to rock him if that's okay with you." He smiled, but his words carried a hint of irritation.

Caleb stirred when Genny held out her arms. Paul slipped his arms under Caleb, and they switched places. Genny stopped in the doorway on her way out of the room. Paul's gaze was fixed on Caleb, and he leaned down and kissed their son's forehead. She crossed her arms tightly against herself when she walked to the kitchen to help Tricia with dinner.

Genny's mind kept going back to the feeling she had when Paul wanted to rock Caleb. If she didn't know better, she'd thought he was criticizing her parenting by wanting to take Caleb from her. It was a silly thought; she knew Paul would never think that about her. What was wrong with her?

"Are you okay, sweetheart?"

Genny realized she'd stopped peeling the potato in her hand and was staring out the kitchen window. "Oh, yeah."

"It's a lot to take in." Tricia patted Genny's arm and smiled. "We had a big scare, and the adjustment can be hard. And you've been holding down the fort since June."

"Yeah, but I had your help." Genny went back to peeling the potato.

"Don't minimize what you've done for your family."

Genny sighed and dropped the potato back into the bowl. She squeezed her eyes shut, pushing tears down her cheeks.

"He's been home a day. Why do I feel so overwhelmed?"

"Give yourself time, sweetheart." Tricia brushed Genny's hair behind her shoulder and smiled.

Tricia was right, but how much time? Her adjustment depended on Paul's adjustment. How long would that take? Six months? A year? Genny eased out a breath. The thought of walking on paper thin glass for a year burned Genny's stomach.

⁓⁓⁓

Early the next morning, Genny zipped her jacket as she walked out the back door, heading for the picnic table. She climbed on top and sighed. Being outdoors was her favorite way to talk to God. It reminded her of the many hours she'd spent outside on her grandparents' old farm as a small child.

Lucy hopped up on the picnic table and sat next to Genny. They'd had Lucy for almost as long as they'd been married. Lucy wasn't just a dog; she was a part of their family. She had been patient with the kids, laying still when they tugged on her ears or pulled her fur. When Katie was younger, she'd tried to ride Lucy a time or two. What did the dog do? Stand still. Genny smiled and stroked Lucy's back. If only dogs lived as long as humans.

"Lord…" She found it difficult to put her thoughts into words. "What's going on with me?" The feeling from the night before worried her.

The back door opened and Genny turned around. Paul was walking toward her and, for an instant, she felt like he was intruding. She needed to reconnect with her husband and wondered if he struggled as well.

"Hey, babe." Paul sat next to Genny and kissed her cheek. "What are you doing up so early?"

"I'm used to it. Your children refuse to let me sleep in." Genny laughed and scratched Lucy's neck.

"Got to take advantage of the grandparents while we can."

"Sure do."

The back door opened, and Brian and Tricia headed their way. Tricia was carrying Caleb, but Katie was nowhere in sight.

"Speaking of grandparents," Genny said.

"It's a family reunion." Paul laughed when they walked up. Paul and Genny climbed down and sat on the bench seat, facing Paul's parents.

"Is Katie still asleep?" Genny looked around Tricia toward the back door.

"Yes," Tricia replied.

"What's up?" Paul looked at his mother, then his father.

"Your transfer to Jersey was canceled, right?" Brian asked.

"According to my squadron."

Tricia swallowed hard and looked at Brian. Caleb reached out to Genny and she took him in her arms.

"Mom and I have been talking." Brian looked at Tricia. Genny saw Tricia draw in a quiet breath.

"Yeah?" Paul said.

"Will you two consider moving to Murfreesboro? Mom and I can help you."

Move to Tennessee? Heat filled Genny's shoulders and spread throughout her body. She didn't want to leave Charleston. Moving hadn't crossed her mind. Was she naïve?

"I think we're getting ahead of ourselves," Paul said.

"Son—"

"There's a lot coming up. Once I get on my feet, I'll go through a medical evaluation board to see if I will be retained or discharged."

"Retained?" Tricia's eyes widened. "You mean you could stay in?"

"Don't worry, Mom. I'll be discharged. Crippled people can't be in the military." Paul groaned and rested his hands on top of the table.

Genny could feel the anger coming from Paul. Lacing his fingers together, Genny glanced at his hands, noticing the tips of his fingers turning white.

"Sweetheart. We love you and your family. We want the best for you. Whatever that may be." Tricia patted Paul's hand.

"I want to finish my degree in accounting. Or something else, maybe, and get a job. I need to take care of my family like I'm supposed to." Paul inhaled hard.

"We honor that," Brian said.

Genny watched Paul relax his hands.

"If you find it difficult, will you reconsider?"

"Of course, I will."

"Hi guys!"

Genny looked between Brian and Tricia and saw Katie walking towards them. Hopefully, she didn't hear Paul's tone and what they were discussing. Especially since she was readjusting to him.

"Come here, baby girl." Paul held out his hands. Climbing onto his lap, Katie turned and looked up at him.

"Want to watch *Sesame Street* with me?"

"I'd love to." Paul picked Katie up and carried her into the house.

Genny couldn't see Paul moving their family to Murfreesboro. That'd mean he'd given up and that was something he'd never do. For a moment, relief flooded through her body. A discharge meant no more deployments. It was a selfish thought; she knew. Closing her eyes, Genny cleared her head. God would provide as He always had. It might not be in the way they thought, but He would provide.

Genny took Caleb into the bedroom to lay him down for his morning nap. Their first morning together once again hadn't been what Genny had expected. She picked up her journal and settled against the pillows.

Dec 13, 2016

Where to begin? Yesterday was different. Not good or bad. Just different. I'm so happy to have Paul home. Katie was standoffish at first, but she warmed up quickly. Mom and Dad brought up moving to Murfreesboro. Paul was angry at first, but he didn't let it escalate. As of now, we aren't moving anywhere. I hope it stays like that. I don't know how many major life changes I can take.

CHAPTER 10

Paul

Paul ran his arm across his forehead. Grabbing the hem of his shirt, he fanned himself and continued his pace. His goal was two more rounds along the perimeter of the backyard fence and then he could rest. At his pace, it'd take another half hour.

The neighbor's back door opened and a little girl ran out shouting, "Swing me, Daddy!"

The man stepped outside and lifted his chin to Paul and Brian. "Welcome home, Paul."

"Thanks, David."

David grabbed his little girl's hands and spun her around, her feet slowly lifting off the ground. She laughed and screamed as her daddy spun her in the air. Would he be able to do that with Katie and Caleb? Paul's heart fell to his stomach.

"I'm proud of you, son. You're working so hard."

"Thanks, Dad." Paul looked at his dad and smiled. He rubbed his thigh muscle as they walked. "I should hear something soon about the medical evaluation board. The holidays may delay it a bit."

"Probably so. Do you know what to expect?"

"From what I found online, the doctor will decide if I have a condition that will keep me from performing my job and forward my medical records to the people who handle medical discharges."

"Which doctor is that? The VA?"

"No, the doctor on base. I have my VA appointment tomorrow. I'll see my Air Force doctor after the first of the year."

"What do you feel they will say?"

"I'm gone." Paul shook his head.

"I'm truly sorry, Paul. I know you love serving."

"Yeah. I guess it's time to dust off the good ole college transcripts and find out what I need to graduate. I don't know if I want to stay with accounting, though."

"You've got to do what makes you happy."

"Yeah, that's what Trevor said. We were talking one time about what I wanted to do when I retired, and I mentioned the accounting degree. Trevor said he didn't see me as a desk person, which I agree."

"I can see that." Brian smiled.

"Last round."

"What's this make? Eight laps?"

"Ten. I've got to work up to wearing the prosthetic most of the day. And let's be honest, I'm lounging on the couch a lot here lately." Paul chuckled.

"Daddy! Daddy!" Paul glanced over his shoulder and watched Katie running toward them, flailing her arms. He and Brian turned around and headed her way.

"Want to color with me?" She panted when she stopped in front of Paul and Brian.

"I'd love to, baby girl." A slither of pink peeked out from the bottom of Katie's heavy winter coat. He picked her up and rubbed her bare legs. "Your legs are cold. You should wear a pair of leggings if you wear a dress when you come outside."

"Okay." She grinned and kissed his cheek.

Paul looked over at his dad, and Brian smiled. "Well, Papa. I think our walk is over for the day."

"No problem. I was getting tired."

"Nah-uh, Papa. Your head ain't wet. Daddy's head is wet when he is tired from walking." She swept her hand across Paul's forehead and held it out to Brian. "See?" Katie giggled.

Paul plopped Katie down on the couch when they went inside. She looked at the coffee table and lowered her brows.

"Did you move my coloring books, Mama?" Katie huffed and crossed her arms.

"I put them away. I've told you several times not to leave your coloring books and colors on the coffee table."

"Daddy is gonna color with me." Katie's eyes narrowed.

"Don't talk to your mother like that, Katherine. Tell her you're sorry."

Katie groaned. "I'm sorry, Mama."

"I accept your apology." Genny pinched her lips together when her eyes met Paul's.

Katie got the coloring books and colors from the small bookshelf next to the TV and placed them on the coffee table. Paul joined her and flipped through a princess coloring book. Picking out a baby animals coloring book, Katie climbed onto the couch next to Paul. Moving close to him, she hummed as she colored. Katie had gone from barely looking at Paul when he got home to gluing herself to his side.

Genny drove under the overhang at the main entrance to the VA hospital to let Paul out. Sliding down, he grunted when his feet hit the pavement. An employee saw Paul and offered to get his wheelchair from the carrier on the back of the SUV and set it up for him. His first thought was to decline, but his leg had been hurting the past few days and he didn't have it in him to walk.

The man opened the wheelchair so Paul could sit and he wheeled through the entrance.

"Hey there, young man."

Paul's focus was on Genny as she parked in a handicap space near the entrance. It was something he'd never get used to. Once he received his permanent prosthetic and could walk normally, he'd have no use for a handicap parking space.

"Young man," the voice repeated. "You, there."

Paul turned around and was eye-level with an older man in a wheelchair wearing a baseball cap with a *veteran* patch on the front. His right leg was amputated below the knee.

"I can't wear them things." He pointed to Paul's legs. "Hurts too bad."

Paul looked down. His pant legs had risen, revealing part of the prosthetic. "Mine's been aching a little. I'm three months post-surgery."

"Hope it gets better for ya. Where'd ya get that? Iraq?"

"Afghanistan." Uneasiness crept up Paul's chest and spread to his shoulders. It was the first time he'd been asked about his leg since returning home. Would someone assume that he'd lost his leg in combat? Was losing his leg in an accident as bad as having it blown off by an IED? Where was Genny? The doors opened, and Paul turned around. Genny smiled as she walked up next to him.

"You got a purty wife. Or is she ya girlfriend?" The older vet eyed Paul's left hand and nodded when he saw the silver wedding band. "Wife."

"I'm sorry. I have an appointment I need to get to."

"No problem, young man, and thank ya for yer service."

"Thank you for your service as well."

The man nodded and wheeled out the doors. Paul and Genny headed to the information desk to find the area where Paul's appointment was located. When they found the orthopedic clinic, Genny sat in a chair and Paul wheeled up next to her once he checked in. There were several patients in the waiting room. Among them was a man wearing a cast, and another was missing his left leg like Paul. One man was missing all four limbs.

"Thompson?" a woman called. Paul and Genny followed her down the hall.

Paul watched as Genny looked around the exam room. It was her first time attending an appointment with him. Her expression told him that the posters on the walls intimidated her. One poster she seemed to linger on showed a silhouette with an amputated leg above the left knee.

A knock sounded on the door and a middle-aged man in blue scrubs walked into the room. He introduced himself as Dr. Watts. He had Paul pull off his prosthetic and compression sock so he could examine the residual leg. He suggested a tighter compression sock, which should eliminate pain so that Paul could be fitted for the permanent prosthetic.

"Do you use the chair often?"

"Oh, no. Just when it's a long way away. And I walked a good bit with my dad yesterday and my leg is a little sore." Leg. Should he still call it that, since it wasn't technically a leg? He watched Dr. Watts scan his medical records on a laptop.

"Dr. Godfrey feels you are a good candidate for the return to duty program."

"What's that?" Dr. Godfrey had said nothing to Paul about returning to duty. He assumed it was impossible. Hope brought out a smile.

"You have a year from the date of injury to be fit for duty. You'd have to pass all the areas of the fitness test, including running."

"Running?"

"You'd run with a blade. I've got someone you can talk to." Dr. Watts reached into his desk drawer and pulled out a business card. "Steve Bond. He's retired from the Army and an amputee. He leads a PTSD group for amputees here at the VA. I highly suggest you attend."

"I don't need a PTSD group. I don't have PTSD."

"One rarely comes through something like you've experienced emotionally unscathed. I'll put in a referral to mental health for the group and get you set up for physical therapy and the prosthetics clinic."

Paul wheeled down the halls as if he were on autopilot. His mind raced with thoughts of staying in the Air Force. It would afford him the ability to take care of his family. He'd have to work harder than he'd ever imagined in order to pass the fitness test, but he could do it. He'd see if Steve Bond would meet with him outside of the VA. A PTSD group was unnecessary.

Paul realized Genny had been quiet since the doctor mentioned him staying in the Air Force. There was no way she could understand. The Air Force was more than a career—it was a part of who he was. Genny stopped when they made it out the front doors.

"Do you want me to pull up here?"

"No. I'm good."

They reached the SUV and Paul wheeled around back to the chair carrier.

Genny sighed. "Should have let me pick you up. The man could have helped."

"I'm fine." He winked.

He stood from the wheelchair and helped Genny lift it onto the carrier. He'd do it himself, but he needed to let his leg rest a few more days before attempting something like this on his own.

"I guess I should workout more." Genny laughed and shook her head.

Paul hobbled to the passenger side, wincing with each step. He'd have to ice his residual leg after they got back home.

Suffocating by the silence in the SUV, Paul couldn't take it anymore. "What's got you so quiet? You haven't said much since we left the doctor's office."

"You're kidding, right?" Genny scoffed.

"No."

"If you stay in the Air Force, you will deploy again, and I can't handle that," she snapped.

"Baby…"

"No. I almost lost you. You should know how that feels, or did you forget that someone tried to strangle me to death?"

"Of course I didn't forget, Genevieve!" If Paul saw the sorry excuse of a man on the street, he would kill him. Or at least do him grievous bodily harm. He rubbed the back of his neck. Genny was right. He wanted to stay in the Air Force but hadn't thought about how it would affect her.

"I'm sorry. I never thought I could stay in and I'm excited to hear that it's a possibility. I have less than four years until I'm retirement eligible and the thought of sixteen plus years going down the drain…"

"I know." Genny pushed out a breath.

To Paul's surprise, she reached over and rested her hand on top of his. He slipped his fingers between hers and smiled at her.

Genny pulled into the driveway and before she shifted into park, Katie tore down the front steps and up to the passenger door. She jerked the handle until Paul opened it.

"Daddy!" She reached in and started climbing onto his lap.

"Katie!" Brian yelled from the front steps and rested his hand on his chest.

"Baby girl, wait a second."

"Okay." She slid down and stood back.

Tricia poked her head out the door. "You need your crutches, sweetheart?"

"Yes, Mom. Thanks."

Tricia walked to the passenger side with the crutches and handed them to Paul. Resting her hand on Katie's shoulders, she pulled her back so Paul could stand. Katie wiggled free and ran up the stairs and disappeared inside.

Paul made it in and started down the hall to change clothes. He stopped at Katie's room and saw her sitting on the bed. Wiping an eye with the back of her hand, Paul watched another tear roll down Katie's cheek. What was going on with his baby girl? He took a step towards Katie's room but stopped and turned around when he heard his mother's voice. She gestured to his and Genny's bedroom.

Paul led the way, lowered himself onto the side of the bed, and looked at his mother as she closed the bedroom door behind her.

"Katie pitched a fit when she realized you had left for your appointment."

"Really?"

"Yes. She sobbed and sobbed. Threw herself on the floor."

"That's not like her. At least not before I left for deployment."

"You haven't noticed the change in her attitude the past few days? It started when you told her she couldn't go with you to your appointment."

"What does that have to do with anything?"

The door creaked open, and Genny walked inside.

"She's scared, Paul," Tricia said.

"Of what?" Paul lifted his shoulders.

"Losing you," Genny walked up next to Tricia.

"But she's four. What do four-year-olds know about stuff like that?"

"She knows what she feels. My therapist helped me realize that our mind knows, even when we can't explain why we feel or act a certain way." Genny sat down next to Paul.

The door creaked open again and Katie appeared in the doorway. Tricia excused herself and coaxed Katie into the room.

"Come here, baby girl." Paul held out his arms. Katie stuck her finger in her mouth and took slow steps to the side of the bed where Paul and Genny were sitting. Paul picked her up and sat her on his lap, facing Genny.

"Do you think I was going away and never coming back?" Paul eased back so he could see her. Katie's little face crinkled, and she started sobbing. He gently pulled her head against his chest and held her tightly as Genny wiped her cheeks.

Genny wasn't the only one that was scared for him to stay in the Air Force. And what about Caleb? He'd be Katie's age when Paul was retirement eligible. Genny ran her fingers through Katie's hair, bumping into Paul's chin. She brushed a finger against the stubble and smiled. As valid as Genny's feelings were, he couldn't shut the door on his Air Force career until he talked to Steve Bond.

CHAPTER 11

Genny

The house was quieter than it had been since Paul had deployed six months earlier. Brian and Tricia had left on January second. Genny missed her in-laws. Their support meant the world to her, and she didn't know where she would be without them. Paul, Genny, and the kids had spent the past five days, just the four of them.

Each time a car passed by in front of the house, Genny went to the kitchen window and pulled back the curtain. Their best friends, Peter, Melissa, and their kids, were spending the weekend with them. Melissa had texted her not long ago to let her know they were fifteen minutes away.

Katie patted Genny's leg. "Are they here, Mama?"

"Not yet." Genny ran her fingers through Katie's hair. Melissa had said their rental car was a white Jeep Grand Cherokee. It'd be hard to miss since Genny and Paul owned a maroon one.

Katie groaned. "I wanna see Asher and Izzy."

"Me too, baby." Genny walked down the hall and stopped in the doorway of their bedroom when she saw Paul with Caleb on his hip staring at the bookshelves shoved together against the wall.

He turned around and saw her. "We need a bigger house. Little man needs his own room." They lived in a small three bedroom, two bath house. The third bedroom was used for an office and guest room, which left no room for a crib, much less a nursery.

Since Paul had received transfer orders, they'd stayed in their house rather than rent a bigger house. Renting a larger house for a few months didn't make sense, so Genny had set up the portable crib in her and Paul's room.

"Can we afford it?"

"I'll still get paid until I'm discharged. If I'm discharged, that is."

Genny's stomach twisted at the thought of Paul being retained on active duty. Caleb reached out and Genny took him in her arms.

"Are we going to rent?"

"Well, yeah. We can't afford to buy a house. Maybe when I figure things out and get my degree." Paul shook his head.

That'd be at least five years from now. Genny pressed her lips against Caleb's cheek and groaned, hoping Paul didn't hear.

"I'll start looking online. Maybe we will luck out. We need at least four bedrooms, but I'm sure the rent would be outrageous."

"Mama! Daddy!" Katie screamed from down the hall. She flew into their room, waving her arms. "They're here!"

"Why didn't you let them in?" Paul asked.

"I can't touch the door, 'member?"

Genny laughed and followed Paul to the front door. Asher was the first one inside, and Katie ran up to him and hugged him. He looked at her and leaned back.

"It's me. Katie."

A slow smile spread across his face, and he followed her to her bedroom.

Melissa pushed past Peter and Paul with Izzy in her arms and made her way to Genny. "Happy New Year!" She hugged Genny, then turned her attention to Caleb. "Oh, my gosh. He is precious. Trade ya." Melissa handed Izzy to Genny and took Caleb from her arms. Izzy was two and a half now, and Asher was turning five at the end of the month. Izzy was six months old the last time they'd seen each other.

Izzy leaned back and stared at Genny and stiffened. She held her hands out to Peter when he walked over to hug Genny. "It's okay. She doesn't remember me." Genny looked at Melissa and Caleb. He'd shoved his hands into her curly hair and grabbed a fist full. It reminded Genny of when Asher did the same to her when he was a baby.

After visiting for a while, Peter and Melissa went to the Airbnb they'd rented for their stay. If Paul and Genny had a bigger house, the Parkers could stay with them if they'd like. They made plans to come over for breakfast the next morning.

Once the kids had their baths, Genny rocked Caleb to sleep and carried him down the hall to his crib. She laid him down and watched as he settled. *Mrs. Baker.* Tears stung Genny's eyes. If they moved, they wouldn't see Mrs. Baker like they did now. There was no need to get upset. It might take some time to find another rental.

Genny walked out of the room, easing the door closed. She heard Katie's voice from the living room.

"What about that one? It's pink." She gasped. "Look. A swimming pool!" Katie giggled and clapped her hands.

So much for that.

"No pools, baby girl."

Katie looked up when Genny walked into the room. "Mama, we lookin' at houses."

"You are?"

"Come see this one, babe."

Genny walked over, picked Katie up and sat her on her lap. She looked over at the laptop screen as Paul scrolled through the pictures. It was a nice house, recently remodeled with all the latest trends. But it wasn't here, on Poplar Street, next to Mrs. Baker.

"What's wrong?" Paul asked.

Genny realized her eyes had filled with tears. She shook her head.

"Baby girl, I think it's time for bed." Paul closed the laptop and placed it on the coffee table. Katie whined but obeyed her father. She kissed Genny and held Paul's hand as he walked her to her bedroom.

When he returned, he sat by Genny's side, and rested his hand on her leg. "Tell me what's wrong, love."

"Mrs. Baker." Tears streamed down her cheeks. "If we move…"

Paul pulled her close. "I know. I've thought about it, too. All the houses in this neighborhood are less than fifteen hundred square feet. Ours is barely over a thousand. Anyway, I looked, and nothing is available for rent in this neighborhood."

"Maybe we can find a rental close to here." *The closer the better*, Genny thought.

"Maybe so." Paul kissed the side of her head. "We should get some sleep. Got that feast to prepare in the morning." He stood and held out his hand, pulling Genny to her feet.

Genny lay in bed thinking about the sweet lady next door. The first day they'd met Mrs. Baker, Genny and Paul knew they'd love having her as a neighbor. She had been a support over the years, being there for Genny when Paul was deployed. And when the kids came along, she became their adopted great-grandmother, as she'd become Genny's adopted grandmother years earlier. The thought of moving had already left a hole in Genny's heart.

The following morning, Genny stood at the stove flipping pancakes and groaned. The kids had distracted her and the pancakes ended up darker than she liked. Peter walked over, holding a strip of bacon.

"Don't worry, Melissa burns pancakes." He laughed when Genny swung the spatula at him.

The level of noise in the house brought both a smile to Genny's face and tightened her stomach. Katie and Asher ran around the house making loud airplane noises as they held up toy airplanes. Izzy tried to keep up with them, but they ran too fast for her short legs. Genny looked Paul's way. Caleb was dozing on Paul's shoulder and oblivious to what was going on around him.

"Does Izzy like French toast?" Genny asked when Melissa handed her a cup of coffee.

"Loves it. Mom makes it every morning for breakfast when we visit."

Genny grabbed a French toast stick that had cooled and handed it to Izzy when she walked up to Melissa. She smiled and took it from Genny's hand. "I can get a few of Caleb's toys for Izzy to play with."

Melissa watched the older kids. "I think that's a good idea."

Genny went down the hall and returned with a bin of toys. She and Melissa sat at the table with their coffee and watched the kids play.

"So how are things?" Melissa tilted her head toward Paul and Peter, deep in conversation.

"It's better. Katie's still attached to his hip. She freaks out when she realizes he's left the room. That is, if she lets him out of her sight, which isn't often."

"Poor baby," Melissa said, and frowned.

"Paul or Katie?" They both laughed. "But seriously, it's hard on both."

"I imagine so," Melissa sipped her coffee as she watched Izzy play with a shape sorter.

Genny had missed her friend. FaceTime, texts, and the occasional call weren't the same. They'd spent a lot of time together before the kids came along. Peter had two years until he retired. Where would Peter and Melissa move once he was out of the Air Force? They had no reason to move back to Charleston.

Later in the afternoon, Genny and Melissa went out to catch the last of the after-holiday sales and left the kids in the care of their fathers. Melissa pulled into Starbucks and shifted into park.

Genny took in her surroundings and laughed. "I feel like I'm cheating on The Roasted Bean."

"Well, we'd be there if it wasn't for the gift card I found in my Christmas stocking from Mom." Melissa grinned and they stepped out of the car.

Melissa found a seat after they ordered, and Genny waited at the pickup counter. Everyone was getting their afternoon caffeine fix after shopping. Genny glanced around and sighed when she saw Melissa sitting at the bar by the windows.

"This was it."

"It's okay. We'll grab a table when someone leaves." Genny pulled out a stool and sat down.

"You mean fight to the death for a table?" Melissa laughed.

They talked about the sales they'd found and what the first few months of the new year held for them.

"Can I ask you something?"

"Of course," Genny couldn't read Melissa, but something was off.

"Is Paul upset with Peter?"

"No, not at all." That came out of nowhere.

"He said that Paul wasn't himself. He considers Paul his best friend and he was trying to let Paul know he could talk to him about what happened and Paul told him he doesn't remember."

"He doesn't."

"Peter should have let it go, but he was asking him about the deployment and he said that Paul raised his voice and shut down the conversation."

"Gosh, Melissa. I don't know. He's been a little snippy, but the doctors said it's normal with a TBI."

"I guess that's it. Peter was a little upset."

"I hate that. I can talk to Paul—"

"Don't say anything, please. Peter will be mad that I told you. I hope things are okay between you two." Melissa sipped her coffee.

"Yes, considering." Genny watched as Melissa's gaze drifted to the street. She knew her friend. Passing cars hadn't grabbed her attention. Genny reached over and laid her hand on Melissa's hand. "Hey. What's got you counting cars?"

Melissa looked at Genny and laughed. "Nothing really." Melissa sighed. "That's not true. Here lately, I've been wishing that I was really pregnant when we had the scare in the fall."

"I'm sorry."

Melissa gave Genny a weak smile and shrugged. "So, what about you and Paul?"

Genny shifted on the stool and eyed her friend.

"Are you going to foster? I know that was important to you two."

"I don't know. Since Caleb came along, we've had our hands full."

Melissa took a sip of coffee, and Genny could tell she was smiling behind the cup.

"What?"

"I don't know. Three seems like the perfect number."

"Of what?"

"Kids." Melissa's eyes brightened.

"For you, maybe." Genny laughed. "I don't think Paul can get recertified now that he's an amputee."

"There's only one way to find out." Melissa brought her cup to her lips and arched her brows.

Melissa was right, but what if she and Paul got their hopes up only to have them come crashing down? It would give Paul more reason to doubt his worth. Four months had passed since he was injured. If they pursued fostering again, how would Paul handle a denial?

———⁂———

Genny sat on the couch beside Paul. She leaned over and rested her head on his chest, listening to the soft thump of his heart. Lately, when she listened to his heartbeat, fear fought its way into her thoughts. She'd come close—too close—to never hearing his heartbeat again. Genny leaned forward and spotted the kids on the other side of the coffee table. Both were stretched out on the floor, asleep. Katie hadn't played this hard since the last visit with Asher. Genny giggled.

"What? The kids?" Paul asked.

"Yeah. They will be up all night, but it was worth it to see Peter and Melissa. The visit went by too fast."

"I sure have missed them. And the kids, of course."

"Yeah, me, too. Gosh, our friendship has come a long way since I entered the picture."

"Ah, the dreaded 'marriage of convenience.'"

"That's how it started out." Genny brushed her hand across Paul's chest. "Hard to believe it's been six years."

"I know. I never would have thought we'd have those two." Paul lifted his chin towards the kids.

"Me either." Genny sighed. "You know? We never talked about what would have happened if we hadn't fallen for each other." She raised up and looked at Paul.

"I prayed like I'd never prayed before. I didn't know what would happen, and I was scared to death, but I knew God was in control. So, there's that." He laughed.

"Mmm. Me, too. But seriously, would you have divorced me?"

"Genevieve!" Paul pinched his lips together.

"Well?"

"There's no reason to go there. I fell hard for you and will love you until the day I die."

Genny leaned over and kissed him. "Me, too."

"Daddy?" Katie sat up and rubbed her eyes. Genny held in a laugh at Katie's hair matted to her head. For a moment, she allowed herself to imagine a third child sitting on the floor. A little girl, maybe. How old would she be? What would she look like? Genny softly sighed. She may never know.

CHAPTER 12

Paul

Paul walked down the steps and made his way to the truck. The Tundra had been parked in the driveway for the past four months, except for the time or two his dad had driven it when his parents were helping Genny.

Opening the door, Paul turned and lifted his right hip, sliding smoothly into the driver's seat. He swung his legs around and shut the door. The old truck was lifted enough that he had to step on the running board to get in the truck, and he was six two. He'd traded it in so it would be easier with the kids. Now that he was an amputee, he was glad about that decision.

Today was Paul's first appointment with Steve Bond. He'd called to talk to Steve directly, but was told that he had to make an appointment. He couldn't help but wonder if Dr. Watts had something to do with it, since Paul was reluctant to attend the group. But he'd do what he had to do to talk to Steve. Paul didn't know any other veteran who had successfully returned to active duty as an amputee.

Paul walked into the clinic and took a seat by the windows. There were a few people in the waiting room. The couple in the corner must be in for marital counseling by the way they were snapping at each other. Several pamphlets were scattered around the room. The stacks on the table next to him covered a variety of topics. Trauma seemed to be the most prevalent, PTSD was slapping him in the face lately. He picked up a pamphlet and laid it back down. A tall man wearing a white short-sleeved polo and tan slacks walked through the doorway to the hall.

"Paul?" the man said, looking Paul dead in the face. Steve didn't look like the image he'd conjured up in his mind. Steve wasn't short, plump, with graying hair and glasses. He was tall, blond, and fit. With the way the sleeves of his shirt pulled tight against his biceps, the man lived in the gym. Paul stood and followed him down the hall to his office.

"Steve Bond." He held out his hand.

"Paul Thompson. Nice to meet you." Paul shook hands with Steve.

"You, too. Have a seat." Steve motioned to a pair of wingback chairs.

Steve gave—what Paul guessed—was the usual spiel about the PTSD group. As he spoke, Paul noticed diplomas hanging on the wall behind him. Glancing at the desk off to the side, Paul saw a nameplate with a group of letters behind Steve's name. With what he knew about Genny's counselor, he was mistaken about Steve.

"Any questions?"

"You're a counselor?"

Steve chuckled. "Yep. I got good use out of tuition assistance and the GI Bill. I finished my master's degree when I was on terminal leave before retirement."

"Wow, I assumed the group was peer led. I apologize."

"Oh, no problem." Steve reached for a bottle of water on the side table next to him. He tilted his head to a bottle of water on the table next to Paul.

"Thanks." Paul picked up the bottle and took a long drink.

The two men talked briefly about their military backgrounds before Steve brought out his laptop and began asking questions that Paul was adamant didn't apply to him.

"No, I don't have nightmares. My wife hasn't said I've yelled out. No startle response." Paul strained to remember the symptoms Genny experienced because of the assault. "No flashbacks." Paul sighed and drank the rest of the water. He sat quietly for an uncomfortable moment. Why was Steve staring at him?

"The last thing I remember is standing at the back of the plane. Then I woke up at Walter Reed. When I found out what had happened and that one person died, I…I don't know. How could I forget something like that?" Paul stared at the empty water bottle in his hand. The plastic crackled when he tapped it against his knee. He sat up straight and looked at Steve.

"It's the mind's way of protecting you. That's why we have to pay close attention to see if anything surfaces. We don't only talk about PTSD; the group is actually a group for amputees. But PTSD is prevalent among the members."

Paul leaned back against the chair. He felt like a balloon that'd had the air let out of it before it was tied. He had no control over where he was going. Paul had no choice but to attend the group.

"Sign me up." He tapped the empty bottle on the arm of the chair.

"Good deal. How about Monday?"

"Sure."

On the way home, Paul drove in silence. Usually, he'd have the radio on one of the Christian music stations in the area. Sometimes, he'd listen to eighties rock. Today, he needed to get his thoughts out of his head. Why all the obstacles? He was physically injured, not mentally. Attending a therapy group was unnecessary, but what could he do about it? Nothing. Paul knew God had a plan, but what purpose could be served by him being in an accident he didn't remember and losing his leg?

Later in the evening, Paul sat on the couch with his laptop and logged into the bank's website. He gritted his teeth when the account popped up on the screen. Genny had renamed all the accounts. What once was Checking, Savings, and Money Market, were now Bill collectors, An unexpected event, and House on the beach. A fire started in his chest and spread throughout his body.

Slamming the laptop closed, he tossed it on the coffee table and jumped to his feet. As he passed by Katie sitting on the floor watching *Sesame Street* for the tenth time today, he noticed her wide eyes. Genny turned her head towards him when he walked through the bedroom door. She fastened Caleb's diaper and sat him up on the bed.

"What the heck did you do?" Pain shot through Paul's jaws when he clenched his teeth.

"What are you talking about?" She rested her hand on her throat.

"The bank account! Why did you rename the accounts?"

"My gosh, Paul. I thought it was funny and I thought you'd think it was funny, too."

"Well, I don't." He flared his nostrils.

Genny's eyes glistened.

Paul's arms shook as he balled his hands into fists. He knew he was overreacting, but couldn't stop himself. "First the glasses, then the lamp, then this? Oh, and you moved the Keurig and rearranged the cabinets." His deep voice boomed off the walls. Caleb cried, and Genny picked him up. Wiping her cheeks, her chin trembled.

"I'm sorry. I'll donate the glasses and lamps. I saw the old ones at Walmart, and I'll put everything in the cabinets back where they were. And the Keurig. You can change the name of the accounts back. I'm sorry."

Paul relaxed his hands, his heart rate slowing. "I feel like I'm walking into your world," he cried. "You don't need me anymore."

"What?" Genny's mouth fell open.

Paul walked over and sat on the edge of the bed next to where Genny was standing and dropped his head in his hands. She sat down and slipped her arm across his shoulders.

"I feel so useless," he sobbed. "I have to put my leg on before I can get out of bed. Do you know how ridiculous that sounds?" Paul pushed out a breath, and wiped his cheeks.

"Is that what this is about? The glasses, lamps…" Genny shifted Caleb on her lap.

"Honestly? I don't know. I've never had these feelings before. It scares me, Genevieve."

"Remember what the doctor said about your symptoms?"

Paul sighed.

A muffled cry came from the bedroom door. Katie was holding her hands over her mouth, her eyes wet with tears. "Come here, baby girl." Running to Paul, Katie climbed onto his lap and rested her head against his chest.

Caleb quieted and reached out and slipped his fingers in Katie's hair. Babbling, he tugged.

Paul unwound the strands from his fingers and smoothed Katie's hair down. "Steve told me today that I have to attend the PTSD group. Well, he highly suggested it since the group is for amputees. He said that most have PTSD. Since the medical board will want my VA records, they'll see I'm in a mental health group. I think it will benefit me to drop the group to protect myself."

Paul stared at his hands and let out a long, low sigh. "I have to try. Four years until retirement. Four years. I feel so useless and lost. The Air Force is all I know. I can't throw it away. If there is the slightest possibility that I can stay in, I have to take it. I'm afraid when the board sees I'm attending a therapy group, it'll all be over."

"But you might deploy again."

"What, Mama?" Katie sat up.

"That means Daddy would leave for a while."

"That's part of military life." Paul rested his cheek on the top of Katie's head. Genny sighed.

"Daddy, are you leaving?" Katie's voice rose an octave.

How could he explain this to his little girl? "We don't know if or when I would leave."

Quiet for a moment, Genny spoke up. "I think you should go to the group. It will help to be with other amputees."

Paul shook his head. "We'll talk about this later."

Honestly, Genny was right. A war was looming in the background. Every time Paul thought about losing his career, he felt as if he would waste sixteen years of his life. When he thought about the return to duty program, the crying faces of his wife and children appeared in front of him. It seemed like an impossible decision. Sometimes he wished God would come down from Heaven and stand before him and tell him what to do.

Paul lay staring at the ceiling. The earlier conversation with Genny and Katie played in his head. The fear in Katie's eyes strengthened his guilt for considering returning to duty. Paul closed his eyes and opened them when he heard Caleb stirring in his crib. Taking a deep, pained breath, he closed his eyes and felt himself drifting.

A tap on Paul's chest opened his eyes, and he laid quietly for a moment. It was his imagination. Closing his eyes, he rolled over. The feeling that he was being watched raised the hairs on his neck and he rolled back over. He could make out a small silhouette close to the side of the bed.

"Daddy?" Katie whispered.

"I'm here, baby girl."

"Are you leaving?"

"No, baby." Would he? The answer was yes if he stayed in the Air Force. "Do you want to sleep with me and Mama?"

"Uh-huh."

"Okay." He reached out and picked her up and laid her between him and Genny. She snuggled up to his side and exhaled. Paul closed his eyes and felt himself drifting to sleep.

Paul's eyelids fluttered open. He closed them and rolled over. Checking the time on his phone, he grimaced at the bright numbers displaying one thirty in the morning. He'd woken up after sleeping for an hour and a half. Rolling over facing Katie and Genny, he softly sighed and closed his eyes. Their breathing filled his ears, making it hard to relax. Rolling onto his back, he stared at the ceiling. That wasn't working, so he rolled over facing his nightstand, focusing on the lampshade.

"Paul," Genny hissed through clenched teeth. "You're going to wake up Katie."

Paul sighed and threw back the covers and slipped on his prosthetic. "I'm sorry," he whispered. Genny mumbled and rolled over.

Settling on the couch, Paul picked up his laptop and began browsing the news webpages. The headline of a report on low test scores in the school district stretched across the top of one page. In a few years, his kids would attend one of the elementary schools. Would their test scores be low? He couldn't do that to his children. Tears burned his eyes, distorting the words on the screen.

Closing the laptop, Paul opened the back door and followed Lucy outside. He picked up one of her balls on the way to the picnic table. Climbing on top, he rolled the ball around in his hands as he thought about what lay before him. If he didn't pass the fitness test, what was next? He should explore college programs. He had the GI Bill and could get his bachelor's degree for free.

Drawing in a long breath, he released it as tears filled his eyes. Genny would be disappointed in him if he failed the fitness test because of his disability. She'd made suggestive comments about his athleticism and how it had shaped his physical features. What would she think of him if he couldn't exercise like he used to and let himself go?

Paul shook his head. Genny would love him no matter what. And because he failed his fitness test wouldn't mean he couldn't be active. He'd at least be able to walk around the neighborhood to keep himself in shape. Where were these thoughts coming from? He cried over test scores that had nothing to do with his kids, and the possibility he would gain weight if he was discharged.

Paul hopped down from the picnic table and headed inside. When he looked at the clock on the mantel, he sighed. It was three o'clock and he was wide awake. He should try to get some sleep. Pushing the bedroom door open, Katie had sprawled out and was covering half of his side of the bed.

Turning around, he made his way back to the living room. He could research TBIs until he was tired. Pulling up a search page, Paul typed in traumatic brain injury and glanced out the window while he waited for the results to show on the page.

Was he truly taking into consideration how his family felt about his desire to stay in the Air Force? It wouldn't be an issue if he failed the fitness test. He felt like he was being pulled in half. His thoughts were all over the place. It had to be the TBI. Looking at the search page, he clicked on the first link, hoping to figure out who he was now.

When he read to the bottom of the home page, Paul closed the window and set the laptop on the coffee table. Fear of the future had clouded his thoughts. Making a quick trip to the guestroom, he grabbed his small Bible, journal, and his favorite pen and headed back to the living room.

First, he opened the Bible to a random page and stared at the words. Nothing leaped out to him, and he set the Bible aside. Thumbing through the journal to the last entry, he focused on the next blank page, noting the light blue lines stretching from one edge of the paper to the other.

January 12, 2017

The thoughts in his head were as blank as the journal page. Forcing himself to concentrate on a thought, it began fading until it disappeared, leaving nothing to write. The next best thing was to let it all out and make sense of it later.

I'm scared, overwhelmed, a failure.

Failure was a strong word. What had he failed at? Nothing yet. Shaking his head, he continued.

I'm mad at God.

It was the strongest thought. Maybe that's why it kept disappearing. He didn't want to admit the way he felt. A Christian wasn't supposed to get mad at God. Closing his eyes, he breathed in deep.

"Father, I know your plans are perfect. Why is it necessary for me to lose a part of myself, physically and emotionally? And if you take my career away from me, how am I supposed to take care of my family?"

Leaning his head back, he closed his eyes and imagined his family packed into his parents' three-bedroom house.

CHAPTER 13

Paul

A few vehicles were in the parking lot, most with handicap license plates or placards. One truck had an electric scooter carrier attached to the back. The sight stirred something inside Paul. Losing his leg was devastating, but at least he could walk. He headed inside, and the woman at the front desk gave Paul directions to where the group was meeting. A group for amputees with trauma, she called it. Trauma was a fancier way of saying PTSD. Or maybe less traumatic. He chuckled under his breath and grimaced. There were people in the group with genuine PTSD. He wasn't one of them.

Straight down the hall, Paul saw the open door to the group room. As he made his way toward the door, the walls of the hall closed in on him, choking the air from his lungs. A man pushing a mop cart was walking toward him. By the crispness of his light blue button-down shirt and navy pants, he took pride in his appearance. He inclined his head to Paul.

"Afternoon."

"Afternoon," Paul replied.

From his vantage point, Paul could see a few of the group members. A man opposite the door sat in a wheelchair. A prosthetic hand peeked out from the cuff of the long-sleeved shirt of the woman sitting next to him. When he walked through the door, he recognized the man in the wheelchair as the man who'd spoken to him when he came to the VA for his first appointment.

The man looked up. "Well, hello there, young man. Nice ta see ya upright," he chuckled. "As ya see, I'm still sittin' down." The man spread his hands out.

"Hello, sir."

"Call me Craig." He smiled, revealing a missing front tooth Paul hadn't noticed the first time he saw the older veteran.

Paul sat in the seat next to the woman with the prosthetic hand, the first vacant seat he saw.

"Hi, I'm Karla." The woman with the long, blond hair extended her prosthetic hand.

"Paul." He paused, then shook her hand, the cool metal brushing against his fingers.

"Oh, sorry. I'm left-handed—or was—and I catch myself using it first."

"No problem." Paul shifted in the chair. He took a quick look around the circle of veterans. Steve was sitting where Paul could fully see him, and he nodded at Paul. Breaking out in a cold sweat, Paul fought the urge to run for the door. Attending this group felt like having a root canal with no anesthesia—excruciatingly painful.

"Alright, brothers and sister." Steve smiled at Karla. Paul imagined it was tough being the only woman in a group of ten men. *Eleven*, he corrected himself. "Let's go around the room and tell as much as comfortable so that Paul can get to know his fellow vets."

The next twenty minutes held stories of IEDs, mortar attacks, and suicide bombs. The man in the electric scooter had lost his legs up to his hips because of an IED. Craig, the man in the wheelchair, spoke next. He was the only group member who had not served in Operation Iraqi Freedom or Operation Enduring Freedom. During Desert Storm, he'd lost his leg to a bullet fragment that shattered the bone. He finished his story with encouragement for the younger veterans.

"It don't matter what able bodied folk think. Hold ya head high. Walk, or wheel, or ride with purpose. If they give ya problems, tell 'em where to go. Straight to h—" Craig stopped and looked around the circle of people. "I'll behave. They can go fly a kite." The group broke out into laughter.

Karla slumped. How many times had the vets told their stories? When was the last time someone joined the group? Steve had said it was up to them what they shared. Maybe Karla was tired of talking about what had happened to her.

"I was in explosive ordnance disposal in the Army. I'd been called to deactivate an explosive and I realized a split second before snipping a wire that it was the wrong one."

Karla rubbed the fingers on her prosthetic hand as she talked.

"I'm surprised I'm not dead. It blew my left arm off." She looked at Paul and raised her prosthetic arm. "This goes to my shoulder. I've had too many surgeries to count. But at least twenty on my stomach and chest alone. Third-degree burns stretch from my thighs to my neck." Paul hadn't noticed the scars on her neck when he first sat down. Karla looked at him. "Your turn." She gave him a weak smile.

The underarms of Paul's t-shirt clung to him. This was the first time he would talk about the accident that'd claimed his leg outside of the hospital and his family and friends. He swallowed down the nausea that had pushed its way into his throat. *Lord, please don't let me throw up.* But then again, it would get him out of the room.

"Um, well. My injury isn't like the rest of you. I–I lost my leg in an accident in Afghanistan." Paul scanned the faces around the circle. "I'm in the Air Force. Well, for now. I was on the ramp of a C–5 Galaxy aircraft when its hydraulics failed. Several pallets fell off the ramp." Should he continue? Paul was suddenly exhausted, as if he'd run a marathon, but he couldn't stop now. Everyone else had given details. But he didn't remember.

"I heard about that," Nate had lost his right leg below the knee when the Humvee he was riding in was hit by a roadside bomb.

Paul's face felt hot. What would Nate say?

"My best friend witnessed it happen. He said it was crazy. Troops trying to get all the cargo that had fallen off the pallets out of the way so the medics could get to the injured. I'll ask if he remembers you."

Please don't. He didn't want to know. Like Steve said, it was his mind's way of protecting him, and he was fine with that. Steve announced it was time to wrap up for the day. He mentioned a family picnic in the summer. Socializing outside the group was unnecessary, in Paul's opinion.

The group ended and Paul's intention was to make a run for it, but Nate came up and started talking about the accident. When Paul said that he didn't remember and knew only what he'd been told, Nate changed the conversation to military service in general. Craig and Devon came over and joined in. When Paul glanced toward the door, he saw Karla heading in that direction. Excusing himself and walking to the door crossed his mind, but he stayed, despite feeling trapped. Might as well get used to conversing with these vets since he was spending the next however many months with them.

—ee—

Paul heard Caleb sobbing when he stepped out of the truck. In the living room, he saw Genny holding Caleb, bouncing him on her hip while holding a teething ring to his mouth. Caleb turned his head to the side, avoiding it. Fresh tears rolled down his wet cheeks. Katie stood next to Genny, rubbing Caleb's back, surprising Paul. When Caleb cried, she'd cover her ears and run to her bedroom and shut the door until he stopped.

"He's teething again. This ring is thawed, and I can't find the other one."

Paul opened his mouth to speak.

"And before you ask, it's not in the freezer. I moved everything around." Genny blew a wisp of hair out of her face.

Katie gasped and ran down the hall. Paul heard her throwing things around in her room. He started toward the hall but stopped when she ran into the living room holding the other teething ring. "It was in my toy box."

Genny groaned. "Katie wasn't this bad." Genny let out an exhausted sigh. "What about the Baby Orajel?"

"We're out." Genny puffed out her breath each time she bounced Caleb.

"Should've bought a new tube before the other one ran out."

"Well, that doesn't help us now, does it?" She rolled her eyes.

Paul pulled out his phone and did a quick internet search. He grabbed a few ice cubes from the freezer, wrapped them in the thin dish towel they kept in the back of the drawer, and pounded the ice with a heavy glass. He held the ice filled towel against Caleb's gums when he opened his mouth to cry. A few moments later, Caleb's sobbing turned into a whimper.

"Who knew the least favorite towel in the drawer would come in handy?" Genny laughed under her breath.

"Yep." Paul smiled at Caleb and took him from Genny's arms. Sitting on the couch, he lightly bounced Caleb on his legs. He stopped when a muscle cramped in his residual leg. When would he be able to do the things he did before the accident? Like comforting his children?

"How was the group?"

Okay? Tolerable? Excruciatingly painful like a root canal without anesthesia? Paul held in a laugh. "Okay." It was the truth.

"That's good." Genny brushed her hand over Caleb's hair. He quieted a few minutes later. "Thank goodness the Tylenol kicked in." She leaned over and kissed Caleb's cheek, then Paul's cheek.

Paul carried Caleb to their bedroom and laid him in his crib. A printout of a rental house was next to Genny's laptop. Probably another rental house she wanted him to look at. It was the fourth one this week. He picked up the paper.

"Hideous interior, huh?" Genny laughed.

He looked at the monthly rent out of habit. It was three-hundred dollars more than what they were paying now. He skimmed over the details. It was two thousand five hundred square feet, with four bedrooms and two and three-quarter bathrooms—perfect for their little family. Each could have their own bedroom and an extra room for an office.

"Yeah, looks like it jumped out of the nineteen seventies." Paul laughed. Thirteen hundred dollars a month was too much, anyway. Paul blinked and brought the piece of paper close to his face. Three acres? An apartment over the garage? Now it made sense.

"It was built in the early eighties." Genny clasped her hands in front of her and turned side to side like Katie did when she wanted ice cream at eight o'clock in the evening. "It's for sale, Paul. No down payment for you as a veteran, right?" She smiled sweetly.

Paul focused on the sale price he hadn't noticed before. "Genny, we don't know what the future holds for us. We can't buy a house now." He groaned.

Her smile evaporated and her eyes glistened.

"We have a month-to-month lease here. If I am discharged, our income will disappear. If necessary, we can get out of the lease and—"

"Move to Tennessee?"

"I didn't say that." He didn't want to admit that it was a strong possibility. "We both want to stay here. I can work on my degree and we'd have the monthly stipend from the GI Bill. Please look at rentals." Paul laid the paper back on the bed. "I'll start dinner." He left Genny standing by the crib. It would be nice to buy a house, but not one you'd have to spend fifty thousand dollars to remodel.

⌁

Paul settled into the wingback chair, looking out the window. The office door opened, and Steve walked in with a cup of coffee in each hand. He handed a cup to Paul.

"Two teaspoons of sugar and a splash of creamer?"

"That's it." Paul took a small sip and raised his brows. "Perfect."

"How ya been?" Steve set his cup on the table between the chairs.

"Ah, good. My wife wants to buy a house. Can you believe that? My career is in limbo, and she wants to commit to paying thirteen hundred dollars a month for thirty years. And it's old and needs a lot of work. Like we have the money for that." Paul said. Taking a breath, he sipped his coffee.

"Try not to get ahead of yourselves. Less anxiety that way."

"I wish she felt that way."

"So, what about your first group meeting?"

"Okay, I guess." Three days wasn't enough time to judge the group.

Steve watched Paul as he drank his coffee. He felt as if he was at the end of Steve's rifle scope. Paul was half tempted to walk across the room to see if Steve's steel gaze followed him. Steve set his cup down and walked behind his desk, bending over as if he was getting something. Paul's shoulders rose as he leaned forward to see what Steve was doing. A moment later, he stood up, holding a running blade. The metal blade was attached to the back of a prosthetic and mimicked the curve of a foot.

"Wow, that's bigger than I thought it would be." Paul slid to the edge of the seat. Steve walked over and held the blade out to Paul.

"Want to try it on? It was made for me, but we are about the same height and our residuals are close to the same length."

"Sure." Paul grinned. Steve helped him slip on the prosthetic and held onto him while he stood. Guiding Paul around the chair, Steve let go. Paul fell forward, catching himself on the edge of Steve's desk. "Whoa!" Paul laughed. "People run with these things?" He gripped the arm of the chair as he walked around and sat down.

"You'll get used to it." Steve smiled and sat down. He picked up his coffee cup. "How's PT?"

"It's going great. I should be able to get my permanent prosthetic in a few weeks. Then I can give this thing a try." Paul lifted the prosthetic blade.

"Have you talked to your wife about your desire to stay on active duty?"

"She knows I don't want to give up, but we avoid the subject."

"You can't avoid it forever." Steve angled his head.

"I know."

The men were quiet for a moment. "What's keeping you from talking about it?"

Paul sighed. "She'll do everything she can to change my mind."

"Why is that?"

Paul looked down at his left leg and back at Steve as if he was oblivious to Paul's missing leg.

"Besides that."

What did Steve want him to say? Paul lowered his head and focused on his pants, brushing his finger across a snag in the fabric.

"Does it matter what she thinks?"

Paul jerked his head up and set his jaw. "Of course it does."

"Look, Paul, I know how you feel. It seems like an impossible decision. You ask yourself many questions. Are you being selfish? How dare your wife hold you back? What about your kids? You have—fill in the blank—more years until you retire; do you want to throw it all away?"

Exactly.

He couldn't give up. Paul stared out the window at the cars passing by. What if he did a trial run of the fitness test to see if he could pass? He would know if he had what it took to be the person he was before the injury, or close to it. The thought of throwing away his career was unbearable. What about his family? There was no need to get ahead of himself; he might not pass the fitness test and all this worrying would have been for nothing.

CHAPTER 14

"I'm going to take Lucy out for a little while. Do you want to come, Katie?" Genny asked.

"No, I'm staying with Daddy and Bubby."

"Okay." Genny wasn't surprised. When Paul was at the VA or running errands, Katie spent time with Genny. Once Paul walked through the door, Genny felt as if Katie threw her to the side.

Lucy yipped and bolted to the back fence when Genny opened the door. She made her way to the picnic table to watch Lucy play. She thought about everything that had happened in the past five months. Paul had seemed to adjust, but Genny worried it was a front. And what about Katie? She'd been coming to their bedroom most nights. Maybe she felt left out since Caleb slept in their room. Maybe she was scared since she went to Paul's side of the bed every time.

Lucy jerked her head up and she turned her ears when she heard Mrs. Baker's back door. Genny smiled when Felix shot by Mrs. Baker and up to the fence, teasing Lucy.

Hopping down from the picnic table, Genny made her way to the fence where Mrs. Baker was standing.

"Hello, Genny."

"Good afternoon. How are you?"

"Ah, can't complain." Felix yapped at Lucy and darted from side to side. "Would you like to come over for tea?"

Tea was Mrs. Baker's way of saying that she wanted to talk. Genny had learned a lot by having tea next door.

"I'd love to."

"Are you available now?"

"Oh, yeah. Give me a minute to tell Paul and I'll be over."

The setting was the same as it had been over the years. A floral porcelain teapot with two matching teacups and saucers was placed in the middle of a silver tray placed on the table between the couch and loveseat. Genny sat on the loveseat and picked up the tin of tea bags, choosing Earl Grey as she did every time.

Mrs. Baker dunked a tea bag in her cup several times and used a pair of small tongs to squeeze the tea out of the bag. Genny watched her as she prepared her tea. Something about her was different. They'd talked about heavy topics in the past; there was no reason for Mrs. Baker to be nervous. Settling in her seat, Mrs. Baker let out a weary breath.

"I want to let you know," Mrs. Baker looked over at Genny, "Susan, Alan, and I have been talking." She took a sip of tea.

A nagging feeling rose from Genny's stomach. Sipping her tea, she listened as Mrs. Baker talked about getting older and not living around her children and grandchildren.

No. She can't leave.

"We think it's best if I move in with Susan."

Genny stared at Mrs. Baker, replaying the past years in her head. She'd showed up on their doorstep with an apple pie on the day they'd moved in. Genny had spent her first Christmas in Charleston with Mrs. Baker while Paul was deployed. She'd been there for them many times.

"Honey?"

Genny shook her head and felt a tear roll down her cheek. Mrs. Baker pulled a tissue from the box on the side table and handed it to Genny. Blotting her face, Genny closed her eyes. Mrs. Baker's moving was like losing a family member. People say that they'd visit, but how often did that actually happen?

"I'm sorry. I–I understand." Fresh tears filled Genny's eyes.

"You are special to me." Mrs. Baker reached over and took Genny's hand in hers.

"I'm going to miss you," Genny's voice broke. She stood and went to Mrs. Baker. She found herself on her knees with her head on Mrs. Baker's lap as she sobbed. She loved this woman and would miss her terribly.

When Genny made it home, she kissed Paul and the kids and went straight to her bedroom. Tears filled her eyes, making it hard to see her journal in the nightstand drawer. Wiping her eyes, she found the journal and opened it, flattening the spine.

Feb 13, 2017

Mrs. Baker is moving. What am I going to do? She's so much more than a neighbor. I've known her forever, it seems. Who am I going to have tea with?

Genny studied her words. She and Katie would have tea parties, but she needed the type of conversations she had with Mrs. Baker. Closing her eyes, a moment, Genny opened her eyes and continued writing.

I feel that everyone I love leaves me. My parents, grandparents, Brandon, and now Mrs. Baker. Lord, please don't take Paul or the kids.

Caleb was napping, and Katie was sitting on the floor coloring. Grabbing her laptop, Genny thought she'd surf the web for a while. Noticing the tabs at the top of the browser, she clicked the tab for the real estate company that had listed the house. She'd been torturing herself by looking at the listing several times a day, but it had been close to a week since she last looked at the listing.

Waiting for the page to refresh, Genny figured the house had sold to an investor and flipped for fifty thousand dollars more than the current listing price. The house was old but had "good bones" she'd decided, making it a prime candidate for flipping.

A new picture was featured for the house and the listing had been updated. The house was still for sale and the price had dropped by fifteen thousand dollars. "Fifteen thousand dollars?" Genny's mouth hung open.

"Mama?"

"It's okay, honey. Go back to coloring the picture for Daddy." A few more pictures had been added of the backyard and the apartment over the garage, along with information about the apartment. "Five hundred square feet, living room, eat in kitchen, one bedroom and a three-quarter bath." What was a three-quarter bath? She did a quick search. "Toilet, sink, and shower stall. Hmm." What would they do with an apartment?

Genny scrolled through the pictures of the house again. She wasn't sure how much it'd cost to replace floor covering, paint walls, and buy new appliances and bathroom fixtures. It shouldn't be over ten thousand dollars. Maybe fifteen. She pulled up Home Depot's website and started browsing.

A little while later, a notebook with prices scribbled down lay next to the laptop. Genny tapped the pencil against the page. New appliances alone cost close to five thousand dollars with tax and delivery. That left ten thousand dollars to replace the floor covering, which could cost over ten thousand dollars, according to the contractor on an episode of *Fixer Upper* she'd watched the other day. And with the bathroom fixtures…her estimate was way off. Paul was adamant they wouldn't buy soon. She deleted the page from her favorites and closed the laptop.

Katie headed down the hall to her room. "Mama, Bubby's awake."

Genny went to her room and picked Caleb up from the crib and sat down on the bed. "Are you ready for a snack?" She kissed Caleb's cheek.

"Yes!" Katie clapped from the doorway.

"Let's see what we can find for you, Sissy. Bubby gets a banana."

"Chocolate chip cookies!"

Genny had baked chocolate chip cookies the day before. She'd have to make sure they weren't all gone. Cookies were one of Paul's weaknesses. Genny opened the plastic container. She pulled the top off and shook her head at the lone cookie laying on the bottom. Katie stood next to her, holding out her hand.

Standing at the counter mixing cookie dough, Genny's thoughts drifted to Mrs. Baker. She'd told Genny that Susan had sent two moving companies for estimates. This was happening faster than Genny could process.

Half an hour later, Genny pulled the first pan of cookies from the oven and set the pan on the cooling rack. The deadbolt on the front door snapped back. Katie ran up to Paul when he walked in the door.

"Daddy! Mama's making cookies!"

"Good." Paul looked at Genny and winked. He bent down and picked Katie up. "I'm gonna eat 'em all up."

"Nuh-uh." She kissed his cheek.

Caleb squealed from the highchair. He smacked his hands on the tray, squishing pieces of banana between his fingers. Genny grabbed a towel and wiped

Caleb down. The house was on the tip of her tongue, but she held it in. It was pointless. No need to get herself worked up.

"Guess what, babe?"

"What?"

"I'm getting my permanent prosthetic!"

"Oh, my goodness." Genny rushed to Paul and slipped her arm around his neck. Katie groaned when they pressed her between them. "I'm so happy for you."

"Dr. Godfrey was right. It's been almost six months since the accident."

"You've worked so hard for this, babe." Genny kissed him.

Paul stood Katie on the floor, and she ran to the pan on the cooling rack and grabbed a cookie.

Paul put on a movie and sat on the couch with the kids. Genny had been putting off cleaning the desk and figured that it was a good time since the kids were distracted. When she walked into the guest room, she grimaced. Papers, folders, and books covered the top of the desk and had spilled over onto the bed. She was going to be busy for a while.

Picking up a stack of papers, Genny found the folder that Anna had given them when Paul was in the hospital. She pushed aside some papers and sat on the bed. A few of the handouts referred to programs at Walter Reed. She balled them up and tossed them on top of the trash pile on the floor.

Information on the amputee program at the VA, a handout on PTSD, and other programs Paul qualified for were added to the pile. He'd received the same information at the VA. The last handout was information on a grant to remodel homes for veterans.

"Huh." Genny stared at the piece of paper. A web address was listed at the bottom of the page. She folded the paper and shoved it in her back pocket. Later, she'd look up the site and get more information.

"Babe?" Paul poked his head in the door.

Genny gasped and rested her hand on her chest. "You scared me."

"I'm sorry, sweetheart," he said as he was walking towards her. "I'm going to grab dinner. Maybe Chinese or pizza. I'll take the kids and give you a little break."

"Really?"

"Yep." Paul leaned in for a kiss.

She followed Paul to the living room and got the kids ready. Paul kissed her and headed out the door, carrying Caleb on his hip and holding Katie's hand. Paul had done things like this regularly. She'd take the opportunity for a bubble bath, but it was a perfect time to check out the website for the grant.

When she pulled up the website, the first thing she saw was an application deadline for the next day. Before she thought it through, Genny clicked the apply button. Scanning the page, she noted that family and friends could apply on behalf of the veteran. Checking the clock, she realized she had a little over half an hour to complete the application.

Twenty minutes had passed and she had five more questions to answer. Genny heard the truck door close in the driveway. She filled in the last requirements and hit the send button as Katie sprinted into the room waving a pack of bread sticks. Genny exhaled and followed Katie into the kitchen. Why did she apply for a grant for a house they didn't own?

Later, when everyone had turned in for the night, Genny opened her eyes when she felt the comforter pull tight. Paul was sitting up in bed, staring at himself in the dresser mirror. She tugged on the comforter, but he didn't move.

"Babe," she whispered, trying not to wake Caleb.

Paul didn't move for a few moments, then he turned to face her. "I smell it."

"What?"

"I smell it. I swear I do." He looked in the mirror again.

The only thing she smelled was the fading lavender and vanilla air freshener from the bathroom.

Paul drew in a deep breath. "Don't you smell it, Smith?"

Smith?

She touched Paul's arm, and sweat covered her fingers. Running her hand over Paul's side of the bed, she felt the dampness of the sheet.

"Every time I take a breath, it burns my nose. You can't tell me you don't smell it." Paul scoffed.

Genny touched his shoulder, and he jerked his head to face her.

"Need me to change Caleb?"

What in the world? "No, you were talking in your sleep."

"I was? What did I say?"

"You kept saying you smelled something and you said 'Smith.'"

Paul turned his head and looked in the mirror again. "I guess I was dreaming."

"You don't know what you were smelling in your dream?"

He looked at her again. "It was a strong smell of fuel."

"Fuel?"

"For planes."

"Oh." She ran her hand down his arm. "Are you okay, honey?"

"Yeah."

He didn't sound okay. They laid back down and Paul pulled her close. He'd never talked in his sleep. She thought about what the neurologist had said. A traumatic brain injury could cause several symptoms. Was talking in his sleep one of them?

CHAPTER 15

Paul

Paul was no longer the new guy. A young man in his early twenties walked into the group room. He spotted the vacant chair next to Paul and took a tentative step and stopped. Paul waved him over and he sat down, shifting around in the chair.

"Hey, I'm Paul." He offered his hand. "Nice to meet you."

"Gabe."

Paul shook Gabe's hand, dampness brushing against his skin.

"Oh, nice to meet you." Gabe cleared his throat and shifted in the chair again.

Paul's gaze followed Gabe when he bent down. He saw the left prosthetic leg showing between the hem of Gabe's jeans and his sock. Gabe pulled up the cuff of his sock and tugged on the hem of his jeans. When he sat up, the hem and sock cuff separated again. Gabe scoffed under his breath.

Steve asked everyone to introduce themselves and share what they felt like sharing. This time, introductions started with Gabe. Good way to scare off the new guy. Paul wouldn't be surprised if he never showed his face again.

"I'm Gabe." A few veterans nodded to the younger vet. "I'm not like the rest of you." He rubbed his hands on his knees. "I don't know if I belong here. My…my therapist thought it'd help."

Gabe's uneasiness was palpable.

"I was on base, heading to the dorms after work. It'd been raining all day. My rear tire—I was riding my Kawasaki—it hit standing water and I hydroplaned. I landed on my back pretty hard. When I came to, my motorcycle was on top of me, and my left leg was a mess. Mangled, I guess you could say. It was crushed from the knee down. This thing goes up to here." Gabe tapped the cuff mid-thigh.

Being the only one with a non-combat injury had put Paul in a difficult place, admittingly self-imposed. Not one of the therapy group members had said anything negative about his injuries. Now that Gabe was part of the group, Paul's opinion of his injuries had begun to change. After the therapy group ended, Paul stayed for a little while, talking. He'd thought about inviting Gabe to coffee, but decided it was best to save for another time.

Walking out the doors, Paul squinted in the bright sunlight. As he approached his truck, he saw Karla parked a few spaces down talking on the phone. Her face was flushed and she pounded her fist on the steering wheel. Not wanting to appear as if he was eavesdropping, he picked up the pace to his truck, and slid behind the steering wheel.

"Danny!"

Paul turned his head slightly and saw her holding out the phone, gritting her teeth. She looked in his direction and noticed him. Shaking her head, she repeatedly tapped what he assumed was the button to end the call and tossed the phone aside. Backing out of the parking space, she punched the accelerator, heading towards the exit. Tires squealing, Paul was afraid she'd lose control of the car and run into the ditch or someone else. Karla was the quiet one in the group and it surprised Paul to see her act out. Who was Danny? Probably her husband or boyfriend. What happened to her to act that way? It wasn't his business.

Paul pulled into the driveway and peered out the windshield at the front door. After a few moments, he shut off the engine and opened the driver's door. Where was Katie? She was usually pulling on the door handle of the truck by now. Paul headed up the steps and went inside.

Genny's bright smile welcomed him as she walked into the living room with Caleb on her hip.

"Dada." Caleb reached out for Paul.

Katie ran into the living room and up to Paul. "Where have you been, Daddy? I missed you."

"I missed you, too. I stayed to talk with my friends." Paul took Caleb from Genny. He grabbed a hold of the gold cross on Paul's necklace and studied it for a moment before letting it go.

"Oh. Did you get my message?" Katie frowned.

"I'm sorry, baby girl. I didn't check my messages before I left for home." Lately, he'd been receiving texts from Genny that she'd sent on Katie's behalf.

Tears filled Katie's eyes.

Bending down, Paul looked into Katie's eyes. He stood Caleb on the floor, and he toddled away. "I'm sorry. We'll spend some extra time together, okay?"

Katie nodded, but the frown stayed firmly in place. She walked to where Caleb was sitting on the floor and eased down next to him.

"Her appointment is in two weeks." Genny slipped her arms around Paul's neck and kissed him.

"Good." Paul pulled Genny close.

Paul prayed the therapist could help reassure Katie. He loved his daughter and didn't want her to be afraid every time he walked out the door. She was no longer following him around the house like she did in the beginning, but she wanted constant contact with him when he was away from home, and it was getting to him.

How would she handle him going back on active duty? What would happen if he was discharged and had to enter the civilian working world? Paul pushed the last question out of his head. Lord willing, working in the civilian world would be at least four years away—after he retired.

⁓ℓℓⁱ⁓

During Paul's quiet time the following morning, he thought about Karla. What he had witnessed stuck with him. God had blessed him with a compassionate spirit; maybe He was nudging Paul towards Karla to minister to her. A soft knock sounded on the door.

"Daddy?" Katie whispered from the other side.

Normally, he'd send Katie off to play since she knew not to disturb him during his quiet time, but with her emotions lately, he let it go. When he opened the door, he noted her pink princess nightgown, fuzzy pink slippers, and tangled hair. A faint smile showed on her lips.

"Good morning."

"Hi, Daddy." Katie clasped her hands behind her back and twisted from side to side. They had a brief staring contest before she spoke. "Are you gonna see your friends today?"

Genny walked up behind Katie with a *Jeep Girl* mug in her hand. "Katie, don't bother Daddy. He's doing his Bible study." She pushed out an exasperated sigh.

"But.."

"It's okay, Mama." Paul arched his brows at Genny.

She shrugged and walked away.

Paul opened the door wide, and Katie walked over to the guest bed, taking a seat. Looking around the room, her eyes fell on Paul. Tilting her head, she said, "Are you seeing your friends?"

"Not today."

She nodded, and her gaze fell to Lucy when she walked into the room.

Now they were having a "no talking" contest. Fear and disappointment must have Katie's tongue. "Would you like to do something today?"

A wide smile brightening her face. "Uh-huh. Wanna play Memory?"

"Let's do it."

Katie slid down from the bed, took Paul's hand, and led him to the living room where the game was set up on the coffee table. Pointing to the couch, Paul sat and Katie dropped to her knees on the other side of the coffee table and turned over a card. She looked up at him and smiled wider than she had in a while, showing all of her front teeth.

A minute or two into the game, Paul realized Katie had revealed twelve pairs of cards and he had one. It used to be the other way around. Brushing the thought aside, he hadn't played the game with Katie since he'd left for deployment. It made sense that she was better at matching pairs close to six months later.

At the end of the game, Katie hummed and tilted her head from side to side as Paul counted her cards. Thirty-one pair of cards versus five. He was on the lower end, concerning him. The first few pairs he missed, Katie laughed or giggled, but she must have sensed his frustration. After that, she'd encouraged him and praised him when he found a pair, like he and Genny did for her when they played as a family. How could he have failed miserably at a child's game he'd breezed through in the past?

Paul went back to the office and resumed his study. He turned to the book of John and stared at the first chapter. The letters seemed to jumble together, as if he'd scooped them in his hands and dumped them on the page. A four-year-old had beaten him at a game of Memory. It wouldn't have happened before the accident. Setting the Bible aside, he opened his journal and wrote an entry.

Feb 24, 2017

Am I losing my memory? Will I forget my family or how to feed myself? I'm trying not to overreact, but it's hard. I wish I knew so I can prepare myself and my family.

Some brain injuries could bring on cognitive conditions like dementia and Alzheimer's. What if that was happening to him? Paul ran his hands over his face. He'd do what he always did—rely on God. Paul pushed out a breath, and for a moment, his lungs failed to draw in fresh oxygen. Panic increased his heart rate. His breath came quick, bringing relief, but making the room spin. "Lord, please take these thoughts from me," he whispered.

CHAPTER 16

Katie climbed onto the small couch and pressed herself against Genny. She watched the woman as she pulled out a small chair and sat at the child size table off to the side of her desk.

"Hi Katie. I'm Miss Hailey."

Katie slipped her finger into her mouth and looked up at Genny. She looked at Hailey again and pulled her finger out of her mouth. "Hi."

"Did you bring your toys? I'd love for us to play if that's okay?"

Genny handed a small tote bag to Katie, and she slid down from the couch and joined Hailey at the table. Unzipping the bag, Katie dumped the few toys out on the table.

"These are some of your favorite toys?"

"Yes." Katie turned around and glanced at Genny. She turned back around when Hailey spoke.

"Can you tell me about them?"

The first toy Katie showed Hailey was the Barbie with one leg.

"Oh no, what happened to Barbie?"

"Her leg is gone like my daddy."

Hailey looked up at Genny, then back at Katie.

"Lucy chew it."

"Our dog," Genny said.

"What about your daddy?"

"My daddy got a owie in Aflan…." Katie looked at Genny.

"Afghanistan." Genny smiled.

"Af…Aflaniann." Katie picked up the Barbie and smoothed down her frizzy blond hair.

"I bet that was scary."

Katie looked at Hailey and nodded. She rolled Barbie's right pant leg up to her hip joint. "Daddy's leg ain't all gone like Barbie."

"How do you feel about Daddy's leg? Does it scare you?"

Katie shook her head. "It's okay."

"It did at first," Genny whispered.

Katie turned around to face Genny. Her small brows furrowed. "No, Mama."

"Okay." Katie turned back around and Genny nodded at Hailey.

For the rest of the session, Katie focused on playing and Hailey didn't press.

Genny had been afraid that Katie would clam up, but this was the most she'd talked about Paul's accident.

The hour went by fast. Hailey wanted to meet with Genny alone at the beginning of their next session to get a feel for what was going on with Katie and to set goals. She also wanted Paul to join at least one session.

"I like to start off by playing to help set the kids at ease. It's important to build trust so she feels she can talk about what's going on in that little head of hers." Hailey smiled.

"I'm glad she opened up."

Hailey led them down the hall to the lobby, and Genny waited behind a woman at the scheduling counter. A little girl with long blond hair standing next to the woman looked up at Genny and slipped her finger in her mouth. Genny smiled, but the girl didn't react.

The girl looked at Katie, flinging the one-legged Barbie around. Genny leaned down and whispered, "I think it's time for Barbie to rest."

"Aww…Okay, Mama." Katie tucked the Barbie into the toy bag. She noticed the girl and smiled. The girl didn't react to Katie, either.

The woman at the counter turned around, and her eyes brightened when she saw Genny. Genny's lips parted when she recognized her as their foster care social worker, Tina.

"Genny!"

"Hi, Tina."

"Oh my gosh, is this Miss Katie?"

Katie grinned and slipped her finger in her mouth. "So, was Paul's transfer canceled?"

"Paul was injured in Afghanistan—

"My daddy has one leg." Katie reached into the toy bag and pulled out the Barbie.

Tina's eyes widened. "My gosh."

"He's okay, but we're waiting to see if he'll be discharged."

"I'm so sorry. How's the baby?"

"He's great. He turns one the end of April."

"Already? Wow, time flies."

"Miss Tina."

Tina angled her head at Katie. As she listened to Katie's comparison of Paul and Barbie, Genny looked at the little girl still holding her finger in her mouth. She dropped her gaze to her pink tennis shoes. Tapping her toe, Genny smiled when pink lights danced in the soles. Most kids would at least smile as their shoes put on a show, but the little girl did nothing.

"Well, under different circumstances, I'd beg you to foster. We are hurting for families." Tina's eyes shifted to the girl.

"I wish we could. Maybe once we find out what's going to happen with Paul. Only the Lord knows."

"You're right there. Well, take care."

"You, too."

Tina took the girl's hand and headed to the door. The little girl glanced at Genny before walking out the door in front of Tina.

In the car, Genny fastened Katie into her booster seat and pulled out of the parking lot. Her thoughts ran wild with the urgency to foster. How could they be foster parents? Paul was disabled. Did they let disabled people be foster parents?

"Mama?"

"Yes?" Genny glanced in the rearview mirror, noting Barbie dancing across Katie's lap.

"Did that girl's daddy get an owie in his leg?"

"I don't know, sweetie."

On to another topic, Katie chattered the rest of the way home, but Genny couldn't concentrate enough to fully take part in the conversation. What was

God's plan in seeing Tina today? Why now when their lives were hanging in limbo?

—— *eee* ——

"How'd it go?" Paul picked up Katie when she reached for him.

"We played." A smile brightened Katie's eyes.

"Did you?"

"Uh-huh. And we talk about you and Barbie's leg."

"Is that so?"

"Uh-huh."

"She wants you to attend a session." Genny laid her purse on the side table.

"Of course, anything for our baby girl."

Katie giggled when Paul brushed his nose against hers. Genny watched as he carried Katie into the living room and sat on the floor with her. Genny no longer worried about Paul sitting on the floor. He'd mastered the art of standing from wherever he was sitting.

With each day that passed, the dread over Paul's career worsened. He was athletic, and she knew he'd pass the fitness test. The image of her and the kids watching him walk up the stairs to board a military plane filled her thoughts. How would she survive another deployment?

"How's that sound, Mama?" Paul's voice broke into her thoughts.

"Huh?" Genny's focus shifted to Paul.

"Somewhere else?"

"I guess. What did you say?"

"Tacos!" Katie shrieked.

"Shh, you'll wake Bubby," Genny said.

Katie held her hand over her mouth and giggled through her fingers.

"Tacos sound good."

"Let's go outside, Daddy." Katie stood and tugged on Paul's hand. He rose from the floor with ease.

Caleb began babbling and Genny made her way to the bedroom. She picked him up and sat on the bed. Leaning against the pillows, Genny sat Caleb on her lap, facing her. Focusing on his full, round face, she widened her eyes and stuck out her tongue, bringing out a giggle from him.

"What do you think, little man?"

He clapped his hands and wiggled like he was dancing.

"Is that so? I should leave it alone?" Genny breathed out. "I don't know if I can. It's hard to give up control, even when you don't have any."

Caleb grabbed his foot and squealed.

"Sometimes I wish I was a little kid again. Not a care in the world. Everyone waits on you hand and foot; mostly your mama, or granny, in my case." She brought him close and kissed his forehead. She wasn't a kid and there wasn't anyone to do things for her. She had to work through this on her own.

Genny carried Caleb to the living room and put him in his highchair. Now that he was walking, she couldn't keep an eye on him and cook at the same time. Something caught Genny's eye and she saw Paul walking up to the back door with Katie on his shoulders. He stood her on the patio, and she blasted in the door. Caleb giggled and clapped.

"Let's set you free, little man." Paul got Caleb from the highchair and sat on the couch with the kids.

Genny watched Paul interact with the children. For a moment, she imagined herself as a widow, raising two kids on her own. She sighed and turned her attention to the browning ground beef. Why couldn't she let it go? Every time she put her fears in God's hands, she snatched the fears back, and it was exhausting.

After dinner and settling the kids in for the night, Genny got ready for bed and checked her phone. A few minutes later, she opened her journal and began writing.

Feb 28, 2017

Katie had her first therapy appointment today. She seems to like her therapist. I saw Tina today. I can't help but wonder what God's up to. Of all the people in the world, why her? I'm finding myself getting more irritated with Paul and I don't know why. Yes, I do. He's pretty much made up his mind that he's going to try to stay in the Air Force. I can't blame him, though. I guess I'd do the same thing if I were in his shoes. But it doesn't make it easier for me.

Mrs. Baker is leaving on Monday. My heart hurts.

Returning home from church, Genny saw Susan's car in Mrs. Baker's driveway. Her heart dropped. Mrs. Baker would leave the next day.

They'd taken her out for dinner the night before. Genny knew the day was coming, but it didn't make it any easier.

"I'm going to go over."

"Okay. I'm going to get him to take his nap."

"I want to go!" Katie hurried over to Genny.

"Slip your shoes on," Genny said.

Katie made it to Mrs. Baker's house before Genny and she cringed when Katie pounded on the door. As Genny walked up, the door opened and they were greeted by Susan's welcoming smile.

"Hi, Miss Katie." Susan waved Katie and Genny inside. "How are you?"

"We're good."

Katie's face brightened when she saw Mrs. Baker sitting in her recliner. She held out her arms to Katie.

"Careful," Genny said when Katie climbed onto Mrs. Baker's lap.

"She's okay, honey."

Genny walked over and kissed Mrs. Baker's cheek. "How are you?"

"I'm good. I hate that so much has to go into storage, but Susan is going to help me with everything once I'm settled."

"That's great."

"Want to see Felix?" Susan asked Katie.

"Yes!" Susan took Katie's hand and led her outside to where Felix was lying on the patio. Genny watched as Katie held out a chew toy. Katie giggled when Felix snatched it.

"I have something for you." Mrs. Baker walked over to a large box on the dining table.

Genny joined her and peered into the box when she pulled back the flaps. Reaching inside, Genny pulled out something wrapped in packing paper. Removing the paper, tears spilled down her cheeks as she held one of the porcelain teacups from Mrs. Baker's tea set in her hand.

"Everything's in there."

Genny swallowed hard and nodded.

"You know? Katie's not too young. Start having *real* tea parties with her."

"I will." She smiled and wrapped her arms around Mrs. Baker, breathing in the faint scent of roses.

Mrs. Baker was a special person. At dinner last night, she'd given Paul and Genny a check. They could save it or spend it any way they'd like, she'd told them. Paul tried to give the check back but she shared that she'd planned to leave the money to them after she passed, but wanted to give it to them herself.

Genny sat next to Mrs. Baker in the living room. She watched her as she talked about her grandchildren and the first expected great-grandchild. Close to eighty now, she looked young for her age. Genny studied Mrs. Baker's face, memorizing every line and the curve of her chin. Pictures weren't the same. She had to remember her face.

Mrs. Baker's gentle hand rested on Genny's. She reached up and brushed a tear from Genny's cheek. "You know I love you, honey."

"I love you, too." Fresh tears filled Genny's eyes. She glanced out the window again. Katie's head was leaning back and a laugh that shook her little body came from her mouth. She didn't understand the full extent of Mrs. Baker's move. It differed from her grandparents. Brian and Tricia were always on a visit where Mrs. Baker had been a constant for Katie since she was born.

One last hug and Genny and Katie headed back home. Genny held it together until they walked into the house. Falling to the couch, Genny dropped her head in her hands and wept. Paul sat next to her and slipped his arm around her shoulders and pulled her close.

A few moments later, Paul kissed Genny's temple. "We'll visit. I promise you that, okay?"

Genny nodded against his shoulder. Caleb crawled to the coffee table and pulled himself up, toddling over to the couch. Genny picked him up and sat him on her lap. They may not see Mrs. Baker in person often, but they could FaceTime or Skype. Enveloped in her husband's arms, peace filled Genny's heart.

CHAPTER 17

Paul

Paul hung up with the prosthetics clinic and pumped his fist into the air. "I have my appointment!"

Genny eyed him, her brows pinching together. "What appointment?"

He walked to the couch where she was sitting, took hold of her hands, and pulled her to her feet. Wrapping his arms around her waist, he gave her a tender kiss. Easing back, Paul stared into her green eyes. "My permanent prosthetic and running blade are in."

"Running blade? I thought that'd take a while." Genny's body relaxed. Paul would say it was from relief, but it felt more like resignation.

Caleb cried out from their room. Genny removed Paul's arms from around her waist. "I need to get him."

Would they ever be on the same page? He could see it from her view. She'd lost her brother and come close to losing him. Could she see it from his view? Sixteen years down the drain? Sixteen years was a long time.

Caleb grinned at him as Genny brought him into the living room.

"Dada." Caleb wiggled in Genny's arms when she walked up to Paul. As soon as he took Caleb from her, Genny went out the back door.

He watched her as she headed to the picnic table, her shoulders sagging as if he'd heaved the weight of the world on top of her. Why was God silent in this? He felt the way he did when he'd prayed about marrying Genny over six years earlier. But that decision turned out to be the best decision he'd made in his life. What kind of decision would he be making if he passed the fitness test and was cleared to return to active duty? That was a big "if." According to Steve, he was teetering on the edge of a career-ending PTSD diagnosis.

Paul walked out back with Caleb on his hip and sat down next to his wife. Lucy jumped up, taking her place between them. Reaching down, Caleb grabbed Lucy's ear and she licked his hand. They sat quietly, focusing on nothing in particular.

"All I hear you say is 'sixteen years', 'sixteen years', 'sixteen years,'" Genny's voice held no emotion, confusing Paul.

It was as if Genny was revealing her heart, but protecting it at the same time. Why did she feel the need to protect her heart from him?

"Do we mean anything to you?" Her tone hadn't changed.

"Of course, Genevieve." Paul's voice was louder than he intended. He swallowed hard and held his breath to slow down his climbing heart rate. Lucy looked up at him, hopped down, and ran to the back fence.

Caleb reached up and grabbed the cross dangling from Paul's necklace and gave it a light tug. Paul pulled Caleb's hand away and kissed his fingers. "I'm not Brandon."

Genny slowly turned her head to face Paul, red flooding her upper chest and climbing up her neck. Without saying a word, she stared at him for a good ten seconds. She faced the back fence again, where Lucy was dragging a stick around.

"Genevieve?"

"Mama." Caleb reached out and patted Genny on the shoulder.

"Sometimes I feel the Air Force is more important to you than us."

"Never." He focused on Genny as she watched Lucy play. Her jaw tightened. He was sure it wasn't from anger; she was trying to stop herself from crying.

"I'll get Katie from school," Genny said.

"Okay."

Genny kissed the top of Caleb's head and paused, inches from Paul's face. Her lips met his, then she said, "I know this is hard for you, but it's hard for me, too. I feel like I'm holding my breath until I know what's going to happen."

"So do I, baby."

Genny closed her eyes and breathed out. "I love you."

"I love you, too."

She hopped down from the table and made her way to the back door. He sighed. The feeling that his family had a hold of one hand, while the Air Force had a hold of the other, was weighing him down. He prayed an answer would become clear before he was ripped in half.

⁓ℓℓ⁓

All throughout the group therapy session, Paul's thoughts centered on Genny. Revealing her feelings to him earlier, he felt Genny pulling away and it terrified him. How would she handle him returning to active duty? *If* he returned to active duty. Attending this group was a reminder that it might not happen.

After the group ended, Paul hung around and chatted with some veterans before heading out the door. On the way to the parking lot, he saw the hood of Karla's car raised and walked over. She was sitting in the driver's seat talking on the phone. She spotted Paul and rolled her eyes.

"What's it doing?" he asked when she ended the call.

Karla sighed and turned the key. One click told Paul that Karla needed a new starter. "The starter's pretty much dead. We stretched it as far as it will go. My husband was supposed to bring our daughter today, but I found out he's not coming until tomorrow." She leaned her head against the headrest and sighed.

"I can take you home. How far do you live?"

"Twenty minutes." She said it as if it was an hour away.

"Okay, lock her up and hop in." Paul pulled out his phone and sent Genny a text letting her know he was taking Karla home.

Karla was mostly quiet during the drive. Probably calculating the cost of a new starter in her head. As she directed him where to go, Paul realized they were going towards the shady side of town, as Genny called it. Paul pulled into the parking lot of a duplex. The building looked at least thirty-years old. The roof sagged and the exterior looked as if it hadn't been painted since the building was completed.

"Thanks for the ride," Karla said when Paul parked in front of her unit. "Hopefully, my husband will be here in time to take me to my appointment in the morning."

"Let me give you my number. Call me if you need a ride."

"Okay, thanks," Karla said and they exchanged numbers.

112

Paul pulled into the driveway and headed for the steps. A sign was taped to the door. Written in Genny's handwriting with a green crayon, the sign read: "*Close your eyes.*" He grasped the knob, but it didn't budge. When he unlocked the front door and pushed it open, he saw Katie standing in the hall grinning. She was wearing her favorite pink princess dress up dress.

"Close your eyes, Daddy!" She wagged her finger at Paul.

"Sorry." Paul closed his eyes.

Katie took his hand and led him down the hall. Paul grunted when he bumped into the back of the living room chair. "Now open your eyes!"

Paul opened his eyes. In the middle of the living room was their folding card table with two tiaras, two boas, and two teacups perched on matching saucers from the set Mrs. Baker had given to Genny. Standing off to the side, Genny was holding Caleb, smiling.

"It's a tea party, Daddy."

"I see that. Where's Mama going to sit?" Paul looked at the two folding chairs.

"She's not invited." Katie walked over to the table and picked up one tiara and placed it on her head.

Paul laughed and looked at Genny.

"It's okay. It's a daddy/daughter tea party. Caleb and I will go to the bedroom and watch something on TV."

Paul pulled out a chair and helped Katie sit down. She grabbed the pink boa and wrapped it around her neck.

"Put yours on, Daddy."

"Okay." Paul noticed Genny holding up her phone, grinning. He watched his little girl prepare their tea as he wrapped the blue boa around his neck and placed the tiara on his head. Reaching for the teacup, the tiara fell off of his head and landed on the saucer. He blew out a breath, relieved to see that the saucer hadn't chip.

Katie leaned her head back and laughed. Paul put the tiara back on his head and took a sip of the lukewarm tea. As he watched Katie playing hostess, the thought that he was the reason she was in therapy stung. What was he doing and why did he feel the need to exhaust all of his options? Sacrificing his family for his career was not one of those options, so why the desire to fight to stay in the military?

When Paul walked into the main entrance of the VA, he saw the familiar older woman wearing a red vest sitting at the front desk. She smiled at him as he passed by. On the way to the prosthetics clinic, Paul passed several veterans in the halls. A few were his age or younger, but most of the veterans were older and donned *Vietnam Veteran* caps decorated with campaign ribbons and pins. Paul walked into the clinic, checked in, and took a seat. He pulled out his phone and smiled when he saw a text from Genny.

"Well, hello there, young man."

He looked up and saw Craig wheeling in. He referred to Paul by his name during the group therapy sessions, but always greeted him outside of the group by some variation of how he greeted him when they first met.

"Hey Craig. How's it going?" Paul smiled at the older veteran.

"Ah, ya know. Same ol', same ol'." Craig grinned. "I decided to give it another try." He patted his residual leg. "I'm gonna get me one of them." He pointed to Paul's left leg.

"That's great, Craig. I hope it works out for you this time."

"Figured with advancement with prosthetics and all, I'll give it another shot. Tired of sitting. My backside stays numb."

Paul held in a chuckle. "I can imagine."

"Paul?" Clark, the man who'd been helping him with his temporary prosthetic, called out. He saw Paul and smiled. "Come on back."

As Paul followed Clark to the workout area, Paul spotted two prosthetics—one regular and the other with a running blade attached—leaning against the wall by a set of chairs. A wide grin spread across his face when Clark pointed to one of the chairs. Paul pinched his lips together to keep from squealing like Katie when she found out that they were going to Dairy Queen.

"All right. Let's take it for a spin," Clark said.

Paul slipped off the old prosthetic and slipped on the new one and stood. Shifting his weight to his left leg, he took a tentative step. A moment later, he walked a few yards down and back. The prosthetic felt like a natural part of him, as if he'd never lost his leg.

"How's it feel?"

"Perfect."

"Good to hear. Now, time for this." Clark held up the running blade.

Paul slipped off the new prosthetic and took the running blade from Clark's hand and slipped it on. Taking a step, he let out a little laugh. "I literally feel like I have a spring in my step."

Clark chuckled and led Paul toward the back wall of the room where a few veterans were taking turns running from one end of the room to the other. Paul took his place and closed his eyes. This was it, the moment of truth. He opened his eyes and stepped off, pushing himself to make it to the other end of the room. His muscles burned, reminding him how out of shape he was.

Nausea rose to his throat, and he slowed his pace. The opposite wall seemed to move further away with each step. He had six months to get back in shape in order to pass the fitness test. He pressed harder, wincing when a pain shot through the end of his residual leg.

"You need to take it slow at first," Clark shouted.

Slowing down, Paul rested his hands on his waist and walked around for a few seconds.

"Now, run back," Clark said, elevating his voice above the clatter of the workout room. "Don't push yourself."

Paul softly groaned. He jogged back at a leisurely pace to where the others stood, waiting their turn to run. He steadied his breath and followed Clark.

"Good job, Paul. You need to start off slow, so you don't overdo it. You'll get there sooner than most. You are determined and have a goal to work toward."

Paul carried the running blade as he headed down the halls toward the parking lot. He garnered a few nods and smiles. One younger veteran stopped him, surprised that the VA provided a running blade.

Close to the front doors, Paul spotted a familiar face. She smiled and walked up to him.

"I see you got your blade," Karla said.

"Yep. Now to get back to my average run time in six months." A slow smile spread across his face.

"You can do it, Paul." She patted his upper arm. "I have faith in you. See ya."

Paul made his way to the truck and headed home. Nothing could wipe the smile off his face. In the afternoon, he went to the guest room for his study time. He opened his journal and made a list of prayer requests and spent time in prayer. Now it was time for his personal entry.

March 16, 2017

I have my permanent prosthetic and running blade. I don't know which one I like better. I'm leaning toward the blade since it will help me save my career.

Paul glanced at the prosthetics leaning against the wall and smiled. He trusted God that he would be in shape and pass the fitness test with no problem.

Less than a week after Paul received his running blade, he had his first therapy appointment with Katie. The office was set up like a play room complete with everything from dolls to games to an area for the kids to express themselves with drawing, coloring, and painting. What caught Paul's attention was the sand tray. Memories of him and Brandon playing in the dirt behind Brandon's grandparents' house brought a kind of sadness he hadn't felt for a while. Grief spells were what he called it. The time in between his grief for Brandon had been widening, but it affected him when he didn't expect it. Usually, it was something that reminded him of Brandon. A sand tray in a therapist's office, for example.

"Hi, Daddy," Katie said in the high-pitched voice she used for Barbie.

Barbie's tiny hand brushed down Paul's forearm. He forced himself out of his memories to pay attention to his daughter. "Hello, Barbie."

Katie pranced Barbie's singular leg on top of Paul's prosthetic, causing a thud with each step. The door opened, and in walked a young Asian woman who didn't appear old enough to be a therapist.

"I'm so sorry. Thanks for your patience. I'm Hailey," the woman said and held out her hand.

"No problem. I'm Paul." Paul shook Hailey's hand and settled against the back of the couch.

"He's my daddy, Miss Hailey."

"Thank you for telling me, Katie."

"He has one leg like Barbie," Katie said and held Barbie out, making her dance from side to side.

"That's what you and your mama told me." Hailey angled her head and smiled at Katie.

"Oh, yeah." Katie giggled.

Swallowing hard, Paul eased out a soft breath. Katie had no qualms about informing everyone they met he was an amputee. The problem was he had no ownership of his injury. Keeping it to himself was no longer an option because of his little girl.

Hailey focused on Paul, and he felt as if he was on a stage with a thousand pairs of eyes staring at him. As they talked, Barbie's hand caressed Paul's arm. His first thought was to get on to Katie, but he let it go. They were there because of her insecurities and the last thing he wanted was for her to have a setback.

"Daddy likes to see his friends." Katie focused on Barbie and smoothed down her hair. Hailey looked at Paul.

"I have group therapy twice a week and individual therapy once a week."

"Oh, okay," Hailey said. "Katie, what do you think about Daddy going to see his friends?"

"He likes them more than me."

"I don't like them more than you and never would. You're my baby girl."

Katie didn't look away from her doll.

"Anything else?" Hailey asked.

Katie began humming as she played with Barbie's hair. "He's not coming home," she said, a tremble in her voice.

Paul looked over at Katie and wiped a tear from the corner of her eye. Wrapping his arm around his baby girl, he gave her a tight hug. How could he calm her fears? Many people left home and never came back—like her Uncle Brandon. If Paul stayed on active duty, it was a guarantee that he would deploy again.

Hailey worked with Katie on techniques she could use to ease her fears. Paul appreciated her recommendations weren't restrictive for him. Taking care of his family was important to him, but so was taking care of himself. It was difficult to balance his family and his recovery. If he wanted to stay on active duty, he had to work hard to make that happen. But was that fair to his family?

CHAPTER 18

Genny

Genny listened to Paul and Katie's conversation about his new running blade. He acted like a teenager who'd gotten his first car. It'd been a week and it was all he talked about. Of course, he was excited. It was what he needed to pass his fitness test.

Paul hadn't woken in the night screaming or thrashing in his sleep. But there was the weird fuel smell he'd dreamed about. And the time he woke up from a dream where he said he felt scared. He wasn't socially isolating or had anger outbursts. Genny thought about Paul's overreaction to her changing the names of the bank accounts. That was not the Paul she knew. It could have been the TBI, since irritation was a symptom. But he had no symptoms of PTSD as far as she could tell.

Genny herself struggled with startling easily since she was assaulted. The night before, when she was cooking dinner, she screamed when she turned around and saw Caleb standing a few feet from her holding out his stuffed bear.

She thought about what Dr. Watts had said to Paul at his first appointment at the VA. He either believed that Paul was keeping his symptoms to himself, or he had repressed his symptoms. Paul wouldn't flat out lie. According to her therapist, not all trauma caused PTSD. Was that possible with what happened to Paul? Genny sighed. Was she looking for something that wasn't there?

"Hey, babe."

Genny smiled at Paul as he walked into the bedroom. Announcing himself was one way to keep from startling her.

"Hey." She kissed him when he leaned down. Laying her book aside, Genny scooted over, and Paul stretched out beside her.

"You've been quiet," he said when he rolled onto his side to face her.

"What do you mean?"

"About me getting my blade." Paul ran his finger along her jaw.

"I'm happy for you."

"But…"

Genny breathed out and sucked in her cheeks, holding back the words floating around in her head. But she had to say something. "I'm worried, that's all. So much going on, you know."

Paul rolled onto his back and focused on the crown molding where it met at the corner. "A husband needs his wife's support."

How could she support him by doing something that frightened her?

Katie cried out, and both Genny and Paul sprinted down the hall. When they got to the living room, Katie was standing by the couch, holding her wrist. The running blade was lying on the floor next to Caleb. He smacked the blade and giggled.

Heat flushed through Genny's body, and she tensed. The prosthetic could have hit Caleb's head. Paul never should have left it unattended.

"What were you doing, baby girl?" Paul asked.

"It…" Katie pointed at the prosthetic. She rubbed her wrist and sniffed. "It hit me."

"Did you reach over for it?" Paul brushed his hand across the top of Katie's head.

"Uh-huh. It hit me."

"You need to put that somewhere!" Genny hurled the words.

Paul looked at her, his features pulling tight. He looked back at Katie and said, "Baby girl, you have to be careful. It almost hit your brother. You can ask me if you want to look at it, okay?"

Katie nodded and reached for Paul. He picked her up and she rested her head on his shoulder.

Genny eyed the prosthetic as if it was the serpent in the Garden of Eden. Her gaze shifted to Paul. He was her husband and she loved him with all of her heart, but she was seeing him as someone else and it scared her. His desire for a last chance to save his military career was, in her eyes, slowly turning him into her enemy.

Caleb patted Genny's leg and she picked him up, heading down the hall. He grinned, studying her with his blue eyes. Lucy jumped up on the bed, and Caleb's face broke out in a wide grin. Aside from ear infections and teething, Caleb was such a happy baby.

"Can you say Lucy?"

He shook his head and giggled when Lucy sniffed him. Paul cleared his throat and Genny looked up as he carried the prosthetic into the closet. She turned away and wiped her eyes before Paul came out.

"You're right, love," Paul said and sat on the side of the bed.

She felt his hand on her arm and turned to face him.

"I need to keep it away from the kids." He brushed his fingers across her cheek. "I know the thought of me finishing out my enlistment scares you, but I have to try to make it to retirement, if I can. Do you understand that? I mean, truly understand?"

"I don't have a choice," she whispered.

Paul sighed and focused on Caleb as he reached for Lucy's ear. Katie climbed onto the bed and sat next to her brother. She looked at Genny and asked, "Are you mad at Daddy?"

"No, baby," she lied. Anger had become a part of her everyday life. Each time she saw Paul walk out of the bedroom wearing his running gear, her entire body tensed.

"Okay." Katie wrapped her arms around Lucy and gave her a bear hug.

Paul picked Caleb up and headed down the hall, with Katie and Lucy following behind. Genny rolled over and looked at the ceiling. Feeling as if she had no control was one of the worst feelings she'd had. She wanted comfort from the Word, but not any Bible would do.

Genny walked into the closet. She found the box she was looking for. Getting comfortable on the bed, she took the top off and pulled out the Bible Paul had given her not long after they married. Underneath, she found her old journal. Thumbing through the pages, she stopped when she found the entry she was looking for

August 13, 2011

Paul has feelings for me. I never imagined that I would write these words today. We've been friends since we were kids, and I can't expect that to change overnight. Our

relationship is not the typical relationship so we need to do what we can to make up for that. I feel like I'm dreaming. I've never been in love. This feeling is amazing. Paul is unlike any guy I've ever met. He has always been such a kind and considerate person…

Genny closed her eyes, pushing tears down her cheeks. Deep down in her heart, she knew Paul wouldn't intentionally hurt her or the kids. So why did she feel God was telling her his career was over? And it was obvious that Paul felt God was leading him to fight to stay in the Air Force. Either way, someone would be hurt. What did that mean for their family? Pulling out her journal, she wrote a short entry for the day.

Mar 23, 2017

I despise that running blade. I want to throw it in the trash. I know that's my flesh talking. I would never do that to Paul.

Genny signed Caleb into the church nursery and walked Katie to her Sunday school room. As she headed to the foyer, she spotted Paul talking to several men, including their pastor, Ryan. His expression told Genny that he was talking about his running blade. Heat burned deep inside her chest. Taking in a breath, she released it as she reminded herself that she should be supportive of Paul.

"Got some sun, Genny?" Ryan said as she walked up next to Paul.

Genny covered her neck with her hand. "Oh, no. Just a little warm." She fanned herself for effect.

Paul's brows drew together. He knew what it meant when her neck flushed.

"I'm going to find a seat," she said, reaching for his Bible.

Genny found a pew and laid Paul's Bible next to her. She spotted Ryan's wife walking towards her.

"Hey, Gen," Ashley said.

"Good morning." Genny put on her best smile and hoped her neck was no longer red.

"We need to get together. Just us. Ryan can take a few hours away from his desk. Maybe he can go to your house or Paul can bring the kids to our house."

"That'd be great." Genny tucked her hair behind her ear. She loved Ashley and spending time with her always lifted Genny's spirits, but she wasn't sure she was ready for someone else's sympathy. Honestly, she wasn't ready to admit her fears to someone else. She'd keep it inside her heart for now.

Paul slipped past Genny and sat beside her. Draping his arm across her shoulders, he pulled her against him. Any trace of irritation from earlier was gone. Removing his arm, he held her hand until after the service ended. Conflicting emotions were getting the best of her. She loved this man and should support him. Fear had a habit of holding her down, and it was exhausting.

After church, they joined Ryan and Ashley and their kids for lunch. The subject of conversation was Paul's running blade. Ryan was full of questions, which fueled Paul's excitement and Genny's anger. Her chest warmed again and she took deep breaths to slow down her pulse. What was wrong with her?

"Mama!"

Genny cleared her thoughts. "Yes?"

"Can I have cake?"

Why not? Genny deserved a piece of cake for listening to running blade talk all day. "We'll share a slice, okay?"

"Okay."

Paul looked at her and winked when she flagged down the server. She smiled, hoping it hid her feelings. It'd worked in the past. What would she do to hide her feelings if he was cleared to wear the uniform again—smile twenty-four hours, seven days a week?

~ell~

Because of the negative feelings she'd been feeling over the past few months, Genny decided it was time to see her old therapist again. Lizbeth had been a godsend years ago and she hoped it would be the same this time. Flipping through a magazine, Genny thought about the first time she'd sat in the same waiting room after her brother's death.

A woman walked in holding a little girl's hand and carrying an infant carrier. The baby's cries filled the small waiting room. Genny recognized the distressed look on the woman's face. The infant began crying louder and the little girl patted her mother's arm, jumping up and down.

"Mommy, I have to potty!"

Genny glanced at her phone; five minutes until her appointment. The woman sat on the small loveseat against the wall and looked between the baby and the little girl.

"I can hold the baby while you take her to the bathroom. I have a four-year-old and almost one-year-old," Genny said when the woman's lips parted.

Her shoulders relaxed, and without saying a word, she lifted the baby out of the carrier and handed him to Genny along with a bottle she'd pulled out of the diaper bag. He settled down once he began drinking from the bottle. The woman and girl disappeared down the hall. A moment later, Genny heard Lizbeth's door open. She walked into the lobby and looked at Genny.

Genny grinned. "His mama will be right back."

The woman returned a few minutes later and smiled at Genny. "Thank you so much. My husband is deployed, and my mom went back home after helping with the baby for a little while. So, I'm on my own."

"I can relate." Genny handed the baby to his mother and followed Lizbeth to her office. She'd be that mother if Paul deployed again.

Genny talked about everything except what was consuming her. Lizbeth's gaze fell to Genny's hands, and she realized she'd been pulling her wedding set up to her knuckle and pushing it back down since she'd sat on the couch.

"When you called, you said that there's been some tension between you and Paul."

"Yes. Um…" Genny let out a little laugh. Where to start? "Paul wants to stay in the Air Force, and I want to stand by him as his wife, but…"

"That's possible as an amputee?"

"Yes."

"That's great," Lizbeth said and smiled.

The tears Genny had been holding back for the past few days spilled down her cheeks. She covered her face and sobbed. Lizbeth sat patiently. It was one thing Genny liked about her. She didn't press her to talk until she was ready.

"If he stays in, he will deploy and…"

"And what?"

"He might die, and I'll be left to raise the kids by myself."

Lizbeth was quiet for an uncomfortable amount of time; her gaze fixed on Genny. Genny crossed her legs and ran her fingers through her hair.

"What if you die on the way home today and Paul is the one that has to raise the children by himself?"

Genny's eyes widened. She'd been fixed on something happening to Paul but hadn't once thought about her being the one that died.

"Constantly asking yourself "what if" will steal your happiness. Let go."

"How do I do that?"

"Focus on the things that make you happy. Not just your family, but you. Do you have any hobbies or interests?"

Genny took a few moments to think about the question. Everything seemed to revolve around the children and Paul. She loved spending time with her family, but Lizbeth was right. "I used to love taking pictures when I was younger."

"All right, then. To ease into it, you can take pictures of the kids first." Lizbeth's facial features turned serious. "I want you to do something."

Genny lifted her brows and tugged the hem of her shirt. "Okay."

"I want you to make a "what if" plan.

"A what?" A knot formed in Genny's stomach.

"Write down your fears and make a plan of what to do if those fears come true."

The knot in Genny's stomach rose to her throat.

"I know it'll be hard, but I think it will help you feel you have more control. Your fear is that if Paul stays in the Air Force and deploys, he will die, right?'

"Yes."

"Write out a plan. What will you do if he dies? Will you move close to your in-laws so they can help or stay in Charleston?"

Genny's arms went limp. Heat rose from her stomach and spread throughout her chest. What *would* she do?

"I know this sounds harsh, but it will answer the "what ifs.""

If Genny put her fears on paper, it would increase the chances they would come true. She was being ridiculous. "I'll try."

"Good."

Genny pulled a tissue from the box on the table next to her and wiped her eyes and cheeks. Why was it hard for Genny to let go and give it to God?

On her way home, Genny thought about the uncertainty they were facing. It seemed like every time life was on track, something happened. Genny pulled into the neighborhood and topped the hill before their house. A moving van was parked in front of Mrs. Baker's old house. Immediately, her eyes filled with tears.

Mrs. Baker's absence had left a hole in Genny's life and in her heart. As she slowed to turn into the driveway, Genny spotted a man and woman standing at the back of the moving van. When she turned off the engine, she heard rock music pumping from a stereo inside the house.

"Great." She stepped out of the car and made it to the front steps before the new neighbors saw her.

It was a perfect time to move, but that was in limbo, like Paul's career. When she thought about the future, what she saw was a long, deserted road stretched out before them. It was a feeling she wouldn't wish on anyone.

CHAPTER 19

Paul

Genny looked up from the book she was reading to the kids when Paul walked into the living room. Today he was heading to the Air Force base to run on the track with the blade for the first time. He hadn't been on a track since before he deployed. Admittingly, he had high hopes for a good runtime.

Katie sprang to her feet and ran up to him. She slipped her small hand in his. "I want to go with you, Daddy." Katie's eyes brightened with excitement.

"Not today, baby girl. I'm going to run on the track. You know, the circle by my work?" Katie pulled her hand free and sat back down by Caleb. She sniffed, sending a sharp pain through Paul's chest. She was too young to understand what was going on around her.

"Really?" Genny's encouraging smile surprised him. Usually when he talked about running, a flame flickered in her eyes.

"Yep." Paul walked over and kissed her before he headed to the truck.

Maybe when he was used to the blade, he could bring Genny and the kids so they could cheer him on from the sideline. But today was about building stamina, so he could get back to where he was before he was injured.

Paul pulled into the parking lot of the running track. It was mid-afternoon and the sun was out in full force. He walked to the bench on the sideline and sat to change prosthetics. There weren't many people out since there was an hour and a half left in the duty day. Setting out at a leisurely walk, Paul picked up speed until he was just shy of jogging. Sweat beaded on his forehead and back as he panted. Why was the track harder than the gym at the prosthetics clinic? Paul drew in a deep breath and took off in a full-on run. He slowed, gasping for air. Running again, he set his pace, and his breathing evened out.

As Paul made his first lap, he noticed a group of people heading to the track. They must be attending squadron fitness training. It was something he didn't miss. He'd always preferred running by himself. On his second lap, he heard someone call his name. He slowed and turned around and was met with a familiar smile.

"Is that you?" the young airman asked.

"Brody?" Paul grinned. "How are you?" Paul walked over and shook Brody's hand. Brody reminded Paul of Brandon. They had similar mannerisms and smiles. He had taken Brody under his wing not long after the young airman arrived at Joint Base Charleston.

"Great. What about you?" He looked down at Paul's prosthetic running blade.

"Trying to get back out there. I'm shooting to return to duty by September seventeenth, which will be a year since I was injured."

"I've heard about that program. Good for you."

"Thanks." Paul watched the squadron gather to do push-ups and sit-ups. Seeing everyone together stirred Paul. He missed the camaraderie. The desire to stay in the Air Force had just multiplied by a thousand.

Over the next six weeks, with running seven days a week, Paul's runtime had surpassed his time prior to his injury. Today, he was meeting with the head of the base Air Force fitness program for his fitness test. Paul walked into the living room carrying the running blade. Genny looked up from the book she was reading and smiled.

"Daddy! Are you taking your running test?" Katie said when she looked up from where she was sitting on the play mat with Caleb.

"I am." Paul leaned down and kissed Genny.

"Knock 'em dead, babe." Genny smiled, but there was a reservation in her voice.

"I will." Paul kissed the kids and headed for the Air Force base.

A man dressed in athletic clothing walked up to him. Paul's prosthetic gave him away as the person whose career was in this man's hands.

"Sergeant Thompson?"

"Yes," Paul said and offered his hand.

"I'm Sergeant Madison," the man said as he accepted Paul's hand.

Let's get this over with.

Sergeant Madison gave Paul instructions that he was already familiar with. He pumped out as many sit-ups and push-ups as he could within the allotted time, earning a perfect score for both. Two obstacles down, one to go.

Paul walked up to the starting line and waited for the signal. Sergeant Madison looked at him.

"Ready?"

Paul nodded.

"*Go!*"

Paul tore away from the starting line and slowed a few seconds later, reminding himself to pace his steps. He breezed through several laps with no problem. As he approached where Sergeant Madison was standing, the look on the man's face confused Paul. His eyes were wide and he grinned when Paul ran by. Grunting, Paul pushed himself until his chest burned with each breath.

"Last lap!" Sergeant Madison yelled out when Paul passed by on his eighth lap.

Paul bore down and pushed himself. Nausea rose from his stomach as streaks of light flashed in front of his eyes. When Paul was in the homestretch, he noticed someone in uniform standing next to Sergeant Madison. As Paul passed by, he saw Sergeant Madison click the timer.

Paul made it to the grass in time to vomit.

"Sergeant Thompson, you okay?" Senior Master Sergeant Johnson, the superintendent of Paul's squadron, said when he walked up to Paul.

Paul straightened and rested his hands on his hips. Sergeant Madison walked over to Paul, wide-eyed and smiling.

"Sergeant Thompson. You made a perfect fitness score. I've never had anyone run a mile and a half in ten minutes."

"Huh?" Paul's heartbeat had slowed, but was still pounding.

"You're kidding?" Senior Master Sergeant Johnson said. He walked up to Paul and clapped him on the back, causing him to stumble. "Sorry." The superintendent grabbed Paul's shoulder.

"No, sir." Sergeant Madison showed Senior Master Sergeant Johnson the timer.

"Sergeant Thompson. You're a superstar."

Paul inhaled slowly and breathed out to keep from vomiting again. "Is it because of the blade?" Paul drew in another deep breath. "I've heard there's controversy because it can give someone an upper hand."

"If the Air Force says it doesn't matter, then it doesn't matter," Sergeant Madison said. "I'll get this paperwork turned into the medical group today. The package should go to the medical evaluation board soon."

"Okay, thanks Sergeant Madison."

"They're crazy if they don't recommend retention," Senior Master Sergeant Johnson said.

At least one person had faith in him. Three hurdles jumped. One incredibly high hurdle to go.

"Hey, can we grab a cup of coffee or something once you're finished here?" Senior Master Sergeant Johnson removed his hat and ran his hand over the top of his shaved head.

"Yes, sir. I'd like that."

Paul pulled up to the small coffee shop on base and looked around when he walked inside. He spotted Senior Master Sergeant Johnson and the man held up his hand and smiled. He was a black man in his mid-fifties, Paul guessed. Short in stature, he was intense, but would go to bat for anyone as long as they deserved it. Paul bought a soda and smiled as he slid into the booth opposite the senior master sergeant.

"How are you doing, Sergeant Thompson?"

"Actually, I'm doing well. Especially after today." Paul sipped his drink and grinned.

"I bet so." Senior Master Sergeant Johnson smiled. After a recap of Paul's fitness test, his face took on a serious tone. Paul was halfway expecting a scolding. "I want to apologize to you."

"For what, sir?" Paul thought back to his encounters with the man and recalled nothing negative.

"That I didn't check up on you. I already had orders to deploy, and I left a week after you arrived at Walter Reed."

"I understand, sir. 'Service before self.'"

"Still…" He sighed and looked out the window. He looked back at Paul. "You are resilient. You've worked your rear off to get to this place. I'm proud of you."

"Thank you, sir. I've got less than four years until I'm retirement eligible. I have to do what I can."

"What about your wife? How does she feel?"

A faint laugh escaped from Paul's mouth. "Not too well, I'm afraid." Paul explained Genny's losses and her fears of what might happen to him. He also mentioned Katie's difficulties.

"Do what's best for your family, but you have what it takes to finish your enlistment. You proved that today. That, along with your performance reports speak volumes about the man sitting across from me." Senior Master Sergeant Johnson drank the last of his coffee.

"Thank you, sir." Paul fought the tears filling his eyes. The words coming from Senior Master Sergeant Johnson were an inspiration and the boost of confidence Paul needed to sustain him as he fought for his career.

CHAPTER 20

Genny

The front door flew open, and Paul sprinted into the living room. The wide grin on his face spread heat throughout Genny's chest. *He passed.* Why was she surprised? She gasped when he pulled her into his arms and spun her around.

"Congratulations, baby!" She planted a firm kiss on his lips to keep from choking out a sob. "What's the next step?" She fought the tears building in her eyes.

Katie ran into the living room with her hands in the air. "Daddy! Did you win?"

Paul put Genny down and picked up Katie. "Yes I did, baby girl." Paul looked at Genny, his gaze falling to her upper chest and neck. "Gen."

Resting her hand on her neck, she felt the heat seeping through her fingers.

Paul sat Katie on the couch and rested his hands on Genny's shoulders, looking into her eyes. "I know you're scared." He kissed her forehead. "But there are several steps in the process. Passing the fitness test is the first step."

"I know."

"Put your fears in God's hands. It'll all work out the way it's supposed to."

A sudden feeling that she was suffocating was settling into her lungs. She needed to get out of the house for a bit. "I'm going to go…" Genny tilted her head towards the backyard.

"Okay, love."

Slipping on her jacket, she walked out to the picnic table. Making herself comfortable, she sighed. Her thoughts twisted together, but she was at least able to pull some words loose. The one word that was as big as a billboard was "death." Everyone dies, though. Like Lizbeth said, what if she was the one that died? But being in the military upped Paul's chances of dying first.

What was she doing to herself? Genny groaned. Taking a drive would help clear her thoughts. When she walked inside, Paul had Caleb on his lap and Katie was sitting next to him. Genny softly let out a breath. Paul's phone was on speaker and Genny heard Tricia's and Brian's congratulations.

"I'm going for a drive," Genny said, when Paul looked up at her.

His brows inched together. "Okay."

Kissing everyone on the cheek, she stopped at the key holder and grabbed the keys to the SUV, accidentally knocking off the Jeep keys. The *Jeep Girl* keychain caught her eye. Hanging up the SUV keys, she picked up the Jeep keys and headed out the door.

Genny didn't make it far before she headed back home. She'd volunteered to bake cookies for Katie's preschool class and she'd put it off. It was a few minutes past eight now and the kids should be in bed. She had at least an hour of work ahead of her. Maybe she should stop by the grocery store and buy a couple of rolls of cookie dough.

When Genny came in the front door, she heard Paul talking on the phone. Placing the two rolls of cookie dough on the counter, she realized he was talking about his fitness test.

"Got to go, Peter. Genny just got home. Thanks again." Paul ended the call still wearing his smile. "I saw you were at the grocery store on the app. Katie got a little miffed when you left and told me about the cookies. I'll take care of it." He walked over and kissed her forehead.

"Really?"

"You bet."

Genny got ready for bed and decided to do what Lizbeth had suggested. Pulling out her journal, she turned to the next blank page and stared at it for a while. Drawing in a deep breath, she began writing.

Apr 20, 2017

Paul passed his fitness test today. I knew he would. A small part of me wanted him to fail. Gosh, I'm a horrible wife. Why couldn't he have made it home from the deployment as planned? I don't know what else to write. All that comes to my mind is anger. I'm mad at the Air Force for not making sure their plane was safe, I'm mad at the military doctors because they couldn't save Paul's leg, and I'm mad at Paul for wanting to save his career even thought he knows how I feel. Yep, I'm a horrible wife.

Genny stared at the words and thought about what she'd been pushing aside since her appointment with Lizbeth. She puffed her cheeks and forced out her breath. "Here goes."

What I will do if Paul dies:

Genny studied the words and swallowed down the knot, trying to close off her throat.

1. *I will get a degree and take care of my children.*

2. *I will move in with Mom and Dad.*

She couldn't think of anything else. Either she'd rely on herself or rely on her in-laws. There was no in between, and it scared her. Glancing out the window, she considered what she'd written. Guilty that it wasn't her first thought, Genny renumbered her list and put God at the top. He should have been her first thought. He'd take care of her if Paul died. She didn't know what that looked like, but she knew God wouldn't leave her and the kids to walk through life alone.

CHAPTER 21

Paul

The past few days since Paul's fitness test were spent walking on eggshells around Genny. She said she was proud of him, but her actions said otherwise. Yesterday, she'd said that she needed to make a quick trip to the store to get a gallon of milk. After she left, he went to the fridge to get a snack for Caleb. What was the first thing he saw? A nearly full gallon of milk.

Paul sat on the couch and scrolled through a list of on-demand documentaries, trying to decide which one he wanted to watch next. He had gained an interest in homesteading and clicked on a recent documentary.

Caleb grunted and Paul caught sight of him teetering around the chair with his arms wrapped around one of Paul's combat boots. Chuckling, Paul took the boot from Caleb before he dropped it on his foot.

"You've been in Mama and Daddy's closet again, little man." Paul playfully scowled at Caleb and picked up the boy, tickling his stomach. Carrying Caleb and the boot, he made his way to the bedroom and put Caleb down. In the closet, Paul placed the boot next to its mate in the back corner of the closet.

The sleeve of one of his uniform overshirts peeked out from behind his coat. Reaching out, he rubbed the stiff fabric between his fingers. Pulling the hanger off the rod, Paul held the shirt up in front of him. Would he wear the uniform again, or were those days about to be over? The odds were in his favor. He blew the physical fitness test out of the water. There was no reason for the medical evaluation board to discharge him.

But there was always a chance. Why was he doing this to himself? He had to think positively so his mood wouldn't plummet.

Paul and Caleb walked into the living room as Genny and Katie came in the back door.

"We had fun, Daddy."

"It looks like it." Paul shook his head at the smudges of dirt on Katie's dress and dirt on her fingers. "Babe, I think I'm going to visit the guys at the shop."

"Really?"

"Yeah, I've got a few texts, and I think it'd be good for me to show my face."

"Well, okay. But it's getting late."

"I'll grab dinner on the way home." He walked up to her and slipped his arms around her waist.

"Okay, but don't be too long."

"I won't. Two hours tops."

"One."

"One and a half?" Paul grinned.

Genny sighed. "Fine."

He could visualize the brush strokes as she painted on a smile. Kissing her and the kids, he headed out the door for the truck.

The clock on the console showed it was getting close to five. The shop was twelve minutes from the gate of the base. Paul pulled into the parking lot and pushed open the truck door, situating his prosthetic so he could step out. When his feet hit the ground, the first note of Retreat sounded throughout the area.

Paul stood at attention and rendered a salute toward the American flag flying at the Air Force headquarters building. He couldn't see the flag, but it didn't matter. A flash of camouflage caught his attention. Lowering his brows, Paul clenched his teeth when he saw an airman running for his car. Blatant disrespect of the flag and the country boiled Paul's blood.

Each duty day began with Reveille and ended with Retreat. Both called for standing at attention facing the American flag—wherever it was on base—for a minute at the most. Was that too much to ask? Paul held his salute until the last note played.

Pulling the door open to the shop, the first face he saw was Brody Alexander. The young airman's face lit up as a smile spread across his face.

"Sergeant Thompson. I didn't know you were coming by today."

"Yeah, I thought I'd see what everyone was up to."

"Ah. I heard the good news."

Word traveled fast. "Yeah, just waiting on the board's decision."

"Nothing to worry about." Brody smiled.

"Sergeant Thompson."

The familiar voice had Paul straighten and roll his shoulders back. "Colonel Torres, ma'am. Nice to see you." Paul held out his hand.

"It's so nice to see you. Glad to hear that you'll be coming back. You'll get clearance. I saw those perfect scores." Her smile brought warmth to Paul's chest. To have the backing of his commander meant the world to him.

Paul walked with Brody around the shop as he talked to his co-workers. He met a few new faces that regarded him as if he'd won a gold medal at the Olympics. There was nothing wrong with being proud of accomplishments, and Paul was proud of how far he'd come.

A few of the co-workers he was close with were on the flight line. A shiver ran down Paul's spine when Brody opened the door and held it for Paul. He brushed it off and walked with Brody to where airmen were checking a plane.

Paul spotted a group of full pallets on the edge of the flight line waiting to be loaded. The familiar sound of a forklift powering on sent tremble after tremble over Paul's body. His pulse raced as he watched the forklift load a pallet and head to the plane. It stopped and Paul heard voices call out, but he couldn't understand what was being said for the aircraft engines.

Paul and Brody made it to the edge of the flight line. Brody waved at someone, whose face brightened when he saw Paul. A moment later, the ramp of the cargo plane hissed and lowered. The air around Paul stood still. Gasping for air, Paul's chest tightened. A pounding in his head traveled to his chest, making his heart feel as if it was splitting his chest open. The hands of death slipped around his throat, blocking oxygen from reaching his lungs. He desperately grabbed at his throat to free himself.

"Sergeant Thompson!" Brody shouted.

Darkness swallowed Paul as he floated down a cold, narrow tunnel.

"Sergeant Thompson!" Brody's voice faded and the world went quiet. Paul stretched his eyes wide and stared into the darkness.

"Sergeant Thompson, hold on. Don't give up." The man's breath brushed against Paul's ear. "Hurry!" he yelled above Paul.

Voices called out in the distance. The noise. It was so loud that Paul couldn't think. Pressure built in his chest as if a tank had parked on top of him.

"Hold on," the man whispered in his ear. "We're getting you out from under here."

"Push!" someone shouted. "Push!" Grunting and groaning sounded above Paul. "Come on! We got to get this pallet off him! Hold on Sergeant Thompson. Count!"

"One. Two. Three." the men yelled at the same time.

The weight that had been bearing down on Paul evaporated. He sucked in a deep breath and let out a scream. His left leg felt as if it had been dragged away with the weight. Tears gathered in his eyes and rolled down the sides of his face. He screamed, losing his breath. Gasping for air, he screamed again.

"Sergeant Thompson," a woman's muffled voice said. "His blood pressure's dropping," her voice raised as if she was talking to someone nearby. Paul closed his eyes; the pain was unbearable. His body felt like it was being ripped apart. He screamed until his throat was raw.

CHAPTER 22

Genny

Genny's body shook as she paced the small room, counting the beeps of the heart monitor. A panic attack triggered by a flashback was the doctor's diagnosis. Brody had said that he was scared that Paul would have a heart attack before the EMTs could make it to the flight line. Brody was shaken up, and Genny had sent him home.

A soft knock sounded on the door, and the doctor walked inside. "Mrs. Thompson, I'm Dr. Sanders. We've reserved a bed for your husband on the behavioral health floor. He'll be transferred once he's cleared through the ER."

"Behavioral health?" Genny crossed her arms over her chest, hugging herself.

"Yes. This flashback was serious. The EMTs reported that his blood pressure was one eighty-five over one twenty when he came in. That's a heart attack range. They also said he talked about being crushed and asking if he was dead. He called out your name and they think your children's names. He would pass out and wake screaming, trying to get out from under the straps on the stretcher. Has he been depressed? Any odd behavior?"

"Well, just a few dreams. I won't consider them nightmares. He doesn't remember the accident when he was deployed."

"Mrs. Thompson, I've treated many military members with PTSD in the emergency room and your husband, by far, is the worst I've seen."

"PTSD?" Paul would be devastated if he lost his career after fighting hard to pass his fitness test.

"You don't have a flashback like that without PTSD. He's been suppressing it, but now that it's out, he may struggle. The good news is the VA has the top PTSD treatment program in the US. Maybe the world." He patted Genny's arm and excused himself.

Genny eased down on the chair next to the bed and leaned her elbow on the edge of the mattress. Her thoughts went back to the phone call from Paul's superintendent she'd received earlier. She felt as if she was re-living the nightmare from September when Paul's commander had called.

The door opened and a nurse poked her head in. "Hello." She walked over to Paul, checking his vitals. "Once he's cleared here, we'll get him up to behavioral health."

"What will happen?"

"He'll talk with the psychiatrist and attend therapy groups. He'll be here for a few days until he's adjusted to the medication."

"Medication?" Heat filled Genny's chest.

"You'll need to talk to a nurse at behavioral health." The woman clicked her pen and slipped it into the pocket of her scrub top. "You can stop by the front desk and they'll give you a contact number."

"Okay. Thank you." Genny looked at Paul. Leaning over, she kissed his cheek and left the room.

Walking down the hall to the front desk station, Genny felt as if she was floating like she did at Walter Reed when she found out about Paul's injuries. Behavioral health? A classmate of hers had spent time in a behavioral health hospital and told horror stories when she came back to school. "Please, God. Don't let Paul experience anything like that." Genny stopped at the desk and sucked in a quick breath. A woman smiled at her.

"I would like to get the number to the nurse's station in behavioral health." Genny thought she saw a flash of judgment cross the woman's face. She was imagining things. Paul wasn't a special case. The employees in the emergency room dealt with this type of situation all the time, right?

Genny pulled into the driveway with no memory of driving home. How would Katie react to Paul being in the hospital again? Genny unlocked the front door and walked in. Katie ran up to her, wearing a wide smile.

"Where's Daddy?"

"Baby, he's sick and has to spend a few nights in the hospital."

Katie's face paled. Her bottom lip trembled and moisture filled her eyes.

"Hey, he will be fine, okay?" Genny picked Katie up and walked into the living room where Tamika was sitting on the couch with Caleb on her lap.

"Honey, you look exhausted. Want me to make you a cup of coffee?"

"Yes, I'd love that."

Tamika sat Caleb on the floor and went into the kitchen. When Genny put Katie down, she reluctantly joined her brother. The women sat on the couch with their coffee. The smell of Genny's favorite brew always soothed her, but it did nothing for her now.

"They are admitting him to behavioral health," Genny whispered in Tamika's direction.

"I know it's scary, but he will get the help he needs."

Tamika gave Genny a supportive smile and sipped her coffee. Caleb grinned when he turned around and looked at Genny.

Brody had said that it was like a switch had flipped when the hydraulics on the ramp sounded. Paul hadn't been around a cargo plane since the accident. Was that why he'd had no problems before now? What did that mean for his Air Force career? Cargo and planes were part of his job. Genny sighed and took another sip of coffee, watching her children play.

Katie looked at Genny and lowered her gaze when Genny's eyes met hers. Prayers that this setback wouldn't undo Katie's progress filled her heart. Genny's chest tightened. All this time, she'd been selfishly praying that Paul would be discharged. It didn't matter that he'd made a perfect score on his fitness test. This flashback would end his Air Force career.

Paul stared out the passenger window most of the trip home. A two-day hospital stay had turned into four days. Genny's bright, funny, loving husband was a shell of the man he was before. It could be the slew of medications the doctor had prescribed. Paul faced forward and blew out his breath.

"I didn't know I was depressed. I guess I was, though."

"Why do you say that?" Genny glanced in his direction.

"Everything the doctor asked me. It makes sense."

If Paul was depressed, he hid his feelings well.

"I cried a few times. You know? Thinking about losing my career. Letting you and the kids down." He let out a laugh that sounded more like a sob. "Well, it's gone now."

"You don't know that."

"It's gone, babe. Gone. Poof." Paul flung his fingers in the air, mimicking a puff of smoke.

"No matter what happens, you'll never let us down. I know you will do whatever you can to take care of us."

"I'll get a job at Walmart. I hear they are always hiring." Paul chuckled.

"I can get a job."

"*No!* Absolutely not."

"Why?"

"God will provide."

Maybe that's through me getting a job. He was right, though. After high school, she worked a job for a month and worked a part-time job when she attended a couple semesters of college. What could she do to bring in the amount of money Paul made?

Genny bit her lip, pulling into the driveway. Paul climbed out of the car and met Katie at the door. The switch flipped again and he was all smiles, as if nothing had happened when he picked up the kids. Katie asked questions about Paul's stay in the hospital. He gave her vague answers, which satisfied her curiosity for now.

Genny headed down the hall. Staring at herself in the bathroom mirror, she lifted her brows at the red lines that stretched across the whites of her eyes. Grabbing a bottle of eyedrops, she squeezed more than the recommended drops in each eye. Since September nineteenth, Genny had felt herself steadily aging because of the stress. Now she felt like she was a hundred years old. Anxiety was holding her down. If something didn't give, she'd be gone soon. Not dead, but a zombie aimlessly walking through life.

CHAPTER 23

Paul

Paul watched the clock on the fireplace mantel as the minutes ticked by. The VA was twenty minutes away, and he needed at least five minutes to find a parking space, even in the handicap area. A yawn watered his eyes. He woke up every hour during the night. It reminded him of when he was a kid, and it was the night before the first day of school. Anxiety was a beast. He looked at the clock again. He should go.

On his drive, his thoughts went back to the flashback. He didn't remember the events of that day, but he did remember what had happened in Afghanistan. And now he was on his way to the hospital discharge appointment with one of the VA psychiatrists.

When he arrived at the VA, he sat in the truck for a moment before exiting. He drew in a deep breath and blew it out. Might as well get it over with.

He sat in the same waiting room where he'd met Steve. The couple he'd seen on his first visit sat in the same corner as before. Except this time, they were smiling and holding hands. Paul closed his eyes and prayed that the Lord would calm his nerves.

"Mr. Thompson?"

Opening his eyes, Paul saw a woman standing in the doorway. She was wearing scrubs and smiled when he walked up to her. The woman led him to a small room with a chair and a machine to take his vitals. He glanced at the badge on the lanyard around her neck. She was a nurse. It must be standard procedure to take vitals before an appointment with a psychiatrist since they were medical doctors. Did this mean that she would keep him on the medication?

The nurse led Paul to an opened office at the end of the hall. A woman was sitting behind the desk. Her hair was twisted up like Genny wore her hair at times. She smiled when Paul walked in.

"Hello, Paul. Please have a seat." She stood, pushed the door closed and motioned to the two armchairs close to the window. The tan leather chairs were separated by a wooden table with a lamp on top. A coffee table was in front of the chairs that held a few décor items, a dish of peppermints, and a laptop.

Paul chose the chair closest to the desk and the woman took the other chair. He grabbed a peppermint and opened it, slipping the plastic wrapper in his pocket before putting the mint in his mouth. In the sunlight streaming through the window, Paul guessed the woman was in her late forties, which he didn't expect. He assumed she'd be older. Kind of like the female version of Sigmund Freud.

"I'm Tisha Wilson." She reached out and offered her hand. The name badge around her neck fell forward, revealing the yellow veteran badge hanging out from under the name badge. Another thing he didn't expect—she was a veteran as well.

"Nice to meet you, ma'am," Paul said, shaking her hand. Relief and anxiety swirled together. He was still apprehensive. He didn't mind talking with Steve, but as a psychiatrist? She intimidated him like the psychiatrists in the behavioral health unit.

She picked up the laptop and informed Paul that she would fill in some blanks from what he'd been working on with Steve and what the hospital had sent her.

A half-hour later, the doctor had gathered all the information she needed. It wasn't as bad as Paul had thought it would be. She was thorough in going over anything related to PTSD and depression. She had asked dozens of questions and paused thoughtfully after his responses. Closing the laptop, she placed it on the coffee table and settled into the chair.

"Paul, did you have any PTSD symptoms before the flashback?"

"No. Not that I can remember."

"Has your wife said anything about forgetting things, snapping at her or the kids, not understanding what she or anyone else said?"

"Well, yes. We thought maybe it was the TBI."

"It could be. Or it could be a combination. Depression, PTSD and TBI share a lot of the same symptoms."

"Really?" Why didn't the staff at the hospital say anything?

The doctor nodded. "Irritability, insomnia, out of character emotions, feeling run down physically, crying easily…"

Paul listened to the symptoms as the doctor spoke. He'd had the two nightmares and several times he'd woken in the middle of the night not able to fall back asleep. Then there was the time he cried over low test scores and thinking Genny would leave him because he gained weight. And his overreaction to the name of the bank accounts.

PTSD was the one diagnosis he didn't want. It was a career ender. A notice of an extension of the medical evaluation board had come through because of the flashback. Who was he kidding? He was as good as gone.

"Paul?"

He looked up at the doctor. "I'm sorry, ma'am. Just a little overwhelmed."

"I understand." Dr. Wilson spent the rest of their session answering questions Paul didn't know he had. Talking with her had eased some of his fears as far as his diagnoses, but the uncertainty of his career still hung over his head like a two-ton weight. What would he do when it fell on him?

Standing in the closet, Paul leaned against the wall and noted his uniforms. Six sets of ABUs–airman battle uniforms–hung in front of him. It was the camouflage uniform airmen wore in deployed locations. For his job, it was the uniform he wore every day. He'd received notice of his discharge the day before. Knowing it was coming didn't help his mood.

A garment bag was tucked in the back of the closet. Paul pulled it off the rod and held it up. Walking out of the closet, he laid the bag on the bed. Staring at it for a while, he pulled the zipper and pushed the bag off the hanger to get a better look. It was his service dress uniform. Genny had said it looked like a dark blue suit a man would wear to church.

Slipping out of his clothes, Paul stepped into the slacks and fastened the waistband. The relaxed fit of the pant legs hid his prosthetic. No one would know that he was an amputee. Putting on the light blue button down shirt, Paul buttoned it as he walked into the bathroom. Fighting with the necktie, he jerked it from around his neck and grabbed the clip-on tie.

Shrugging into the jacket, Paul buttoned the silver buttons and stared at his reflection in the mirror. He turned slightly; the light catching the silver occupational badge. His eyes shifted to the ribbon rack above the left breast pocket. It was a collection of awards and decorations he'd earned since he'd enlisted into the Air Force on August fifteenth of two thousand–just over a year before the terrorist attacks on September eleventh. He rarely wore the service dress uniform. He could donate it to Airmans' Attic thrift store. A young airman could use the uniform more than he could.

He brushed his fingers over the patch that signified his rank. Technical sergeant meant nothing and neither did his pending promotion to master sergeant. He was a veteran now. Rank didn't matter.

Paul drew in a shaky breath. Maybe he should hang onto it. Veterans could wear the uniform for special occasions like Veteran's Day, Memorial Day, or Fourth of July celebrations. Even weddings and funerals. He could wear it when he walked Katie down the aisle.

Paul sat on the bed and slipped on his socks and shoes. Grabbing a tissue, he bent down and buffed the smudge from the toe of his left shoe. Like the slacks, no one would know he was an amputee since the sock covered the prosthetic foot when he was sitting. Dropping his head in his hands, a strangled sob slipped from Paul's lips. It was over. His sixteen year career was gone.

"Baby?"

Paul looked up and wiped the tears from face.

Genny stood Caleb on the floor and walked over to the bed. She pushed aside the empty garment bag and sat next to Paul. Taking his hand in hers, she draped her arm across his shoulders.

"I'm okay."

Genny angled her head. She wasn't convinced.

"I was looking at my uniforms and…maybe I'll donate this one to Airmans' Attic." Paul sniffed and wiped fresh tears from his cheeks. "My ABUs are a little worn, so I'll trash those, or maybe keep them."

"Keep at least one set. One day you'll wish you had."

"Yeah. Maybe." Paul's stomach knotted. Caleb walked over and rested his hands on Paul's knees. His grin was a balm to Paul's hurting heart. He squeezed his eyes shut and opened them when he felt Caleb climbing onto his lap.

"Daddy. Wanna see my picture I drawed?" Katie said, as she walked up to Paul waving a piece of paper. She opened her mouth and paused, opting to slip between Genny and Paul. Katie said, "Are you sad, Daddy?"

"A little."

Katie gave Genny a serious look. "Mama, you need to get Daddy some ice cream."

"Oh, yeah?"

"Uh-huh. You give me ice cream when I'm sad."

"We bought a gallon of chocolate chip cookie dough." Genny raised her brows and smiled.

"Thanks, babe."

Katie tossed the paper at Paul and ran out of the room, shouting," I'll get it for you, Daddy."

Genny got up and followed Katie into the kitchen.

Paul picked up the piece of paper and turned it over. Katie had drawn their family, including Lucy. Paul's hair was spiky, as Katie called it, and Genny's legs were at least five inches long. He chuckled. What caught his eye was the prosthetic. Katie had drawn it on the right leg, but it didn't matter which leg. She saw who he was now—an amputee.

⁓ℓℓℓ⁓

Staring blankly had become Paul's recent hobby. He shook his head and continued reading the Bible. He'd always clung to the Lord's Word in the middle of a dark storm, bringing comfort to the deep recesses of his heart. This was one of those times. A week and a half earlier, he'd received notice that he was medically retired. Expecting the outcome didn't keep him from being punched in the stomach.

Thankful for a medical retirement instead of a medical discharge, it was still the end of his career. Wearing the uniform had been how he had started the workday for the past sixteen years. It was physically a part of him. Now he was slipping into athletic pants and a t-shirt. Who would he be now? For nearly two decades, he'd been an airman, a member of the military.

Flipping the page, Paul found one verse he'd claimed as his own when he was in the hospital after he was injured. Second Chronicles chapter fifteen, verse seven, read: "But as for you, be strong and do not give up, for your work will be rewarded."

Paul remembered what the chaplain had said when he was in the hospital in Maryland. He didn't know God's reason, but he took comfort in knowing God's plans were perfect. Paul looked out the window and noticed a small bird hopping across the top of the picnic table. Peace filled his heart when he felt God calling him to minister to someone who carried deep, emotional pain.

Paul pulled into the neighborhood he'd become familiar with as much as his own. A smile spread across his face when he saw Trevor's Jeep with the hood up. That man was always tweaking something on the engine. He pulled into the driveway and shut off the truck. Trevor ducked out from under the hood and grinned.

"Brother," Paul said when he walked up to Trevor and hugged him.

"Hopefully, I didn't get any grease on you."

"It'll wash out." Paul said and gave his shirt a quick once over.

"Come on in. Tamika made a pot of coffee and banana bread before she left."

"Thanks."

After getting their coffee and bread, Paul followed Trevor out onto the deck and sat in the chair next to him.

"Is Zach getting nervous?" Paul bit into the banana bread and held in a moan. He'd never tell Genny that Tamika's banana bread put hers to shame.

Trevor sighed. "Yeah." He looked at Paul and shook his head. "Why the Army?" That was all Trevor had to say. He was a part of a Navy family and when Zach had talked about joining the military, Trevor was certain he'd choose the Navy.

Paul took another big bite of banana bread and a sip of coffee. "I know it's hard, but—"

"Nah, I might complain about the Army, but I'm proud of my son." He looked at Paul and smiled. "Enough about me and my woes. How about you?"

"Well. I got *the* diagnosis." Paul looked at Trevor, then turned his attention to the backyard.

"I'm sorry, Paul. I hate to say it, but I expected it."

Paul looked at Trevor. "Really?"

"With what you've been through, I was surprised that you came out of Walter Reed without a PTSD diagnosis."

Paul exhaled hard and sipped his coffee. "I guess I repressed it all. I was surprised when it spewed out of me. At the shop, no less." Paul looked at Trevor. "Do you have any experience?"

"Oh, yeah." Trevor lifted his chin. "Started with Desert Storm. Went through Iraqi Freedom. Navy Seabees are on the ground, not in the water, so we see as much as the Army and Marines do. And sometimes the Air Force." Trevor laughed.

"Yeah, yeah, yeah. At least Seabees don't call us the Chair Force, like the Army does."

"Hey, it's because they're jealous."

Paul shook his head and smiled.

"Iraqi Freedom was by far worse. It's hard to build a camp when snipers are taking potshots at you."

Paul had known Trevor for years, but they'd never talked about his combat experience.

"A guy next to me was shot in the head." Trevor cleared his throat and drew in a deep breath. "I was covered with his blood and…and…"

"You don't have to say it. I know what you are talking about." Trevor's splotchy skin slowly faded to his normal skin tone. Why did he ask and put Trevor through this?

"What about your symptoms? My worst trigger used to be fireworks. I've come a long way with exposure therapy."

"Does it work?"

"Did for me. Don't get me wrong, I still have a lot of triggers but I try to avoid those that I can."

"I hear ya." Paul watched two kids playing ball in the neighbor's yard.

"What's next? Have you thought of something besides accounting?"

"No."

"You should get your degree in IT and come teach with me at the community college." Trevor raised his brows when Paul eyed him. "No? Okay." Trevor laughed. He sat forward and clasped his hands between his knees. "You have my number if you ever need me. You never know when something will trigger a flashback or something else. Trust me."

"Thanks, man. I appreciate it."

Paul left Trevor's house thankful that he knew someone who'd been where he was at. But why Trevor? He wouldn't wish these feelings on anyone, much less his friend.

Once Genny and the kids were in bed, Paul picked up his journal from the desk next to his Bible and walked into the living room. The past few weeks had put him through the ringer. The flashback, being in the hospital, and the discharge from the Air Force. It was like an avalanche. He didn't have time to catch his breath before he was knocked off his feet again.

May 16, 2017

Life has been rough. I've tried to keep God in the center, but it's been hard with everything that's happened. I still believe that one day, and hopefully soon, I'll learn why all of this has happened. I am blessed with a medical retirement. At least I can take care of my family financially. I am reminded of what Chaplain Zhang said. I am here for a reason. Hopefully, I will figure that out soon.

CHAPTER 24

Genny

From the living room window, Genny watched Paul and the kids in the back-yard. Paul was sitting on top of the picnic table while Katie pulled Caleb in the wagon. Genny released a breath and headed down the hall to tend to the laundry. As she folded, she thought about Paul's demeanor when he had come home from his appointment with the psychiatrist.

Defeated was the word that kept surfacing in her mind. Paul was defeated and Genny was full of guilt. Something that she'd hoped and prayed for had become reality. What would this mean for Paul and what would it mean for their family?

Genny flinched when the back door slammed. Katie's feet pounded down the hall and she ran up to Genny, holding a bouquet of dandelions.

"Here, Mama!" she said and shoved the flowers at Genny. "Smell 'em,"

Genny sniffed the flower and kissed Katie's cheek.

"I'm gonna put them in some water." Katie strolled down the hall with the flowers. A moment later, Genny heard one of the dining chairs scrape across the kitchen floor. She dropped the shirt she was folding and sprinted down the hall as visions of Katie laying on the floor unconscious flashed through her mind.

"Here, let me get it, baby girl," Paul said.

"I didn't hear you come in," Genny said as she made it to the kitchen. Caleb walked over to Genny, holding a single dandelion.

"Caleb and I snuck in." He smiled.

Paul went into the living room and sat on the couch.

"Wanna play dolls with me?" Katie asked when she ran up to him.

"I'm going to see if I can find a documentary."

"Oh." Katie stood next to Paul for a moment, then lowered her head and went to her room.

"I guess she doesn't like documentaries either." She grinned at Paul as she sat next to him. He flashed a smile and turned his attention back to the on-demand shows.

Paul clicked on a documentary about homesteading. "Maybe I can become a farmer. We can get a house with some acreage and a tractor." He looked at her and wiggled his eyebrows.

Usually, she could tell when Paul was joking, but not this time. Did he really want to homestead? He set the remote on the side table, leaned back, and slipped his arm around her shoulders, pulling her close. What would life look like for them a year from now?

—ell—

Genny watched Julie balancing a cup of coffee on a saucer and smiled when she walked by the table. Genny glanced out the front window and spotted Tamika's car. The two hugged when Tamika reached the table. Pulling out the chair across from Genny, Tamika blew out her breath and sighed when she sat down.

"The Army, huh? How did that go over with Trevor?"

Tamika laughed and shook her head. "It was rough at first, but he finally came around. Trevor was glad that Zach enlisted in the military since he wasn't doing well in college."

"Zach will fit into the military."

"Yeah, but I'm going to miss my baby." Tamika poked out her bottom lip and laughed. "I'm going to order my coffee." Tamika stood and headed to the counter.

Genny thought about the kids. Katie would graduate from preschool soon. It seemed like yesterday she was a newborn. She sighed and sipped her cup of Americana as she waited.

Tamika sat back down and placed her purse in the empty chair next to her. She rested her forearms on the table and laced her fingers together. "How's Paul?"

"Quiet. I think he's still depressed." Genny sighed. "The doctor said the meds take up to eight weeks for him to feel the full effects."

"He'll be okay." Tamika rested her hand on Genny's hand.

Genny blew out a quiet breath. Tamika was right, but it could be a long road. Tamika leaned back when Julie walked up with her order.

"You look frazzled," Genny said to Julie.

"Two baristas are out sick." Julie groaned.

"Sorry girl." Genny eyed the chocolate croissant on the plate Julie placed in front of Tamika.

The drive thru beeped and Julie's eyes narrowed. "Ugh. See you ladies later."

"Bye." Genny and Tamika said at the same time.

Genny leaned back and wrapped her hands around her cup, bringing it to her lips. She sipped her coffee and set the cup back on the table. "I feel bad."

"About what?"

"I've been so scared that Paul would stay in the military. I never thought about how being discharged would affect me, not him. I was selfish."

"Fear can do that. Try not to beat yourself up. You have to let him grieve."

"Grieve?"

"Grief isn't only for death. It's any loss. Paul has lost a part of his identity."

"Yeah." Fear and guilt had been fighting within Genny for far too long. She was glad they had an answer regarding Paul's career so that they could get on with their lives.

When Genny arrived home from her visit with Tamika, she headed down the hall to their bedroom and smiled. Caleb was napping in his crib. Katie would be at preschool for another hour, so she had time to spend with Paul. She walked into the dining room and glanced out the window. Paul was sitting on the picnic table, throwing Lucy's ball towards the back fence.

Lucy bolted towards Genny when she walked out the back door. Genny gave him a tender kiss when she sat on top of the picnic table next to him.

"How was your visit?"

"It was great. Zach has to report to the military processing station next Friday."

"Mmm. It's good for him. Trevor is proud but a little disappointed that he didn't choose the Navy."

"Yes, that's what Tamika said." Genny leaned her head against Paul's shoulder. The surrounding air stilled, and Genny could feel the sadness emitting from Paul. She drew in a slow breath. "I'm sorry."

"For what?"

"Wishing you'd be discharged from the Air Force." Despite her attempt to hold back tears, a sob slipped out.

"Babe," Paul whispered against her hair, and pulled Genny into his arms. "Yes, I was hoping and praying that things would work out, but that flashback was the defining moment. God has better plans for us. I have no idea what those plans are, but I trust Him."

"So do I." Genny slipped her fingers between Paul's. God's plan might have been for Paul to be discharged from the military, but it didn't take her guilt away.

She had to forgive herself for not supporting her husband during a difficult time in his life. And the hardest realization for Genny was that God's will all along was what she'd been praying about. It was time she let go of the guilt and helped Paul adjust to their life going forward.

Holding up Katie's swimsuit, the corners of Genny's mouth lifted. Katie had grown since last summer and with two tall parents, she'd gotten leggy. And there was no question Caleb needed a swimsuit. The front door opened, and Genny heard Paul talking to Lucy. He walked into Katie's room where Genny was and kissed her.

"Whatcha doing?" he asked.

"Preparing for the beach."

"Oh." Paul's gaze dropped to the floor.

"Trevor said the Jeep club is meeting next weekend, but I figured we could go during the week since it won't be that busy."

Paul shifted his gaze out the window.

Genny looked down and noted the athletic pants he was wearing. It was then she realized he'd been wearing pants all summer. Paul had lived in shorts during the summers before the accident. Being self-conscious was understandable, but they'd seen amputees around. Katie pointed out people wearing a prosthetic and announced that her daddy was wearing one, too.

"Wanna come?"

"Maybe next time."

"Suit yourself," Genny said, and held up Katie's swimsuit.

Paul smiled as he headed out of the room.

Genny shoved the swimsuit back in the drawer and decided she'd check on the plants on the patio. At least half a dozen tomatoes should be ready to pick. She was tending to the tomatoes when she heard the back door open.

Paul stuck his head out and said, "I'm going to get baby girl. Want me to stop by the store?"

"Yeah, the list is on the fridge." Genny followed him inside. She buckled Caleb in the highchair and cut up an apple for his snack. Her phone chimed, so she went to the living room and grabbed it. The notification was a price drop on the house she had been dreaming about. A thrill traveled through her. She'd given up and figured the house had sold by now.

Placing a few cubes of apples on the tray of Caleb's highchair, Genny grabbed her laptop. Her mouth hung open when she saw that the price had dropped by ten thousand dollars. The sellers must be desperate. Glancing out the living room window, the wheels in Genny's head turned with each second.

Paul was now discharged from the Air Force, and they'd gotten one retirement deposit. The VA claim was still in process. He was told that between the two, they should be fine financially. Did that mean that they could afford a house? Genny looked at the listing again.

"Is it this house, Lord?" Genny sighed and sat the laptop on the coffee table.

"Mama." Caleb grinned at Genny when she walked over to him.

"It would be nice not to have to ask permission to hang a picture. Isn't that right?" She had no complaints. The property manager had been wonderful to work with. Genny wiped Caleb's hands and got him out of the highchair. "You want your own room, don't you?"

Caleb nodded as if he knew what Genny was talking about.

She carried Caleb to the couch and eased down with him on her lap. Pointing to the laptop with the listing of the house up, she said, "Look at that yard. You, Sissy, and Lucy would have so much fun." A car door slammed out front. Was it at their house or the new neighbor's? Genny heard Katie's voice on the other side of the front door and closed the laptop. Now wasn't the time. Hopefully soon they'd be in their own house, and Genny prayed it was 300 Apple Orchard Way.

CHAPTER 25

Paul

At group therapy, Paul joined Steve off to the side of the room. He glanced at the people as they made their way to their seats.

"How are you doing?" Steve asked.

"Better. The first day was rough. Deep down I knew I would be discharged, but to see it on paper…"

"No matter the reason for discharge, it's hard to leave the uniform hanging in the closet."

"Yeah."

The men joined the other vets in the group, and Paul settled into the chair next to Gabe. The veterans had given updates around the circle when the door creaked open. Karla snuck inside and found the last vacant chair.

"Nice of ya to grace us with yer presence," Craig said and grinned.

"Sorry guys." She slipped her purse under her chair.

Paul sat quietly as a few group members talked about what was going on in their lives. It seemed everyone was dealing with something.

When it was his turn, he sighed. "I got the official notice. I'm now medically retired." Paul gave the group a faint smile.

"So ya gonna stay with us, young man?"

"Yep, you're stuck with me, Craig." Paul laughed, but his insides twisted. When he started attending the group several months ago, he figured it was temporary. Becoming a permanent fixture had never crossed his mind.

"Anyone feel like sharing their experience with Paul? The good and the bad," Steve said. The room was quiet for a moment before Devon spoke up.

"Well, I'd been in the Marines for twelve years and had planned to retire. But fate said no." Devon looked down at his wrecked body. "If they had the return to duty program back then, I'd have worked my tail off to stay on active duty."

Paul's gaze fell to Devon's residual legs and right arm.

Devon laughed. "I was no candidate, obviously. The desire was still there, so I know how you feel." Devon's compassion and understanding shone in his eyes.

Paul stared at his hands, fingering his wedding band. "I passed the fitness test. It was a sure thing. You all know." He scanned the crowd. "That flashback killed me."

"You can appeal it," Karla said. "The discharge." She leaned forward, eyes sparkling.

"I already signed and waived my right to appeal." Paul released a breath. "I don't want this to follow me. You know, PTSD?" He looked at each face around the group. Several nodded.

"Yeah, like at the grocery store, everyone backs away from you when you voice your frustration a little too loudly when the cashier chats more than she scans," Nate said.

"Ya gotta find sum'in' to do. Sum'in' to give ya purpose. Ya sit around and that dang depression'll set in and kill ya," Craig didn't always joke. His words made sense. "I'll say it, may the VA prove me wrong, but ya be sittin' pretty between ya military retirement and the VA disability. Don't matter, though. Ya don't seem the type to sit around all day watchin' soap operas." Craig laughed.

"What do you like doing? Any hobbies?" Karla asked.

"My wife would say watching documentaries." Paul's laugh lightened his mood a bit. "I know what you mean. I'll have to think about it."

Paul got suggestions from woodworking to being a professional poker player. The latter was Craig's idea. The group ended and everyone made their way to the parking lot, but Karla stopped at her car

"Want to go for coffee?"

Paul looked at his watch. He had about an hour before Katie was released from preschool. "Sure." He texted Genny and followed Karla out of the parking lot.

Karla found a table while Paul ordered the coffee and waited at the pickup counter. He glanced in her direction. What was going on in her life? She hadn't talked about her marriage and why she didn't live with her husband and daughter.

Paul handed Karla her coffee and sat down. They talked about their kids and how the kids were adjusting to the changes in their lives. Karla quieted and stared at the cup in front of her.

"How old is your daughter?"

"Three. She lives with my soon-to-be ex in Charlotte."

"That must be hard." Paul noticed Karla rub the ring finger of her prosthetic hand.

"It's very hard."

Not seeing his kids every day was something Paul couldn't imagine. And he didn't want to think about living life without Genny by his side.

"I know you don't want to ask, so I'll tell you." She dropped her arms under the table and leaned forward, bracing herself against the edge of the table. "It's PTSD and my new appearance that ran my husband off. I understand PTSD, but to me, the appearance thing is shallow. It was supposed to be in sickness and health, you know?" She held up her prosthetic arm.

"You're right."

"This is nothing." Karla pointed to her throat where disfigured skin rose from under the neckline of her shirt. "I don't have what makes me a woman up here." She pointed to her chest.

Paul picked up his cup and focused on the coffee as it flowed towards his lips. He winced as the hot liquid slid down his throat.

"I'm sorry. That's TMI."

"No, it's okay."

Karla sighed. "In the group, when I said I was scarred, I meant it. I've had so many skin grafts that my skin no longer stretches, so I'm not a candidate for reconstructive surgery." She took a long sip of coffee. "In the middle of an argument, Danny said I disgusted him. I think he's using PTSD to cover his shallowness. And like the guys said in group, everyone is scared of PTSD, so it's the perfect grounds for divorce and custody of Sophia. I'm not mentally stable, you know. According to society anyway." She shook her head.

"Karla, I'm so sorry." Suddenly, Paul's grief over losing his career seemed trivial.

"I'm used to it. I'm glad my family still loves me." She smiled and finished her coffee. "So, what about you?"

"In no way does what I'm dealing with compare to what you've been through."

"Both of our lives have changed because of our military duty. It's hard for you, too. Men are providers. I don't mean just financially. You want to make sure your family is happy and healthy. And I'm sure you've struggled with things like how your wife and kids see you now."

"Yeah, Katie was standoffish at first, but she came around pretty quickly. Caleb was two months old when I left, so he doesn't remember the old me."

"Like my family." The love for her family was clear in Karla's smile.

"My main issue is feeling as if I've lost a large part of myself. I enlisted when I was eighteen. Sixteen years of my life were spent in uniform. I'm not sure I can be someone else." Tears stung Paul's eyes. He looked out the windows at the traffic passing by to hide his emotions.

"I understand."

The warmth of Karla's hand turned his focus. Slowly, he pulled his hand out from under hers. The compassion in her eyes turned to embarrassment.

"I'm sorry."

"Don't worry about it." Paul's phone buzzed and he saw the preview of a text from Genny on the lock screen, and swiped.

Genny: Did you forget about our daughter? <smiley face>
Paul groaned. "I need to run. I'm late picking up Katie."

"Okay. Thanks for having coffee with me. It helped."

"You're welcome. See you at the next group therapy session." Paul grabbed his half-empty cup, smiled at Karla, and headed for the truck.

As Paul expected, when he pulled up to the school, Katie stood next to her teacher with her little brows scrunched together and a scowl on her face. The teacher opened the back door of the truck and helped Katie into her booster seat. As soon as the teacher shut the door, Paul received quite the tongue lashing.

"Daddy. Where were you?" The sharp tone in her voice would have gotten her into trouble, but he was giving her grace.

He glanced in the rearview mirror and saw Katie's arms tightly crossed over her chest.

"I'm only fifteen minutes late, baby girl. I was having coffee with a friend and lost track of time."

"You gotta lot of coffee friends," she snapped. "You like you friends more than me." She sobbed.

Paul found a store and pulled into the parking lot. He turned around to face Katie. "That's not true, baby girl. I like you a million times more than my friends."

"You always with them." Katie sniffed.

She wasn't wrong. The therapy group was twice a week and most of the time, at least one veteran asked him to coffee afterward. Sometimes, several of them would meet up somewhere after the group. Genny knew Paul's need to spend time with others who dealt with the same things he dealt with. But she wasn't a four-year-old who didn't understand why her daddy wasn't home with her all day.

Katie's therapist had been working with her about her clinginess. As her therapist had said, kids' behavior was their language. They acted out since they didn't know how to put their feelings into words. There were times Paul didn't have the words to express how he felt about the new chapter in their lives and wanted nothing more than to scream in frustration. Those feelings pushed Paul to be patient with Katie.

Paul watched from the kitchen window as Genny folded back and secured the soft top of the Jeep. She grabbed the beach bag next to Caleb's car seat and pulled something out of the bag. He chuckled as Genny began applying sunblock on the kids. Katie giggled and Caleb cried when she slathered them with the lotion.

Genny had brought up going to the beach a few weeks earlier and had asked him several times since then if he wanted to go. He glanced down at his prosthetic. He wasn't ready. Around the house he wore shorts, but in public he wore pants. Glancing out the kitchen window, he saw Genny staring in his direction. She shook her head and cranked the Jeep. Katie raised her hands above her head and clapped at the sound of the mufflers.

Changing his mind, he sprinted toward the front door and jerked it open in time to see Genny turn her head toward the house after she backed out onto the street. He motioned for her to pull back into the drive. A smile spread across her face.

"Are you coming, Daddy?" Katie's voice was barely audible above the sound of the mufflers.

"Yes, baby girl. Let me change clothes."

"Yeah!" Katie leaned toward Caleb, but Paul couldn't make out what she was saying.

"Give me five minutes," Paul said to Genny. She nodded, still wearing a smile.

He looked down at his legs and pulled a pair of athletic pants from the dresser drawer. Slipping them on, he stopped mid-thigh. What if he wanted to carry Katie or Caleb into the water? Paul sighed, pulled the pants off, and dug his swim trunks out from the bottom drawer.

Genny was sitting in the passenger seat when Paul made his way to the Jeep. Pulling open the driver's door, he paused a moment before hoisting himself into the driver's seat. It wasn't as difficult as he'd thought. Genny had pulled her auburn hair into a high ponytail. She smiled when he looked at her. Shifting in reverse, Katie raised her arms and cheered when they headed down the road.

Paul pulled into a handicap parking space when they reached the beach. He wanted to park a few rows back, but with the kids and the beach gear; it made sense to take advantage of the handicap space. Paul reached in to unbuckle Caleb.

"Unbuckle me, Daddy!" Katie's smile brightened her face.

"I'm here next to Bubby."

Katie's smile fell and she raised her arms for Genny to lift her out of the Jeep. He pushed his thoughts of Katie's behavior from his mind. She was dealing with what happened in her own way.

Carrying Katie on one hip and Caleb on the other, Paul followed Genny as she looked for a space for them to set up. She spread the blanket out and Paul stood Katie on the blanket and sat Caleb next to her. Katie started jumping up and down and pointing to the water. Setting up the sunshade, Paul moved Caleb under it and looked around. A woman to his left not far away turned her head when he noticed her. *I should have stayed home.*

"She's not looking at your leg."

Paul shaded his eyes to see Genny.

"You're a sexy man, Paul Thompson." She lifted her eyebrows.

"If you say so." His cheeks warmed, but he couldn't blame it on the sun.

"I do." Genny pulled a sippy cup out of the small cooler and handed it to Caleb. "Why do you think I married you?" She laughed.

"Take me to the water, Daddy!" Katie grabbed his hand and tugged on his arm.

"Okay, baby girl." Paul swept Katie up in his arms. He felt like he was going to lose his balance a time or two, but got used to the shifting sand under his prosthetic foot. Katie squealed when her dangling feet touched the water.

The frigid ocean claimed his breath when he lowered himself to cool off his shoulders. Katie gasped and coughed when the water flowed into her mouth.

"You can wear you pretend leg in the ocean?" Katie's teeth chattered as she spoke. Her arms tightened around his neck.

"I wear it in the shower."

"Oh, yeah." She giggled and wrapped her legs around him. He felt her small body shaking.

"We need to warm up."

"No, Daddy!"

"You're cold. We'll come back out once we're warm."

Katie groaned. "Okay."

Paul passed by Genny on the way to the blanket. Caleb wore a sun hat and his new swimsuit. Paul laughed when he jerked off the hat and threw it on the wet sand. Genny looked at Paul and shook her head. She placed the hat on Caleb's head and gave it a good tug. Holding his hands, Genny walked Caleb along the shoreline. He squealed and drew up his legs when a wave rolled toward him.

Paul sat on the blanket, digging his feet in the sand. He groaned when Katie walked onto the blanket and plopped down behind him. While he brushed as much sand off the blanket as he could, he felt her running her finger across his shoulders and down his spine.

"Why do you have this on your back, Daddy?" Katie had seen the cross tattoo that covered his back many times over the years, but it was the first time she'd asked about it. "To show everyone how much I love God."

Katie was quiet for a moment. "Do you love Mama?"

"Yes, very much. But we are supposed to love God more than anyone else."

"Oh." She traced the tattoo again. "Why?"

The conversation was getting deep for a four-year-old. Caleb's giggling caught Paul's attention and he watched Genny walking toward them with Caleb in her arms. She sat him under the sunshade and handed out the sandwiches she'd prepared. They sat quietly, eating.

"Mama, Daddy loves God more than you."

Genny looked at Paul and laughed under her breath. "That's how it's supposed to be."

Katie shrugged and bit into her sandwich.

It was time to change the subject until Katie was old enough to understand. "How about I rent an umbrella?" Paul asked.

Genny wiped her forehead. "Sounds good to me. It is getting hot out here."

Katie begged to go, but Genny made her stay and finish her lunch. Paul slipped on his t-shirt and made his way down the beach to where a vendor was set up. Several people glanced at him as he passed by. Would the stares be something he'd have to deal with for the rest of his life? Standing in line, he heard a feminine voice behind him.

"Hello."

Paul turned around. The woman was wearing a red bikini that left nothing to the imagination. Seeing her reminded Paul of how grateful he was that Genny dressed modestly. The bottom of Genny's two-piece looked like shorts, and her tank top covered her midriff.

"Hello." He gave her a faint smile.

"If you don't mind me asking, how did you lose your leg?"

Every ounce of him wanted to tell her it wasn't her business, but he couldn't. It wouldn't be the first time he would be asked by the public.

"I was injured in Afghanistan."

"Oh, so you're in the military."

"I was. I recently separated."

"Ah." She glanced at his left hand. Neither he nor Genny wore their wedding rings when they went to the beach. Paul turned his attention to the vendor.

"How are you today?" The woman had moved to Paul's side.

The man in front of Paul took his turn, and Paul stepped up. "Blessed. You?"

"Bored." She tipped her chin and smiled. Her gaze swept over him.

The vendor called Paul and he picked out an umbrella. On his way back to his family, he puffed up a little and said, "Got to keep the wife and kids out of the sun." He glimpsed the woman's frown as he passed..

Two cranky kids and an hour and a half later, they headed home. Paul looked over and smiled at his beautiful wife. Her eyes were closed and her head wobbled when he made a turn or hit a bump. Taking a quick glance in the rearview mirror, Paul smiled when he saw Katie and Caleb's eyes closed and heads wobbling like their mother's.

Slipping his hand around Genny's, Paul thought about his life. He had to trust that God had their family's best interest in mind. He didn't know what tomorrow would bring. Or next year, for that matter. But he took comfort knowing that God was in control.

When Paul walked into the group room, the first person he spotted was Karla. She smiled when he sat next to her.

"Got some sun?"

"Yeah, we went to the beach yesterday. All four of us got a little redder than we had planned."

"I see that." Karla drew in a long breath and forced it out. "I'll never be caught dead on a beach. No one wants to see this." She looked down at herself.

"Who cares what others think?" The question was hypocritical. He had thought the same thing yesterday.

"You're kidding, right? All you're missing is a leg. You are as attractive as you were before your accident. I used to be pretty." She dropped her gaze to her lap and brushed her fingers over her prosthetic.

"What in the world?" Craig said when he hobbled in and took a seat next to Paul. "Ya look like a lobster."

"We went to the beach yesterday."

"You and Karla?" Craig chuckled.

Paul liked Craig, but the man didn't have a filter. Plus, his sense of humor was drier than the driest desert.

Paul shook his head and eyed Karla. Checking the clock on the wall, they had ten minutes before the group started. Was now a good time to say something? The gaggle of group members making their way through the door answered his question. He'd ask Karla for coffee after the group.

An unfamiliar face walked through the door behind the others. The woman sat on the other side of Craig. A brief thought of sympathy went through his mind, and he had to hold back a chuckle.

"Okay everyone. We've got a new member. Karla, you're no longer by yourself." Steve smiled. "This is Beth. But before we got started, don't forget about the picnic. Who's coming? We need a headcount for the dogs and burgers."

Steve looked around the circle of veterans. Paul noted that every group member had raised their hand, including Beth.

"Paul, mind if we start with you?" Steve asked.

"Not at all." Paul gave his history for the third time since he'd joined the group. He thought about Gabe. His wife had given birth last week and he was taking some time off from the group to be there for his wife and bond with his baby boy.

"Well, I guess it's my turn," Beth said, and smiled briefly. She was, from Paul's guess, in her early to mid-thirties. She cleared her throat and pushed her red hair behind her shoulders. "I lost both my legs early in the War on Terrorism."

Paul fought to keep his gaze from falling to her legs.

"I got my commission in mid two thousand and two. I was the oldest in my class by five years and my nickname was Mama." Beth grinned.

"Wow, young lady. You don't look *that* old!" Craig chuckled and slapped his thigh.

"I'm forty-three now. It'll serve me well when I'm seventy."

"Sure will, young lady."

Beth shared she was in a helicopter crash less than a month after she arrived in Iraq. Her legs had been severely injured. She'd developed sepsis and had to undergo a double amputation.

Many stories affected Paul on a personal level. But the group had more than injuries in common. They had a camaraderie through their losses, whether the loss resulted from combat or a motorcycle accident. The effects of such a loss were something no one except another amputee could completely understand. Especially one who lost his or her military career because of something beyond their control.

CHAPTER 26

Genny

Genny wrapped a sheet of foil across the cheesecake and pushed out her breath. She'd thought about making her granny's potato salad. It was her go-to dish for potlucks and get-togethers, but she'd done something different for the therapy group's picnic.

"Mama!" Katie shrieked.

Genny took off down the hall and groaned when she saw that Katie had pulled all the clothes out of her dresser drawers. "Katherine Kelly Thompson! What did you do?"

"I can't find it." Katie gritted her teeth.

"What?"

"My purple dress." Katie whined.

"Honey, it's in the hamper."

Katie's shoulders fell and she began sobbing.

Genny bit her tongue and counted to ten. "It's okay. Come here."

Genny took Katie by the hand and led her to the master bedroom. Pulling each item of clothing out of the hamper, Genny sighed when she found Katie's beloved purple sundress close to the bottom. She sniffed and grimaced. Katie stood next to her, whimpering.

Making a vow to tell no one, she sprayed the dress with body spray. Katie pulled it out of Genny's hands and inhaled deeply.

"Mmm." She smiled.

Genny shook her head and helped Katie get ready. Paul walked in with Caleb on his hip.

"Ready?"

"We ready, Daddy!" Katie grinned and skipped down the hall.

"She's in a good mood."

"What? You didn't hear her screaming from the backyard?"

Paul lifted his brows.

"Let's go. I'll tell you about it in the car."

There weren't as many people as Genny thought there would be. It made sense. This was a therapy group, not a military squadron. She guessed there were less than thirty-five people with the group members, significant others, kids, and the employees. Genny made her way to the food table and placed the cheesecake next to a container of brownies.

"Hello," said the woman standing on the other side of the table. "I'm Missy. Nate's wife." The woman tilted her head toward the man talking with Paul.

"Genny. Paul's wife."

"Ah, Paul's wife." She grinned. "Nate talks about Paul all the time."

Genny smiled and spotted a woman walking up to where Nate and Paul were standing. Caleb wiggled in Paul's arms and he stood him on the ground. Caleb grinned as he toddled over to Genny.

"That's Karla." Missy smiled and waved at Karla when she looked in their direction.

As she walked their way, Genny noted Karla's long-sleeved shirt and capris pants. It had to be close to ninety degrees today. When Karla came closer, Genny spotted the burn scars on her neck.

"Karla, this is Genny. Paul's wife."

Karla smiled warmly and offered her right hand. "It's nice to finally meet you, Genny. Paul talks about you and the kids all the time."

"Nice to meet you, too." Genny glimpsed the prosthetic fingers poking out from under the hem of Karla's left sleeve. Caleb ran up to her, and Genny swept him up in her arms. "This little guy is Caleb."

"He's adorable," Missy said.

"Sure is," Karla agreed. She reached over and rubbed Caleb's back.

"Katie's over there somewhere." Genny angled her head toward the playground.

Karla had beautiful hazel eyes and thick, long blond hair. Her makeup was caked on but Genny figured it was to help cover the scars. A breeze whirled around them, pushing Karla's hair away from her face. Genny caught sight of the scars that stretched from the bottom side of her neck to above where her right ear used to be. Karla quickly grabbed her hair and held it tightly against the side of her face, revealing a small bald spot where her hair was parted.

"It's okay, girl," Missy said, and rested her hand on Karla's arm.

"Yes, don't worry about it," Genny added.

Karla smiled slightly and walked to the food table, swiping a brownie. "Can he have this?"

"Sure."

Karla handed the brownie to Caleb and got one for herself. Genny and Missy helped themselves to a brownie and the three women talked for a few minutes.

Genny and a few moms made their way to the playground and shared a picnic table to watch the kids play. Thankfully, there was a play area for little kids next to the picnic tables and Genny let Caleb loose to have fun with the other younger kids. She heard laughter coming from a group of veterans. Karla and Paul were standing next to each other. Karla laughed again and nudged Paul with her shoulder. He stumbled and she grabbed his arm to steady him.

Turning her focus to the playground, Genny rubbed her temples. What was that about? She shook her head. Nothing. Some people didn't think about others' personal space. What was Paul's personal space with someone besides his wife? That was a dumb question. She knew he had defined boundaries with—

"Mama?" Katie said, whimpering.

Genny turned around and saw Katie holding up the hem of her dress, revealing a skinned knee. "Oh, honey. Are you okay?"

"I wanna go home."

"I have a Band-Aid in my purse." One wife began digging around in her purse. She pulled out a Barbie Band Aid, bringing a smile to Katie's face.

Genny put the Band-Aid on Katie's knee and she ran off to the slide. Glancing over to the group again, conflicting thoughts sprang to life in Genny's head when she saw Paul and Karla off talking by themselves. Suddenly, she didn't feel comfortable about Paul and Karla going to coffee. Even if it was for Paul to witness to Karla. What if Karla saw it as more? Genny realized she'd zoned out when Paul's smiling face came into view.

"Hey, babe. Ready to go?"

"Sure, but you can be the one to tell the kids." Genny laughed.

In the early evening, Genny took her journal with her to the picnic table. Rarely did she journal anywhere besides the bedroom, but she felt like being out in nature.

May 26, 2017

Today was the picnic for Paul's therapy group. Paul introduced me to all the vets. It took a little to get used to Craig. He's jokes a lot. Karla is the woman Paul took home from the group when she had car trouble. I don't know what I was expecting, but my heart goes out to her. She has a prosthetic hand (or arm, maybe) and lots of burns. I wanted to ask what happened, but there's no way I would. I probably wouldn't if I knew her well. It kind of rubbed me the wrong way that she and Paul went off by themselves to talk. I'm sure I'm overreacting as usual. It's not like they were out of my sight. Anyway, he knows her and if he feels led by God to witness to her, who am I to stand in the way?

CHAPTER 27

Paul

Paul leaned his head back against the headrest and closed his eyes, letting the lyrics of the song playing on the radio fall over him. "We Won't Be Shaken" by Building 429 had become his theme song since the accident. The memory of Genny humming the song the first time she saw him in Walter Reed hospital filled his heart. "Lord, thank you for bringing that woman into my heart and my life."

A knock on the driver's side window startled Paul and he opened his eyes.

"Oops, sorry." Karla held her hand over her mouth.

"It's okay. I was listening to my favorite praise and worship song."

Karla downcast her eyes for a moment. She looked up and smiled. "Ready?"

"Yes. Me and my stomach are ready for some Chick-fil-A."

They stood in line to order and when it was their turn, Paul stood aside so Karla could order. The clerk rang her up and gave Karla the total.

"I got this," Paul said.

"You paid last time. I have money." A slight smile showed on Karla's face, but her eyes said something else.

Had she been offended, or was it sarcasm? This was the first time they'd had a meal together. He didn't see her as a charity case. It was the gentlemanly thing to do.

"Sir?"

"Sorry. Twelve-piece nugget meal please."

Karla laughed.

"What? I'm a big guy."

They got their food and found a table. "I'll say the blessing."

Karla's brows lifted before she bowed her head. Bowing his head as well, Paul said a quick blessing and they talked in between bites of food.

"So far, we've talked mostly about being veterans, our kids, and our injuries. How did you and Genny meet?" Karla took a bite of her chicken sandwich.

"Childhood friends." Paul took a long drink of lemonade.

"Really? That's so sweet."

Paul told the story of Brandon's death and that Genny had no one. As usual, he left out the part of their marriage, starting out as a way for Genny to have medical insurance. Instead, he told the story like they'd told so many people before—they fell in love through their grief. It was true, though it happened months later.

"What a story for you two to tell your kids one day."

"Yeah, that's what we've said." Paul popped the last waffle fry in his mouth and washed it down with the rest of his lemonade. "Your turn." He grinned.

"Not much to tell. I grew up in Texas and my dad's a rancher. They weren't too happy when I enlisted in the Army, but they have been supportive. Danny and I met in Advanced Individula Training school and married as soon as we finished. Sophia was born nine months later."

Karla talked about her life as if she was reading a book report. All factual with no emotion. After they finished eating, Paul bought two coffees and prayed it was a good time to witness. "Is there anything I can pray about?"

Karla pushed herself into the back of the chair. "Why would you ask that?"

There was that look again. He'd offended her like he did at the order counter. But it was obvious that she needed God in her life. She appeared lost. "It's what I do." He chuckled and cleared his throat when her expression remained the same.

"You can pray my husband brings our daughter home and we are a happy family again. While you're at it, pray that my body will look like it did before I deployed." She forced out her breath and shifted her gaze out the windows.

This was going to be challenging. That was okay though, Paul loved a good challenge.

"Anyway, a God who would do something like this to me isn't worth my time," she said without shifting her focus.

"God doesn't do bad things to us. Some things are because of our choices or—"

"So, because I chose the wrong wire to snip, this happened to me? You did nothing but be in the wrong place at the wrong time." Karla looked at him, her face colored with pain. "How do you do it? Stay so positive about life?"

Her expression softened. "I'm sorry, Paul. I understand what you're doing and a part of me is touched, but I don't see things getting better. My husband is in Charlotte with our daughter and the only money I have coming in is my VA disability. All I can afford in the Charleston area is on the bad side of town. My neighbor sells drugs." She crossed her right arm over her middle and glanced at a family of three sitting in a booth by the wall. Karla's cheeks glistened in the sunlight streaming through the windows.

"I will pray for you when I say my daily prayers."

"Thanks," Karla said, her tone full of sadness. She leaned forward and rested her forearms on the tabletop. "Maybe He'll listen to you 'cause He sure ain't listening to me." She let out a sad laugh. "I think I'm going to head home." She grabbed her purse and slid to the end of the booth.

"Okay." Paul gathered the trash and threw it away on the way out the door.

Karla walked up to her car and stopped. "I enjoy spending time with you. You are the bright light in the middle of my storm. See you next week," Karla said and got in her car.

Paul climbed into the truck and cranked the engine. Turning off the radio, he sat thinking about the last hour. Karla was the second most damaged person he'd seen. Genny had been the first. He'd spent many nights on his knees covering her in prayer, and he'd do the same for Karla.

⁂

Paul was sipping lemonade when Ryan walked into the restaurant. He spotted Paul and joined him at the table. The hostess took Ryan's drink order and he placed his Bible on the table next to him.

"How are you doing, brother?" Ryan rested his arms on the table.

"I'm doing well," Paul replied.

Ryan sat back when the hostess brought his sweet tea. "Good to hear,"

The men sat quietly, sipping their drinks. Ryan looked Paul in the eyes. Paul could tell that Ryan was trying to find the right words. Paul smiled and shook his head.

Ryan exhaled. "You know me too well." He laughed. "I have felt the Lord leading me to start a support group at the church. It'd be open to anyone. Not only members of the church."

"What kind of support group?"

"I've been thinking about a group for people who have been injured in the line of duty like police officers, EMT, firefighters and the military."

Paul leaned back when the server came by to take their orders.

After the server left, Ryan took a drink of his sweet tea. "I know you already attend a group, but this is a little different. You know my brother is a pastor in Nashville?"

Paul nodded.

"One of his parishioners was a firefighter. He experienced severe smoke inhalation on a call that scarred his lungs. He'd had chronic bronchitis off and on since. Losing his career sent him into a deep depression. Tom called me last night. The man committed suicide yesterday afternoon."

Paul's heart constricted. It didn't matter that the man had been a firefighter; he had dealt with some of the same feelings that veterans experienced. "That breaks my heart. What can I do?"

"I would like you to co—lead the group. Everyone—group members and group leaders–will have had an injury that ended their careers."

"Who's the other co-leader?"

"Clyde Martin."

"Clyde?" Paul thought about the older gentleman. He was one of the friendliest members he'd met since he and Genny joined the church years ago. As far as he knew, Clyde had retired as a CPA.

"He's an amputee. Lost his leg when he was shot as a beat cop."

Paul's lips parted. "Oh wow. I did not know."

"He doesn't talk about it. I think I'm the only one that knows." Ryan gave Paul a faint smile.

"I need to pray about it. And talk to Genny."

"Of course."

"I'll get back to you soon."

Ryan nodded.

They talked about Ryan's plans for the group. Paul asked lots of questions, so he knew how to pray and give Genny all the information she needed. Paul felt a spark of excitement. From what Ryan said, the group shouldn't interfere with the VA group, which was a relief. He'd formed a bond with the VA group he didn't want to break.

May 30, 2017

I think the support group Ryan wants to start would be a blessing for many people. I need to pray that it's the Lord's will. Leading a group takes a lot of preparation and between the VA group, my personal therapy and my family, I don't have a lot of free time. Plus, I need to throw time for myself in there somewhere.

Karla is struggling. She has a lot of anger about what has happened in her life. The bitterness will eat away at what's left of her heart. I have to reach her before it's too late. Lord, lead me.

CHAPTER 28

The kitchen was a mess from Paul and Katie's attempt to make finger paint. Genny had offered to clean while Paul was out for a run. His discharge from the Air Force didn't stop him from keeping active. Steve had mentioned something about the Department of Defense Warrior Games. It was the military's version of the Paralympics, and Paul was seriously considering entering.

Paul's phone chimed and Genny rinsed her hands and walked over to the dining table, wiping her hands on her shirt. She glanced at the screen in time to see the message preview before it disappeared.

Karla: Thank you for being there for me.

"Hey, babe." Paul came in the front door, startling Genny. He walked up to her and kissed the side of her head.

"You got a text from Karla." She handed the phone to Paul.

"Oh." He swiped the screen and walked into the living room. A moment later, he placed the phone on the side table.

A quick rush of heat filled Genny's face. What did 'Thank you for being there for me' mean? A second later, the heat faded. Paul was doing what he did best, witnessing. And from what he'd said about Karla, she could use the Lord right now. Genny breathed out. She was overreacting.

"Daddy!" Katie ran into the living room with Caleb on her heels. He grinned, pulling both kids onto his lap. Katie scrunched up her nose.

"Don't worry. I'm about to take a shower." Paul laughed. His phone chimed again, and he picked it up and grinned. "Mom said they want to visit."

"Mimi!" Katie cheered and clapped her hands. "Bubby, Mimi and Papa are coming!"

"Whoa, girl. We don't know the details yet. But they will come soon." Paul's gaze swept over the living room. "Maybe it's time."

"For what?" Genny asked as she walked into the living room.

"A bigger rental."

A pang of disappointment filled Genny's chest. So much for Apple Orchard Way. She put on a brave face. It was now or never. "That house is still for sale. It dropped another ten thousand dollars."

Paul forced out his breath.

"I know all we have is your retirement now, but it shouldn't be much longer for the VA, right?"

Instead of going into why it was a bad idea, he sat quietly for a few moments. Genny held her breath as she watched Paul grab his phone. He tapped repeatedly on his phone, and she presumed he was adding figures. *Please, Lord.*

"You still got that link?"

"Yep." Genny grabbed her phone from the dining table and had the link emailed to Paul in less than ten seconds. He looked at her when his phone chimed with an email notification. Shaking his head, he smiled, giving her a tiny ray of hope.

⁓ℓℓ⁓

Genny tensed and her heart was about to beat out of her chest when they pulled onto Apple Orchard Way. The past week had been the longest week of her life. *Please, God. Please, God. Please, God. If it's Your will, of course.* What was she doing? The house could be a dump. Like the real estate agent had said, sellers' agents used the best photos on the website, hoping to draw in potential buyers.

"Remember, show no emotion."

"So, I can't be excited to see something? What if there's a swimming pool in the basement? If it has a basement, that is."

Paul rolled his eyes and got out of the truck and met Genny on the passenger side. Their agent Brad made his way to them, wearing a wide grin. Slipping his fingers between hers, Paul and Genny headed to the front door. Genny's heart banged inside her chest as the butterflies fluttered in her stomach like they were caught up in a tornado.

A slight dog smell hit Genny when she walked inside. Lucy would fit right in. Genny held back a giggle. She knew what Paul was thinking. Dollar signs were floating around in his head as they toured each room. To replace all the carpet would cost thousands of dollars.

Walking into the living room, Genny's eyes were drawn to the brick fireplace that stretched across the outer wall. She couldn't help but grimace. They'd be stuck with that brick monstrosity for a while. Glancing back at Paul, she bit her bottom lip. She could almost see the figures as he added them up in his head.

They stood on the low deck overlooking the backyard. Genny braced herself on the railing and pulled back when it moved. Another cost. Hope filled her heart when she heard Paul tell Brad that the deck could be torn down and graduated steps built down to a patio. She followed Paul down the steps and walked out into the yard.

"At least the backyard is fenced. Lots of room for the kids and Lucy."

Genny glanced up at Paul and smiled. Surprising her, Paul leaned down and gave her a gentle kiss. Another good sign. After listening to some figures and advice from Brad, Paul and Genny made their way home. Rather than talk about finances and facts, Paul opened the conversation with what would be demoed first and how they'd handle a remodel with the kids and Lucy. It took everything in Genny not to scream. Was this really happening?

"Don't get too excited, babe. There's so much to do. Got to look at comps in the area and crunch some numbers. And let's not forget applying for a mortgage." Paul sighed.

"It'll be okay. You'll see. I have a good feeling about this."

"You could be right."

"I am." Genny gave Paul a cheesy grin.

Holding hands, he brought her hand to his mouth and kissed the back. "I love you, Genevieve."

"I love you, too."

Finally, a home of their own. Maybe.

Paul stood at the stove making pancakes. He placed a few small star-shaped pancakes on the tray of the highchair. Grabbing one, Caleb shoved it into his mouth. Genny placed a strip of bacon on Katie's plate. Setting the plate in front of Katie, Genny grabbed the remote and turned off the TV.

"Mama, turn it on! Me and Daddy was watching *Sesame Street*."

"Katherine Kelly," Paul said. "You know we don't watch TV at the dinner table. Apologize to Mama."

Katie pinched her lips together and stabbed her fork into the small pancake, shoving it into her mouth. "Sorry, Mama," she said, her words muffled by a mouth full of pancake.

Genny finished eating and made her way to the bedroom to gather up the laundry. Memories of Genny's school years brought tears to her eyes. She'd been on the receiving end of exclusion back then and it was happening again. Except this time it was her daughter who was excluding her. Genny poured the detergent into the washer and closed the lid. When she turned to leave the laundry room, Katie ran up with the phone in her hand.

"You got a message, Mama." Katie handed the phone to Genny.

"Thank you, baby girl."

"Uh-huh." Katie's eyes brightened and she ran back into the living room.

Genny followed Katie and sat on the couch. A Facebook message bubble was at the bottom of the phone screen, and she tapped it. "Zoe Daniels?" she muttered to herself. She didn't know anyone with the last name, Daniels. But… This person couldn't be her Zoe, could she? Her brother's daughter. Zoe would be fourteen now, but Daniels? She brought the phone closer to her face. The profile photo was of a popular boy band. She tapped on the message and breathed out.

Hi. My name is Zoe Daniels. My last name was Jones until my mum got married and my stepdad adopted me when I was 11.

Genny gasped and her phone slipped out of her hand, bouncing off her leg and landing on the floor with a thud. She grabbed it and turned it over, relieved that the screen didn't crack.

"You okay?" Paul asked, banging pots around as he washed the dishes.

Genny stared at the message. Legally Sarah could sign papers for her husband to adopt Zoe since Brandon wasn't alive to contest it. Genny's heart felt heavy.

I've been thinking about my real dad. I know he has a sister named Genny. Are you her? If you are here, please write me back. It may take me a while to write to you. My mum doesn't know I have Facebook. She will make me delete it if she finds it. But I can use my best friend's phone if she does.

Genny's hands began trembling. "Zoe messaged me."

"What?" Paul turned off the water and joined Genny on the couch. "Are you sure?"

"Who's Zoe?" Katie walked up and tried to look at Genny's phone screen.

Paul looked at Genny, then told Katie to play in her room. She poked out her bottom lip but did as her daddy told her.

"Look." She handed the phone to Paul.

His eyes widened as he read. He looked at her. "No way."

"That's what I thought. How should I respond?"

"Babe, I don't know. Maybe…"

Genny tightened her jaws. "Maybe what? I figured she'd forget about me over the years. This is a miracle." Tears burned Genny's eyes and she lowered her head, covering her face with her hands.

"Come here, baby." Paul wrapped his arms around her and held her for a while. "I think we need to pray about it. What if Sarah deletes her account and tells the friend's mom not to let her use her friend's phone? Then what?"

"I don't know." Tears spilled down her cheeks.

"Da-dee!" Caleb called out.

Paul went to the dining room and got Caleb from the highchair and sat him on the play mat among his toys.

"Maybe we should wait and see what happens," Paul said.

"What do you mean?"

"If Sarah finds the account, will she drop off the face of the earth again? I don't want to see you hurt, babe."

"What do we tell Katie?"

"Nothing right now."

What would Zoe think if Genny didn't respond? She planned to write Zoe back, if for no other reason than to let her know she was her aunt. She prayed Zoe would get the message before her mother found her Facebook account. If Sarah wouldn't allow her and Zoe to communicate, Genny would lose her niece and the only part of Brandon she had left.

Paul went back to the kitchen and Genny felt like spending some time outside. After getting her journal, she made her way to the picnic table and thumbed through it until she found a blank page.

June 1, 2017

Zoe messaged me. I never thought I'd hear from her. I haven't seen her since she was little. Sarah's husband adopted Zoe. At first I was mad, but I guess I can't blame Sarah. Paul doesn't think it's a good idea to respond to Zoe, but I don't think I agree.

Genny pulled out her phone and read Zoe's message again. Breathing deep, she tapped to reply.

It's me, Zoe. I'm your Aunt Genny. I am so happy you messaged me. I want you to know I had no idea where you were or I would have contacted you.

The backdoor closed, and Genny looked over her shoulder and saw Paul walking towards her. Tapping the send button, Genny closed her journal and slipped her phone into her back pocket. If Zoe responded, she'd write again. For now, Genny tucked Zoe deep inside her heart.

CHAPTER 29

Paul

Paul pulled up in front of a small ranch house that reminded him of his own home. Clyde's house was at least ten years newer and the brick was painted an off-white color. With the shutters and front door painted red, and the immaculate landscaping, the Martin's house was one of the nicest in the neighborhood. Shifting into park, Paul shut off the engine and reached for the door handle, but stopped when his phone chimed.

Karla: Hey, I was wondering if we can grab a coffee or something. I've been thinking about what you said about God. Just let me know.

Karla was opening up to the possibility of having God in her life. She'd been texting him more frequently lately—a good sign. He tapped to reply, but decided it could wait.

The sound of the doorbell reminded Paul of his grandmother's house. He hadn't heard the sound in years. Nostalgia was threatening tears when the door opened.

"Hello, Paul." Celia pulled the door back and Paul walked into a cozy living room that also reminded him of his grandmother. The furniture and decorations were different, but the placement was the same and he was sure that the Martin's fireplace was the exact fireplace in his grandparents' home.

"You'll have to excuse me, Paul. I'm on my way to meet the ladies at Hobby Lobby."

"Sure, Mrs. Martin."

"Call me Celia."

"Celia." Paul couldn't help but smile at the woman. She was the epitome of grace.

"Hello, Paul," Clyde said when he walked into the living room.

"Hello, sir."

"Clyde. Call me Clyde." A smile spread across Clyde's face.

"Your home reminds me of my grandparents' home down to the doorbell and fireplace." Paul sat on the couch, and Clyde sat in a chair across from him. "And Miss Celia reminds me of my grandmother."

"The good Lord blessed me with a sweet, godly woman. Much like yourself."

"Oh, yes. I'd be lost without Genny." Paul smiled. His phone vibrated in his pocket. Ignoring it for a few seconds, he pulled it out when Clyde checked his own phone before laying it on the side table. Taking a quick glance, he saw it was another text from Karla.

I'd really like to meet today if that works for you.

"Can I open with a prayer?" Clyde asked.

"Of course."

The older gentleman prayed for their meeting and the future of the support group. When Clyde raised his head after he said amen, he looked at Paul. "Oh, goodness. I forgot about the coffee. Be right back." Clyde stood and made his way to the kitchen.

Paul sent Karla a quick text.

Paul: I'm visiting with a friend. Can I get with you later today?

Karla: Sure

Paul pocketed his phone when Clyde came into the living room carrying a tray with two full coffee cups and a container each of cream and sugar. The men spent a few moments preparing their coffee before they settled in.

"I think we should get to know each other a little better before we hit this thing head on. You go first." Clyde chuckled when Paul's eyes widened. "I'll go first." Clyde took a sip of his coffee and leaned back, crossing his ankle over his knee. "I remember the day you and your wife came to church with the Parkers. You two have grown over the years. I've noticed maturity in you in the men's group. And from what Celia has said, Genny is quite the young woman."

"I think so." Paul sipped his coffee.

"I joined the Army when I was eighteen. Spent my enlistment as a military policeman at Ft. Hood. Came back here to Charleston and married Celia. I took a few odd jobs here and there, but felt the calling to go back into law enforcement. I was on the force for close to fifteen years when I was shot. It was a domestic call." Clyde picked up his coffee cup and took a sip, then stared into the cup. "I was shot in the leg and near about bled to death. My partner was shot in the head. He didn't make it."

It was the most Paul had heard Clyde say since he'd first met the man. "I'm sorry. That must have been tough."

Clyde slowly nodded. "Survivor's guilt is real."

Paul thought about the one fatality in the incident that took his leg. From what he was told, a pallet fell on that man as well. Why did the person die and not Paul? Like Chaplain Zhang had said, God wasn't finished with Paul.

"Do you see what's happened here?" Clyde slid to the edge of the chair and leaned forward with his hands clasped between his knees. "Now that we have trauma and amputation in common, we've opened up to each other. This is why Ryan and I feel this group is so important."

"I attend an amputee group at the VA. There's something about being around people who deal with the same thing you're dealing with. Not just losing a limb, but all of us were discharged because of what happened to us. It was out of our control, you know?"

"I do. Devastating injuries happen to people every day, but like you said, it's tough when the injury ends your career. Especially those of us who have a heart for helping people in crisis. It could be a house fire, a domestic violence situation, or to liberate people in a foreign land."

Clyde was quiet for a long moment. He reminded Paul of the character John Coffey in *The Green Mile*. Clyde wasn't just tall; he was a big man. Clyde was as tall as Paul, and Celia was barely five feet. He and Celia were on opposite ends of a yardstick, as his grandmother would say.

The men spent the afternoon making plans for the group and discussed ways of getting the word out. Paul's only social outlet was the VA group, and he didn't feel right inviting anyone from that group to the support group. Clyde was right about the commonality of people who help those in crisis, but there was something different about the VA group.

On the way home, Paul's thoughts went to Gabe. He had attended the group a couple of times since his son was born, but it had been several weeks since he'd talked to him. Gabe had voiced his views that he didn't belong in the group since he wasn't injured in combat. Maybe the new group would be a better fit.

Paul walked into the house, and both kids ran up to him. Katie flung her arms around his waist and Caleb grabbed his left leg. Pulling back, Caleb poked Paul's prosthetic.

"Weg," Caleb said. The word was muffled by his pacifier.

"That's Daddy's pretend leg, Bubby." Katie released Paul's waist and poked at his prosthetic. "See."

"Okay, kids." Paul laughed and shook his head. When he sat on the couch, both kids piled onto his lap.

Genny came into the living room with her hair wrapped in a towel. She leaned down to kiss him and laughed when the towel fell off her head and landed on the kids.

"How'd it go with Mr. Clyde?"

"It went really well. We've got a game plan. Our first group is scheduled for early next month. We've got four weeks, which should be enough time."

"That's good, babe."

Paul's phone rang and he saw their real estate agent's name on the screen. He answered and looked at Genny, mouthing to her who was calling. She stood back and crossed her arms over her chest, hugging herself.

"Congratulations, you're a homeowner," Brad said, excitement coloring his tone.

"What? That was fast." Paul looked at Genny. "We got the house!"

Genny held her hands over her mouth and squealed.

"What is it, Daddy?"

Genny grabbed Katie's hand, pulling her off the couch. "We got the house!" Genny said when she picked Katie up.

Katie grinned. "I want a pink bedroom, Mama," she whispered.

"They want a thirty-day closing," Brad said.

"Wow. That doesn't leave much time for the VA appraiser."

"I have my connections."

At dinner, the family talked about their new house. Paul and Genny discussed necessities like appliances and fixtures, while Katie chatted about a pink bedroom and the backyard. Caleb sat in his highchair, looking back and forth between Katie and his parents. Once the kids were in bed, Paul and Genny sat on the couch watching HGTV.

"I wonder if we'll be in the house thirty years from now," Paul said.

"Probably. It'll take that long to finish the remodel." Genny laughed.

Paul pulled her onto his lap and kissed her. It didn't matter where they would be in thirty years, as long as she was by his side.

The next month was filled with pre-closing repairs, inspections, and appraisals. Not to mention getting the rental house ready to vacate. They'd gotten estimates for movers and priced a new living room set and fridge. Paul and Genny sat with Brad, waiting for the mortgage company's representative and notary so they could sign away the next thirty years of their life.

The mortgage company representative came into the room carrying a stack of papers. Paul rubbed his hands on his jeans and picked up a pen. A half hour later, they were presented with the keys to the house and had their picture taken with the representative and Brad.

"Now comes the fun part," Paul said as they walked to the car. They had two weeks left at the rental house, which meant they couldn't waste a day.

They talked about where the furniture would go in each room and what remodeling project they would tackle first. Paul's phone rang and Genny picked it from the center console.

"It's Karla."

"Oh, let it go to voicemail."

"She calls you?"

"No."

"Why would she be calling now?" Genny turned her head to the passenger window.

"Not sure." They'd always texted. Maybe it was an emergency. Paul cleared his thoughts. She'd call again if it was an emergency.

Paul hadn't been able to attend the VA group like he normally had because of everything with the new house. In the past month, he'd made it to four group meetings and he had to cut out immediately after each one for one house-related reason or another.

Karla had been mostly quiet in the group. Most group meetings, they'd have a few minutes before the session to talk, but it was never anything of substance. She'd texted again about coffee a few days ago, but he'd told her he couldn't with a promise to have coffee once they were in the new house. He'd call Karla later in the day to check on her.

Genny drew in a deep breath and blew it out. He could imagine what was going on in her head. She'd made a comment or two about the increase in Karla's texts. How could he get her to understand the importance of obeying God in this situation? Paul strongly felt that God had called him to care for and minister to one of His children. Someone that suffered from deep emotional damage. That person was Karla. He was sure of it.

After group therapy, Paul chatted with Nate and headed out. Every once in a while, he liked to stop by a store on the way home to pick up a few surprises for his family. Would today be a good treat or something they could treasure for a while?

Walking up to the truck, he spotted Karla sitting on a bench in the break area. Concerned about her mood lately, he walked over to check on her. Tipping her head back, she blew a puff of smoke that stretched over her head. She glanced in his direction and smiled.

"What are you up to? I figured you'd be on your way home to your family by now." She snuffed the cigarette and tossed it into the ash bin.

Was that a jab? "Thought I'd say hello since I didn't get a chance before the group."

"Yeah, I was running a little behind. Danny let me talk to Sophia and I couldn't pass that up."

"I don't blame you." Paul stood for a moment, then joined Karla on the bench.

"Sorry, I've been quiet lately. The stress has been getting to me. Danny hasn't been letting me see Sophia like he promised."

"Don't you have an agreement?"

"Not officially. We're still married. He was good about it in the beginning, but here lately…"

"I'm sorry. I can't imagine how you feel."

"I've been trying to pray, but it's not working. I must be doing it wrong." She pushed out a laugh.

"There's no wrong or right way to pray. There are times I can't find the right words, but God knows."

Karla's groan was soft, but Paul heard it.

"If Danny wants a divorce, fine. But not being able to see Sophia is something I can't handle."

"Have you talked to a lawyer?"

"My parents said they'd help. I wanted to do this on my own, but I guess I need to take them up on their offer. I can't believe it's come to this, you know?"

"Yeah, I get it."

"Settled in the house?"

"Mostly."

"I've really missed our talks."

Paul thought of Karla's many texts over the past month. Part of him felt she was reaching out because she was struggling, and the other part thought she was becoming dependent on him and not learning to stand on her own.

"Yeah. The new house has taken more time than we thought it would. We are first time homeowners, so we were relying on our real estate agent to hold our hands. It's taken some adjustment for the kids, too."

"I bet."

They were quiet for a few seconds. "Do you have a Bible?" Paul asked.

"Used to. I don't know what happened to it. Maybe it was lost in a move or something."

"I'll get you one."

"You don't have to."

"No, it's no problem."

"Well, okay."

"In the meantime, you can use an app on your phone. I'm old school and like it in print." Paul smiled.

"I will." Karla glanced off into the distance. "I've been thinking a lot about what all's happened to me. It's not just military related." She let out a slow breath. "I was assaulted by a guy I was dating in high school."

"I'm so sorry, Karla."

"It was a 'he said, she said' situation." Karla shook her head. "My therapist said that along with my military trauma, has caused complex trauma. Lucky me. Why did all this happen to me? I think I'm a good person."

"Being good or bad has nothing to do with what happens to us. Trials lead to a closer relationship with God."

"Hmm. I must not be a Christian then. I mean, I believe there's a God. It's just…I have a hard time understanding why this has happened." Karla pushed her hair behind her shoulders and held her arms out. "What man is going to want me?"

"Karla, life isn't about having a romantic relationship. It's about drawing closer to God and spending eternity with Him."

Karla looked down and rubbed her fingers over the prosthetic hand.

"Some people never have a relationship and that's okay. I'm not saying you're one of these people. God brings people into our lives at the right time. It might be a mentor, friend, or a love."

"Genny's lucky."

"What do you mean?"

"She grabbed you before anyone else had a chance." A brief smile passed over her lips.

"It was all God. But if His plan was for me to be single, I was okay with that."

Paul had to help her understand that if it was God's will to bring someone into her life, it would be at His timing, not hers. But first, she needed to fully rely on God to get her life straight.

CHAPTER 30

Genny

It took Paul less than two days after they'd moved into the house to set up the office. Genny shook her head. Here she was, struggling to get all the kitchen boxes emptied. She laid the mail on Paul's desk and headed to the kitchen to unpack the last two boxes.

In the kitchen, Genny was leaning into a box, reaching for a spatula on the bottom, when her phone rang. Sighing, she stood and grabbed it from the kitchen counter. Tina's name showed on the screen. Why would Tina be calling? They couldn't take a child. She was sure that the state wouldn't approve them with Paul's disability.

"Hey, Tina."

"Hello, how are you guys doing?"

"We're good."

"Great. Well…I'm calling to see if you two would consider fostering."

"You don't beat around the bush." Genny laughed.

"No, I guess not." Tina laughed as well.

"Tina, I wish we could—"

"If it is still something you two would like to do, a physical disability won't necessarily prevent Paul from being a foster parent. As long as he is medically cleared."

"What about mental health issues?" The question came out before Genny could consider the implications. "Paul has been diagnosed with PTSD."

"If he is cleared by his psychiatrist."

"Really?"

"Uh-huh."

"I don't know. We bought a house and are still settling in."

Tina was quiet for a few moments. "We've got a special little girl and I thought of you."

"Yeah?" Genny walked into the living room and sat on the couch. Tina was gently pushing, something she was good at.

"She's three and recently lost her family in a car accident. Her parents, brother, aunt, and maternal grandparents."

"Oh, my goodness." Genny's chest tightened.

"I thought of your history. But I have to let you know that she's mute."

"Mute?"

"The psychiatrist says it's because of the trauma from the accident."

"That's so sad." Genny paused. Did they want to take on a child so traumatized she couldn't speak? If Paul would agree, that is.

"Genny, this will probably be a permanent placement."

"Adoption?" How could no one want to care for a child? What kind of people were this child's family?

"Kendall was living with her paternal grandmother, but she's in poor health. She has an aunt but she travels abroad for work and isn't prepared to care for a child. If nothing else, it can be a temporary placement until we find a family for permanent placement."

"I need to talk to Paul and, to be honest, I'm not sure what he will say."

"I understand. Let me know as soon as possible. Her grandmother is bringing her back at the end of the week."

Bringing her back? Like a return at the grocery store?

A connection with Kendall took shape. How was it possible when Genny hadn't met the child? An urgency overtook her. If not their home, where would she go? "I'll talk to Paul tonight."

Ending the call, Genny went to the kitchen to finish unpacking. Paul's coffee cup was sitting by the sink, and when she picked it up, she focused on the verse hand-painted on the cup. Matthew, chapter nineteen verse twenty-six, had spoken to her many times over the years, but it had never seemed more fitting than now. "'With man this is impossible, but with God all things are possible,'" she said and read the verse again.

Was God telling her something about the little girl? Genny washed and dried the mug and placed it in the cabinet. She wanted to spend some time outside. Being out in nature helped her see things through a different lens.

"Let's go outside," Genny shouted down the hall. She heard Katie cheer and did a double take when she ran into the living room wearing her Easter dress. Caleb came in behind her wearing the black jacket from his Easter suit.

"We was having a tea party." Katie grinned.

"I see that." Genny slipped off Caleb's jacket, but Katie ran out the back door before Genny could get to her.

Pick your battles, Genny.

As Genny approached the picnic table, for the first time, she noticed it was weathering. The wood had turned a grayish color and a few of the boards had small cracks. Climbing on top, she lightly brushed her hand across the wood and smiled. The table meant a lot to her. Paul had bought it for her at one of her lowest points and it had given both of them comfort over the years.

"Mama." Caleb reached for the tabletop and Genny pulled him up and sat him on her lap.

Caleb pointed at Katie and Lucy, giggling as they chased each other around the yard. Katie was finally at a point where she was comfortable with Paul being out of her sight. Did she want to risk Katie's progress by bringing an emotionally injured child into their home? Kendall would take a lot of her and Paul's attention.

The back door closed, and Caleb grinned at Paul when he climbed on top of the picnic table.

"Daddy!" Katie ran towards them, Lucy bounding along with her.

Paul pulled Katie onto his lap when she climbed onto the table. Lucy found an old ball and carried it to Paul, so he threw it toward the fence and she shot off to fetch it.

"Tina called today," Genny said.

"Really? That's random."

Katie slipped off Paul's lap and climbed down from the picnic table. Pulling the ball from Lucy's jaws, Katie ran around the yard laughing while Lucy chased her.

"Kind of. I saw her when I took Katie for her first therapy appointment. She was surprised since she thought we'd moved to Jersey. They need foster parents—"

"Gen."

"We just need to update our certification."

"Things have changed. There's no way the state will let me foster with my disabilities."

"Tina said it didn't matter as long as you are medically cleared by your doctor and psychiatrist. Anyway, there's a little girl—"

"Genevieve."

"You won't even consider it? You could see your doctor." Genny bit the inside of her cheek when Paul looked at her, a scowl forming on his face. He was quiet for a bit.

He looked in Katie's direction and said, "Do you think it's worth it? Katie could have a setback. We don't know how a foster child will affect her. And I'm sure the little girl has problems herself."

"Tina said that she's got some issues. She was in a fatal car accident. She lost her parents, brother, aunt, and grandparents."

Paul's shoulders slowly fell. He was quiet for a while and she knew it wasn't because of frustration this time.

"She's mute."

"Mute?" His gaze shifted to her. "As in no communication?"

"Tina said it's because of the trauma."

Paul released a slow breath and watched the kids. Katie ran after Lucy and Caleb was trying his best to keep up, but his chubby legs wouldn't cooperate.

"It's a potential foster to adopt placement."

Paul shook his head. "If, and that's a big if. If we were to consider this, I may get denied. And where are we supposed to put this girl?"

The office.

Genny looked down and shook her head, hoping Paul didn't see her. "Ok, I'll call Tina."

"I'm sorry, babe."

"No, you're right. I don't know what I was thinking." Tears filled Genny's eyes and she hopped down from the table.

Katie ran up to them, panting. "Can we have KFC?"

"Sure, baby girl," Paul said, and looked at his watch. "It's only four, but what the hay?"

"Yay!" Katie grabbed Paul's hand and tugged until he got off the picnic table.

Katie tore away, heading to the back door, her yellow Easter dress swishing around her legs as she ran. Sighing, Genny wrangled Caleb and Lucy inside. While she was gathering glasses and paper plates for the chicken, Genny wondered what life would be like this time next year. Would the little girl be in their home and one day, would she be their daughter?

Flopping down on the couch, Genny sighed and savored the time she had to herself while Paul took the kids to grab dinner. Leaning her head back, she closed her eyes for a moment. When she opened her eyes, her focus fell to a Bible in the center of the coffee table. Sitting up, she opened the cover. The presentation was filled out the usual way with the current date. Paul had written a note at the bottom of the page.

Karla,
Keep your eyes on God and everything will fall into place.
Blessings,
Paul

Genny closed the cover and stared at the Bible for a moment. The pit of her stomach bubbled with heat. Paul was a thoughtful person, especially when he was ministering to someone. It wasn't uncommon for him to buy the person a Bible.

Genny pulled back her hair into a ponytail. Paul's phone rang and she glanced around and spotted it on the dining table. He had a habit of forgetting his phone and it was one of Genny's pet peeves. What if something happened and she needed to get in contact with him? Or he with her?

Genny walked over to see who was calling. Karla's name showed on the screen and she let it go to voicemail. Less than half a minute later, the voicemail notification dinged. Tapping on the voicemail app, Genny's muscles tightened as she listened to Karla's voice.

"Hey, just wondering if everything is okay. You left the group in a hurry. Talk to you soon."

"He came home to his family," Genny yelled into the phone as if she was talking to Karla.

Why was this getting under Genny's skin? She placed the phone where she found it and walked into the kitchen. Lucy's collar jangled when she walked up beside Genny.

"Comprehension problems from the TBI. Can that be it?" Genny asked Lucy when she leaned down and took the dog's face in her hands. "That's kind of silly, huh? Is it possible that Daddy is all mixed up about Karla? What if she's not the person God is leading him to?" Did he see he was taking away from their family? Taking time from her?

In the living room, Genny sat on the couch and Lucy hopped up next to her. Kendall filled her thoughts. What if *she* was the one God was sending to Paul? The person didn't have to be an adult. Could God have sent both Kendall and Karla? It had been a while since Genny had written in her journal. Anytime she felt she and Paul weren't on the same page, she'd journal to work out her thoughts. Retrieving her journal from the bedroom, she glanced out the back window before settling on the couch and opening her heart.

June 19, 2017

Tina called today about a placement for a little girl. Paul thinks a placement will make adjusting to our new life difficult. At least right now. Is this a true concern or his fear? I get that adding a new person to our family could complicate that. What about Karla? He has no issues pouring himself into ministering to her. Why not Kendall? She's a CHILD. Karla can find someone else.

Genny closed her journal and tossed it and the pen onto the coffee table. Was Karla capable of finding someone else? Paul hadn't talked much about her struggles, but Genny admitted God had blessed Paul with the heart for and knowledge of ministering. He'd ministered to her, after all. Genny heard a car door shut and Katie's voice sounded from the front door. Genny sighed, grabbed her journal and pen, and headed to the bedroom to put them away. She'd keep her concerns tucked in her heart for now.

CHAPTER 31

Paul

Clouds formed overhead, giving a reprieve to the heat. The smell of rain was soon followed by a few sprinkles, then a steady drizzle. The kind of rain that tickled and brought out a smile. Paul closed his eyes and turned his face towards the sky. The corners of his mouth curved and he inhaled deeply.

Jingling opened Paul's eyes. He watched Lucy hop up on the picnic table and sit next to him. Licking his chin, she settled and seemed to watch the rain, surprising Paul. Usually, she'd run for the door at the first sign of rain. His phone dinged with a text and he picked it up. Pastor Ryan had sent out an emergency prayer request. A drunk driver had hit a family of four head-on and there were no survivors.

Paul thought about Genny's parents. They were killed by a drunk driver on their way home from celebrating their anniversary. Sorrow surrounded him. The amount of damage the loss had caused Genny over the years broke his heart. If it wasn't for God, who knew where she'd be now.

Paul's thoughts went back to the conversation he'd had with Genny a few days earlier. The little girl had recently lost her family in a car accident. Genny had said nothing since then, but he knew the little girl had been occupying her thoughts. Genny's heart went out to anyone who'd suffered the loss of their family as she had. She wasn't much older than Kendall when she lost her parents.

What kind of future would Kendall have? Genny's grandparents were there to step in. Who did Kendall have? Her grandmother couldn't care for her and her aunt couldn't take custody. She had no one. Paul drew in a deep breath and breathed out slowly. How would a hurting foster child—potentially a permanent placement—fit into their lives? Paul turned around and looked at the back of the house. Now wasn't the time. They were getting used to their new normal. If he was approved, maybe they'd get back on the list one day. Paul looked at his watch and hopped off the picnic table, heading inside.

"Hey, baby," he said when he walked up to Genny as she was washing dishes and slipped his arms around her waist. "Do you mind if I take Karla to coffee after the group? Her divorce is final and she's a little emotional." To erase the emotional tension between them, Paul felt it was important that Genny was onboard with him, spending time with Karla outside of group therapy.

"Does she have any friends here?"

"No. She's from Texas and that's where her family is."

"How did she end up in Charleston? I mean, her ex lives in Charlotte, right? Why isn't she there with her daughter?"

Paul sensed the irritation in Genny's voice. "The burn center at MUSC."

"Oh." Genny dried her hands and turned around to face Paul. "I think Caleb is getting another ear infection."

"I was afraid of that. He's been tugging his ears for the past few days. Okay, love. I'll get home right after. Oh, unless you want me to stay home."

"No, it's okay. I'm going to make an appointment for tomorrow."

"Sounds good."

Paul headed to the truck and made his way to the VA. He pulled into the parking lot and went inside. Karla's face brightened when she saw him. Beth was sitting between Karla and the last empty chair. Disappointment filled her face when she realized Paul would have to sit on Beth's other side.

Karla leaned forward and said, "We can try out that new sandwich shop."

"Oh, Caleb has another ear infection and he's cranky. I'm going to head home after the group. I think it's time the little guy got tubes."

"I hope he feels better soon. Hopefully, it doesn't come to tubes."

"Welcome everyone," Steve said.

Karla sighed and leaned back. Beth glanced at Paul for a moment before looking at Steve.

"Ya hear from that young man? The Hispanic one?" The rattling in Craig's chest sounded like he had pneumonia.

"Oh, Gabe," Steve said. "He has a lot going on, so he's decided not to continue with the group."

"Aw, too bad. He was a nice kid." Craig wiped his mouth with a handkerchief.

"You need to go to urgent care, Craig?" Nate joked.

"Nah. Quit smokin' last week 'n' this here is the result."

"Good for you, Craig," Paul said.

Karla was quiet during the group. Paul was surprised that Craig didn't make a comment. But then again, he was busy coughing mostly. At the end of the group, Karla slipped out before Paul could catch her. He could go after her, but let it go. He'd send her a text later.

Paul pulled into the driveway and before he got to the front door, he could hear Caleb crying. Genny was standing in the living room bouncing him in her arms. Paul took him from her and rubbed his back as he eased down on the couch.

"He feels a little warm."

"I gave him Tylenol about fifteen minutes ago."

"Okay." Paul kissed the side of Caleb's head. "Aw, little man. You'll feel better soon." Paul caught sight of Katie and laughed. She wore a pair of his old headphones on her head, the earpieces twice as big as her ears.

"She found them in the cabinet under the TV."

"Smart girl. Why don't you take a break, babe? I'll lay him down once the Tylenol works."

"Okay. Oh, his appointment is at ten in the morning."

"I'll go with you." Paul went to Caleb's room to rock him until he settled down. His phone rang and heard Genny sigh. She appeared in the doorway to Caleb's room a few moments later.

"It's Karla." The dim light in Caleb's room didn't hide the red creeping up her neck.

"Let it go to voicemail."

Genny disappeared down the hall. Paul heard her say something to Katie, but he couldn't understand what she said. Katie tiptoed into the room with Paul's phone in her hand.

"Mama said check your text messages." Katie held out the phone.

Paul took the phone from Katie and she left the room. Tapping on the message, Paul's heart sank when he read the words.

Karla: Danny wants my engagement ring back. He said it wasn't like I could wear it.

Caleb fell asleep and Paul eased up from the rocking chair and laid him in his crib. Genny was sitting on the couch when he walked into the living room. As he got closer, he saw that her neck and face were still flushed. Lowering himself to the couch, he rested his hand on her leg.

"Why is she always contacting you? Is something going on?"

"What?" Paul's nostrils flared.

He looked at Katie. She was oblivious to what was said since she was wearing the headphones again, but he didn't know where the conversation was going. Genny had the same thought. She stood and reached over the coffee table and tapped Katie on the shoulder and she pulled one earpiece away from her ear.

"Why don't you go see if we have a ripe tomato?"

Katie grinned and pulled off the headphones, darting out the back door.

"Do you have feelings for her?"

"*No!* I don't think of her in that way. We've been through the same thing. She has PTSD, too. And she's searching, babe. I honestly feel that God has put her in my life to lead her to Christ."

"Well, I think she has feelings for you. I read your messages. She's definitely emotionally attached to you."

"You are searching for something that's not there."

Genny stood, wrapping her arms around herself. She walked to the back door and sighed. Turning towards him, her gaze fell to his phone on the coffee table.

"You know what I want to do? I want to take that thing to the driveway and run over it a hundred times."

"Genny."

"Paul, what is important to you?"

"What do you mean?"

She shook her head and went out the back door. Paul jerked his head back. Had his wife accused him of having an emotional affair? What had he done that led her to that conclusion? His and Karla's texts had been anything but inappropriate, and neither had their interactions. He grabbed the baby monitor and headed outside.

Paul passed Katie on his way to the picnic table and shook his head. She had a basket full of half-red tomatoes. As soon as Paul sat next to Genny, she spoke.

"I may not have lost a part of my body, but I know what it's like to experience trauma."

"I know you do."

"I feel that you've forgotten what I went through. My scars might not be visible like yours and Karla's, but they are there."

"Genevieve, I'll never forget being called into my superintendent's office and seeing the commander sitting in a chair. I knew something had happened to you." He rested his hand on top of hers. "And listening to Dad as he told me what that monster did to you and seeing your face…" Paul drew in a sharp breath. "Do you know what I do every night for you?"

She looked over at him and shook her head.

"On my nightly rounds, I check each door and each window twice. I also test your pepper spray every so often to make sure it still works."

"You do?"

Paul nodded and slipped his fingers between Genny's. "I want you to feel safe."

"Why you and why her?"

"I don't know. I feel God wants me to help someone who has been through unimaginable pain. I don't know why, but I honestly believe it's her. I hope you trust me."

"I do. I guess I'm going back to my insecure stage from years ago."

"No need. You have my heart."

Genny rested her head on his shoulder.

Paul was sure the enemy was trying to wreck his attempts to reach Karla and he was using Genny in the process. Genny took Katie inside and Paul found himself alone on the picnic table. A faceless little girl appeared in front of him. What were God's plans for her? If the state denied his certification, why had God laid her on his heart?

When Paul pulled into the church parking lot, he was surprised to see Clyde's car. He walked into the fellowship hall and he saw Clyde standing in the middle of the circle of chairs. He lifted his chin when he saw Paul. He had evenly spaced the chairs and aligned the backs. Paul wondered if he had used a ruler and laughed to himself.

The men helped themselves to coffee as they waited for the group to start in half an hour. Clyde took a sip of his coffee and lifted his chin. "Something on your mind?"

Paul looked at the older man. Was it that obvious? "Things have been a little strained at home."

"Yeah? If you feel comfortable talking, I'm here to listen." Clyde smiled at Paul.

Paul talked about meeting Karla, and how he felt led to minister to her. Genny's reservations became the focus of the conversation.

"She read the text between me and Karla. She sees something I don't."

"Is that so?"

"She thinks Karla is emotionally attached to me."

"Is she?"

Paul leaned back against the chair. He thought about the times they'd met for coffee or lunch. Karla had mentioned several times that she was happy that they were friends. And there was the time she laid her hand on top of his. Though he felt it was harmless, it still made him uncomfortable.

"No. I don't think so." Paul looked down into his cup of coffee.

"Maybe you were meant to minister to her for a season and now it's someone else's turn."

"I didn't think of it that way." Paul had been putting pressure on himself to reach Karla. He'd planted the seed. Perhaps it was up to someone else to nurture that seed.

"It's clear that you have a heart for the Lord and ministering is one of your gifts. But God doesn't want you to sacrifice your family to witness to someone. Like I said, God will put someone else in her life."

"You're right." Paul sighed. The door opened and he saw Gabe and another man walk in. He smiled at Paul and walked over.

"Gabe. You got my message. How's the baby?"

"Growing too fast."

"I hear you."

Paul introduced Gabe and Clyde. The other man walked over to the coffee bar, and Paul joined him for a second cup.

"I'm Paul, one of the co-leaders of the group. Clyde's the other co-leader." Paul pointed to Clyde.

"I'm Chuck. Nice to meet you."

The men sat in the circle, well-spaced apart. Clyde waited until ten past seven before he opened with a prayer for those interested. Paul and Clyde shared their stories first, and Gabe shared his story. Paul saw the familiar expression that told him Gabe still felt the same way about his injury as before.

"I was a firefighter," Chuck said. "The truck was out getting a wash down. Our firehouse was on a slight incline and we always chock the tires. I was walking down the incline to my car and I heard the crew yelling. Before I knew what was happening, the truck rolled and clipped me and I went down. Ends up, someone forgot to chock the tires. Now I got this."

Chuck raised his left arm to his lower chest. "This is as high as I can raise it. No more fighting fires. I'm a manager at Target. It pays the bills and I've worked my way up. It's not what I dreamed of doing."

Gabe looked up at Chuck. Paul could imagine what was going on in his head. Chuck's story was similar. He was off work and heading home.

As Paul drove home, he thought about his conversation with Clyde. Maybe Clyde was right. God had planned to use him to reach Karla for a season and that season was ending. Would God bring another person into his life to minister to? Paul believed so and he wondered if that person was a three-year-old girl named Kendall.

CHAPTER 32

Genny

The process for foster parent certification went quickly. With Paul actively attending therapy, his psychiatrist had recommended certification a few days after his last appointment, and his primary care physician had signed off less than a week later. After a home study, they were approved and were preparing for Kendall's placement in their home. A permanent placement was up in the air. Paul had agreed to temporary placement to see how well Kendall adjusted.

The bedsheet floated to the mattress, reminding Genny of her childhood. Anytime her granny would put fresh sheets on the bed, Genny would lie on the mattress, and watch the sheet as it floated down on top of her. She tucked the bottom under the mattress and flung the comforter over the top. Katie had picked out a cream-colored comforter with pastel flowers. Genny straightened the pillows and sat on the side of the bed.

Caleb walked into the room with Mr. Floppy, Katie's stuffed rabbit, in his hand. She'd have to be sneaky to get the rabbit away from him. Katie had been told several times to keep Mr. Floppy in a place her brother couldn't reach the rabbit. Caleb squealed and narrowed his eyes at Genny when she tugged on Mr. Floppy's leg. Holding in a giggle, Genny and Caleb came to an agreement. Caleb would give up Mr. Floppy for an apple. A pretty good trade off, she thought.

"Mama?" Katie said when she walked into the dining room where Caleb was in his highchair eating bits of apple.

"Yes?"

"Is the little girl going to be like Caleb?" She spotted Mr. Floppy at the end of the dining table. "Why's he there?" She snatched the rabbit off the table and glared at Caleb.

"Make sure you keep him put up and Bubby won't be tempted."

Katie tucked the rabbit under her arm and snuck a piece of her brother's apple, popping it in her mouth.

"What were you asking about Kendall?"

"Will she be my sister?"

The average child wouldn't think to ask the questions that Katie had been asking about Kendall. As an inquisitive child, their answers satisfied her until the next question popped into her head—usually a few minutes later. But it wasn't the right time to tell Katie about Kendall's family. Besides, there was no guarantee that Kendall would be a permanent placement. They did, however, tell her that Kendall was mute. That brought up all kinds of questions.

"Come here," Genny led Katie to the couch.

"We don't know what God has planned for Kendall."

Katie nodded and rubbed Mr. Floppy's faded black nose. She glanced at Caleb as he ate the last piece of apple.

"Mmm." Caleb grinned and pumped his hands in the air, wiggling.

Genny got Caleb out of the highchair and sat on the couch next to Katie. Wrapping her arms around her children, she closed her eyes and thanked God for answering her prayers to be a mother. Joy filled her soul, bringing a smile to her face.

"Is Daddy gonna bring pizza home?"

"No, I've got lasagna in the oven."

Katie gasped. "Yah!"

Genny noticed the time and the smile disappeared. Maybe Paul stopped by the store. He'd usually call to see if they needed anything. Her mind went to a place she'd been trying to keep it away from. If he stayed after the group to talk to Karla, he would have texted or called. Genny stopped the thought before it could bring her mood down.

"Daddy!" Katie hopped off the couch and ran to the living room windows.

Genny looked out front and saw Paul driving towards the house. Where had he been? Katie ran to the front door and waited for Genny to give her permission to unlock the door. When Genny nodded, Katie turned the lock and swung open the door. She met Paul on the sidewalk and grabbed something large from his hand.

"Mama! Look what Daddy got me." Katie came into the house lugging a bag of popcorn that was as big as her.

"That's for all of us, baby girl," Paul said as he walked through the door. "The kettle corn truck was at the intersection again and I couldn't resist. I forgot to call." Paul walked up to Genny. "Hey, beautiful." Smiling, he tilted his head and kissed her. Warmth flowed through Genny's chest.

Katie sat on the floor, trying to tear the bag open.

"Wait." Genny grabbed the bag before popcorn ended up covering the floor. "You're going to spoil dinner."

"Come on, Mama. One bowl won't hurt," Paul said.

"A small one." Genny rolled her eyes. Why did she allow the thoughts from earlier to take up residence in her head? Even if Paul and Karla had coffee after the group, she trusted her husband.

Warm air swirled around Genny as she walked out to the garden to pick a basket of tomatoes. Why hadn't she planted jalapenos and cilantro? Or onions and garlic? They'd at least have fresh tomatoes for the salsa. On her way to the house, she went over the menu in her head. Paul was grilling the usual hamburger and hotdogs and had decided to grill chicken wings as well. She was making a salad and Tamika was bringing a variety of side dishes.

Genny had asked Paul if he was going to invite anyone from the VA group to their house-warming and Fourth of July celebration. He'd said he wanted to keep it to their closest friends. In her head, Genny had cheered as if she'd won the lottery since it meant Karla wouldn't be there. That would have been awkward, plus Genny would have been in a foul mood all day.

When Genny stepped inside the back door, she spotted Katie sitting on the couch chatting with Tamika. A bit of chocolate stretched up the corner of Katie's mouth.

"Katherine, have you been into the chocolate bars?"

Bright red filled Katie's cheeks and she licked her lips, trying to erase the evidence.

Ashley laughed when she saw the candy wrapper in the trash can. "At least she threw it away. Bethany leaves wrappers everywhere." The little girl sitting on the other side of Katie sulked when her mother looked in her direction.

"Katie, why don't you and Bethany go to your room and play?"

"Okay, Mama." The girls slid off the couch and Caleb squirmed on Tamika's lap. "You're not invited, Bubby!" Katie grabbed Bethany's hand as they ran down the hall.

Genny glanced out the kitchen window as she washed the tomatoes and smiled when her eyes met Paul's. She noticed Ryan and Ashley's ten-year-old son playing fetch with Lucy. Keith, Julie's boyfriend, was the new guy, but the others treated him like he'd been a part of the friend group for years.

Genny placed the bowl of tomatoes on the counter and got the cutting board and chopper from the cabinet. As she watched her friends, her heart was heavy. One person was missing. Mrs. Baker had joined them at their Fourth of July celebrations every year since they'd moved into the rental house several years ago. She fought back tears.

Genny slammed her hand on the chopper and scoffed when the tomatoes turned to mush.

"You need to do it by hand or they'd get squished," Tamika said, walking into the kitchen with Caleb on her hip.

"I see that." Genny rolled her eyes.

"Why didn't you tell me you have a chopper?" Julie said and wiped her eyes with her upper arm. "These onions have been making me cry for the past five minutes."

"Sorry," Genny held the chopper out to Julie.

"Any news on Kendall?" Tamika grabbed a carrot from the vegetable tray.

"Our social worker will bring her by next Friday."

"Are you ready?" Ashley asked.

"We've moved Paul's office to the apartment and I've got her room set up."

"Ooh, I want to see." Tamika stepped into the hall and peeked into the bedroom. "Oh, my goodness, it's cute."

"Katie picked out the bedding."

"What about her being mute?" Ashley leaned forward when Genny looked her way.

"This is Paul and Genny we're talking about." Julie scraped the onions into the bowl of salsa and stirred.

Genny shook her head. "How do you prepare for a mute child? Sometimes I ask myself if I'm crazy for wanting her placed with us. But I've been there, you know? The details are different, but I've lost my family, too."

The back door opened, and Lucy trotted inside, followed by Paul. He set the pan of hamburger patties and hotdogs on the kitchen counter and scratched Lucy's head. Katie and Bethany blasted past Genny into the kitchen. She turned around in time to see Katie holding out a hotdog to Lucy. Biting her tongue, Genny went to the kitchen and placed the pan of food into the oven to keep warm.

"Wings will be ready in ten minutes tops," Paul said to Genny as he walked towards the back door.

"Okay. We'll start bringing out the sides." Genny went to the fridge and got the potato salad Tamika had made.

"It's not your granny's."

"It's still good," Genny smiled and made her way out to the picnic table. Arranging the side dishes on the picnic table, Genny thought about Kendall. What would she be like? Tina had said she showed no emotion and didn't respond to questions. Would she be the same in their home? How would they handle it if she never communicated?

Later in the evening, the kids played with sparklers as the couples sat around the firepit roasting marshmallows. Genny noticed Trevor watching fireworks shooting into the sky in the distance. They were far enough away where all they heard was a soft boom. Paul had told her what Trevor had dealt with and that fireworks could be a trigger. Together they'd decided to keep their celebration to sparklers for the kids.

"Look, Mama!"

Genny smiled at the wide grin across Katie's face as she twirled the sparkler making it resemble a ring of fire. "That's so cool, baby girl."

Caleb squealed at the flaming marshmallow Genny pulled from the fire. She blew out the flames and put together the S'more. Caleb reached for the treat before Genny squished it together. Squealing, he cried and flailed his arms when she wouldn't let him hold the S'more by himself.

"It's past his bedtime," Paul said and stood, taking Caleb from Genny and heading to the house.

"I'm not tired." Katie gave the group a toothy grin.

"I guess not with all that sugar. How many has she had?" Trevor asked Genny.

"Two," Genny said.

"Four, Mama."

Genny grimaced. Katie would be up past midnight with all that sugar in her system.

"When do we get Kendall?" Katie angled her head at Genny and shoved the rest of her S'more into her mouth.

"She's coming next week."

"Okay," Katie said, her grin revealing brown teeth in the fire's light.

"We'll keep your family in our prayers," Ryan said. "It's going to be tough, but I know you two will be a blessing to Kendall. You've been through a lot and the Lord has seen you through."

Genny prayed they'd put their fears and frustration—and Genny was sure there would be frustration—in God's hands. Not knowing what they were facing, they had no other choice. "Thanks."

"You know we're here for you," Tamika said. Keith agreed, surprising Genny. He and Julie had been dating for a few months. But from what Genny and Paul saw, Keith was good for Julie. He was a Christian and they'd noticed that he was gently guiding Julie back to the faith of her childhood.

Katie cried out, speeding up Genny's pulse. "What is it?"

"Lucy ate my cracker." She sobbed, barely getting the words out.

Paul walked up and said, "Looks like it's someone else's bedtime."

"No, Daddy." Katie sobbed louder.

"It's okay," Tamika said. "I think it's getting close to everyone's bedtime."

Genny glanced at Jamie and Bethany. Both were having a hard time keeping their eyes open. It was a few minutes past ten, but the kids had played hard in the afternoon.

"Yeah, I think it's that time," Ryan said and stood.

Paul and Genny saw their guests off, and Paul headed to the bedroom. On her way down the hall, Genny stopped in the room's doorway that Kendall would call her own. She drew in a deep breath and exhaled. Closing her eyes, she prayed Kendall would trust and open up to them. She had to eventually, right?

CHAPTER 33

Genny

Genny reclined against the pillows on her bed and covered a yawn with the back of her hand. Pulling out her laptop, she went to Brandon's profile on Facebook. He'd been gone for six and a half years now. She felt close to him when she browsed his Facebook timeline and photos. As she scrolled, she smiled at the many photos of Katie and Caleb. Genny tagged Brandon in any pictures she'd posted of the kids. She knew it was silly—it wasn't like he'd see the pictures—but she did it, anyway.

The kids' photos covered most of his timeline. Early on, a string of his friends and former military coworkers would post heavenly birthday messages, but it had dwindled down to mostly Genny's posts over the years. She clicked on his photos tab and scrolled through the pictures she'd seen a thousand times since his death. A picture of Zoe caught her eye. She had to be around three years old. Genny hadn't gotten a reply to the message she'd sent Zoe a few weeks back. Optimism wasn't her strong suit. She was more aligned with pessimism—something she was working on.

A message notification popped up at the bottom right corner of the screen. Genny held in a squeal when she saw Zoe's name; she didn't want to wake Caleb from his nap. God's timing was perfect. Her heart jumped in her throat when she read the message.

Genny, this is Sarah.

Genny's heart raced as she watched the dots dance, showing that Sarah was typing again. A whole minute must have passed when the words finally popped up on the screen. She swallowed hard and began reading.

The first thing I want to say is that I'm sorry. I never should have done the things I've done. All I can say is that I was a different person back then. I wholeheartedly regret keeping Zoe from her father. When I found out that Brandon had died, my pettiness hit me like a truck. I stole my daughter away from her father and that's something I have to live with for the rest of my life.

Genny saw the dots again. Her throat tightened when she read what Sarah had written.

I see you're online. Can we video chat?

Genny stared wide-eyed at Sarah's request. Did she want to video chat with Sarah? It would be awkward. She leaned her head back and closed her eyes. A moment later, she had a sense of peace. She agreed and hovered her mouse over the telephone icon at the top of the message window. Before she could press it, Sarah's call rang in. Genny blew out her breath and answered.

Sarah's face appeared and she gasped, covering her mouth. "Genny. Zoe looks so much like you," Sarah said. Her British accent wasn't as thick as Genny remembered.

"Really?"

"Yes." Sarah nodded. "And you have grown into a beautiful woman. It's funny how memories work. I know you are no longer a kid, but I half expected to see the eighteen-year-old Genny." Sarah laughed. "But you left me guessing with the profile picture of the beautiful dog."

"That's Lucy." Genny smiled. They loved Lucy and Genny loved posting pictures of her as much as she loved posting pictures of the kids, but using a photo of Lucy as her profile photo was to protect her from the man who assaulted her. It was the same reason she used her maiden name on social media.

"Genny, I have absolutely no problem with you and Zoe having a relationship. You are her aunt and her blood."

Genny blinked back tears.

"Zoe and I had a nice long talk. That girl went through fire to find you. I was quite surprised when she told me you and Paul were married." Sarah let out a little laugh. "And it's lovely that you two have children. Zoe has a grown cousin with his own family from my brother, and my husband's sister has no children. I'm so happy that Zoe has your little ones."

"Me, too." Genny wiped her eyes. "I'm glad they have Zoe."

The women were quiet for a moment. Caleb cried out, breaking the silence.

"Oh, the little boy or little girl?"

"Caleb. Katie's at preschool. Be right back."

Sarah nodded.

Genny slipped off the bed and headed to Caleb's room. A minute later, she was back in front of her laptop, holding Caleb. He grinned when he saw Sarah's face on the screen.

"Oh, my goodness, he is precious. I wish I could pinch his cheeks. How old is he?"

"Fourteen months."

"He's a beautiful little one. How old is Katie?" Sarah smiled.

"She turned four on December first."

Sarah's smile fell. "December first?"

"Yes. My mind doesn't go to the anniversary of Brandon's death since she came along."

What Genny would describe as guilt and regret crossed Sarah's face.

"We can't change the past, but we can change the future." Sarah smiled again.

Why was this going so smoothly? Sarah was a stranger to Genny. She had no way of knowing if Sarah was being genuine. But Sarah could have deleted Zoe's account and moved on. This was one of those times that Genny had to put it in God's hands.

"My husband, Jim, is stationed at the Pentagon."

"Oh." Genny grabbed Caleb's hand and kissed the back.

"He's an American soldier. We met in Germany, where he was stationed. I worked on the base. Anyway, I said that, so you'd know that I'm in the states. I think Zoe would love to come down to Charleston to see you and the kids."

Genny's breath hitched. Sarah would come to Charleston for a visit?

"Zoe said that you live in Charleston. Is that not correct? Did Paul get orders or something?"

Sarah didn't know. How could she since Genny didn't tell Zoe?

"Paul was medically retired."

"Is…is he okay?"

"He was injured in Afghanistan."

Sarah's lips parted.

"He lost his left leg."

"Oh my goodness, Genny. Please tell him I'm thinking about him."

Genny glanced at the clock on her laptop. "He should be home anytime now. He went to pick Katie up from preschool. Maybe he could say a quick hi."

Sarah's eyes went wide. "Oh, he won't want to talk to me." She let out an awkward laugh.

Huh?

"I need to get going, anyway. Zoe will get out of school soon, and I need to leave to pick her up."

"Okay. Well, it was nice talking to you."

"Yes, Genny. We'll talk soon about arrangements for Zoe to visit."

"Okay. Thank you, Sarah." Genny heard the front door unlock.

"Da dee." Caleb clapped.

"See you soon." Sarah disconnected before Genny responded.

Weird.

Katie's feet pounded the floor as she ran down the hall to the bedroom. She stood on the bench at the bottom of the bed and crawled up to where Genny and Caleb were sitting.

"Look, Mama!" Katie shoved a sheet of paper in Genny's face.

"Careful, baby girl. Mama's going to get a paper cut on her eyeball." Paul laughed. He leaned down and kissed Genny on the lips and kissed Caleb's head.

Genny took the paper from Katie and smiled as she looked over the perfectly written capital letters. "Good job, baby girl." Genny held up her hand and Katie high fived her.

Paul picked up Genny's laptop and glanced at the screen. "Videoing with Melissa?"

"Nope. Sarah."

"As in Sarah Sarah?"

"Yes. She found Zoe's Facebook account, but believe it or not, she would like for Zoe to have a relationship with us." Genny grinned.

"Zoe?" Katie angled her head at Genny.

"We'll talk about it later, okay?"

Katie sighed and traced the letters on the sheet of paper with her finger.

"Sarah acted a little weird when I told her you would be home soon."

"Yeah?" Paul closed the laptop and slid it under the bed. He picked up Caleb and sat on his side of the bed.

"Yeah. When I said you might want to say hi, she said that you wouldn't want to talk to her and kind of hung up on me. What's that about?" Genny angled her head.

Paul rubbed the back of his neck and shook his head. "Baby girl, go change your clothes and I'll make you an ice cream cone."

"Okay, Daddy." Katie slid down from the bed and ran to her room.

Genny eyed Paul, waiting for him to fill her in.

"Remember when I went to England to visit not long after they got married?"

"I think so."

"Brandon had something he had to do at work, so it was me and Sarah. Well...um..." Paul's face paled and he grimaced. "I-I went outside to..." He sucked in a quick breath through his teeth. "Smoke."

"What? Paul Tyler! You used to smoke?" Genny glanced at Paul's mouth and couldn't imagine a cigarette between his lips.

"Only for about a month."

Genny lightly smacked him.

"Sorry." Paul rubbed the sting away.

"Continue," Genny said and pinched her lips together.

"Sarah came outside not long after I did."

Genny didn't like where this was going. Caleb reached for her, and she pulled him into her arms. Katie came into the room and Paul sent her to the kitchen to get the ice cream cones out of the pantry.

"So anyway, she moved her chair close to me and said something about how 'hot' I was and laid her hand on my upper thigh."

Genny clenched her teeth.

"I pushed her hand away, of course. Then she said it was okay and Brandon would never know. Baby, that was a long time ago. I'm sure she's not the same person."

I hope so. Genny was quiet for a moment. "Well, this is about Zoe. If it becomes too weird, we'll sit down and talk about it like adults."

"That's right, babe," Paul said. His phone chimed and he grabbed it from the nightstand.

Genny eyed him as he read the text and responded. It was some crisis or another. Paul laid the phone back on the nightstand and headed down the hall after Katie called out to him. When Paul was out of sight, Genny grabbed his phone and swiped the screen.

Karla: Danny brought Sophia so I won't be in the group. Just wanted to let you know in case you looked for me. Talk to you soon.

Paul: That's awesome! Another answered prayer. God is good.

Genny rolled her eyes and sighed, placing the phone back on Paul's nightstand. Caleb giggled and Genny saw Lucy sniffing his socked feet. She picked up her son and went into the living room with visions of giving Paul's phone to Lucy for a chew toy. Why was Paul blind to Karla crossing boundaries? As terrifying as the thought of Paul staying in the military, if he'd stayed, there'd be no Karla.

❧

Genny's stomach clenched when the doorbell rang. She slowly blew out her breath and ran her hands down the front of her shirt. Paul walked up by her side and rested his hand on the small of her back. With a trembling hand, Genny opened the front door. Tina stood on the porch holding the hand of a petite little girl with long blond hair. Genny drew in a quiet breath. She was the same girl that was with Tina the day of Katie's first therapy appointment. Kendall slipped her finger in her mouth, reminding Genny of Katie's habit when she was nervous.

"Miss Genny and Mr. Paul, this is Kendall." Tina tugged Kendall's hand, urging her to walk inside.

For a moment, Kendall glanced at Genny, then her gaze went to Paul. The fear in her eyes showed as she looked at him from head to toe. He must seem like a giant to her.

Genny held her hand up to Katie when she ran towards Kendall. "Slow down. You'll scare her," Genny whispered.

"Okay, Mama." Katie studied Kendall. She reached out and brushed her hand down the length of Kendall's hair. Kendall's face twisted and she moved closer to Tina. "It's okay. My name is Katie and I'm your friend."

Tension left Genny's body when Kendall's expression relaxed.

While Paul went to Tina's car to get Kendall's suitcase, Genny and Tina walked Kendall to her room. Sitting on the edge of the twin bed, Kendall traced a flower on the comforter while she took in her surroundings. Glancing at the pillows, her eyes fell to the doll Katie had picked out laying on the pillows. Kendall's finger was still in her mouth, and Genny guessed it would be for a while.

Katie walked into the room with a doll tucked under her arm. Inching up to the side of the bed, Katie pointed to the doll on the bed. "That's Ruby and this," she held out the rag doll with a head full of frayed brown yarn for hair, "is her sister, Miss Peggy."

Kendall stared at the doll. She pulled her finger out of her mouth and hesitated before taking the doll from Katie's hand. Picking up the other doll, she held them together and looked at Katie. Genny glanced at Tina and smiled.

Caleb wobbled into the room and up to Kendall. She scrambled to the other side of the bed, pushing her back against the wall. Paul came in, set down the suitcase, and swept Caleb up in his arms.

Tina left a little later, leaving Kendall alone in a strange house with a couple she didn't know and their two curious kids. Genny's heart went out to her. They made the first night easier for everyone, and Paul made a quick trip to grab dinner.

Paul cleaned the kitchen while Genny got the kids ready for bed. She stood outside the bathroom, asking Kendall questions through the door. By some miracle, Genny was sure Kendall would answer. She didn't. Kendall emerged in a pair of pajamas, the wet ends of her hair soaking the pajama top.

"Sorry, sweetie." Genny sighed. She wasn't used to taking care of hair as long as Kendall's hair, since Katie's hair was above her shoulders. "Did you brush your teeth?"

Kendall glanced at Genny a second and turned and looked into her room.

"Go ahead." Genny pointed to Kendall's room. She tucked Kendall into bed and Paul came in to say goodnight. They prayed over her and studied her for a moment before they left the room. Tina had told them that Kendall's family was Christian, but they felt it was best to take things slowly in bringing her into their family's faith practices.

Paul and Genny tucked in Katie and Caleb and made their way to Kendall's room. The only way they knew she was in the bed was the bit of hair sticking out from the edge of the comforter. Genny sighed and they headed to bed.

Turning the lamp off, Genny and Paul talked about the day's events. They prayed for Kendall again and Genny's mind kept going back to Kendall's losses. When Genny lost her parents, she had her grandparents. Kendall had no one to comfort her.

Genny rolled onto her back and stared at the ceiling. All she could think about was the sweet girl down the hall. Easing out of bed, she grabbed her pillow and a blanket from the closet and made her way to the hall. Kendall's bedroom door was slightly open and the nightlight brightened the room enough to where she could see Kendall staring at her through the crack. Not saying a word, Genny spread the blanket on the floor, and laid down, wrapping herself in the blanket. She would not let Kendall be alone.

"Babe."

Genny opened her eyes and saw Paul hovering over her.

"What are you doing?"

"I don't want to leave her alone. I'm sure she's scared to death."

"Okay, baby. Let me know if I need to help you up off the floor in the morning." Paul laughed under his breath.

Genny shook her head and pulled the blanket over her shoulders. Closing her eyes, she drew in a deep breath and wondered what was going through Kendall's mind. Not long after, Genny felt herself drifting to sleep.

A noise startled Genny and her eyelids flew open. A shadow stretched up the wall across from Kendall's room. Rolling over, Genny saw Kendall standing inside the doorway looking at Genny. Kendall sniffed and Genny realized that Kendall's sniffing was what woke her.

"Are you scared?"

Kendall's face was shaded by the shadow of the door, keeping Genny from seeing any expression on her face.

"I'm here, okay? If you get scared, you can…" What could Kendall do? It wasn't like she would run into Genny's arms. "I won't let anything happen to you. Okay?"

Kendall stood still for a second, then went back to bed, pulling the covers over her head. Did she trust what Genny said? The child's world had been turned upside down. She had been abandoned not once, but twice. The people that loved and cared for her were gone. Her grandmother couldn't care for her and her aunt wasn't prepared to raise a child. What would happen to Kendall? Genny closed her eyes and drifted in and out of sleep as she listened for any sign that Kendall was in distress.

CHAPTER 34

Paul

Pushing back the curtain, Paul smiled as he watched Katie go from hugging a porch column to fidgeting on a chair. A flash of black lifted Paul's gaze and he saw his parents' Escalade pulling into the driveway. Katie leaped off the chair and ran out onto the sidewalk, jumping up and down. Paul laughed and let the curtain fall back into place.

"They're here, babe."

"Oh, good." Genny wiped Caleb's mouth and hands and picked him up. "They must have left Murfreesboro at three this morning." She laughed. "Let's go see Mimi and Papa. Want to come, Kendall?"

Paul glanced at Kendall sitting at the dining table eating an apple. She looked at him but didn't move. "It's okay, you can stay here." He smiled, but inside, his heart hurt for her. He held the door for Genny and followed her to the car. Katie had already opened the passenger door and climbed onto Tricia's lap. Paul grabbed her and stood her on the ground. "Let Mimi get out."

"Sweetheart." A smile spread across his mother's face.

Paul helped Tricia out and she wrapped her arms around his neck. "You look well."

"Thank you, Mom."

Genny walked up with Caleb on her hip. Tricia covered her mouth with her hands.

"My grandbaby is so big. Hello, little man." Caleb smiled. He leaned toward Tricia and she took him in her arms. "Where is she? Kendall?" Tricia looked past Paul to the front door, where Kendall was standing with her finger in her mouth. A moment later, she disappeared back inside the house. "How's it going?"

Genny shrugged. "It's been hard. She makes no sounds. At least not around us. She plays with Katie, eats with us, and watches TV. She takes a bath on her own. It's heartbreaking." Tears filled Genny's eyes.

"Prayer and patience." Paul said, slipping his arm around Genny.

"That's all you can do," Tricia added.

Paul heard Brian and Katie talking. He walked over to the driver's side and saw that Katie was pointing to the backyard, where Lucy was staring at them through the fence.

"Let's go see Lucy, Papa."

"Baby girl, give Papa some time to recover from their eight-hour trip." Paul gave his dad a hug.

"Let me get this luggage in and I'll go see the house and yard with you and Lucy, okay?"

"Okay, Papa."

Once Brian and Paul brought the luggage into the living room, Katie, Paul, and Genny took them on a tour of the house.

"The house is big. All the rooms are spacious and I love the front porch," Tricia said as she looked around the living room.

"Let us show you to the apartment," Genny said, motioning to the garage. Paul helped Brian with the luggage. They walked around the last few moving boxes in the garage. Paul made it to the stairs before everyone else.

"Can you walk up the stairs, sweetheart?"

"Yes, Mom." Paul rolled his eyes.

"She doesn't know, babe," Genny whispered.

"Brace yourselves. It's the worst, as far as cosmetic, as you say, Mom," Paul warned.

"Oh, my," Tricia said when she walked into the living area. "That carpet has to go."

"It has a separate bedroom and bathroom," Paul said. "And this kitchenette is like the ones in hotels." He pointed to the mini-fridge, microwave, and bar sink. Paul turned around and spotted Kendall standing in the small living room close to the door. She came in and stood close to Katie.

"Nothing a little paint and new carpet won't fix," Brian said.

Katie ran into the bedroom, climbed onto the bed, and began jumping up and down.

"Katherine Kelly!" Genny narrowed her eyes at Katie.

"Aww," she hopped down and lowered her head. When she walked back into the living area, Brian swept her up in his arms.

They made their way downstairs and Lucy met them at the back door and led the way into the yard.

"My gosh," Brian said. "How many acres? Three? Four?"

"That's what we were told, but it's closer to five. Two back fence panels were loose, and we didn't want Lucy to get out. Had a contractor fix it and he told me that the property corners are about two hundred feet into the woods. We thought it was state property, I looked at the deed, and sure enough, it's four and three quarters acres."

"You two have yourself a nice place here. The kids are going to love living here. Lots of adventures to be had." Brian looked at Paul and smiled.

"Hopefully, it won't take too long to remodel," Genny said.

"We're taking it one step at a time. Probably replace the carpet first." Paul lifted his brows.

Caleb whined to be put down. Genny stood him on the grass, and he sat down, running his hands over the blades. Kendall stood off to the side, but Katie got her to run around.

"Oh, we want to treat you to dinner tonight to celebrate the house," Tricia said.

"You guys drove eight hours." Paul shook his head and laughed.

"We're fine." Tricia smiled.

"Hey, anything not to cook." Genny laughed.

Paul watched his parents love on their grandkids. Brian began talking to Kendall, being sure to include her. She stood, twisting the hem of her shirt as she listened. Genny came up next to Paul and slipped her arm around his waist.

"I wished we lived closer. The kids are missing out on so much with their grandparents."

"Yeah." Paul sighed.

Maybe they should have moved to Murfreesboro when Paul's parents suggested it. But it didn't feel right then and it didn't feel right now. God had them in Charleston for a reason. His gaze shifted to Kendall.

—*ele*—

The waitress made her way around the table refilling drinks, and smiled at Caleb when she grabbed Paul's glass. He grinned at her and took the stuffed mushroom from Paul's hand. Spitting it out, Caleb grimaced.

"Not a mushroom fan, huh?" Paul said and shook his head. "What about this?" Paul handed Caleb a small piece of roasted Brussels sprout that'd been cooling on the edge of his plate.

Caleb stuffed it in his mouth. Lifting his small brows, he made a noise and smiled.

"More?" Paul said, holding up a sprout. Caleb nodded, and Paul gave him another piece.

"How's school, Katie?" Brian asked.

"It's preschool, Papa. I'm not big enough for real school."

Brian laughed. "It's still school. And what about you, Miss Kendall?"

"She'll start next year. If…" Genny cleared her throat and took a sip of lemonade.

She wanted permanent placement, but Paul knew it was too soon to make that decision. Paul's phone vibrated in his pocket and he pulled it out.

Karla: Hey. How are you? How's Kendall? I've missed seeing you in the group. And coffee.

Genny's fork screeched across her plate, and Paul glanced at her. The hateful look on her face sent a chill down his spine. He looked up and was met by his father's gaze. He looked from Paul to Genny. Paul sighed and pocketed his phone.

Kendall sat next to Paul. Most of the food on her plate had been eaten. Paul saw her eyeing a roasted Brussels sprout on the edge of his plate.

"Want to try one?"

She looked up at him. He wondered what was going on behind her sad hazel eyes. He stabbed the sprout and held the fork out. She pulled it off and put it in her mouth.

"Is that good?" Brian asked. Kendall looked at Brian and back at Paul.

They finished their meals and the dishes were removed. Caleb reached for Genny and laid his head on her shoulder when she pulled him into her arms.

"We should get going," Paul said. "It's late and Mimi and Papa are tired."

The family walked out to the parking lot and got into the car. Paul took Genny's hand in his.

"What's wrong, baby?" Paul asked. Her attitude had changed when he got the text from Karla.

"Did Karla text you?" Genny's tone had a bite to it.

Paul sighed. "Yeah."

"What did she want?"

"Checking on me since I haven't been in group therapy much."

"She is inserting herself into our lives, Paul. It's not her business why you haven't been in group therapy. You are giving too much of yourself." Genny turned and looked out the window.

Tricia made a comment about a building they passed, and Paul was relieved to have the tension dissipate between him and Genny. But he knew she was right about Karla. He needed to pray for guidance on how to step away from Karla. He thought about the look his dad gave him at dinner. Brian was a perceptive man. Paul was sure he sensed the tension between them after the text from Karla.

Paul's thoughts kept him distracted and he didn't realize they were close to home until his dad pulled into the driveway. They got the three sleeping kids out of the car and in their beds without waking them. Paul and Genny said good night and Brian and Tricia headed to the apartment.

Settled into bed, Genny faced Paul and let out a long breath. "Do you think the TBI has anything to do with…this?"

"What? What's 'this?'"

"Nevermind." Genny rolled over.

"No, I want to know what you mean."

"I don't know." She rolled back over. "A TBI can cause comprehension problems. Maybe that's why you can't understand what's going on with Karla. What about the little girl down the hall? Don't you think she needs you more than a grown woman needs you?"

Paul's jaw muscles tightened. "So, I'm mentally slow?"

"I didn't say that." Genny groaned and rolled over.

Yes, you did.

Genny said nothing else and before long, her breathing evened out. Paul focused on the bedroom door and slipped out of bed. Making his way down the hall, he eased open Kendall's door. In the dim light of the nightlight, he saw her facing the wall. She had pushed the covers down to her waist, and Paul walked over and covered her back up.

Genny was right. Karla was a grown woman and knew how to get the help she needed. Kendall was a helpless child, lost in an unfamiliar world with people she didn't know. Paul wanted that to change.

— ℓℓℓ —

Paul's eyes opened when he heard a door close. For a moment, he found himself in fight mode, but remembered his parents were visiting. Rubbing his hands over his face, he glanced at his watch. Why would his parents be up this early? Now wide awake, Paul slipped on his prosthetic and got dressed, making his way to the living room.

The light over the stove dimly lit the kitchen. Paul heard shuffling and saw Brian hovering over the Keurig. He grumbled when the Keurig groaned, hissed, and sputtered.

"Genny says it sounds like a street bike," Paul said, keeping his tone low.

Brian whirled around, eyes wide. Relief flooded his face.

"Sorry, Dad."

"It's okay. I was trying to be quiet."

"I heard something and figured it was you or Mom. Why in the world are you up so early? It's five Tennessee time."

"Over ten years retired and my body still thinks I need to get up and go to work."

"Want to have our coffee on the patio?"

"Sure. Lucy and I will head out."

Paul put in a K-cup of his favorite coffee and looked out the window as he waited for it to brew. Brian must have foregone the patio for the picnic table. Paul prepared his coffee and headed outback. They sat quietly for a moment as the sun made its way over the horizon. Paul loved watching the sun rise more so than a sunset. A sunrise represented a new day in Christ.

"How are you doing with the discharge?" Brian sipped his coffee.

"I'm alright."

"Honestly?"

"Yeah."

"If you could, would you go back in?"

220

Paul contemplated what his dad asked. Would he? "If you'd asked me two months ago, I'd say yes, but that's not the case now." A pain shot down Paul's left leg and he sucked in a quick breath.

"You okay?"

"Yeah, phantom pain. That was a mild one."

"It blows my mind that the brain thinks your leg is still there."

"Yeah, me, too." Paul laughed. He took slow, deep breaths until the pain subsided. "I love being with Genny and the kids every day. Katie has made progress with her separation anxiety and I get to see Caleb grow and learn. Now we have Kendall. I don't know what would happen if I went back on active duty." For a moment, Paul thought about how returning to active duty would not only affect his family, but Kendall as well.

"I'm here if you want to talk."

"Huh?"

"I can feel the friction between you and Genny."

"You still got it." Paul smiled. Lucy came up to him with an old ball in her mouth. Paul tugged it until she released her jaws and he threw it towards the back fence. She took off after it and returned to Paul for another go.

"I know my son." Brian turned up his cup to drink the last few drops of coffee.

Paul placed his cup on the picnic table in front of him and began telling his father about Karla and the VA group and Genny's feelings. Brian was quiet until Paul was finished.

"You are a good man and love the Lord. Genny and your kids are your world. For the sake of your marriage, you need to let this go. It's causing problems I can clearly see. I'm sure your children sense the tension as well. All that said, ministering to Karla was not a mistake. The Lord wouldn't have put her into your life for you *not* to minister to her. Maybe that time is over." Lucy walked up to Brian with her ball. He pitched it towards the back fence, and she took off after it.

Paul looked at his dad.

"You aren't the only one capable of leading her to Christ. Trust that He'll put the right person in her life."

Paul had missed his dad's counsel. Since he'd joined the military and left home, it had been hard to find anyone as wise as Brian. Hearing what his dad had to say could be trying but Paul appreciated his dad's candor.

"You need to let it go not only for your wife and kids, but for that sweet little girl that the Lord has placed in your care. She's hurting. She doesn't need the tension. None of you do."

"I know." Paul scratched Lucy's head when she bumped him with her nose. Genny said it, Clyde said it, and now his dad said it—he needed to turn Karla over to someone else.

The light came on in Caleb's room and Paul made out Genny's silhouette through the closed blinds. It was close to six thirty. He figured the kids would sleep in, since it was late when they got home the night before. The back door opened and Genny walked out onto the patio holding Caleb's hand.

He spotted his daddy and papa and toddled out to the picnic table wearing a wide grin. Lucy ran up to him and licked his hands, bringing out a giggle.

"I'm getting ready to start breakfast," Genny said when she walked up to the picnic table.

"The works?" Brian grinned.

"You know it," Paul said. "We'll be in soon, love. I'll make the pancakes and bacon if you do the omelets."

"Okay." Genny smiled and reached for Caleb's hand. He jerked away and rested his hands on his grandfather's knees. "Fine. I see how you are," she joked and headed for the house.

"Thanks for the talk, Dad."

"Anytime."

As Paul and Brian strolled to the back door, Brian stopped at the garden and picked a red tomato. He held it up and looked at Paul. "For my omelet." He chuckled.

Paul looked past him and saw Katie and Kendall standing at the back door. Kendall's eyes found him and he smiled. Katie pressed her wide-open mouth against the glass and puffed out her cheeks. Paul shook his head and held the door for Brian to walk inside.

Brian had recently turned seventy-four. How many years would they have together? The longing to live closer to his parents overwhelmed Paul. Even so, he knew that God wanted them in Charleston.

—ele—

Paul and Katie headed to Lowe's after his parents left a few hours earlier. The parking lot was full, bringing up the dread Paul had been pushing down since before he'd left the house. His eyes were drawn to the garden center. A man pulling a pallet of soil outside the greenhouse sent heat over Paul's body. Heart racing, Paul broke out in a cold sweat. Grabbing the steering wheel, he squeezed until his knuckles burned. A groan came from the backseat.

"Daddy?" Katie's seatbelt released and she slid to the edge of the seat. "Are we going inside?"

Paul's pounding heart stole his voice. Releasing the steering wheel, he closed his eyes and drew in a deep breath.

Katie leaned up and whispered in his ear, "Are you okay, Daddy?"

No, he wasn't okay. It wasn't just working around cargo that could trigger a flashback. Steve had said that Paul needed exposure to places—retail or other—that used pallets. Pallets were used by all kinds of businesses, not just the military. Was he going to avoid places like Lowe's and Walmart because the stores used pallets to move merchandise around?

Steve had assigned homework for exposure therapy. Paul was to go to a store that was likely to have pallets out on the floor. He was two weeks behind on his first attempt, and his next therapy appointment was in two days. Why did he bring Katie? Genny had tried to get her to stay home with Kendall and Caleb, but she truly looked like she was going to cry. Now wasn't the time to admit that his little girl had him wrapped around her finger.

Paul's breathing quickened. Katie's small, warm hand brushed over his cheek. He opened his eyes and turned his head. Her smile was inspiration enough to get him out of the truck after fifteen minutes of sitting in the parking lot. Katie slipped her hand in his and they made their way to the entrance.

The store was brighter, louder, and more crowded than he'd remembered. Funny, it never bothered him before. A high-pitched noise sounded above him and he realized he could hear the hum of the fluorescent lights. Something he'd never been able to hear.

A distorted sound came from Katie, as if Paul was listening to her from underwater. Tugging on his hand, she looked up at him and smiled, leading the way to the appliance section. Katie inspected each fridge, chatting to Paul the whole time. Engaging in conversation with Katie, Paul realized that his heart rate had slowed down.

A little while later, they'd ordered the fridge he and Genny had picked out online. When they walked outside, Paul glanced in the direction of the garden center and spotted the pallet of soil the garden employee had been pulling earlier. It stared back at him as if it was about to charge at full force. He knew his mind was playing tricks on him, but it was still a terrifying thought. A wave of nausea passed over him, but his sweet baby girl pushed the fear away as she talked about the different flavors of ice cream he and Genny were going to put into the freezer for her, Caleb, and Kendall.

Paul came up with a plan for more exposure, this time by himself. He couldn't drag his four-year-old along. This was something he had to do by himself. According to Steve, he would get to where seeing a full pallet didn't bring on a strong emotional reaction. Paul had his doubts.

~ell~

Paul woke after a good night's sleep, despite his trip to Lowe's the day before. A few of the guys in the VA therapy group had talked about suffering for days after a trigger. He decided sleeping through the night was a sign of progress.

Grabbing a cup of coffee, he headed to the picnic table. On the way across the yard, the grass reached above his ankles. Mowing would be a good way to release anxiety.

Finishing the last section of the yard, Paul pulled the lawnmower into the shed. As he headed down the hall to the master bedroom to shower, he passed by Katie's room and glanced inside. Kendall was sitting on the floor next to Caleb and they were playing with blocks while Katie played with her one-legged Barbie.

He braced himself on the bedroom wall and kicked off his shoes. When he turned to head for the bathroom, he saw Kendall standing just outside the doorway. Wide-eyed, she slipped her finger in her mouth. A moment later, Paul realized why. He'd been wearing pants since she'd been living with them, but he couldn't stand the thought of mowing in pants. She was seeing him in shorts for the first time.

Should he say something? She would probably run off if he walked up to her. Kendall stood as if she was too afraid to move. He couldn't leave her standing in the hall.

"That's Daddy's pretend leg," Katie said as she walked up next to Kendall. "He was in an accident and got an owie like Barbie." Katie danced the doll in front of Kendall's face.

"Katie, please take her back to your room. I don't think she's ready to see my leg."

"Okay, Daddy." Katie grabbed Kendall's hand. "Come on."

Paul considered the right time and how he'd go about introducing Kendall to his prosthetic. Katie had a short adjustment period and with Caleb being a baby when he was injured, he'd only known Paul as an amputee.

Paul walked into the living room and plopped down on the couch. He pulled out his shirt several times to push cooler air onto his skin.

"Mama?" Caleb asked when he walked up to Paul.

"Here I am, little man," Genny walked into the living room with a laundry basket on her hip. He grinned and toddled over to her. "Missing that tiny backyard?" She asked Paul.

"Just when I mow." He laughed.

Genny sat on the other end of the couch and began folding the clean towels.

"She saw my prosthetic," Paul whispered, and tilted his head to Kendall. "I think it freaked her out."

"Oh, no."

Paul propped his left elbow on the arm of the couch and rested his head on his hand.

"She's going to see it, eventually. We'll ease her into it." Genny tossed a towel on top of the stack on the coffee table.

Kendall looked up at Paul from where she and Katie were playing. Paul raised his head when she stood and walked over to him. Focusing on his arm, she lifted her left arm, exposing the lengthy scar on her forearm where a broken bone from the accident had been repaired. Reaching out with a shaky finger, she pointed to the scar on Paul's forearm that stretched from below his elbow to his wrist. Genny widened her eyes when Paul looked in her direction.

"I have another owie from my accident." Paul brushed his finger down his scar.

Kendall looked at her arm again, then rejoined Katie. Paul considered Kendall and her situation for a minute. God brought her to them for a reason. Paul took comfort in knowing that He wouldn't leave them to figure this out on their own.

CHAPTER 35

Genny

Lucy barked from the backyard, causing Genny's muscles to tense. She scanned the living room, quickly brushing her hand over the top of one of the side tables by the couch. Katie gasped and sprinted into the living room from her bedroom.

"They're here, Mama!"

Genny glanced at Katie and saw Kendall next to her, looking out the window. She ran her hands through her hair and tugged on the hem of her shirt. What was she doing? Truthfully, Zoe was a stranger, but she was her niece. Maybe it was Genny's former hateful, vindictive sister-in-law who raised her heart rate. The last time she saw Sarah, Genny was eighteen. She didn't know if the person she had talked to on video was who Sarah was in real life.

The room spun, and Genny broke out in a cold sweat. Closing her eyes to regain her balance, her lids flew open when she heard the deadbolt on the front door snap back. Katie was already standing on the sidewalk grinning when Genny made it to the porch.

Sarah climbed out of a large, white BMW SUV. Genny had studied a few old pictures she'd had of Sarah and Zoe the night before. Sarah looked the same except her hair was lighter and she had gained a few pounds. Genny glanced at the passenger side but didn't see Zoe.

"I'm Katie!"

"Hi, Miss Katie. I'm Sarah, your cousin Zoe's mum. I think Zoe just fell in love with your dog." Sarah smiled and tilted her head towards the fence. Without hesitation, she walked up to Genny and wrapped her arms around her. "It's so good to see you. You are so beautiful. The video didn't do you justice. And that precious little girl." Sarah glanced toward the fence, where Katie and Kendall had joined Zoe and were bent down, poking their fingers through the fence at Lucy. Sarah tilted her head and looked at Genny when she saw Kendall.

"That's Kendall. Our foster daughter."

"Oh, how wonderful that you two have opened your home to a child in need." Sarah's eyes brightened when she smiled.

"I'm Katie."

"I'm your cousin Zoe."

"This is Kendall. She's our foster child," Katie said, pointing at Kendall.

"Hi, Kendall." Zoe got down to eye level with Kendall and gave her a wide smile. She grasped a lock of Kendall's hair and rubbed it between her fingers. Kendall stared at Zoe wide-eyed.

Genny could detect a slight British accent when Zoe spoke. She'd been in the States for over seven years and Genny figured her accent had faded over time. Katie giggled and looked at Genny. When Zoe stood, Genny's breath caught in her throat. She was close to Genny's height. Their likeness was uncanny. Genny would swear she was looking at herself if not for the shape of Zoe's chin. That was pure Sarah.

Zoe walked over and hugged Genny. "You remind me of my dad," she whispered when she pulled away. Genny smiled and blinked back tears.

"That's little Paul in a dress." Sarah laughed as she looked at Katie. "Except for her eyes. That's all you Genny. Where's the little one?"

"Bubby is napping. Come inside." Katie said and grabbed Zoe's hand.

"Yeah, come inside. I've got the Keurig warmed up." Genny took Kendall by the hand and they went inside.

Genny fixed three cups of coffee and place the cups along with cream and sugar on the silver tray Mrs. Baker had given her. She placed the tray on the coffee table and sat on the loveseat. Sarah sat on the couch and surveyed the living room. Genny pulled her shirt away from her neck and swallowed hard. Katie sat next to Zoe and grinned at her while they talked. The child was enamored with her cousin.

"I love your house," Sarah said.

"Oh, we've got a lot to do. New floor covering, appliances, plumbing fixtures, window coverings, to name a few." Why did she list off what was wrong with the house? Sarah had not showed that she disapproved of the house. "We just bought it and are still settling in."

"Well, it sounds like you have a good idea of what you want to do to make it your own. It looks like you've got a good bit of land."

"Close to five acres."

"Oh, wow. That's nice."

Genny smiled and took a sip of coffee. The women sat quietly, while Katie and Zoe chatted about anything and everything. Kendall sat next to Genny, twisting the skirt of her dress.

Sarah watched Kendall for a minute and looked up at Genny. "Is Paul working?"

"Oh, no. He's in the apartment over the garage doing some work."

"An apartment? I bet that's nice for visitors."

Genny smiled and nodded. They turned their attention to Zoe and Katie. Genny was glad to see that Zoe was genuinely interested in Katie. Katie had made plans for the visit the week before and would have been devastated if Zoe seemed uninterested. The garage door opened and Katie squealed.

"That's my daddy!" She shot off the couch and met Paul as he walked into the living room. "Come meet my cousin and her mama."

Genny heard Sarah suck in a quiet breath. Paul smiled and walked over, leaning down to give Genny a kiss.

"Sarah," Paul said, and stepped over to shake Sarah's hand.

Red bloomed in Sarah's cheeks.

To Genny's surprise, Zoe stood and hugged Paul. "It's nice to meet you, Uncle Paul."

"You, too." Paul sat on the arm of the chair where Genny was sitting.

"My daddy has a pretend leg," Katie said after a short period of silence.

Kendall looked up at Paul.

"Katherine," Genny said, and narrowed her eyes at Katie.

"He does, Mama."

Paul chuckled. "She's right, Mama."

"If I didn't know, I'd never guess that you are an amputee," Sarah said.

"He's worked hard to get where he is."

Genny heard Caleb's whimper down the hall, breaking the tension.

"Guess who's awake." Paul stood. "I'll get him."

Paul brought Caleb into the living room and stood him on the floor. A few trusses of his hair were sticking up and a red mark covered his cheek where he'd been sleeping. He spotted Zoe, then Sarah. Walking to the end of the coffee table, Caleb stood staring at Sarah.

"You two have such beautiful children," Sarah said and reached to grab hold of one of Caleb's hands.

Katie stopped chattering and looked at Sarah. "Caleb grew in another lady's tummy."

"Boy, she's on a roll," Genny said. The adults laughed and watched pink fill Katie's cheeks.

"Wanna go outside and play?" Katie said when she walked up to where Zoe was sitting on the couch.

"Sure," Zoe said and stood. Katie took Zoe's hand and led her towards the door. "Let's not forget Kendall."

"Oh, yeah." Katie grinned and let go of Zoe's hand, heading to the couch where Kendall was sitting. Katie grabbed Kendall's hand, then Zoe's hand, and led them outside to the patio.

"She's going to be too wound up to sleep tonight," Paul said and smiled.

After the girls went outside to play with Lucy, Sarah talked some about the years since her and Brandon's divorce. Sarah hadn't made eye contact with Paul since he greeted her. Tension was hanging in the air around them.

After half a minute of painful silence, Genny heard Paul release a heavy breath. "Okay, I'm going to put this out there. What happened was a long time ago and we are different people now. Let's push past it for all our sakes, but especially the kids."

Sarah's shoulders relaxed. "Yes, let's."

"Sounds good," Genny said, although she felt like an outsider in the situation.

Genny was setting the table when she overheard the conversation between Sarah and Zoe in the kitchen.

"Mum, do we have to go home in the morning? Can we stay another day?"

Genny heard the emotion in Zoe's voice. She and the girls had played in the backyard for the past few hours. When Genny was preparing the side dishes for dinner earlier, she glanced out the kitchen window and smiled when she saw Zoe standing next to Paul as he grilled. Paul, Genny, and the kids were more than a lost connection to Zoe and Genny's chest tightened hearing Zoe's conversation with her mother.

"Zoe, we have to get back. Dad has that dinner and I have to be there."

Zoe walked into the dining room and placed the potato salad in the middle of the table. "He's not my dad," she whispered and looked up at Genny, her eyes glistening in the light.

Zoe's expression broke Genny's heart, but because of their new relationship, Genny didn't feel it was right to step on Sarah's toes and invite them to stay longer. It was a weekend trip and Sarah had said earlier that Zoe had commitments. The back door opened, and Paul walked in with a tray of barbeque chicken.

"Yum yum," Caleb said and clapped.

"It does look yum," Sarah said when she walked in with a plate of dinner rolls.

Paul said a prayer and everyone began preparing their plates. Genny had turned to place a plate in front of Caleb when Zoe got her attention.

"Aunt Genny, do you mind if we stop by in the morning for breakfast before we leave?"

"Zoe Camille." Sarah's features tightened.

Genny slowly released a deep breath. She'd forgotten that Brandon and Sarah had used her granny's first name for Zoe's middle name. It had been years since she'd heard her grandmother's given name. Everyone had called her Millie.

Genny glanced at Zoe. She was pushing potato salad around on her plate with her fork. Genny hated feeling like she was walking on thin ice. One wrong move could land her in freezing water, and she'd never see Zoe again. It would break all of their hearts.

The room was quiet except for forks scraping on plates and jangling ice when someone took a sip of their drink. Katie looked at each person around the table and scrunched her brows. Caleb squealed, his voice bouncing off the walls. Katie threw her head back and giggled, relieving the tension.

Katie brought up playing Candyland after dinner and Paul was setting up the game while Sarah helped Genny clean the kitchen. Sarah loaded the last few dishes into the dishwasher and closed the door. Turning to Genny, she said, "Can I see the apartment?"

That's out of the blue.

"Sure." Genny led the way through the garage and up the stairs. "Now, it's worse than the house. Think shag carpet." Genny laughed.

Sarah grimaced when she spotted the pile of green shag carpet against the wall. "I can only imagine what it looked like spread over the floor." She laughed.

After Genny gave Sarah the tour that took less than a minute, she paused when Sarah sat on the small loveseat in the living room.

"Genny, I didn't know how this would go. That's why I didn't let Zoe video chat or to be your friend on Facebook. I was looking out for her best interest. We don't know each other. I have to protect my child. As a mother, I'm sure you feel the same way."

"I do, and I get where you are coming from." How did Sarah feel after spending the day with them?

"This is why it took me so long to agree to a time to visit. Zoe had already fallen in love with your family and I was so scared that she would be disappointed. But after today, I see I had nothing to worry about. Oh, and Jim really has to attend a dinner and I have to go with him. Trust me, I'd rather stay in Charleston. I can't stand to be around all those stuffy people." She laughed. "If it's okay, we'd like to stop by for breakfast before we head up north."

"That's perfectly fine."

Thankful that her kids would have their cousin in their lives, Genny could get to know her brother's only child, something he never had the chance to do because of Sarah's selfishness. Genny thanked God for softening Sarah's heart.

After Sarah and Zoe went back to their hotel, Paul got the kids ready for bed and Genny got out her journal.

Aug 12, 2017

Zoe is a sweetheart, and Sarah seems like a nice woman. I'm trying to get over my reservations about her. People change. I am not the same person I was fifteen years ago. I'm happy that Sarah is putting aside her feelings about her marriage to Brandon, for Zoe's sake. I can't wait to see Zoe again. Maybe we can visit her.

My heart breaks for Kendall. I've noticed that she withdraws when anyone visits. It's probably because of unfamiliar people. They try to include her and I'm sure that doesn't help. Too many strangers, I guess. Sometimes I wish I could get inside her head. I'm sure it would break my heart to see her thoughts.

CHAPTER 36

Paul

Heading home, Paul had turned up the radio and was singing along with Def Leppard's "Pour Some Sugar on Me." He pulled up to the house and found Genny in the garage digging through boxes. She readjusted her ponytail and blew the strands of hair out of her face.

"What are you doing, babe?"

"Looking for a few of Katie's books. We were picking out a book to read tonight at bedtime and the girls were asking about a specific book and I can't find it. Can you bring that box inside?" Genny said, pointing.

Paul gasped. "They?"

"Well, Katie did."

"I was excited there for a minute."

"Babe, if Kendall had talked, I would've called you screaming."

Paul picked up the box and carried it inside. On the way across the garage to the apartment, he spotted a box that had been in the office at the old house. Grabbing the box, he headed up the stairs. Fumes from fresh paint claimed Paul's breath when he walked into the apartment. Placing the box on his desk, he shut off the AC and opened the windows. He had a few minutes until a massive headache came on from the paint.

Curious, Paul sat in the desk chair and pulled back the flaps of the box. Reaching inside, he pulled out a stack of award citations. Rubbing his fingers over the Air Force logo embossed on the cover of the folder that held an award, Paul opened the folder and read the words the commanders had written about him over the years.

Going through the rest of the awards, Paul reached the bottom of the stack. Tears filled his eyes, blurring his vision when he saw the folder before him. Squeezing his eyes shut, he opened the cover of the folder and began reading out loud. "Brandon William Jones." He drew in a sharp breath. "United States Air Force...for military merit and for wounds...wounds received in action." Paul blew out his breath. "Resulting in his death."

Paul hung his head and wept. Tipping the box over, he saw the small hinged box that held the medal on the bottom. He grabbed it and opened the top, his breath catching in his throat. The gold profile image of George Washington stared at him. Removing the medal from the box, he held it up and studied it.

The Purple Heart was awarded to military members who were injured or killed by enemy action. In Brandon's case, he was among four people killed by a terrorist while eating breakfast in the dining facility in Iraq. Conflicting thoughts warred inside Paul. Brandon dying by the enemy's hand and Paul losing his leg by a falling pallet were vastly different. As challenging as his new life had been, he was thankful his and Brandon's circumstances weren't different. If Paul had been killed while on deployment, it would have destroyed Genny. Especially if by a terrorist.

"Daddy?"

Paul looked up and saw Katie standing inside the door. "Mama said it's time to eat." She walked over to where he was sitting and tilted her head. "Are you crying, Daddy?"

"Umm. Yes, I am. I found something of Uncle Brandon's and it made me sad."

Katie climbed onto Paul's lap and laid her head on his shoulder. "I get sad too, Daddy."

According to doctors, Genny's odds of conceiving were less than a percent. But God proved them wrong. He entrusted Paul and Genny with this precious gift. Katie already possessed the kind of love that was hard to contain in her young heart. And she was sassy to boot. Paul laughed under his breath.

"Are you not sad anymore?"

"Just a little bit." Paul packed everything in the box except for the Purple Heart.

On the way to the house, Paul held two precious things in his hands. In one was his daughter's hand and in the other hand represented his best friend's sacrifice for his country.

"Mama. Daddy's got something from Uncle Brandon."

"He does?" Genny looked up from setting the table. When Paul saw her face, he knew she recognized what he was holding. "You found it. I was afraid it was lost. There's something I've been thinking about."

"Yeah?"

"Let's talk about it after dinner."

"Okay, babe," Paul said and tousled Caleb's hair. Giggling, Caleb grabbed Paul's hand and looked up at him with smiling eyes. Caleb was another gift the Lord had placed in their care. Paul looked around the table as they finished their meal. Kendall picked up the un-eaten biscuit on the edge of her plate. He watched as she slipped her finger inside to scoop out the fluffy middle. She looked up at him and stopped. Lifting his brows, he smiled. Kendall was another gift from the Lord, no matter how long she would be in their home.

Paul helped Genny clean the kitchen and get the kids ready for bed. Genny sat on the couch and picked up the hinged box that held the Purple Heart medal. Paul joined her and watched as she opened the box and studied the medal, turning it one way, then the other. Lifting it out of the box, she shook it so it dangled from the ribbon.

"I used to think this was an award for Brandon's death."

Paul thought about what to say, but if there was one thing he'd learned over the years, it was best for him to listen to Genny and not try to fix her heart. Brandon had been gone for over six years, but sometimes, it hit Genny like it'd happened the day before.

"We should give this to Zoe." She dangled the medal again. "It was supposed to go to her, anyway."

"That's a wonderful thing to do. Maybe you should call her."

"I think I will." Genny put the medal back in the box, and leaned forward gently placing it on the coffee table as if it held Brandon himself.

Slipping his arm around Genny, he held her for a while. Her breathing slowed, and he figured she was asleep. Releasing his arm from around her, he made his way to the apartment to close the windows and turn the air conditioner back on. As he walked into the kitchen from the mudroom of the house, his phone chimed. Glancing at the screen, Paul wrinkled his nose when he saw Karla's name.

Karla: Sorry it's late, I just found out that Danny has a girlfriend. I need your shoulder. Can we go for coffee in the morning?

"Let me guess."

Paul looked up and saw Genny standing not far away. She knew.

Genny scoffed and rolled her eyes. "It's almost ten. She should be concerned with her own life, not interrupting ours."

"You're right, Genevieve, and I'm sorry. I'm going to talk to her."

Paul headed to the office after Genny went to bed. Opening the window helped to lessen the paint fumes. The earlier conversation with Genny surfaced. A Purple Heart award could be painful for the surviving loved ones. For him, it brought back the devastating effects of Brandon's death. He opened his journal and let his feelings flow.

August 23, 2017

I found Brandon's Purple Heart. When I read the words, my mind went back to the images that had haunted me right after he died. The images I created in my head weren't pretty. I'm not going to dwell. Brandon is with the Lord and is no longer in this fallen world. I wonder what he'd think about what happened to me.

Genny doesn't understand my feelings regarding Karla. I've tried to be mindful. The last thing I want is for this to come between me and my wife. I know God has put someone in my life to witness to. I thought it was Karla. She's hurting.

Paul focused on the framed family photo on his desk. It was taken a few days before Kendall's placement. They were sitting on the picnic table with their backs to the woods behind the property. Genny held Caleb and Katie knelt next to Paul with her hand on his shoulder. One day, would Kendall be kneeling on his other side? He returned to his journal.

The more I think about Karla, the more I think about Kendall. Maybe I should move on like several have suggested. That would be hard with us being in the same therapy group. Maybe I should leave the group…

CHAPTER 37

Paul

Paul stopped at the end of the driveway to check the mail. There was mostly junk mail, but on the bottom of the stack was a large manilla envelope. It was addressed to him and the return address was from The Lewis Manuel Foundation in Jacksonville, Florida. It was probably junk mail, too. Since they'd bought the house, they'd been bombarded with unsolicited offers from new gutters to refinancing the mortgage they'd had for two months.

Inside, Paul placed the mail on the side table and settled on the couch with the large envelope. Slipping his finger under the flap, he opened it and pulled out the letter.

The letter referred to a grant for disabled veterans he'd applied for. What grant? He hadn't applied for a grant. Paul shifted his eyes to the body of the letter.

Sergeant Paul Thompson,

Thank you for applying for The Lewis Manuel foundation grant, which was created in 2010 to provide disabled veterans financial assistance in converting their homes into handicap accessible homes.

"What?" Lucy raised her head next to him and he rubbed her back and continued reading.

We are happy to inform you that you have been awarded fifty-thousand dollars to aid in converting your home. Please visit our website for further instructions…

Paul read the letter again, then a third time. It made no sense. How could he be awarded a grant that he hadn't applied for? They probably had him mixed up with someone else. But that wouldn't explain how they got his address and the last four digits of his social security number. The garage door opened and Katie ran into the living room.

"Bubby got a shot like me and Kendall, but he's cranky." Katie climbed onto the couch and squeezed between Paul and Lucy.

Genny came inside with Caleb asleep in her arms, and Kendall walking behind her. "There are a few bags of groceries. I'm going to lay him down."

"Okay, sweetheart." Paul put the letter aside and headed out to the car.

After he brought in the bags, Genny came into the kitchen and they put away the groceries. Paul sat on the couch and picked up the envelope again. Katie climbed down and called Lucy to sit by her on the floor, where she rolled a ball across the living room floor and laughed when Lucy bounded after it. Kendall walked over and stood by the living room chair.

Genny joined him, and he handed her the envelope. "Do you know what this is?"

She read the return address and pulled out the letter. Gasping, Genny grinned and waved the letter. "You got the grant!"

"You applied for this?" Paul pointed at the letter.

"Yes. A pamphlet was in the folder you got from Walter Reed. I decided to apply. I don't know why I did since we didn't have a house then. But I never imagined that you'd get a grant. They only give out a few a year." Genny looked around the living room and her eyes fell on the brick fireplace wall. "We can get rid of that thing."

"Did you read the letter?"

A deep crease formed between her brows. Paul took the letter from her hands and read one paragraph and emphasized the requirements.

"Oh. I didn't know."

"You didn't see that the grant was for a handicap accessible house when you applied?"

"No, but can't we can have the house converted to handicap accessible? It means a total remodel."

"No."

"Why not? What if you have a problem with the prosthetic and have to use your wheelchair?"

"Like what?"

"I don't know. Anything can happen. Irritation or whatever."

"I'd use crutches before the wheelchair. We are not having this house converted just so it can be remodeled, Genevieve."

"I didn't say that. I said it would be remodeled in the process. Gosh." Genny pushed out her breath and stood. "I need to fold the laundry." She headed toward the hall. Paul stood to follow her, but stopped when he spotted Katie and Kendall sitting on the floor coloring.

Katie looked up at him. "Are you mad at Mama?"

"No."

"You yelled at her."

"I didn't yell." Did he yell? Katie was probably overreacting. But if his daughter felt he yelled, then he yelled. Thinking over his conversation with Genny, he was sure he had raised his voice, not to mention the look on his face, which he figured was none too pleasant.

He knew Genny was trying to be helpful, but in no way was he letting the house be converted. Technically, he was handicapped, but he didn't need his house to remind him daily of his disability. He'd contact the foundation and decline the grant. Someone with a greater need could use the money.

Katie grabbed Paul's hand and led him to his and Genny's bedroom. When he walked into the room, he saw Genny wiping her eyes. She continued to fold laundry until he walked up behind her and slipped his arms around her waist. Leaning her head back, she let out a breath he was sure she'd been holding since their conversation.

"I'm sorry. I didn't mean to be a jerk. I was caught off guard."

"It's okay. I should have asked, or at least told you I applied. I won't do anything like that again." She continued folding clothes.

"We can do a little in the house at a time."

"Yeah." Genny sighed.

Paul stood for a moment and walked back into the living room. The brick fireplace wall stuck out as if it was a hundred feet tall. The money from Mrs. Baker would take care of it, but he wanted to do the sensible thing and invest it, mainly for the kid's education.

Paul pulled his laptop out from under the couch, brought up the browser, and began a search.

Remodeling contractors in Charleston.

The estimate for the remodel added up to over three-quarters of the figure in his head. What could they do to cut the price? Paul laid the document down and leaned against the counter, glaring at the brick wall. The labor to demo the eyesore was ridiculous. Maybe he could get Trevor and Ryan along with some men from church to come over one day with their sledgehammers.

"Da-dee?" Paul looked down at the sweet smile of his son.

"Yes, little man."

"Gurl," he said, and pointed toward Kendall's room.

Paul made his way to the room and paused when he saw Kendall sitting on the floor facing the wall. When he walked over, he saw Katie's doll, Peggy, on her lap. Releasing a quiet breath, Paul sat on the floor next to Kendall. Strands of hair were hiding her face, but Paul could make out tears running down her cheeks. How could he comfort her and help her feel safe? If only she would talk.

Out of the corner of his eye, Paul saw Lucy walk up behind Kendall and press her nose into Kendall's hair. Raising to her knees, Kendall froze when Lucy pushed herself between her and the wall. Lucy sat in front of her and nudged her hand.

"She wants you to pet her," Paul said and rubbed Lucy's head.

Kendall stared at the dog for a moment, then hovered her hand above Lucy's head. Bumping her head into Kendall's hand, Lucy's body began swaying from side to side when she wagged her tail. Kendall patted Lucy's head and jerked her hand away. Standing, she darted over to the bed and climbed under the covers, head and all. Paul sighed and headed to the door.

Curious why Lucy hadn't trotted past him, he turned around and his mouth hung open. Lucy was stretched out on the bed next to Kendall. The girl's head was still under the covers, but at least she didn't appear bothered by Lucy's presence. Progress? Paul thought so. He spotted Peggy on the floor by the wall and picked up the doll, slipping her under the edge of the comforter.

By the time Paul stepped into the hall and looked over his shoulder to see if Lucy was going to follow him, Peggy was gone. Smiling, Paul headed down the hall to text Trevor and Ryan about helping him demo, hopefully dropping the estimate by a few thousand dollars.

The garage door flung open, and Katie ran into the living room. Stopping in the middle of the room, she looked around and said, "Where's Kendall?"

"She's taking a nap. She had a rough morning."

"Oh." Katie skipped towards the hall.

"Leave her alone, okay?" Paul warned.

"I am Daddy." Katie groaned.

Genny walked in carrying a coloring page and held it out to Paul. Caleb squealed and ran up to her.

"How'd counseling go?" Paul asked.

"Better than I expected. I thought that she'd say something about us spending a lot of time with Kendall, but Hailey said that all she talked about was how sad Kendall was."

"Hmm. That's good, though."

"Definitely. Oh, Tina is setting Kendall up for her counseling. I know they use the clinic where Katie goes, but I'm not sure if Hailey will be her therapist."

Paul filled Genny in on what had happened with Kendall when she and Katie were out. Genny glanced around the living room, then at Lucy's empty bed.

"Lucy's still with her," Paul said.

"Really?"

He nodded and walked up to Genny. "I think she's good for Kendall."

"Lucy has helped us. I hope she can help Kendall, too."

"So do I, love." He slipped his arms around Genny's waist and gently kissed her.

Genny walked to Kendall's room, opened the door a crack, then went inside. Paul's phone chimed, and he stepped over to the side table and tapped the message.

Karla: How's the little girl? I hope everything is going okay. I miss seeing you in the group.

Paul sighed and typed a quick reply.

Paul: Keep us in your prayers. I'm not sure when I'll be back. Things are tough right now.

Karla: Okay, I will.

He placed his phone back on the side table and focused on the brick wall. Maybe they could paint it. What made it less than desirable was the dated brick color. Paul saw Genny step into the hall and slowly close the bedroom door.

"She's still asleep," Genny said as she walked towards him.

It had been nearly four hours since he'd left Kendall in her room. He'd checked on her half an hour after she hid under the covers and gently pulled the comforter away from her face. She'd looked like an angel with her blond hair spread across her pillow. He'd closed his eyes and prayed over God's precious child and for him and Genny as they did their best to care for her physically and emotionally.

Tossing the kids' toys off the couch, Paul pulled up the couch cushions and groaned. His keys had to be at the apartment; he'd looked everywhere else. Paul set out in a sprint towards the garage door, bumping into Caleb. Grabbing his arm, Paul kept Caleb from falling to the floor. He whined and Paul stood him up straight and continued to the garage.

In the apartment, Paul shuffled through everything on his desk, in the bedroom and the bathroom, even though there was no reason his keys would be in there. Where were they? Paul headed back through the garage to the house and, as he reached for the door, he heard Caleb crying. When he pushed open the door, Genny looked up and glared at him.

"What are you doing?" she snapped.

"I'm looking for my keys. I'm going to be late for my appointment with Steve."

"Caleb said you pushed him."

"It was an accident. Have you seen my keys?"

Genny's eyes shift past him.

"Did you check the key holder?"

"They're not there."

"Did you check?" She tilted her head and crossed her arms over her chest.

"Of course, I did, Genevieve!"

Genny stepped over to the key holder by the garage door and lifted Paul's keys from a hook. Walking up to him, she held the keys out, wearing a smirk. The keys weren't on the holder when he went to the apartment.

"Maybe one of the kids—"

"What Paul? You think one of the kids dragged a chair over and hung your keys up after they played with them while you were in the apartment?" Genny rolled her eyes.

Paul breathed out and drew in a calming breath. Genny must have had the keys. What was he thinking? It was absurd that he would accuse his children of playing with his keys or his wife playing a trick on him. What was wrong with him?

The TBI? PTSD? Both?

"I'm sorry. I shouldn't have snapped. I know you struggle with your memory," Genny said and grabbed Paul's hand. "Steve's working with you, right?"

"Yeah. Oh, speaking of Steve, I need to run." Paul took the keys and gave Genny a quick kiss before heading to the door.

Pulling into a parking space at the VA, Paul made his way to the entrance. Wasting no time, he darted around those walking slowly. An older man mumbled something when Paul slipped between him and someone walking in the middle of the hall. Paul gritted his teeth when pain traveled down his left leg. Slowing his pace, he drew in slow, deep breaths as he rubbed his residual leg.

"That's what you get," the man hissed at Paul as he ambled by.

Holding back a moan, Paul bit his bottom lip until the pain subsided. He continued on his way, slowing his pace when he caught up to the elderly gentleman.

"I'm sorry, sir. I'm late for my appointment."

"Leave earlier," the old man snarled.

Lord, hold my tongue. Paul took another step and cried out when his residual leg felt like it was on fire. He grabbed his leg and squeezed.

"Are you okay, sir?" a nurse said as she wove her way through the people in the hall towards Paul.

"Phantom pain. It'll pass." Paul slowly pushed out his breath and looked up at the people eyeing him as they walked by. The cranky old man had stopped a few feet ahead of Paul and was watching him and the nurse. When the pain had eased, Paul took his time as he continued down the hall. He glanced at his watch and groaned. He was five minutes late for his appointment.

"You an amputee?" the man asked and looked at Paul's legs as Paul walked up to him.

"Yes, sir. Left leg above the knee."

"My goodness. Right below the knee."

The man stayed by Paul's side as they took their time walking down the hall. Neither mentioned their exchange earlier. Parting ways with the older veteran, Paul opened the door of the mental health clinic and rushed to the counter.

"I'm sorry I'm late. I had some phantom pain in the hall and it stopped me in my tracks." It was true, but he wouldn't have been late if he'd first looked at the key holder. He'd barely taken a seat when Steve called his name.

Steve leaned back and rested his ankle on his knee as he watched Paul settle into the chair he'd called his own for the past several months.

"You look flustered."

"You can say that." Paul choked out a chuckle.

"Tell me about it."

Paul gave Steve the rundown of the morning, including nearly knocking Caleb to the floor.

"What strategy did we come up with last time to help prevent this?"

Paul leaned his head back, then looked Steve in the eyes. "Hang my keys on the key holder as soon as I walk in the door."

"Trust that."

Steve was right. Katie had been reminding him to hang his keys up. So much so that it had got on his nerves. "Yeah." Paul puffed out his cheeks and blew out a long, heavy breath.

"How's Kendall?"

"Gosh, she's hurting, Steve. I have some experience with loss because of Genny's parents. Genny was five and doesn't remember much about it, but she knows how she feels, if that makes sense. Not specifics, but fear and sadness."

"That's not uncommon for children."

"It's different with Kendall. There's no family to take care of her. Her paternal grandmother gave up custody, so here she is with a strange family."

"Really? Did the grandmother give a reason?"

"Health problems."

"Do you two regret it?"

"Genny doesn't."

Steve angled his head.

"That sounded bad. It's hard balancing her needs with Katie and Caleb, and it's been almost two months since she came to live with us. Sometimes I wonder if she is a good fit, you know? I must sound like a terrible person."

"No. It's perfectly normal."

Paul glanced out the window. "I know she's here for a reason. And it could be for a short period." A feeling came to Paul that Kendall was going to be with them for longer than a season. But how long? Peace filled his heart at the thought that they wouldn't be doing this alone. God would make sure they had the help they needed to give Kendall the best chance at recovering, and one of those helpers had four legs and fur.

CHAPTER 38

Genny

Paul headed out to the small grocery store a couple miles down the road to buy a gallon of ice cream and a box of cones for an afternoon snack for the kids. Genny went outside to check the tomato plants. She turned on the spigot and unwound the hose from the hose cart as she headed to the garden.

The tomato plants flourished. Paul had joked that Genny watered and fertilized them too much. As if that were possible. Memories of helping her granny in her garden brought a smile to Genny's face. Her granny's tomato plants were almost as tall as Genny's plants, but not as full. Genny looked out over the row of ten tomato plants and twisted the hose nozzle.

She aimed the nozzle at the bottom of the plants, taking her time watering each one. The plants were loaded with ripening tomatoes. The kids had eagerly watched one tomato as it matured ahead of the others. Katie had begged her to let her pick it when it was still half green. Genny reached to pick the tomato and paused. She'd wait until later in the evening and let them pick it with Kendall. Dropping the hose, she walked to the other side of the garden to check the rest of the vegetables.

A blast of cold water hit her square in the chest, and she screamed. She couldn't see Paul through the thick plants, but heard him laughing. "Paul Tyler Thompson!" Genny ran around the garden towards Paul, still holding the hose in his hand.

"You better not!" Genny shrieked. Paul dropped the hose and Genny ran into his arms, pressing herself against his chest. She giggled at the wet spots on his t-shirt when she pulled back.

"A fire truck is at Yancy's Grocery Store," Paul said.

"Oh yeah? The new fire station must have opened earlier than planned."

"Yeah. Do you think the kids would like to go? Katie would love it, but is Caleb too young?" Paul ran his hand down the front of his damp t-shirt. "And what about Kendall?"

All kids loved fire trucks, right? But it was hard to know what Kendall liked since she wasn't speaking.

"What are you guys doing?" Katie's raised voice came from the patio.

"Thinking about seeing the fire truck at the grocery store," Paul said.

Katie gasped. "I wanna go!" She ran out to where Paul and Genny were standing.

Genny spotted Kendall standing in the doorway and walked over. "Want to see the fire truck?" Kendall stared at Genny. What was going on in that precious child's mind? Three years old and her family was gone. Genny sighed. Caleb's voice came through the speaker on the monitor clipped to Genny's shorts.

"Bubby's awake. Let's load up!" Paul said.

Parking was scarce when the grocery store came into view. Genny spotted a vacant handicap space and eyed Paul. He used handicap spaces as a last resort. With it being Labor Day weekend, he didn't have a choice but to park in a handicap parking spot.

Genny held Katie's and Kendall's hands as they walked through the parking lot. The truck looked as if it'd just rolled off the assembly line—shiny and new, without a dent or scratch as far as Genny could tell. It was smaller than the trucks she'd seen in Charleston. In their rural area, she guessed there was no need for a large truck. Katie's mouth gaped as she stared at the ladder on top.

Paul walked up next to Genny with Caleb in his arms. Near the fire truck stood a man in full gear. The only thing missing was his helmet. His face brightened when he saw them, and he walked over.

"Well, hello there." He squatted down to eye-level with Katie and Kendall. "I'm Firefighter Connor, but you can call me Andrew."

"Say hello to Mr. Andrew." Genny tugged on the girls' hands.

Katie piped up. "Hi, Mr. Andrew, where's your dog with spots?"

The man chuckled and stood. "Do you think all firefighters need a dog with spots?"

Katie nodded.

"Let me see what I can do." He walked around the front of the truck and returned a moment later with a dalmatian on a leash. "Meet Pepper." He tugged on the dog's leash to guide him to where the girls were standing. Katie giggled and Kendall's eyes widened.

Genny bent down to Kendall. "He's kind of like Lucy, but a different color." *And bigger.* Genny kept the thought to herself.

"Do you want to pet him?" Andrew asked.

"She don't talk," Katie said.

"That's okay," Andrew smiled at Kendall.

Paul stood Caleb on the ground and the dog walked up to him.

Kendall moved behind Genny.

"I guess she's afraid of dogs," Andrew said.

"We have a dog, but Pepper is a lot bigger."

Kendall's gaze was fixed on the top of the cab of the fire truck. It was as if she was mesmerized by the dancing red lights.

"You guys actually have a dalmatian?" Paul grinned.

"Pepper is a rescue and is in a foster home. He came from an animal hoarding situation. Right now, he stays with the chief and his family."

Paul scratched Pepper's head and looked at Genny. The sirens on the truck wailed to life, the sound bouncing off the building. The blast of the horn vibrated in Genny's chest. Katie held her hands over her ears and grinned. Paul reached down and covered Caleb's ears with his hands.

Kendall shrieked and clamped her arms around Genny's legs. Paul and Genny looked at each other. Kendall started shaking and wailing along with the siren. Genny pried Kendall's arms from around her legs and picked her up.

"Rogers!" Andrew yelled as he ran to the open passenger window of the truck, hoisting himself up. A moment later, the siren silenced. He hopped down and sprinted over to them. "I'm so sorry."

"It's all right. I think it's time to go home," Paul said and picked up Caleb. Katie groaned. "Katherine." Paul glared at her. She looked at him and frowned.

With the kids in their seats, Paul backed out of the parking lot and headed toward home. Kendall's sobbing drowned out the radio and Genny turned it off.

"What's wrong with her, Mama?" Katie shouted, holding her hands over her ears.

"I don't know, honey." Genny sighed and lowered the sun visor and looked at Kendall in the mirror. Tears filled Genny's eyes. She'd cried so much that her hair had stuck to her cheeks. By the time Paul pulled into the driveway, Kendall's crying had quieted as if all the energy had drained from her small body. Paul picked her up from her booster seat and she rested her head on his shoulder. Genny helped Katie out of the SUV and carried Caleb inside.

After changing Caleb's diaper, Genny walked into the living room. Her heart squeezed when she saw Kendall asleep on Paul's chest. Katie sat next to him, lightly rubbing Kendall's back. Genny eased down in the chair and sat Caleb on her lap.

"This isn't being afraid of a siren and horn," Paul whispered. "She was downright terrified." Paul ran his hand over Kendall's head.

"I know. Could it be the accident?" Genny parted her lips and closed them.

"I think it is."

"Huh?" Katie said.

"Do you remember she was in an accident?" Paul asked. "That's how she hurt her arm."

Katie nodded.

"The siren scared her. It reminded her of the fire truck that helped her the day of the accident," Genny said.

"Oh."

Caleb reached for his sippy cup on the side table and Genny handed it to him. Paul was right, but what could they do about it?

"I think you should call Tina about that therapy appointment."

"I will." Genny watched Kendall as she slept. Her mouth hung slightly open, and with her cheek pressed against Paul's shoulder, her breathing was louder than usual.

"Mama," Katie whispered. Genny's focus shifted to Katie. "How long is she going to live with us?"

"I don't know, honey." The foster care system was too complicated for a child to understand.

Kendall stirred and lifted her head, her face inches from Paul's face. A red mark covered her cheek where she had laid against Paul's shoulder. He pulled his arms away from her and she pushed against his chest to sit up. For a long moment, she stared at him.

"Hi, Kendall," Katie whispered and rested her hand on Kendall's back. "Want to play with Mr. Floppy?" Hesitating for a moment, Kendall reached out and took the rabbit from Katie.

"Anyone hungry?" Genny asked. She sat Caleb on the floor and he crawled over to his toys.

"Me, Mama! Chicken tenders."

"That's what's on the menu." Genny headed to the kitchen and glanced out the window at the backyard. For an instant, she expected to see Mrs. Baker next door on her patio watering her plants. Tears blurred her vision. Sometimes Genny missed Mrs. Baker badly, causing actual pain in her heart.

CHAPTER 39

Paul

Hissing caught Paul's attention. He groaned when he realized he'd forgotten to place the coffee carafe on the burner after he poured the water into the tank of the coffee maker. Paul grabbed a few Styrofoam cups and tried to catch the coffee as it brewed.

"What are you doing?" Clyde laughed. He walked over and pulled the cord from the outlet.

"Why didn't I think of that?" Paul carefully poured the four cups of coffee into the carafe and ran his forearm across his brow. After cleaning up the mess, he put the decaf onto brew, paying attention to what he was doing.

The men took a seat to pray for the group meeting, starting in half an hour. Once Clyde closed the prayer, he looked at Paul and lifted his chin.

"Something on your heart?"

Paul sat up straight. "You sound like my dad. Apparently, my thoughts are etched on my face when I'm around him." Paul laughed. "I've decided to leave the VA therapy group." Paul opened the cover of his Bible and closed it.

Clyde stood and made his way to the decaf coffee maker and poured a cup. "Is that so?"

"I thought the VA group was special because of the military, but through this group, I've learned that's not true."

Clyde slowly nodded. "It's not just the career. Military, law enforcement and other first responders all share a camaraderie. It can be devastating when you lose it. What we are doing is bringing back camaraderie to those who lost it when they lost their careers."

"And spending time with Karla is getting to Genny."

"Remember what I said?"

The door opened and a woman limped in they'd never seen before. The look on her face told them she was about to turn around and take off in a sprint. Both Paul and Clyde stood as she took her time walking to the circle of chairs.

"Am I in the right place for the support group for military and first responders?" she squeaked out.

"Yes, ma'am," Clyde said. "I'm Clyde Martin, and this here is Paul Thompson. We run the group. And you are?"

"Kat." She pushed her flaming red hair away from her face. "I'm Catholic." She swallowed hard.

"Although we meet in a church, this group is for everyone no matter what religion or no religion at all," Paul said.

"Oh, okay." A brief smile crossed her face.

The other men trickled in and took their seats. Disappointment filled Paul's heart at the empty chairs. They had seven members, including Clyde and himself. Each week, Paul set up fifteen chairs and they had yet to come close to filling them.

When the group started, Clyde introduced Kat, and she freely shared her story. Injured as a rookie police officer, she'd bounced from working retail to the restaurant industry to hospitality. Most of the jobs required her to be on her feet for extended periods of time and her leg injury forced her to quit each job. Recently, she was approved for disability and that was what pushed her to join the group.

"Me too," Chuck said to Kat. "I felt worthless and relying on the government for my livelihood caused my depression to take a nosedive. My therapist suggested this support group and I'm glad I joined. We have something special going on here." He looked around the group and smiled.

At the end of the group, as usual, Paul announced a closing prayer and invited those to stay who would like to join in. He smiled inside when everyone remained seated. Asking for prayer requests before starting, Joey lifted his hand and Paul gave him a nod of acknowledgement.

"I'd like to pray for that precious little girl you and your wife are fostering. I'm sure it's an adjustment for all of you."

"Yes, it is. Thank you, Joey."

Once everyone had left, Paul and Clyde put away the chairs and locked up for the night. Walking to his truck, Paul felt his phone vibrate in his pocket. Genny probably wanted him to pick up milk or something on the way home.

Genny: Please pick up milk and dish soap. I love you.

After checking out at the grocery store, he climbed into the truck and placed the grocery bags in the passenger seat. Reaching inside one bag, he pulled out a small stuffed bear. It was soft and cuddly and infused with lavender. According to the tag, lavender was known for its calming and soothing effects. Hopefully, it would help Kendall sleep. He didn't think she'd slept through the night since she came into their home.

Katie's bedroom light was on when Paul walked into the house. Glancing at the clock on the mantel, he noticed it was close to ten o'clock, two hours past her bedtime. He placed the bags onto the counter and made his way to Katie's room, where he heard her whining.

"Daddy!" she said when Paul walked in the doorway. "Mama said I had to go to bed, but I want to wait for you," she said, tears rolling down her cheeks.

"I'm here now, baby girl." Paul walked over and gave her a hug and a kiss. "Night night."

"Night night, Daddy." Katie grinned as her tears disappeared.

Paul looked at Genny, noting her lips pressed together. She pulled the door closed behind them and rested her hand on Paul's arm. "Kendall is still awake."

"I've got something for her." Paul smiled and led Genny into the kitchen. "It's to help calm her. It has lavender in it." He handed the bear to Genny.

She sniffed. "Mmm, I need one of these."

"I'll remember that for your birthday." He winked. "I'm going to give it to her now."

"I'm going to get ready for bed."

"Okay." Paul made his way to Kendall's room.

Pushing the door open, he peeked in and saw Kendall in bed facing the wall. Taking quiet steps, he made it to the side of the bed to see if she was still awake.

Rolling over, Kendall's eyes found the bear in Paul's hand.

"I saw this bear and thought of you. It's supposed to help you sleep." Paul held it out, but Kendall kept her arms under the covers. He let out a soft breath and tucked the bear in bed next to her. When he stood and made his way to the door, he glimpsed a small shadow against the wall outside Kendall's bedroom. But by the time he was at the door, Katie was in her room. The nightlight cast enough light on Katie that he could see her head pressed against the pillow.

Genny was in bed reading when Paul walked into the bedroom. After getting ready for bed, he slid under the covers and took the book from Genny's hand.

"What are you doing?" Her brows came together.

"We need to talk."

"Uh-oh." She gave him a tentative smile.

"I've decided to leave the VA group."

"I thought you liked that group more." Genny sat up and turned to face Paul.

"I feel it's served its purpose."

"Whatever you feel led to do." Genny leaned over and kissed Paul's cheek. As she pulled away, she said, "What about Karla?"

"I plan on talking to her. I can't leave her hanging."

Genny reached for his hand and gave it a gentle squeeze. "Good night."

"Good night, love."

Genny turned off the lamp and laid her head on his shoulder.

Why didn't Paul see what had been happening with Karla? The small warning signs were there, but he kept pushing them down. He'd never considered himself prideful. Was that why he felt it was his job, and no one else's, to witness to Karla?

Glancing in the rearview mirror, Paul saw Kendall staring straight ahead. They were approaching the outskirts of town where the traffic was heavier. Paul could do a pretty good job of avoiding places where a pallet would be, but cars were everywhere. They didn't know the details of the car accident, but Paul imagined it was scary for Kendall to be in traffic.

Paul turned into the parking lot of the counseling center. His heart sank when he opened the back passenger door. Kendall's hands were clamped to the armrest of the booster seat and the tips of her fingers had turned white. Coaxing for a few moments, she released the arm rests. Paul picked her up, stood her on the pavement, and took her by the hand.

On the way to the entrance of the building, Paul barely felt Kendall's hand in his. He was used to Katie's firm grip. Glancing down at her, he wondered who she was before the accident. Was she an outgoing child like Katie, or was her behavior not much different from what it was now?

Inside, Kendall walked up to the play area in the lobby while Paul checked her in. He'd barely settled into the seat when her therapist, Charlie, walked into the waiting room and spoke to Kendall.

"Good morning, Miss Kendall." She looked around the waiting room and spotted Paul. He rose to his feet when Charlie made her way over to him. "Hello, Paul."

"Hello."

Kendall put down the block she had in her hand and stepped over to where they were standing.

"Why don't you go back and play with the blocks while I talk to Mr. Paul for a few minutes? Miss Claudia can come out to play with you."

Kendall looked at Paul as if she was asking his permission. A young woman came out and led Kendall to the play area, and Paul followed Charlie to her office.

Charlie's office resembled the play area in the lobby. His first thought every time he walked into the room was to throw himself onto the beanbag. He stifled a laugh when Charlie saw his face.

"Don't worry, most adults think the same thing." She laughed.

Paul took a seat in an oversized chair against the wall.

"How's Kendall?"

"Pretty much the same. She interacts with us, plays with Katie and Caleb."

"Don't be discouraged. You two are doing a wonderful job."

"Are you sure?" Paul laughed under his breath. "Why is she still mute? I know the accident has a lot to do with it, but I was wondering why it's still happening."

"At first it was the trauma, but it's progressed to a way of being in control. Her life has been out of her hands, starting with the accident. They were traveling when the accident occurred, so she was in a hospital with a bunch of strangers poking and prodding her. Her grandmother came for her and she's ended up in your home. Not talking is the only thing she can control."

Paul considered what Charlie said, and it made sense. "What about when she stays in her room? It's better, but there are days she's in there all day long."

"Depression and grief. Kid's behavior is their language."

Katie's therapist had said the same thing. Paul thought about Katie's behavior after he came home. He couldn't leave the room without her searching the house and backyard for him. It was her fear that he was going to leave her and never come back.

"Tina told me about the fire truck."

"Yeah, it was rough. I'm glad the firefighters were understanding."

"Definitely. So, how has she been since then?"

"It took a few days, but she seems okay now. She and Katie play most of the day except for quiet time."

"Good. What about the dog? Lucy, right?"

"Yes. She's with the girls all the time. Lucy can tell when Kendall is having a bad day. She pretty much stays by her side."

"Dogs are very therapeutic."

"Lucy has seen Genny and I through some pretty rough times." Paul smiled as Lucy's face appeared in his head. "There was something Kendall did that surprised us."

"Yeah?"

"I've worn athletic pants around Kendall since prosthetics can scare kids. We figured it could be worse for her. The girls were busy playing, so I wore shorts when I mowed. I'd just finished and came in to shower. She must have seen me because I went into the bedroom to take my shoes off and I noticed her standing outside the doorway.

"She was shocked, as most kids would be. Katie came about that time and took Kendall to her room to play. A little while later, I went into the living room and the girls were playing with their dolls. Out of the blue, Kendall looked at me and came over to where I was sitting. She pointed to my scar on my left arm and looked at her own scar. Nothing since then, though."

"She connected with you. Give it time." She smiled. "Well, I think it's about time to get Miss Kendall in here. Why don't you hang out in the lobby while we play in the sand tray?"

"Sounds like a plan."

They made their way into the waiting room, where Claudia was playing with Kendall and another child. When Kendall saw Paul and Charlie, she dropped the toy she was playing with and went to where they were standing. Charlie urged Kendall to walk with her toward the hall, but she stayed by Paul's side.

"Go ahead with Miss Charlie." Paul nodded at Kendall when she looked up at him. When Charlie turned to steer Kendall to the hall, she raised her brows at

Paul and smiled. Maybe she was right about Kendall having a connection with him. Time would tell.

CHAPTER 40

Genny

"She's *mine!*" Katie shrieked.

Genny darted into the living room where she saw Katie holding Clementine—Genny's doll when she was a little girl—by the hair, glaring at Kendall. Kendall stood and wrapped her arms around herself. When Genny made it to where the girls were standing, her heart sank at the tears filling Kendall's eyes.

"Put the doll down, Katie," Genny said, forcing her voice remain calm.

"But, Mama."

The garage door opened and Paul walked into the kitchen holding a shop towel with the handle of a paintbrush sticking out. He stopped, realizing something was wrong.

"Give Clementine to me." Genny held out her hand. Katie's bottom lip quivered as she handed the doll to Genny.

"What's up?" Paul asked.

"Katie, go to your room."

Katie reached for the doll.

"I'm keeping Clementine for now, okay?"

"Okay, Mama." Katie wiped her cheeks and looked at Kendall.

Arms still wrapped around herself, Kendall bristled when Genny kneeled next to her.

"Do you want to play with Clementine?" Genny held out the doll.

Kendall's gaze rested on the doll, then shifted to the floor.

"It's okay, you can play with her."

Red crept up Katie's neck—an inherited trait from Genny. Katie forced out a breath and ran to her room.

Kendall turned and walked down the hall to her room.

"It's time," Paul said.

"Yeah."

On the way to Katie's room, Genny peaked at Kendall sitting on her bed. She was picking at her fingernails, and wiped her cheeks. She looked up in time for Genny's eyes to meet hers, filling Genny's heart with sorrow. Paul walked into Katie's room first, and Genny pushed the door closed behind them.

"Am I in trouble, Daddy?"

"We want to talk to you about Kendall." Paul said and they sat on either side of Katie.

"Oh." Katie tilted her head. "When is she going home?"

"She's not, baby girl," Paul said. "She doesn't have a mama and daddy to go home to."

Katie's mouth opened and closed. "She doesn't have a mama and daddy?"

"No, sweetie." Tears burned Genny's eyes. "Her mama and daddy went to heaven like Grandma and Grandpa."

Katie looked at the photo of Genny's parents with Genny and Brandon on her dresser. "They did?"

"Yes," Genny said.

"Is that why she's sad?" Katie looked up at Genny.

"Yes. Her mama and daddy went to heaven recently," Paul said and tucked Katie's hair behind her ear. "She was in the accident with her family." Paul told Katie enough of what had happened so she could understand why Kendall acted the way she did.

Katie was quiet a little while. She slipped her hand around Genny's hand and looked up at her. "Why don't she talk?"

"She's sad and scared. She's in a place she doesn't know with people she doesn't know. And she misses her family."

Katie tilted her head thoughtfully. "I'm sorry I was mean, Mama."

"You need to tell Kendall that you are sorry," Paul said.

"Okay."

Genny handed the doll to Katie and watched as she walked across the hall into Kendall's room.

"I'm sorry, Kendall. Here." Katie said, and held out the doll. "You can play with her." Katie turned to her parents and sighed when Kendall didn't reach for the doll.

"Leave her. She'll play with her if she wants to," Paul said.

"Okay." Katie gingerly laid the doll on the bed next to where Kendall was sitting. She walked out into the hall and looked up at her parents.

"Why don't you take Lucy outside to get some sun," Genny said.

"Okay." Usually, Katie was beside herself when Paul or Genny told her she could take Lucy outside, but not today.

"She has a good heart," Paul said. "She's confused."

"I know." Katie had been adjusting to Kendall's presence the best she could. Genny worried that Kendall's silence would affect Katie negatively, as if Kendall was mad at her.

Kendall had been with them for close to three months, and nothing had changed. She was still mute and withdrawn. What was it going to take to break down her walls? Today was the first time she'd expressed any emotions since the incident with the fire truck. Why did it have to be through tears?

For the past two weeks, Kendall had played with Katie for most days. An improvement from isolating herself in her room. Genny felt that Katie apologizing for the Clementine incident was a turning point. Today was a special day for Kendall—it was her fourth birthday. Paul and Genny wanted it to be a low-key celebration as not to overwhelm Kendall.

Genny bought three flavors of cake mix and figured she'd ask Katie to pick one if Kendall didn't seem interested. She rinsed her and Paul's coffee cups and looked out the kitchen window. A smile crossed her lips at Lucy running zoomies around the backyard. Light footsteps sounded behind Genny and she turned around. To her surprise, Kendall was standing not far away with Clementine under her arm.

"Hi, sweet girl." Genny gave Kendall an exaggerated smile, but Kendall didn't react.

Grabbing the boxes of cake mix from the pantry, Genny lined them up on the kitchen counter and said, "Do you have a favorite? This is chocolate, strawberry, and vanilla," Genny said, pointing to each box. Kendall looked up at her and back at the boxes.

"What are you doing, Mama?"

"Helping Kendall pick out a cake for her birthday."

Katie walked up next to Kendall. "Which one do you like? Chocolate is my favorite."

Kendall looked over at Katie, then back at the cake boxes. She grasped the edge of the counter in front of the chocolate box and glanced at Genny.

"Would you like a chocolate cake?" Genny focused on Kendall's face for an answer, or at least an acknowledgement. Kendall looked at the boxes and back at Genny again. She gave a slight nod. Genny rested her hand on her chest. "She answered a question," Genny said to Katie.

"She did it in my room."

"What? When?"

"When we was playing. She looked at Clementine. I asked if she wanted to hold her & she nodded."

"Katie, why didn't you tell me?"

"I didn't know, Mama."

"Has she done it before then?"

"No."

"Okay. Chocolate it is." Genny smiled at Kendall and picked up the box. She glanced at the clock on the microwave. Paul had another hour until the group therapy was over and it would take at least half an hour for him to stop by the store and drive home.

"Can we help?" Katie grinned.

"Of course."

Though Kendall didn't communicate or show emotion while they prepared the cake, she had followed Genny's instructions and maintained eye contact. This was a turning point for Kendall, and Genny couldn't wait to tell Paul.

Later on, the door opened, and Katie gasped, running up to Paul when she saw him carrying a wrapped present.

"Is that for Kendall's birthday?"

"Yes, it is, baby girl."

"What is it?"

"A surprise."

Katie rolled her eyes. "I know, Daddy."

Paul placed the present on the dining table next to the cake. Genny walked up to Paul with a lighter and leaned over to kiss him. "Kendall nodded when she was picking out her cake," Genny whispered and smiled.

Paul's eyes widened when he looked at her.

The family took their seats at the table and Genny lit the candle. Kendall stared into the flame on top of the number four candle for a long moment. Genny grimaced when wax rolled down the side of the candle, puddling on top of the cake.

"Want me to help?" Katie tilted her head and smiled at Kendall.

Kendall nodded, and Paul counted to three. The flame danced in their breath, then disappeared, leaving a ribbon of black smoke floating above the candle for a couple of seconds.

Genny stood to slice the cake and stopped when she saw Katie's finger swipe a dollop of chocolate icing from the side of the cake and stuck her finger in her mouth.

"Katherine Kelly!" Genny groaned.

"Hmm. I think I will," Paul said, and swiped his finger across the side of the cake.

"Paul." Genny let out a heavy sigh.

Caleb squealed and smacked his hands on the tray of his highchair. Paul dug his finger into the icing and swiped, holding his finger in front of Caleb's mouth. Genny glared at him and shrugged, swiping her own dob of icing. Kendall sat quietly, looking at the finger trails in the icing. Genny closed her eyes and prayed that Kendall would put her finger on the cake like the rest of the family, but she didn't. Was she scared of getting in trouble or didn't want their attention?

"We're four, Mama!"

"You sure are. For a few more months until you turn five."

"Open your present, Kendall!" Katie bounced on the chair and clapped.

Impatiently, Katie reached over and grabbed at the wrapping paper, tearing a small hole. Kendall ripped the paper off the box, revealing a doll.

"Jenny? Really?" Genny looked at Paul, shaking her head.

"I didn't name her, babe." Paul laughed.

Genny opened the box and handed the doll to Kendall. Focusing on the doll's face, Kendall ran her fingers through the doll's blond hair.

"She has hair like you," Katie said. "You can name her Scarlett."

"Baby girl, let her name the doll whatever she wants," Paul said.

"But she can't talk."

"Maybe she has a name in her head. Or she can keep Jenny until she decides if she wants to change it," Genny said.

Katie sank back into her chair and pushed out her bottom lip. She perked up and said, "You can still play with Clementine. She can be Scarlett's sister, okay?"

Genny shook her head. The girls climbed down from the table and ran to Katie's room, where Genny heard Katie talking in her Miss Peggy's voice. Creeping down the hall, Genny peeked into the room and smiled when Kendall was making Jenny dance with Miss Peggy.

"What a blessed day," Paul said when Genny walked into the living room and eased down on the couch next to him.

"Yes. I hope she doesn't regress."

"Babe, have faith."

"You know me. Miss Pessimism."

Paul pulled Genny close and kissed the side of her head. "You've come a long way, Genevieve."

He was right. But Genny couldn't help worrying that the excitement of Kendall's birthday was what had knocked down the walls around her heart and the walls would be rebuilt by the morning.

Genny headed outside with her journal. It was now her favorite place to journal, as long as the weather was nice.

Oct 12, 2017

Today's Kendall's fourth birthday. She gave US *the most wonderful present. She nodded! I'm hopeful it's the beginning of her coming out of her shell.*

It was a short entry but full of emotion.

CHAPTER 41

Paul

"How've you been? Done any more exposure therapy?" Steve asked.

"The commissary is having a case lot sale today and I thought I'd stop by on the way home. Genny asked me to bring home a few grocery items, so might as well kill two birds with one stone, right?"

"Man, are you sure?" Steve chuckled. "A case lot sale equals hordes of people."

Paul hadn't thought about that, just the pallets. Maybe he should go another day.

"Don't mind me. I have faith in you."

Paul shrugged and decided he'd at least try.

"How's the family? What about Kendall?"

Paul filled Steve in on Kendall's progress. As he talked, it felt like a dark cloud was gathering over his head. Telling Steve that he was leaving the group would be difficult. But it was best under the circumstances. Paul was sure that Steve would understand.

"Something bothering you?"

He didn't wear his emotions on his sleeve. He wore his emotions plastered all over his face. "I have decided to leave the group. The support group I started with Clyde has taken off and I feel led to focus on that."

"I hate you are leaving, but I understand. Will you still be seeing me?"

"Definitely." Paul shifted in the chair. "I have to be honest with you. It's not only the support group. Karla has…I don't know…gotten attached to me?"

"I noticed. So did Beth."

Paul opened his mouth and closed it. Was Karla that obvious?

It made sense now. When the group therapy sessions had ended, Beth had been inviting Karla for coffee or to walk around the grounds.

"I know that you have a heart for people who are struggling, but I don't want you to worry. Beth is a strong Christian and I believe she'll be good for Karla."

Paul released a long breath, ridding himself of the anxiety that had been weighing him down since he'd left the house an hour earlier. "I don't know why, but apparently, I've had blinders on for how she saw me. I thought I was the only one who could reach her, but I've finally realized that it's not my responsibility. My family comes first."

"Yes, they do. Don't worry. We won't let her slip through the cracks." Steve smiled.

Leaving the VA, Paul felt lighter. Now he could focus his attention on the support group and, most importantly, his family.

When the commissary came into sight, Paul looked for a place to turn around. He could make a U-turn in the middle of the road. For a moment, he was serious, but kept going. Paul drove up and down the rows in the parking lot until he saw the reverse lights of a van in a handicap parking space. That was the last place he wanted to park, but if that was all that was available, he'd park in the space.

The closer he got to the tent where the cases of products were, the higher his heart rate climbed.

You can do this.

Paul repeated the declaration each time his right foot hit the pavement. The face of a woman walking towards him twisted and heat surged in Paul's body.

"Are you okay?" she asked when she reached him.

"Yes, ma'am. Thank you."

She smiled and continued walking. Paul stopped and gathered himself. The shade of the tent gave him a quick reprieve from the sun, but his body heat continued to soar.

You can do this. You can do this. You can do this, Paul. Paul walked around and found himself in front of a pallet of diapers.

"I can do this," he whispered. A laugh came from beside Paul. The woman grinned at him when he looked at her.

"Wife do all the shopping?"

"Yes, ma'am." Paul forced a smile but found that the woman's attention distracted him from his thoughts. Spending a minute deciding what size diapers Caleb wore, Paul put four cases in the cart and browsed all the aisles. Not to say his anxiety had dissipated because it hadn't. His pulse remained high while he was there, but he finished shopping without vomiting or fainting.

Twice now he'd exposed himself to situations that would provoke anxiety. How many more times would he have to torture himself until he could maintain his senses when he was around pallets? Who was afraid of pallets? Paul shook his head and glanced in the rearview mirror at the boxes secured in the truck's bed. Caleb had enough diapers to see him through until he was potty trained.

Paul's thoughts went to Kendall. She'd come out of her shell but had yet to speak. How long would it take for her to feel secure enough to express herself verbally? He could relate. He was afraid of wood and nails and she was afraid of…what exactly? Death? She had every right to be afraid of death. Paul thought about his family. Everyone except for Caleb struggled with something. Many times, he'd been thankful that Caleb was a toddler. He didn't know who Paul was before the accident. Paul focused on the thought. Was he all that different now?

Just Love coffeehouse had recently opened in the area and Paul thought it would be a nice place to talk with Karla. He found a secluded table since he wasn't sure how she'd take his decision to leave the group. But he figured she'd blame herself. A smile filled her face as soon as she saw him. She sauntered over and pulled out a chair.

"Hey, how are you?" Karla asked.

"Well, thanks. You?"

"Same." She smiled.

Paul took Karla's order and went to the counter. When their drinks were ready, he returned to their table and placed Karla's coffee in front of her.

"I'm happy you texted me. I'm sure you've been busy with the family and Kendall."

Kendall is *family*, Paul thought.

They were quiet for an uncomfortable amount of time. Paul drew in a quiet breath. "I asked you for coffee to let you know that I'm leaving the VA group."

Karla's eyes widened. "You are?"

"The two groups have been taking up a lot of time and I need to focus on what's important to me. That's my family, and…well…the support group." Paul's mouth went dry. He sipped his coffee, but it didn't help.

Karla focused on her coffee and wrapped her right hand around the cup. Looking up at him, she said, "Are you sure it's not because of me?" She glanced out the window.

"I have to do what's best for my family."

"I get it, but if I said or did anything that made you uncomfortable, I'm sorry."

What could he say to that? She was the main reason he was leaving the group. He had to be honest. "Our time together…"

"It upset Genny." Karla leaned back against the chair.

"Yes. But she was right. I got fixated on helping you spiritually, and that was wrong."

She looked out the window again. What was going on in her head? Turning her gaze to him, she said, "I have to be honest. You are easy to talk to and have helped me a lot. It makes it easy to develop feelings." Karla bumped her cup with her prosthetic and she grabbed the cup with her other hand before it fell over. "But I would never intentionally come between you and your wife. I'm sorry."

"I know." Paul looked down at his coffee and drank what was left, grimacing at the lukewarm temperature.

"Thank you for listening to me. I think I'm going to go. Thanks for the coffee, and good luck with the group. With everything." Karla pushed the cup of coffee to the side of the table and stood.

Paul stood and watched Karla walk out, get into her car, and drive away. Paul reminded himself that Beth had taken Karla under her wing. He had peace that Karla was in good hands. Releasing a breath, he closed his eyes and prayed for Karla. Paul's focus was on what was the most important—Genny and the kids and the little girl who God had brought into their lives.

Before turning in for the night, Paul made his journal entry for the day.

October 27, 2017

Today was hard, but I know it's for the best. I need to be fully present for my family, especially Kendall. I know Beth is good for Karla. I have to trust in the Lord...

267

CHAPTER 42

Genny

Genny pulled Kendall's suitcase from the closet. Some of her clothes were snug and Genny had given her a few outfits of Katie's until they went shopping. Unzipping the suitcase, Genny piled the clothes inside and closed the top. A crinkling sound stopped Genny from pulling the zipper. Opening the top again, she slipped her hand into the inside pocket and found a letter sized envelope. When she turned the envelope over, she read the words *Mr. and Mrs. Thompson* handwritten on the front.

Glancing into Katie's room as she passed by, Genny made her way to the kitchen to make a cup of coffee. Settled on the couch, she paused, wondering if she should text Paul to come to the house, but decided not to interrupt him since he was installing new faucets in the kitchen and bathroom at the apartment.

Genny removed and unfolded the letter. Her heart began beating hard as she read the words.

Mr. and Mrs. Thompson,

I wanted to write you this letter, so you know why I gave up custody of my granddaughter. It's not because I don't love her. The Good Lord knows I do. I have rheumatoid arthritis and I am getting worse. Pretty soon I won't be able to dress myself and if I can't take care of myself, how can I take care of a child that depends on me for everything?

Tina Baxter has told me about your family, and I feel the Lord has brought you into Kendall's life to raise her. And by what she said, you are a family of God. That makes me happy. It would make her parents happy.

I love Kendall. She's all I have left of my son. I want Kendall to know who I am and that I love her. Please send me pictures, if you feel comfortable, that is.

Thank you for caring for my grandbaby,

Roberta Cain

Tears blurred Genny's vision. So much love in three short paragraphs.

A car door shut and Genny peeped out the living room window. Tina had opened the trunk of her car and was pulling out a large cardboard box. Genny got up and met Tina at the door, standing aside for her to walk inside. Placing the box on the floor by the couch, Tina blew out her breath.

"It's from Roberta," Tina said when Genny looked at the box and lifted an eyebrow.

"What is it?"

"Some of Kendall's stuff. It came in this morning. She's going to be sending more boxes."

Poor child was having her life mailed to her one box at a time.

"I called her and she said she's going through Kendall's parents' house. She plans to send everything that belongs to Kendall to you and auction the rest."

Was that what Genny's grandparents did with her parents' house? How sad it must have been for her grandparents. It was going to cost Roberta a small fortune to send one box at a time. She and Paul could help.

"I can talk to Paul about paying for a U-Haul or a local moving company. We don't mind if the state doesn't mind."

But it's not official yet. Kendall could leave any day. You're setting yourself up for heartache.

"I can check and let you know. Are the girls in Katie's room?"

"Yeah. Caleb, too. I'm surprised he's not crying yet." Genny laughed. She watched Tina as she walked down the hall. Sitting on the couch by the box, Genny's first thought was to rip it open, but she'd wait until after bedtime. There was no telling what was in the box. Hopefully clothes and a few toys.

Tina came back into the living room and sat on the other end of the couch.

"Can I get you anything? I've got that tea you like," Genny asked.

"Sure."

Genny went to the kitchen to turn on the kettle. She leaned against the counter, looking out the window for a moment before she got cups out of the cabinet. What was in the box? Paul wouldn't be home for a few more hours. Then they'd be into the evening routine with the kids. The thought of waiting that long got under Genny's skin.

Genny carried the cups to the living room and handed one to Tina. "Just the way you like it."

Tina smiled and took a sip, closing her eyes for a moment. When she opened her eyes, she looked at Genny. "Aren't you going to open it?"

"I hope there are clothes and toys." Genny's thoughts took her in a direction that she hadn't considered. Would Kendall's toys and clothes bring comfort or grief? "I wonder how Kendall will react when she sees stuff from home."

"When's her next therapy appointment?"

"Two days."

"Good. Just in case." Tina sipped her tea and shot a glance down the hall when Caleb cried out as he ran out of Katie's room and towards Genny with something swinging from his hand.

"Caleb!" Katie ran out of her room after him, grabbing at the toy in his hand.

Genny glimpsed Kendall when she stepped into the hall. Kendall was gone as quickly as she appeared.

Caleb climbed onto Genny's lap when he reached her and waved the toy at Genny.

"Mama. That's Kendall's."

Genny steadied Caleb's hand and was surprised to see Bea, the rag doll that Brian and Tricia had given Katie for her last birthday. Katie was protective of Bea, and it touched her heart that she let Kendall play with the doll. Did Katie give Bea to Kendall? If that was what Katie wanted, it was fine with Genny. Since Katie had gotten mad at Kendall about Clementine and learned what had happened to Kendall and her family, she'd been more mindful of Kendall's feelings.

Genny gave Bea to Katie and she skipped down the hall to her room. Genny shuddered when Katie slammed her bedroom door. Caleb slid down from Genny's lap and pounded his fists on the top of the box. Taking a few moments to debate when she should open the box, Genny got a pair of scissors and sliced it open.

To curb Caleb's curiosity, Genny put him in his highchair and gave him a snack. When she made it to the living room, Tina had pulled several things out of the box.

"Look at this." Tina held a small photo album in her hand. "It looks like it was something that was recently put together. That was thoughtful of Roberta." Tina handed the album to Genny.

Genny thumbed through the pages. It looked as if they had been printed on a home color printer. That *was* thoughtful of Roberta. Genny closed the album and brushed her hand over the textured cover. "Tina?"

"Yep?" Tina said and placed the cup of tea on the side table.

"Do you think her Aunt Sierra will change her mind?"

"No, but there's always a chance. I know you are worried, and it doesn't help that these things take time. There are rules and laws that have to be followed."

"It was so much easier with Caleb."

"This is the foster care system. It's a whole different animal."

"Yeah." Genny breathed out and laid the album in the box on top of a stack of clothes.

"What's that, Mama?" Katie pointed at the box.

"It's Kendall's things that Ms. Tina brought with her."

Katie's face brightened and she took a step towards the box. Genny held up her hand. "Daddy and I want to go through it first."

"Why?"

"To make sure there's nothing in there that will make her sad."

"Oh." Katie shrugged and returned to her bedroom.

"Charlie said Kendall still isn't talking," Tina said.

"No."

"Anything? Laughing or crying?"

"No, just nodding."

"Hmm."

"I've had my share of mental health issues with everything I've been through, but not talking? How long is this going to last? I asked Charlie and she said maybe Kendall feels she has no control over her life and this is something she can control. How can a four-year-old know that?"

From her own experience as a child, Genny knew people handled their emotions in different ways. She had pulled her hair out starting when she was ten and it had continued into her early twenties. Thank goodness she hadn't gone back to using the coping mechanism after Paul was injured.

~elle~

Genny sat on the couch with a cup of coffee and looked at the documents in the envelope Roberta had sent with Kendall's belongings. She came across an eight by ten photo of Kendall with her family. Genny studied it for a while. Kendall looked like her mother. Kari was petite with long blond hair. She didn't come close to Tom's shoulder. Kendall's brother Carson was his dad's twin. He was tall, with broad shoulders and light brown hair. Who was this family before the tragedy that left Kendall alone with a family she didn't know? She laid the photo aside and planned to frame it for Kendall.

The next document was several pages stapled together. The first page was blank except for rectangles in the middle of the page, with initials next to them. Genny brought the paper closer to her face and gasped when she realized what the initials meant. VH1 was vehicle one, VH2 was vehicle two, and so on. Genny was holding the sketch of where the vehicles had come to rest after the accident. Flipping the page over, Genny's hands began trembling when she read the title of the report: *Fatal Vehicle Accident Report*.

A rush of feelings came back: her parents' death, the late evening knock on the door informing her of Brandon's death, the early morning phone call she received over a year ago that Paul had been critically injured. Nausea filled her throat and she ran to the bathroom. Returning to the living room, she picked the paper up off the floor and began reading the report.

...nine deaths reported: one fatality in a red Ford Fusion sedan (VH1), six fatalities and one non-life threatening injury in a white Honda Odyssey van (VH3), two fatalities in a black Nissan Armada SUV (VH4). Non-life threatening injuries reported in a white Peterbilt 579 semi-truck (VH2), and one in the Honda Odyssey van (VH3) ...

"Six?" Genny whispered the words. She knew this, but it was still a shock. The people in the van were Kendall's family. Genny swallowed hard and continued reading.

VH2 approached VH1 at approx. 70 mph and realized that VH1 was stopped in the road. VH2 applied the brakes, but because of the rate of speed, full cargo and VH1 was immobile, VH2 hit VH1, which caused a chain reaction. VH3 hit the trailer of

VH2. VH4 ran into the back of VH3, pushing VH3 under VH2's trailer. All deaths were reported at the scene by EMT. It was determined that the driver of VH1 was intoxicated with a blood alcohol level of twice the legal limit. Witnesses reported VH1 had come to a stop minutes before the accident, causing several near-misses before VH2 hit VH1.

Genny read the accident report several times. *Six lives lost in a Honda Odyssey,* she thought as she walked to the bedroom. Kendall's family. Moisture filled her eyes as she opened her journal.

Nov 1, 2017

Why? Another drunk driver ruins a family. Will Kendall recover? Losing your family is something that sticks with you forever, but will she get to the point where she feels comfortable enough around us that she can be herself? At least who she is now. I know she will never be the child she was before.

The driver that caused the accident was drunk. A drunk driver had killed Genny's parents. Old wounds—wounds she thought had healed—ripped wide open. She bent over and held her head in her hands, trying her best to muffle her sobs so the kids didn't hear. Losing her family by a drunk driver was one thing Genny wished she didn't have in common with Kendall.

CHAPTER 43

Paul

In the living room, Katie was plastered to the front windows watching for Brian and Tricia's car. Paul stepped beside her and pushed back the curtain as a large black SUV passed on the road.

Katie gasped. "Where they going, Daddy?"

"That's not them, baby girl. They bought a new car. It's white."

"Aww. When will they get here?"

Paul glanced at Kendall sitting in the chair next to the couch. She was straightening Clementine's pinafore and Paul was sure he heard her softly humming. It was wishful thinking.

"Is that them, Daddy?" Katie grinned at Paul and squirmed.

"Sure is," Paul said when he saw his mom waving from the passenger seat of the white Chevy Tahoe when they pulled in front of the house. Paul chuckled and shook his head.

"Come on, Kendall! Mimi and Papa are here!" Katie ran up to Kendall and took her hand, pulling her to her feet. She kept pace with Katie, but stopped before they made it to the passenger side of the car.

Tricia opened the door and stepped out. Katie slipped her arms around her grandmother's waist and squeezed. Paul gave his mother a hug and walked towards the driver's side. He watched them as he walked around the car. His mom bent down and wrapped her arms around Kendall, holding her for a moment. "Hi, Kendall."

Kendall looked into Tricia's eyes but said nothing.

"Mimi, come inside." Katie took Tricia's hand and Tricia grabbed Kendall's hand and they made their way inside.

"Dad," Paul said and hugged his father. "I thought you were getting another Escalade." Paul stepped back, rubbing his chin as he gave the car a once over.

"Time for a change." Paul followed Brian to the back of the car and helped bring in the luggage.

"Bubby had to see the doctor," Katie said to Tricia.

"Mama told me. Hopefully, the doctor can help him feel better."

"Uh-huh. Mimi, Kendall don't talk yet."

"She will, honey. Give her time."

Once Paul's parents were settled in the apartment, Paul returned to the house in time to help Genny get Caleb out of the car.

"Another ear infection."

Paul sighed and took Caleb to his room for a nap. When he headed back to the living room, he caught sight of Kendall sitting on her bed, holding Clementine close. Paul stepped inside and sat on the bed next to her.

"Do you remember Papa and Mimi?"

Kendall looked up at him and nodded.

"You and Clementine can hang out here until dinner's ready. Ms. Genny's making chicken tenders."

Kendall's eyes brightened. Paul could tell that she was fighting a smile. No matter how small the steps were , Kendall was making progress.

Paul headed to the hall and stopped when Katie blasted past him into Kendall's room. "Come on, Kendall. Papa's got candy."

"Um," Paul mumbled. Genny would not be happy. Katie stopped, but he waved her and Kendall past him. If anyone could get Kendall to drop her walls, it was Brian.

The next morning, Paul made his way to the kitchen to get the coffee ready. As he passed each child's room, he took a quick glance inside. Katie and Caleb were asleep, but Kendall was sitting up in bed. It couldn't be later than six thirty. Why was she up this early? Giving the door a light tap, Paul pushed it open.

"You're up early. Did you sleep okay?"

Kendall nodded and reached under the covers, pulling out Clementine. Despite Roberta sending all of Kendall's toys, including several dolls, she chose Clementine every time.

"Want to help with the coffee?" Kendall nodded and slipped out of bed with the doll. As they walked out of the room, Paul glimpsed the baseball glove on Kendall's dresser that had belonged to Carson. Not only had Roberta sent Kendall's things, she had also sent most of Carson's belongings as well.

Paul and Kendall walked into the kitchen as Brian came through the mudroom door.

"Good morning, you two," Brian said.

"Good morning. Coffee?"

"Yes, please." Brian smiled at Kendall and reached for her hand. Hesitating for a moment, Kendall slipped her hand into Brian's and they made their way to the couch. Paul heard Brian talking to Kendall as he prepared their coffee. Yawning, Paul watched the Keurig as it filled the first cup with steaming coffee. Brian was still talking and Paul caught a word here or there.

A smile warmed Paul's heart as his dad talked about the time Paul had monopolized Santa's time during a visit at the mall.

"Have you made a list? Christmas will be here soon. I bet you want one of those new things. What is it? Fidget spinners? Maybe a new doll. Nah, you seem to like Clementine, huh?" Brian's voice softened and Paul strained to hear what he was saying. "There's that pretty smile."

Paul drew in a sharp breath. Peeking around the corner into the living room, his shoulders sagged. Kendall's smile must have lasted for half a beat and he'd missed it. Kendall spotted Paul and smiled. He walked over to her and sat on the couch. His dad was right; Kendall's smile lit up the room. He could think of a million things to say to Kendall, but decided not to say anything. The fear of regression was in the back of his and Genny's minds and they didn't want to do anything to cause Kendall to go back to who she was when she first walked through their door.

Glancing towards the bedroom, Paul's first thought was to wake Genny, but he decided against it. She'd know soon enough.

"Have you and Katie started making out your Christmas wish lists?" Paul asked.

Kendall didn't say a word, but her smile remained. She looked at him as if he was speaking a different language. Studying Kendall's face, her striking hazel eyes were no longer dark and lifeless. It had been five months since she'd come into their home, and in the past two months, they'd witnessed her slowly take apart the walls around her heart one brick at a time.

Kendall nodded and looked past Paul. He glanced in that direction and saw Genny coming down the hall towards the living room. She stopped, nearly stumbling, when Kendall smiled. Genny's jaw hung open and she quickly closed her mouth. Biting her bottom lip, she joined Paul and Kendall on the couch. Tears gathered in Genny's eyes when she brushed her hand down Kendall's arm.

"Good morning, sweet girl."

As quickly as it'd appeared, the smile was gone, and Kendall looked down at Clementine. Rubbing a frayed piece of yarn hair between her fingers, Kendall slipped off the couch and took her time walking to her bedroom. Genny looked at Paul.

"She probably feels uncomfortable with all the attention," Brian said.

"You're probably right," Genny said.

"Mama. Mama," Caleb called out from his room.

"Let me go get him."

Paul watched Genny walk down the hall. She took a quick peek in Kendall's room and smiled. Maybe Kendall had smiled at Genny.

"You two are doing a wonderful job, son."

"Thanks, Dad. It's hard. We don't know what her voice sounds like. I never thought that would be something that'd bother me. You know?"

"I can imagine." Brian drank the last of his coffee and stood. "I'm going to see if Mom's up yet."

"All right, Dad."

Paul walked down the hall to check on Katie. He looked into Kendall's room and stopped before he pushed the door open. Kendall was standing in front of her dresser, stroking her brother's baseball glove. "Oh, Father." He stopped himself before his thoughts got away from him. From his personal experience, it wasn't unusual to teeter between moods. And it was worse for a four-year-old wondering where her own family was. Did she think they'd left her? The thought that she may never feel secure was daunting. It was his and Genny's responsibility to give her a sense of security, and that was overwhelming.

—ee—

Paul and Genny watched a movie after everyone went to bed. Genny rested her head on his shoulder and released a breath.

"What is it, love?"

"I can't believe she's smiling."

"Me either. God is good."

"Yes, He is. He's the only way we're getting through this. It's hard to believe that this young girl is going through something like this at her age."

"You did."

"I know, but it's different. Brandon and I didn't end up in foster care. What if her aunt wants her? Then what?"

"Babe, don't do this to yourself. Tina said she isn't equipped for a child and Kendall's mom was an only child."

"I know. Katie and Caleb seem to have settled into a routine. Katie hasn't gotten mad at Kendall since that night with Clementine."

"Look at her now. Clementine is her favorite toy." Paul pulled Genny close and kissed the side of her head. "Give it to God, Gen. Any fear, you give it to God. He'll take care of it."

Genny slipped her arm across his chest and sighed. Anything Kendall felt, so did Genny. What she had gone through made her hypersensitive to people's pain. And since Kendall was a child, Genny felt it on a deeper level. It would destroy her if Kendall was taken away from them. Deep in Paul's heart, he knew God had put Kendall in their home for a reason, and that reason was to be their daughter.

December 16, 2017

Today has been an awesome day! Our sweet girl smiled today! Praise God! Lord, light a fire under the state. We're ready to make Kendall a Thompson.

CHAPTER 44

Genny

"When does Zoe's plane get in?" Tricia asked Genny.

"A little before three. We plan to leave around one thirty. You can never be too early." Genny wiped Caleb's hands and got him out of the highchair. He toddled over to Tricia, wearing a sweet smile.

Tricia picked him up and sat him on her lap. "I'm so glad that we are here when Zoe visits. I remember seeing her when she was around two. She was such a sweet little girl."

"She has a good heart. I'm glad that Sarah has changed. It kills me that Zoe doesn't have Brandon."

"I know, sweetheart. But she has you and Paul."

Genny smiled and wiped the highchair tray. "That she does. Want a cup of coffee?"

"Did you get the decaf? If not, we brought some."

"I got it. Be right back." Genny went to the kitchen and pulled down two coffee cups and picked out two K-cups. Using a single cup brewer didn't compare to working at The Roasted Bean. She'd memorized every drink and could put together a caramel macchiato with her eyes closed and arms tied behind her back. Genny smiled. Sometimes she missed working there.

"We're ready to get Zoe," Katie said.

Genny heard Tricia giggle and turned around. She bit her bottom lip to keep from laughing. Katie and Kendall looked like two elderly ladies heading to church. Each wore one of Katie's Easter dresses and the dress up hats that Paul had caved in and bought Katie one day when they were at the dollar store. Kendall was wearing the dress from two years ago, which explained why the back wouldn't zip. Genny noted the purses looped over their shoulders.

"Why are you dressed up? I'm wearing what I have on." Genny pointed at her jeans and white pullover shirt.

"Zoe's my cousin."

Bless Katie's heart. Zoe meant a lot to her, although they hadn't known each other long. Zoe hadn't visited since the first visit, but they kept in touch through Facebook and texts and the occasional phone call.

"If you want to wear that, you can."

"Okay!" Katie walked over to the couch where Tricia was holding Caleb and sat next to her. "Where's Daddy and Papa?"

"They went to talk to a man about fixing the house," Genny said as she walked into the living room with the coffee.

"Is Caleb coming with us?" Katie asked, taking hold of her brother's hand.

"No, sweetie. Just us girls. He's going to stay with Mimi."

"Let's go, Mama." Katie jumped up and straightened her hat when it slid down over her eyes.

"Well, I guess we can get a snack before we head to the airport." Genny looked at Tricia and turned around, taking her cup of coffee back into the kitchen.

Genny grabbed her purse and the girls followed her out to the car. When Genny pulled out of the driveway, butterflies danced in her stomach. Zoe was spending Christmas with them and was staying for a full week. Sometimes Genny felt like she was in a dream; married to Paul with two—prayerfully three—children and in contact with Zoe. But it was her life, not a dream, and she thanked God for His blessings.

Genny parked in short-term parking and headed inside, holding each girl's hand. She found a monitor and noted that Zoe's plane was due to land in fifteen minutes, and they headed to the terminal for her flight. In their Easter dresses and hats, Katie and Kendall got a few smiles as they walked.

"Zoe!" Katie shouted and took off running, dragging Kendall along.

Genny's lips parted and she sprinted after the girls. "The monitor showed fifteen minutes until you landed," Genny said as she slipped her arms around Zoe.

"We were a few minutes early." Zoe squatted and hugged Katie and looked at Kendall. "Miss Kendall. You are a pretty little thing." Zoe tapped Kendall's nose and Kendall smiled. She tapped Katie's nose and tickled her. "I'm ready if you are."

"Let's go," Genny said.

Zoe was more outgoing and animated this time, maybe because Sarah wasn't around. Once she'd talked about her trip to Charleston, she spent the rest of the drive home turning around and talking to the girls. Out of the corner of her eye, Genny caught Zoe making faces at Kendall. The next sound Genny heard took her breath. Tears stung her eyes when she heard Kendall giggle.

Don't make a big deal out of it, or she might go silent again.

Katie gasped and said, "Mama! Kendall laughed!"

Genny pulled up to a stoplight and held her breath. A moment later, both Kendall and Katie laughed when Zoe reached back and tickled their feet. Zoe looked at Genny when she turned back around and smiled, lifting her brows. Zoe's aim was to get Kendall to vocalize something, and she was successful. Genny was happy that it was a sweet laugh.

∼ele∼

When they got home, Paul and Brian were sitting at the dining table looking at blueprints for the remodel. They were deep in conversation and didn't hear Genny and the girls come into the house.

"Hi, Uncle Paul," Zoe said, and walked up to the table.

"Zoe, girl, come here." Paul stood and pulled Zoe into a hug. "This is my dad, Brian." To Genny's surprise, Zoe gave Brian a hug.

Tricia came into the living room with Caleb and stood him on the floor. He made his way to Zoe and looked up at her. Picking him up, she kissed his cheek and hugged him.

"This is Tricia, Paul's mom," Genny gestured to Tricia.

"Nice to meet you," Zoe said, and put Caleb down. She walked over and hugged Tricia.

Genny helped Zoe settle into Katie's room and, on the way to the living room, she glanced into Kendall's room. The girls were playing with their dolls. Several of Kendall's dolls and Katie's were arranged on Kendall's bed as if they were in church. Genny smiled and walked to the living room.

Paul and Brian were back to discussing details of the remodel, so Genny gave them time even though she was about to explode. She eased down on the couch next to Tricia and released a breath.

"Genny, Zoe's your twin."

Genny looked at Tricia and smiled.

"But I'm not surprised. You and Brandon looked so much alike. It's no wonder that Zoe looks like you."

A grin spread across Genny's face, raising Tricia's brow. As Genny leaned to tell Tricia about Kendall, the sweetest laugh drifted from Kendall's room. Tricia's mouth hung open. Genny looked up and realized that Paul and Brian had stopped talking.

Paul looked down the hall, then at Genny. She smiled and walked over to the dining table.

"I was waiting impatiently for you two to take a breather. Zoe was playing with the girls on the way home and she got Kendall to laugh. It sounds like she's doing it again."

Zoe belted out a verse from "Amazing Grace" and the girls laughed hard, sounding like they couldn't catch their breath. Paul shot up from the table and sprinted down the hall to Kendall's room. Genny heard him ask what was going on in a teasing voice, and the girls started laughing. Genny peeked in and her heart swelled when Paul picked up Kendall and pulled her close. Kendall buried her face in Paul's shoulder and, for the first time, Genny saw her little body relax.

Paul put her down and talked to the girls for a few moments. When he turned around, Genny saw tears gathering in his eyes. He took her hand and led her into their bedroom and shut the door.

"We've been praying for this."

Genny slipped her arms around Paul's neck and they stayed that way for a while. Pulling back, Paul kissed Genny and they left the room. Paul found his dad and they tied up the loose ends of the remodel. Genny grabbed some towels from the hamper and made her way to the laundry room. When she passed Kendall's room, she stopped and listened.

"Can you say Mama? Mama. Say Mama."

Kendall giggled.

"Ma…ma. Can you say Daddy? Um, what about Bubby?" Katie gasped. "Can you say Katie?" Both girls giggled.

It reminded Genny of when Katie had tried to teach Caleb to talk when he was six months old.

"It's okay. You don't have to talk. Let's play," Katie said. A few seconds went by when Katie used her Miss Peggy's voice and said, "Hi Clementine. Want to go to church? Maybe that nice girl will sing with us."

Genny looked up and thanked God for the day's progress. When she made it to the kitchen, she saw Zoe standing at the Christmas tree, looking at the ornaments. Genny made a quick trip to the laundry room and came back into the living room. Zoe looked in her direction.

"You have a pretty Christmas tree. I love all the homemade ornaments."

"Thank you. I have some from my childhood. In fact," Genny said and walked over to the tree, "your dad made this one when he was around eight or nine." Genny lifted the ornament from the tree and handed it to Zoe. Lightly brushing her finger over the gingerbread man cookie cutout, Zoe placed the ornament in her palm and studied it for a long while.

"I can't believe that my dad made this. His actual hands made this," her voice trembled.

"Aw, sweetheart." Genny rubbed Zoe's back as she stared at the ornament and wiped her eyes.

"It's not fair, Aunt Genny."

"You're right, it's not. I've struggled with what happened to Brandon for years. Uncle Paul helped me pick up the pieces, but I wouldn't be here if it wasn't for God's love."

Zoe pushed out her breath. "I know He has plans for me, but why take my dad? Mum said he was a good man and that he loved me."

"He loved you, Zoe. Very much. We can't change the past. I believe your mother was honest when she told me she regretted how things happened with your dad."

"She is being honest. She talked to me about it not long after I started asking about him. Mum's been different since we started going to church."

"That's good, honey."

"Yeah." Zoe hung the ornament up and gave Genny a hug.

"The ornament is yours. You take it home with you, okay?"

Zoe nodded. "I'm so glad I have you. You make me feel closer to Daddy."

Daddy. Genny's heart swelled.

"I like Jim. He's nice, but he's not my dad."

"I didn't have a dad either. My grandfather was my daddy until he died. I was ten, so I've been without a dad for a while."

"I didn't know that."

"Honey, I'm sure Jim would never consider replacing your dad, but it's okay if you like him as your dad. It's not dishonoring Brandon. He'd want you to have a father in your life. Do you understand?"

Zoe's face twisted and she fell into Genny's arms, sobbing.

"Oh, sweet girl. The pain can lead to joy. Here, let's sit." Genny pointed to the couch, and they made themselves comfortable. "My parents died when I was five. Your dad and I moved in with our grandparents and guess who lived next door?" Genny lifted a shoulder.

Zoe shrugged, but a smile spread across her face when she caught sight of Paul and Brian in the backyard.

"When I was at my lowest after your dad died, God led Uncle Paul to help me through that dark time. Through our pain and grief, we fell in love. Katie is our miracle child. I had some health problems and I was told from the time I was young that I probably couldn't have children. Then God brought Caleb to us when we least expected it and now," Genny's voice cracked.

"Kendall." Zoe smiled when Genny nodded.

"Kendall. She smiled for the first time yesterday and you got her to laugh today."

"She's been through a lot."

"Yes, she has." Genny glanced down the hall. The girls ran out of Kendall's room and up to Genny.

"Mama, we're hungry," Katie said.

"Yeah, I need to get dinner started."

"I'll help, Aunt Genny."

"All right. Let's get to the kitchen. Hey, before you leave, I'd love to get some pictures of you and the kids in the backyard. Uncle Paul got me one of those fancy cameras for my birthday."

"I'd like that and I want copies." Zoe grinned.

As Zoe stood next to Genny at the sink, Genny's thoughts went back to Brandon's death. Not knowing where Zoe was had been one of the worst feelings she had experienced. Now her niece was standing next to her as she peeled potatoes. God was good.

—⁓—

Paul turned on the TV and browsed on-demand movies. Brian and Tricia came in from the apartment and took their seat on the couch. Putting the kids to bed, Genny joined Paul on the loveseat.

"What movie do you want to watch?" Paul asked, looking at his parents.

"We want to talk to you two before we settle into watching a movie."

"Oh?" Laying the remote aside, Paul leaned back and took a hold of Genny's hand.

"Dad and I aren't traveling as much as we have in the past. We have sort of drifted away from our friends or they have passed on. And we're missing out on seeing our grandchildren grow."

Paul sat up straight and gave his parents his full attention. "Are you saying what I think you're saying?"

"That depends. If you think we are moving to Charleston," his dad paused, "Then you're right!" He chuckled.

Genny gasped. "You are? No joking?"

"No joking, Genny," Tricia said.

Over the next hour, they talked about what areas Brian and Tricia were interested in and looked at houses online.

"It's got to be close. We want to spend as much time as possible with our three grandchildren." Tricia said.

"And since you are here, we have no choice but to spend time with you, too."

"Brian!" Tricia swatted at him.

"You two know we love you." Brian winked.

All Genny could think about was that Tricia had said three grandchildren. Three. Not two, but three.

What if Kendall's aunt Sierra changed her mind? Genny sighed. Why did she do this to herself? As soon as her heart filled with hope, her mind crushed that hope.

—⁓—

Genny watched Paul run a soft cloth over the Purple Heart medal and hold it up to the sunlight streaming through the office window. He placed the medal back in the display box and carefully closed the top. The corner of the presentation certificate had shifted in the folder. He tapped the edge of the paper, shifting the corner into place. Paul held the certificate in front of him and drew in a deep breath. They headed to the living room, where Zoe was watching a movie with Tricia and Brian.

"Zoe," Paul said.

She looked his way and smiled.

"We've got something for you."

"Oh, okay." Her face brightened.

Brian picked up the remote and paused the movie.

"Aunt Genny received this from the Air Force after they couldn't find you. It's your dad's. His Purple Heart." Paul handed the certificate folder with the box perched on top to Zoe.

"Do you know what that's for, honey?" Genny asked.

"Yeah," Zoe whispered. She laid the folder in her lap and opened the display box. Tears streamed down her cheeks as she brushed her finger across the gold image in the middle of the purple heart. "I've never seen one, though." She opened the folder and wiped her cheek. Genny could see her eyes shift as she read.

"His middle name was William? I never knew."

"William was our dad's name. He went by Will. Kelly was our mom's name. Katie's middle name is Kelly."

"Thank you for this. It means a lot."

"Of course," Paul said. "We wanted to give it to you before you leave in the morning."

"I love you guys." Zoe walked over and sat between Paul and Genny, slipping an arm around each of their shoulders.

"We love you too, Zoe," they both replied.

"I'm going to miss you. Each one of you, and those kids in there. My family. I'm so happy." Zoe smiled and closed her eyes. Opening her eyes, she wiped her cheeks and said, "I don't want to leave. I'm going to move in. I can share Lucy's doghouse."

Laughing, she walked over and hugged Brian and Tricia. Zoe's act of including Brian and Tricia warmed Genny's heart. She could see a special relationship growing between Paul's parents and Zoe.

A new year meant a new beginning. Zoe had gone home with plans to visit over spring break. Paul's parents had a buyer for their house in Tennessee, and the sellers of the house they were interested in had accepted their offer. Kendall's personality was blossoming, but she still hadn't talked. Her therapist had said not to push her or they would risk a regression.

Genny's phone rang and she saw Tina's name on the screen. Her stomach dropped and she took a deep breath.

"Hi Tina," Genny said and tapped the speaker button so Paul could hear.

"Hey. We checked again with Sierra, and she said nothing has changed. With working abroad, there's no possibility that she can care for Kendall. She'd end up in a boarding school or something, so Sierra feels that it's in Kendall's best interest to stay with you and Paul," Tina said.

Genny's breath caught in her throat. Kendall was theirs.

"Does she want visitation?" Paul asked.

"She wants Kendall to know about her and is open to future visits, if you allow it."

"All right," Paul said.

"I'll get back to you with the next steps."

Genny hung up and stared at Paul. "Why am I still scared?"

"Give it to God, sweetheart. I know it's hard, but that's the only way you'll have peace."

"Yeah." Genny glanced out the window and into the backyard and groaned. She'd forgotten it had rained earlier, and the girls were playing in a hole Lucy had dug a few days ago. Muddy from head to toe, Genny called the girls inside and put them in the bath.

Afterwards, the girls sat on the living room floor playing with Miss Peggy and Clementine. Switching through the TV channels, Genny was looking for something interesting to watch. Caleb slung his leg on top of the couch cushion and Genny helped him up. Sitting on her lap, he rested his head against her chest.

Paul came into the living room a while later and smiled when he saw Katie and Kendall sprawled on the floor asleep. Sitting next to Genny, he stretched his legs out, resting them on the coffee table. He turned to her and smiled, rubbing Caleb's back.

"We're home," Paul said, and brushed his fingers over her cheek. He didn't have to explain what he meant; Genny knew. "It's been a journey, but we're here."

"Yes, we are. I've often wondered what God's plan was in all this. Not just Kendall, but everything."

Paul snuck over to where the girls were laying, and tugged on Katie's foot.

She sat up and pinched her brows together. "Daddy," she whined.

He tugged Kendall's foot and she too sat up. She stared at Paul for a few moments and said, "Daddy."

Genny's mouth hung open when Paul looked at her wide-eyed.

Kendall gaze went from Paul to Genny. A faint smile played on her lips. "Mama."

Genny's heart soared. Paul picked up both girls and sat on the couch. He and Genny wrapped their arms around their children. The fear Genny had of Kendall's aunt taking custody had slowly dissipated since the call from Tina. They were on their way to becoming a family of five.

A new journey filled with laughter and love, school and dance classes, soccer games and middle school crushes stretched out in front of them. There would be high school and college graduations, and if the Lord willed, weddings and grandchildren. Genny leaned back against the couch and closed her eyes. Her thoughts surrounded her children and husband. She'd never felt so blessed.

Epilogue

Six months later

Genny sprayed Katie's hair with hairspray and sighed when she leaped off the step stool and ran out of the bathroom. Kendall was standing by the door and Genny waved her over. Picking her up, Genny stood her on the step stool and began brushing her long, blond hair.

"Curls, Mama?"

"Okay, sweet girl." Genny pulled the curling iron from the drawer and plugged it in.

"Babe, can you tie my tie?" Paul said as he walked into the bathroom carrying a maroon necktie.

"You know I don't know how to tie a tie." Genny rolled her eyes.

"Mom," Paul called out as he rushed out of the bathroom. "Can you tie my tie?"

Genny smiled and shook her head.

"Mama!" Caleb ran into the bathroom. "Sissy hair?"

"Yep. I'm curling her hair. Isn't it pretty?"

"Uh-uh."

Kendall's smile stretched across her face as she stared at herself in the mirror. Turning from side to side, she grinned at the curls that stretched down her back. "Thank you, Mama."

"You're welcome." Genny leaned down and kissed the top of Kendall's head

Over the past months, Kendall had blossomed. She was a bright, outgoing child. Genny often wondered if it was her true personality or if Katie had rubbed off on her. Genny smiled to herself as she sprayed Kendall's hair.

Once everyone was dressed and ready, Paul and Genny got the kids settled in the car and headed out of the driveway. Paul held Genny's hand as they drove towards the city. The closer they got to the courthouse; the faster Genny's pulse raced. In a little over an hour, they'd officially become a family of five.

Paul, Genny and the kids took their place in the courtroom while their family and friends filed into the spectator area. She glanced behind her and noted all the smiling faces. Brian and Trish beamed. Melissa and Peter had made a special trip for the adoption. Julie held up her left hand and wiggled her fingers. Genny's mouth hung open when she saw the new diamond engagement ring glistening in the overhead light. Tamika lifted her brows and smiled when their eyes met.

Disbelief, excitement, and thankfulness filled Genny's heart and she turned back around when she heard the judge's voice. The judge spoke about foster care and adoption, and thanked Paul and Genny for making a difference in a child's life. She smiled and looked at Kendall.

"It is ordered, Kendall, that your forever mom and dad will be Paul and Genevieve Thompson." She called the new family behind the bench and all five held onto the gavel while the judge counted to three. The courtroom erupted in applause when the gavel fell.

Everyone began approaching them to give their congratulations. Genny saw Roberta sitting in the last row of the spectator area and waved. She'd invited Roberta, but wasn't sure she'd come. Kendall spotted her and ran over.

"Nana!"

Roberta groaned when Kendall slid her arms around her shoulders. She'd lost weight and her fingers had gnarled.

"Easy," Genny said when she reached Roberta. "Nana is sick, remember?"

"I'm sorry, Nana."

"It's okay, honey."

"My name is Kendall Thompson now."

"I know. Your Mommy and Daddy are looking down from Heaven. They are happy that Mr. Paul and Ms. Genny are your Mommy and Daddy now."

Kendall giggled. "I call her Mama, Nana."

"Okay, then. Mama." Roberta looked at Genny and smiled.

"You have the address?" Genny asked.

"I do."

"We're getting ready to head home. See you in half an hour?"

"I'll be there."

Kendall's face brightened when she saw Zoe sweep Katie up in her arms.

"Bye, Nana!"

"Bye, honey."

Kendall grinned and ran off after her sister and cousin. Genny smiled as Zoe heave Kendall onto her hip, and carry both girls out of the courtroom.

"Thank you," Roberta said, moisture filling her eyes. "Thank you for loving her."

"Thank you for trusting us with her."

Roberta braced herself on her cane. Pushing to her feet, she hugged Genny, and Genny watched for a moment as Roberta hobbled to the door. Tina had told her that Roberta feared that Paul and Genny would cut her out of Kendall's life. It was something that hadn't crossed Genny's mind. The pain she'd felt over losing touch with Zoe was something she wouldn't wish it on anyone.

Paul walked up next to Genny and slipped his arm around her. He let out a low whistle.

"What?"

"Two girls. I'm in for it, right?"

"Oh, yeah." Genny laughed.

On the way home, Genny smiled as she listened to the siblings and their cousin in the back. God had truly blessed them.

"God's perfect plan," Genny whispered as she looked out the passenger window.

"What's that, babe?"

She turned to Paul. "God's perfect plan."

He glanced in the rearview mirror. "That they are, love." He slipped his fingers between Genny's and brought her hand to his lips.

As Paul pulled down their long driveway, Genny's eyes widened when she saw the number of cars parked along the gravel. He pulled into the garage and Zoe helped get the kids out of the car. People congratulated them as they made their way to the living room. These were the people who loved them and wanted to share in their joy of bringing a child into their home and making her a part of their family. Except one person was missing.

Genny stopped short when she saw Susan. She held her hands over her mouth when Susan looked at her. "Where is she?" Tears filled Genny's eyes.

Susan smiled wide and stepped aside, giving Genny a clear view of Mrs. Baker sitting in the recliner the kids had given Paul for Father's Day. She made her way to Mrs. Baker and kneeled beside the recliner. Wrapping her arms around Mrs. Baker's neck, Genny kissed her cheek and wiped the tears away as she stared at the woman she loved dearly.

Paul walked over and lifted his brow and smiled when Genny stood.

"You knew?"

"Yep."

Genny gasped and playfully hit his shoulder. Noticing the electric scooter by the fireplace, Genny smiled. They'd invited Mrs. Baker, although they figured she couldn't travel the distance because of her health.

"Honey, I'm sorry that we didn't make it in time," Mrs. Baker said.

"There was an accident on the Interstate and we were at a standstill for almost three hours," Susan added.

"At least you're here now." Genny gave Mrs. Baker another hug.

Mrs. Baker watched the kids run by, heading to the back door. "She's a beautiful girl and fits right into your family. She's blessed."

"We're the blessed ones." Slipping his arm around Genny, Paul pulled her close and said, "So, where's our next journey taking us?"

Genny leaned her head against his shoulder. "Only God knows."

Acknowledgments

There are many people who have a part in bringing a novel to life, from the editor to the cover designer. At the top of the list will always be my husband, Rod. He's my biggest supporter and willing to answer my questions and listen to my ideas. Although he's a non-fiction fan, he doesn't hesitate to read my books, which means the world to me.

About Author

Andie Young began her writing journey in 2020 after a recurring dream, and hasn't put down her pen or put away her laptop since. That dream grew into her debut novel, *A Heart's Journey*. She is a therapist and a veteran and likes to incorporate one or both in her writing. When she's not writing, Andie enjoys spending time with her family and their dog, Lucy. Lucy has a cameo in *A Heart's Journey* and *The Journey Home*. Andie is currently working on two standalone books. *Phoebe's Garden* and *The Knitting* Club will be released soon.

Sign up for her newsletter to keep up to date on upcoming releases: http://eep-url.com/hVEPcH

Reviews are important to the success of a book. An <u>honest</u> review with retailers and social media is appreciated. If any grammatical or continuity errors are found, please contact Andie at andie@authorandieyoung.com.

Thank you for your support!

Also By